Canadian **Dani Collins** knew in high school that she wanted to write romance for a living. Twenty-five years later, after marrying her high school sweetheart, having two kids with him, working several generic office jobs and submitting countless manuscripts, she got 'The Call'. Her first Mills & Boon Modern Romance won the Reviewers' Choice Award for Best First In Series from *RT Book Reviews*. She now works in her own office, writing romance.

Michelle Reid grew up on the southern edges of Manchester, the youngest in a family of five lively children. Now she lives in the beautiful county of Cheshire, with her busy executive husband and two grown-up daughters. She loves reading, the ballet, and playing tennis when she gets the chance. She hates cooking, cleaning, and despises ironing! Sleep she can do without, and she produces some of her best written work during the early hours of the morning.

Louise Fuller was a tomboy who hated pink and always wanted to be the prince—not the princess! Now she enjoys creating heroines who aren't pretty pushovers but are strong, believable women. Before writing for Mills & Boon she studied literature and philosophy at university and then worked as a reporter on her local newspaper. She lives in Tunbridge Wells with her impossibly handsome husband, Patrick, and their six children.

More Than a Vow

DANI COLLINS
MICHELLE REID
LOUISE FULLER

MILLS & BOON

First Published in Great Britain 2018
by Mills & Boon, an imprint of HarperCollins*Publishers*
1 London Bridge Street, London, SE1 9GF

MORE THAN A VOW © 2018 Harlequin Books S. A.

Vows Of Revenge © 2015 Dani Collins
After Their Vows © 2011 Michelle Reid
Vows Made in Secret © 2015 Louise Fuller

ISBN: 978-0-263-26699-3

05-0318

MIX
Paper from
responsible sources
FSC® C007454

This book is produced from independently certified FSC™ paper to ensure responsible forest management.

For more information visit: www.harpercollins.co.uk/green

Printed and bound in Spain
by CPI, Barcelona

VOWS OF REVENGE

DANI COLLINS

In my heart, my books are always dedicated to my husband and kids, my sisters and my parents. They've always been incredibly supportive, both emotionally and physically, by doing dishes and making meals so I could write.

When it comes to writing dedications, however, I often look to my editors. Writing is a lonely business. I'm a big enough control freak that I don't ask other writers to look at my work and weigh in. It's all on me until I hit "Send." Then I rely on my editor to ensure I'm not embarrassing myself.

Kathryn Cheshire is my latest wing-woman in the Harlequin Mills & Boon offices. This is our first book together and she's everything an author wants and needs: warm, insightful and encouraging.

I couldn't do this without my family or you, Dear Reader, but a great editor is the linchpin in the whole operation. Thanks for being awesome, Kathryn.

CHAPTER ONE

SURROUNDED BY OLD money and cold-blooded cynicism for the first part of her life, Melodie Parnell wasn't half as ingenuous as she looked. In fact, she actively tried to give off an air of sophistication by straightening her curly brown hair into a shiny curtain, adding a flick of liquid liner to downplay her round blue eyes and painting a bold red lipstick over her plump, pink lips. Her clothing choices were classic business style: a pencil skirt, a sweater set and her mother's pearls.

At the same time, she privately offered people the benefit of the doubt. She believed the best whenever possible and always sought the brightest side of every situation.

That attitude had earned her nothing but contempt from her half brother and more than once resulted in a sting from social climbers and gold diggers trying to get closer to the men in her family. Being softhearted had definitely been her mother's downfall. But, Melodie often assured herself, she wasn't nearly as fragile or susceptible as that. The fact that she'd lost her mother very recently and kept slipping into a state of melancholy as she faced life without her didn't make her vulnerable.

Yet, for some reason, Roman Killian took the rug right out from under her—by doing nothing except answering the door of his mansion.

"You must be the indispensable Melodie," he greeted. She was supposed to be immune to powerful men in bespoke outfits, but her mouth went dry and her knees went weak. He wasn't even wearing a suit. He wore a casually tailored linen jacket over black pants and a collarless peasant-style shirt, three open buttons at his throat.

Not that she really took in his clothes. She saw the man.

He had black hair that might have curled if he let it grow long enough, tanned skin and gorgeous bone structure. Italian? Spanish? Greek? He certainly had the refined features of European aristocracy, but Melodie knew him to be a self-made American. His brows were straight and circumspect, his eyes decidedly green with a dark ring around the irises. He was clean shaven, urbane and acutely masculine in every way.

He met her gaze with an impactful directness that stole her breath.

"Roman Killian," he said, offering his hand and snapping her out of her fixation. His voice was like dark chocolate and red wine, rich and sultry, but his tone held a hint of disparagement. No one was truly essential, he seemed to say.

"I am Melodie," she managed to say. She watched his mouth as he clasped her hand in his strong grip. His upper lip was much narrower than his full bottom one. He smiled in the way men did when confronted with a woman they didn't find particularly attractive, but were forced by circumstance to be polite toward. Cool and dismissive.

Melodie wasn't offended. She was always braced for male rejection and surprised if she didn't get it. It wasn't that she was homely. She had just inherited her mother's catwalk build and elfin features along with her pearls. The attributes were fine for modeling, but came off as skinny and exaggerated in real life. Spiderlike and awkward—or so she'd been told so many times she tended to believe it.

So his indifference wasn't a surprise, but her skin still

prickled and she warmed as though the sun had lodged in her belly and radiated outward through her limbs with a disarming feeling that she was glowing.

She shouldn't be so nervous. She'd still had a pacifier in her mouth when she'd begun glad-handing, and rarely suffered shyness no matter how lofty the person she was meeting. Presidents. Royalty. Such things didn't affect her.

Yet she found herself surreptitiously fighting to catch her breath, aware that she was letting her hand stay in his too long. When she tried to extract it, however, he tightened his grip.

"We've met," he said with certainty. Almost accusingly. His eyes narrowed as he raked her face with his gaze, head cocked and arrested.

"No," she assured him, but her pulse gave a leap while a romantic part of her brain invented a fanciful "in another life soul-mate" scenario. She was very good with faces and names, though, even when a person wasn't nearly as memorable as he was. And he was too young to remember her mother, not that he looked the type to thumb through fashion magazines in the first place. There was an off chance he'd seen her in connection to her father, she supposed, but she was carving that particular man from her life one thought at a time so she didn't bring him up, and only said, "I'm quite sure we haven't."

Roman didn't believe her, she could see it.

"Ingrid and Huxley aren't with you?" He flicked a look for her clients to where her taxi had dropped her next to the fountain in his paved courtyard.

"They'll be along shortly," she said.

He brought his sharp gaze back to her face, making her quiver inwardly again. Slowly he released her and waved toward the interior of his home. "Come in."

"Thank you," she murmured, disconcerted by everything about him.

He was so masculine, so confident yet aloof. Secure, she thought, with a twist of irony. He'd made his fortune in security, starting with a software package but now offering global solutions of all kinds. It was one of the few things she knew about him. She hadn't researched him much, mostly relying on what Ingrid had shared, turned off by the idea she might wind up reading about her half brother if she looked up Roman online.

But knowing he was Anton's competition *had* made her predisposed to like Roman. He also seemed to have a streak of magnanimity, supporting causes from homelessness to dementia research to donating computers to libraries. And he'd offered his home in the south of France for his employee's wedding. Surely that meant he possessed a big heart under that air of predatory power?

"I didn't expect a security specialist to have such a welcoming home," she confessed, trying to ignore the sense that his eyes stayed glued to her narrow shoulders as she took in a modern house built with old-world grandeur. "I imagined something very contemporary, made of glass and stainless steel, all sharp angles."

The high ceilings held glittering chandeliers. A double staircase came down in expansive arms of delicate wrought iron and sumptuous red carpet over yellowed marble. The tiles continued through the huge foyer to an enormous lounge where a horseshoe sofa in warm terra-cotta would easily seat twenty.

Did he entertain often? Something in the way his energy permeated this airy interior so thoroughly made her think he kept this all-comfortable splendor to himself.

"The sorts of things that people want to protect are often attractive. Jewelry. Art," he supplied with a negligent shrug. "Six inches of steel works to a point, but surveillance and alarms allow for designs that are more aesthetically pleasing."

"Are we being filmed right now?" she asked with a lilt of surprise.

"The cameras are only activated when an alarm is tripped."

So it was just him was watching her, then. Nerve-racking all the same.

A formal dining room stood off to the right. It could be useful for the waitstaff, perhaps, since the four hundred wedding guests would eat in tents outside. And yes, the property allowed plenty of room for the ceremony, tents, a bandstand and a dance floor. Arched breezeways lined the house where it faced the Mediterranean. In the court-yard stood a square pool with a quarter circle taken out of it like a bite for a small dining area. Beyond its turquoise water a half dozen stairs led to a long strip of sandy beach. Off to the right a tethered helicopter stood on a groomed lawn. Once it had been removed, that space would be per-fect for the ceremony and reception.

Melodie had grown up in luxury, but nothing as ex-travagant as this. Roman Killian was a very rich man. It was difficult to hide how awed she was.

She brought her gaze back to the bougainvillea train-ing up the colonnades, and smaller pots of roses and ge-raniums and flowers she couldn't identify. They gave off scents of anise and cherry and honey, dreamy and adding to the magical atmosphere of the place.

"This is all so beautiful," she murmured, trying not to see herself as a bride, spilling in a waterfall of white lace down the stairs, emerging to blinding light and a strikingly handsome groom. The sunset would paint their future in rosy pink. Candlelight would burn like their eternal love.

She met Roman's gaze and found him eyeing her as if reading her thoughts, making her blush and look away.

"It's very generous of you to offer it," she managed.

"Ingrid is an exceptional employee," he said after a brief

pause, making her think that wasn't his real reason for offering his home. "Why didn't you all come together? Are you not staying at the same hotel?"

"They're newly engaged," Melodie said wryly. "I've been feeling very third wheel since meeting them at the airport." It was only four days, she reminded herself.

"Job hazard?" Roman guessed with a twitch around his mouth.

She couched a smile, suspecting he had a much lower tolerance than she did for witnessing nuzzling and baby talk.

"It can be," she replied, aiming for circumspect, because this was only her second wedding and her first international society one. Her business was still so new the price tag hadn't been clipped off, but he didn't need to know that. She'd organized state dinners in her sleep, and this was exactly the sort of event she was ready to build her livelihood upon.

"How long have you been living here?" She was highly curious about him.

His manner changed. Their moment of commonality evaporated and she had the impression he stepped back from his body, leaving only the shell before her.

"It was completed last year. What else can I show you? The kitchen?"

"Thank you," she said, hiding her surprise at how quickly she'd been shut down.

He waved her toward the end of the house, where he introduced her to his personal chef. The Frenchman was standoffish but had nothing on his employer. She was able to get a few details about the catering cleared up as Roman stood watch, keeping her on high alert.

Roman expected the single pulse from his silenced watch to be a notification that the rest of his guests had arrived.

One glance at the face told him it was actually a request that he review an important security alert.

Given that security was his business, he didn't take the request lightly, but an immediate threat would have been flagged as such and dealt with at the perimeter. And he had a guest. This wisp of a woman flickering through his home like sunlight and shadow through a copse of trees fascinated him. The conviction that she was familiar was incredibly strong, yet he'd sensed no lie when she'd assured him they were strangers.

Roman had a reliable radar for lies, one he listened to without fail. The one time he'd ignored his gut and convinced himself to have faith, he'd lost everything up to, and almost including, his life.

So even though he should have forced himself to the panel on the wall to review the alert, he stayed with his PA's wedding planner, keeping her under observation—partly, he admitted to himself, because her backside was delightfully outlined by her snug skirt, proving she was round and perky in the right places. He liked listening to her voice, too. Her accent wasn't heavy like Americans from the Deep South, but it had a lick of molasses, sweet and slow with a hint of rough darkness as she elevated and dropped each word. Very engaging.

She puzzled him at the same time. He was used to women being overt when they were attracted to him. He wasn't so arrogant he thought all of them were, but he worked out, wore tailored clothes and was loaded. These were all things that typically appealed to the opposite sex. She was blushing and flicking him nervous looks, fiddling with her hair, obviously very aware of him, but trying to hide it.

She wasn't wearing a ring, but perhaps she was involved with someone. If she wasn't, that shyness suggested she preferred slow, complex relationships. She didn't sleep with men for the fun of it, he surmised, which was a pity because that was very much a quality he looked for in a woman.

Roman had trained himself to keep emotions firmly at bay, but a blanket of disappointment descended on him. He was attracted to her, but apparently it wouldn't go anywhere. That was a shame.

Melodie had noticed his glance at his watch and offered a wry smile. "Perhaps I shouldn't have left the happy couple to their own devices. They're quite late, aren't they?"

"It's not like Ingrid," he allowed. If it had been, she wouldn't be his PA. He wasn't a tyrant, but he didn't tolerate sloppy behavior of any kind.

At the same time, he was fine with having Melodie to himself for a little longer.

"Perhaps you could show me where she'll dress?" she suggested, and showed him her smartphone. "I wouldn't mind taking note of suitable photo locations. The bridal preparations and procession to the groom are always an important part of the day's record."

"Are they?" If he sounded disdainful, he couldn't help it. He had lived hand to mouth for long enough that he didn't see the point in extravagant ceremonies. Did he pay for top quality now that he could afford to? Absolutely. But weddings were already given too much importance without turning them into a Broadway musical—then filming behind-the-scenes footage for others to ooh and aah over. As much as he appreciated Ingrid for all the skills she brought to her work, he was hosting this performance strictly for business reasons.

"I take it you're not a romantic," Melodie said as though reading his cynicism. "Or is it just that you wish you hadn't agreed to having your private space invaded?"

Both, he admitted silently, and realized he would have

to work on controlling how much he revealed around this woman. She was very astute.

Or very attuned to him, which was even more disturbing.

"I'm a dedicated realist," he replied, motioning for her to lead the way from the kitchen up a flight of service stairs to a breakfast room. "You?" he drawled.

"Hopeless optimist," she confessed without apology. "Oh, this room is gorgeous."

It was the second time she'd forced him to take stock of the choices he'd made in his surroundings. Part of him had been willing to go with the sort of design she'd said she expected of him: glass and chrome and clean, straight lines. But he'd spent enough time in an institution—juvenile, so not quite as stark as real prison—along with houses that weren't his own. He'd wanted something that felt like a real home. Of course, it also had to be a smart investment that would fetch a tidy profit if his world ever collapsed again and he had to sell it. Which wouldn't happen, but Roman was a plan B and C and D sort of man.

So even though he ate in this sunroom every morning, he wasn't as charmed as she appeared to be by its earthy tones and view overlooking the lemon groves between the road and the fountain in front of the house. He had agreed with the architect that having the morning sunlight pour in through the windows made sense, as did the French doors that opened to the upper balcony that ran the side and length of the house facing the pool and the sea, but it could rain every morning for all the notice he took.

"I once had a fortune cookie that told me to always be optimistic because nothing else matters."

Her remark caught him by surprise. His mouth twitched as he processed the irony. He quickly controlled it, but couldn't help bantering, "They should all read, 'You're about to eat a dry, tasteless cracker.'"

"Ouch." She mock frowned at him. "I dread to ask what you think of weddings if that's your attitude toward fortune cookies. Dry and tasteless?" she surmised with a blink of her wide eyes.

She was definitely flirting with him.

Time to let her know that if she went down that road it would be for short-term amusement, not long-term commitment.

"The ceremony does strike me as a rather elaborate shell for a piece of paper that promises something about the future but ultimately has no bearing on what will really happen."

His denunciation had her shoulders dropping in dismay. "That would be poetic if it wasn't so depressing," she informed him. "Weddings are as much a celebration of the happiness that has been achieved thus far as they are a promise of happily-ever-after."

"You promise that, do you? Sounds as if you're taking advantage of the gullible."

"Meaning that people who fall in love and make plans to share their lives are suckers? On the contrary—they haven't given up hope," she defended, lifting her chin with pretended insult.

"For?" he challenged, secretly enjoying this lighthearted battle of opinion.

"Whatever it is they seek. How far would you have come with your company if you hadn't dreamed beyond what looked realistic? If all you'd done was aim low?" She gave him a cheeky smile as she walked past him into his private sitting room, meeting his eyes as though sure she had him. "See? Being an optimist, I believe I can convert you."

"I'm not that easy to manipulate," he stated, confident he'd maintained the upper hand. "But go ahead and try," he added with significance.

CHAPTER TWO

"OKAY— OH." THE sitting room took up the corner of the house facing the water. More French doors opened to both the side and front balcony. The rest of the area was clearly the master bedroom.

Melodie had been so caught up in trying to be clever she hadn't realized where she was going. She blushed. "I didn't realize." Why hadn't he stopped her?

"There's a guest room down the hall that Ingrid can use to dress," he said drily.

She should have hurried to find it, but her feet fixed to the carpet as she took in the luxurious room in varying shades of blue. The bed was obscenely huge and was backed by mirrors to reflect the view. The wall onto the balcony was made of glass doors that doubled back on themselves so many times they ended up tucked into the corners. The partition between outside and interior had essentially disappeared.

Filmy curtains hung in tied bunches at the corners of the bed, presumably to afford some privacy to the occupant— occupants, plural?—if they happened to be in the bed with the doors open.

With that thought Melodie became acutely aware of the fact that she was a woman and Roman a man. He was tall and broad and his bed would accommodate his strapping body easily, along with any company he brought with him. She swallowed, trying not to betray the direction her thoughts were taking, even as she felt heat creeping through her, staining her cheeks.

As far as what he might be thinking, it was hard to tell whether he was attracted to her or just amusing himself at her expense.

"Oh, that's very beautiful," she said, letting the view draw her onto the balcony and away from the intimacy of his bedroom. She set her purse near her feet and used two hands to steady her phone while she took a snap. Her faint trembles grew worse as Roman came to stand next to her.

"How do you know Ingrid?" he asked.

Uncomfortable remaining where she could smell the traces of his aftershave, Melodie moved along the upper balcony, trying to pretend her dazzled state was caused by the band of turquoise just beyond the white beach before the blue of the sea deepened to navy. An indolent breeze moved through her sweater and hair, doing little to cool her. It was more of a disturbing caress, really. Inciting.

"Our mothers went to the same prep school in Virginia." Looking for cool in the wrought iron rail, Melodie grasped only heat, but she let the hard cut of metal into her palm ground her as she added, "My mother passed away recently and Evelyn came to the service. It was auspicious timing, with Ingrid recently becoming engaged."

Melodie's father had been instrumental in this new job of hers, of course, not that she intended to broadcast that. After insisting they invite Evelyn to say a few words about Melodie's mother—a request that had surprised the woman when she hadn't spoken to her old friend in years—Garner had insisted Melodie go talk to her. Ask her about her daughter. Melodie had realized after the fact that Garner had been fishing for info on Roman through his PA, but she didn't know why. She'd taken her time following up with Evelyn a couple of weeks after the service and kept it to herself. Her father and brother didn't even know she was here. Heck, they didn't know she was alive. She preferred it that way.

"Helping with the arrangements has taken my mind off things," she provided with a faint smile. "Weddings are such happy occasions. Far better than organizing a funeral."

A pause, then he asked, perplexed, "Are you saying the funeral was so impressive it prompted this woman to ask you to arrange her daughter's wedding?"

Melodie chuckled, even though the subject was still very raw for her.

"Not exactly. It *was* a grand affair," she allowed, trying to keep the disdain out of her voice. Her mother had wanted something small and private. Her father had wanted publicity shots. Melodie had wanted her mother's ashes. She'd done what she had to and the urn was now in her home, where she'd keep it safe until she could complete her mother's final wish, to have her ashes scattered in Paris. "But I think Evelyn was being kind to me, suggesting I get into this sort of thing as a career—"

Oops. She hadn't meant to reveal that. Shooting a glance at Roman, she saw his brows had gone up with that detail.

"Which isn't to say I'm not qualified," she hurried to assure him. This wouldn't be amateur hour with monkeys stumbling around his home overturning his life, if that was what he was thinking behind that analytical expression. Melodie intended to repay Evelyn's faith in her by ensuring each detail of her daughter's wedding went off perfectly and with the utmost taste. "I've done a lot of this type of thing, just hadn't seen it as a career possibility. After she said what she did, I contacted her and we came to an arrangement."

"So you're just getting your company off the ground. There must be substantial investment up front," he commented. "Flying here to scout the location. That sort of thing."

"Some," she replied with suitable vagueness. Complaining about money problems would not inspire his confidence. But the small policy she'd managed to take out on her mother's behalf had merely paid for the worst of her health-care bills. Pretending she could afford a weekend in the south of France was pure bravado and something Melodie would build into Ingrid and Huxley's final bill.

"Your office," she assumed as she moved away from that topic and along the balcony, arriving in front of a pair of open doors. The interior of the room held a desk free of clutter surrounded by large, clear screens she previously had thought were an invention confined to sci-fi movies. "You'll want to secure this on the day, obviously."

A door led off one wall back into his bedroom. The opposite wall was completely covered in large flat screens. A single image of his company logo took up the black space on them.

Melodie stepped into the room, drawn by its spare yet complex setup. A blip sounded and Roman followed to press his thumb pad to a sensor.

"You're quite the secret agent, aren't you?" she teased.

"I like to consider myself the man who stops them," he rejoined drily.

She bit back a smile at his supreme confidence and said, "This would be a stunning angle for a photo, with the water in the background. Would you stand in for Ingrid?"

"Not likely," he dismissed. Then smoothly turned things around with "You'd make a prettier bride. I'll take the photo." He held out his hand for her phone.

She hesitated, far more comfortable behind the lens than in front of it. She always had been, but she really didn't want to cause even the smallest ripple in such a big commission.

"If you prefer," she murmured with false equanimity and readied her camera app, walking back outside again as she did so. "We'll do a series of shots from when the father of the bride fetches her from her room and all the way down the stairs. I had thought she'd come down the interior ones, but these ones are better. The guests will see her approach, and all this wrought iron is so gorgeous. We'll take some couple shots on the inside stairs after the ceremony." She was thinking aloud as she went to the rail and turned to face him.

He fiddled with her phone, then said, "Ready."

After a few of the app's manufactured clicks, he lifted his gaze and commanded, "Smile. You're getting married."

Caught off guard, Melodie laughed with natural humor, then clasped an imaginary bouquet and channeled her best bridal joy, as if the man of her dreams was awaiting her.

Despite being mocked mercilessly through her teens and suffering a self-imposed disaster that had put her off dating into her adult years, she had been telling the truth about being a romantic. She liked to believe a real-life hero existed for her. She *needed* to believe it, or she'd become as depressed as her mother had been.

Her mother's illness had held Melodie back from looking for him, but now, despite the grief abrading her heart, she was open to possibility. Willing to take a risk. For just this one moment she let herself imagine *Roman* was the man made for her. Her soul mate.

Roman's intense concentration lifted sharply from the phone, pinning her in the steely needle of his hard stare.

"What's wrong?" she asked. Heat climbed up her chest into her throat.

"Nothing."

She licked her lips and moved along the balcony toward the outer stairs, trying to escape the moment of silly make-believe, but now that it was in her head she couldn't help wondering what it would be like to live with this savagely beautiful man.

Hard, she thought. *But the right woman might be able to soften him.*

The stairs descended in a curve to the area beside the pool. She stopped at the top and waved behind herself.

"She'll have a train. We'll fan it out here." She twisted as she indicated the puddle of imaginary silk and lace. Lifting her gaze, looking back over her shoulder at him as if this was a bad idea. She was too far into the dream, unguarded and vulnerable. She had accidentally left herself open to his reading her thoughts. Her entire body became paralyzed in a kind of thrilled panic, as though he'd happened upon her naked, but she wasn't afraid or ashamed. She was a nymph caught by a god.

He went statue still.

Her phone looked small in his hand, clicking, but practically forgotten as he looked past it and kept his eyes on her, taking his time as he toured her shoulder blades and waist and bottom and legs. The term *brutally handsome* came into her head and she understood it for the first time in her life. Roman was so gorgeous it was an assault to the senses, squeezing her lungs and pulsing heat under her skin.

He frightened her, but she wanted him to pursue her. It didn't make sense, but from everything she'd heard about hormones, they were never big on logic. They were the opposite, and hers were responding unusually well to him. *That* was what frightened her. Not him, per se, but her reaction to him.

He abruptly glanced at his watch. "Ingrid has been delayed," he said, touching the device. "She thinks she sprained her wrist. She's at the clinic and asks if we can reschedule."

* * *

He could have asked Melodie to stay for lunch, but he didn't. He had his driver take her back to her hotel. He wanted time to consider how he was reacting to her before pursuing her openly.

Powerfully was the answer to how he was reacting. Taking her photo had been an excuse to study her, and he hadn't seen a single thing he didn't like. And even though he was far beyond getting hot over photos of women, clothed or not, for some reason he'd been fixated as he had watched her pose. There was definitely a strong sexual attraction between them, but more than that, he'd found her magnetic.

Why?

He shook off his perplexity as he pressed his thumb pad to the sensor in his office and tapped the screen, bringing up the security report he'd ignored earlier.

He swore aloud as the contents became clear.

Apparently the experts were right. He was a security genius, if late to the party this once. The myriad details that his gatekeeper and even his own eyes had missed had been refined by his closed circuit camera and proprietary software, filtered against online content, then tagged to warn him of an attack even more insidious than the one he'd suffered all those years ago.

A handful of matches had come up. He glanced through them, stomach knotting.

The surname comparison could be dismissed as coincidental. Melodie had given his guard the name Parnell, which had been tagged to Parnell-Gautier. Two and a half decades ago, a model named Patience Parnell had hyphenated to Parnell-Gautier when she married.

He flicked to a dated glamor shot from a defunct fashion magazine. Patience stared at him, young and nubile, her gamine face bearing a striking resemblance to Melodie's big eyes and wide mouth. And there she was holding a baby girl named Charmaine. Not Melodie, but the date would put the baby in her early twenties today, precisely the age Melodie appeared to be.

Roman had met Patience once, very briefly, he recalled now. But he'd never considered her a direct threat because she'd gone into some kind of medical care several years ago.

His war, Roman had always believed, was with Anton Gautier and Anton's father, Garner Gautier. Aside from one recent photograph, the daughter hadn't been linked publically to either man since childhood.

He studied the photograph from a newsfeed dated two months ago. Melodie's profile from her approach in the taxi today had been set against the profile in the news piece where a backlit woman, wearing a black hat with a netted veil, stood next to her American senator father as he bowed his head over a casket. Behind them stood Anton. The caption mentioned that Patience Parnell-Gautier was survived by her loving husband, stepson and daughter, Charmaine *M.* Parnell-Gautier.

How vile and just like Gautier to send his second spawn into Roman's house like this. To use his PA's *mother* to infiltrate his home.

He immediately dismissed any thought that Ingrid could be in on the scheme. She'd proved her loyalty again and again over the years. And it had been his idea to host the wedding, not hers. High-society circles were small and tight. She had connections he didn't. He wouldn't care about being accepted at that level if it weren't for the fact that it was the one area the Gautiers had an advantage on him. He'd volunteered his home to even the playing field.

What he couldn't understand was how Melodie had captivated him to the point that he'd ignored the security alert rather than read it and order her off his property. He wasn't so uncivilized he'd have had her *thrown* out the way he'd been physically expelled from her father's campaign office twelve years ago. Battered and kicked so badly he could barely walk away. Anton had been the thief, but Garner had had the power to turn it around and call Roman the criminal. He'd had the power to ruin Roman, which he had.

A red haze of fury rose with the recollection. He would *not* allow the Gautiers to play him again. Rage urged him to hurt them, deeply, for daring to try.

Despite being a man who actively sublimated everything resembling feelings, he found himself able to taste delicious vengeance on the tip of his tongue. He'd been longing to get back at this family for years, biding his time, wanting to first overtake Gautier Enterprises in the arena that would cause them the most discomfort: financial.

For years, their two companies had been neck and neck in a two-horse race, both improving on the same software that he, Roman, originally had written and that Anton had convinced him his father would back. Instead, the men had stolen his product, finished it, then made a mint while Roman had scraped by for another five years, rebuilding everything he'd lost and finally entering the marketplace so far behind them he'd despaired of ever catching up.

Finally, early last year, he had begun to see parity. It wasn't enough. Not for him. He'd risked everything and had thrown all his resources behind completely reengineered software. The gamble had paid off. Corporations were dropping the dated Gautier knockoff and stampeding to Roman's new, far superior product.

Gautier's bottom line had to be feeling the pinch by now. It followed that they would send in a scout, thinking to once again steal what they wanted and step back into the top position.

Like *hell*.

Roman wasn't just going to win this time. He would

send a message to the Gautiers they would never forget. He would crush them into nothing, starting by flattening their emissary without a shred of mercy.

His first instinct was to have Ingrid fire Melodie immediately, but he forced himself to more coolheaded contemplation. The Gautiers had let Roman believe he was on the path to success right up to the moment when they explained his services with the software design were no longer needed and they would be taking possession of his ticket to a better life.

Therefore, he would ensure he had another wedding planner in place, so there was no inconvenience to Ingrid. Melodie would lose her contract and any chance of continuing in that field. Nice of her to drop the detail that it was a new venture, he reflected. He didn't think for a moment she was serious about making a career of wedding planning, but as with any con artist's ruse, the Gautiers would have put funds behind making it seem real. He was glad to at least cost them their investment.

A few investigative keystrokes later, he saw that Melodie lived alone. Surprisingly modestly, he noted. So had he, back in the day, but he'd still lost his home and all he owned. He knew that his eye-for-an-eye retribution wouldn't have the same impact. Melodie would simply run home to Daddy, but it was the right message, so he started the wheels rolling on getting her kicked out.

The final touch would be the simple, crystal clear message that they'd failed. The sweetest retaliation of all.

Melodie had clearly pulled the rookie move of plugging her phone into the charger without checking that it was properly connected. When she pulled it off, one foot out the door to meet Ingrid and Huxley and leave for Roman's, she saw it had not only failed to charge, but had lost the 4 percent it had had. Dead as a doornail.

Sparing a moment to throw it into the safe with her passport, she wound up putting her whole purse inside. She'd take a credit card as a just-in-case, but it was only going to be a quick lunch in a private home. She didn't need to pack a bag.

Okay, yes, her mind was racing a mile a minute and she couldn't make a rational decision to save her life. She was not just nervous but excited. Last night with Ingrid and Huxley it had been all she could do to keep her chatter confined to the suitability of Roman's house as a venue for the wedding. The whole time she'd been longing to pump her client for more information on Roman, but she'd managed to wait until bed before doing a bit more online snooping. Then she'd lain awake fantasizing about him—creating scenarios in her head she hadn't ever starred in before, but wanted to with him.

A short while later, having met up with Ingrid and Huxley en route, Melodie barely kept herself from dancing in place as Roman opened his door to them.

"I'm so *sorry*," Ingrid moaned as they entered. "I slipped in the tub the other night and didn't think it was that bad, but by the time we were on our way here yesterday, it was like this." She motioned a ballooned wrist.

"She wanted to wait until we'd finished here before going to the clinic, but she was fighting tears in the car," Huxley said. "I couldn't let it go untreated."

"Of course not," Roman murmured smoothly. "I'm glad it's just a sprain, and won't impact your typing and filing once your vacation is finished."

Ingrid giggled. "He's being funny," she said to Melodie over her shoulder. "The office is paperless and we do almost everything talk to text."

Melodie smiled, wishing that Ingrid and Huxley weren't pressed to each other like a pair of bubbles that were about to become one. She really needed them to diffuse all this aggressive male energy coming her way. It was as if Roman had developed a ten-fold power of masculinity overnight and it was now all beamed directly at her.

"Excellent photos, by the way. You have a hidden talent," Ingrid said to her boss, thankfully drawing his attention for a brief moment.

He only said, "The camera loves her," then trained his intent gaze back onto Melodie as though searching for something.

Huxley wanted to know what they were talking about and Melodie immediately regretted showing the photos to Ingrid. She'd been trying to explain the potential for wedding photos, but now had to brush aside Ingrid's gushing with a brisk "I was hamming."

The final shot, where she'd been looking back at Roman, was the most disturbing. Her slender figure against the ivory backdrop of the mansion's west wing had projected elegant femininity while her expression had been one of sensual invitation. She hadn't meant to be so…revealing.

Embarrassment struck once again as yesterday's unfounded yearnings welled anew. This was why she hated having her picture taken. Too much of herself became visible.

"Why don't we go outside and you can take a few photos yourself?" she suggested, trying to distract everyone.

As they sat down by the poolside for a light lunch, Roman continued to study Melodie, biding his time, confident yet highly cautious. She was a surprisingly dangerous woman beneath that projected innocence.

He'd thought her pretty yesterday, which had apparently been enough to mesmerize him. Today, having seen the glimpse of unfettered beauty in her photos, he now caught flashes of stunning attractiveness in her as she smiled and exchanged banter with Ingrid and Huxley.

The truth was he was having trouble remembering why he shouldn't be drawn to her. He told himself he was giving her enough rope to hang herself, but deep down he wondered if he was putting off the denouement of his plan so he could spend a few more minutes admiring her.

It was sick and wrong. She was his enemy. Yet he suddenly found himself ensnared in the meaningful look she was sending him. She practically spoke inside his head as she flicked a rueful glance toward the couple, who had had to take a break from eating to rub noses. *See? It never stops.*

It was an odd moment of being on exactly the same wavelength. An urge to chuckle over their private joke rose in him while the sparkle in her eye and the flash of her smile encouraged him.

What the hell? How could he be gripped by anything except the fact she was here to commit a crime against him?

"Now that you've seen the place, shall I tell my staff it's set in stone?" he asked Ingrid, pulling them all back to the supposed business at hand. Trying to put his train of thought back on its rails.

"Please," Ingrid said, offering him a look of earnest gratitude. "And I can't thank you enough. I'm still reeling that you've been so kind as to offer this. It's his fortress of solitude," she added in a teasing aside to Melodie. "No one is ever invited here."

Roman brushed off the remark with a dry smile, but felt the weight of Melodie's curiosity. He ignored the prickle of male awareness that responded to the intrigue in her gaze, set his inner shields firmly into place and wrote off a trickle of anticipation as a premonition of threat that he would heed.

"We all need a retreat where we can work in peace," he said, partly to tantalize her—*your move*, he was saying—

but his house was more than a sanctuary. It was a statement that he had arrived, and hosting the wedding would publish that headline.

"Well, it helps a great deal having a central location to bring the families into, since they're coming from far and wide," Huxley went on. "We appreciate it."

Roman offered another vague smile, covering up the fact that he was *very* aware that Huxley's father was a highly placed British ambassador in the Middle East, and the rest of his relations were blue bloods from the UK. Ingrid's were old money Americans, including an aunt married to a German sitting on the EU Council of Ministers. Ingrid's maid of honor was the daughter of a Swiss banker. The event was a who's who of the international renowned and elite.

Being hosted by the son of a New York prostitute.

This was his entrée, he reminded himself dourly, wishing he felt more enthusiasm, but feeling more taken with the cat-and-mouse game he was playing with Melodie. What did it say about him that base things such as competition and survival still preoccupied him?

"How did you get into security software development?" Melodie asked, nearly prompting a sarcastic "really?" out of him.

He didn't allow himself to be suckered by her solemn expression of interest. It struck him that she might not be here to steal, merely to damage. Her family had threatened to use his background to discredit him once before. They wouldn't be above trying it again. Perhaps she intended to sabotage his hosting of the wedding, removing his chance to grow acquainted with the world's top influencers.

He met her quietly lethal question head-on, neutralizing any bombshells she might be poised to detonate by getting there first.

"I was arrested at fourteen for hacking into a bank's network server."

"Are you serious, Roman?" Ingrid cried on a gasp of intrigue, cutlery rattling onto the edge of her plate. "I had no idea," she exclaimed, eyes wide with delight in the scandal. "You're getting information out of him I never did, Mel!"

Melodie's ridiculously long lashes swept down in a hint of shy pleasure, betraying that she enjoyed the thought of having power over him.

Irritated by the amount of truth in Ingrid's remark— Melodie *was* the reason he was going against habit and bringing up his past—Roman finished the story. If it left this table he was determined it would be framed as closely to the truth as possible, and not twisted to annihilate him the way Melodie's father had threatened.

"Once I realized I could outsmart adults, the game was on to see how far I could go," he said frankly. "The security specialist who caught me, a tough ex-marine named Charles, was impressed, especially because I was self-taught. Once I did my stint in juvenile detention, he brought me onto his payroll. Taught me how to use my talent for good instead of evil," he summed up with mild derision.

Melodie's surprise appeared genuine.

"You weren't expecting honesty?" he challenged.

"It's not that. I've just never met anyone with a natural ability for programming." A shadow flickered behind her eyes, something he barely caught, but it colored her voice as she said, "I thought that sort of thing was a myth."

She was talking about her brother, he was certain of it, but her smile wasn't sly. She wasn't trying to trick him or win him over. No, her comment was more of an inward reflection and a hint of confusion. Wondering if Anton was really as good as he'd always claimed?

Hardly.

As quickly as Roman formed the impression, her expression changed and he was looking at a different woman, one who seemed open and engaging, her cares forgotten in favor of enjoying a lively conversation.

"I'm certainly not intuitive with them. Someone had to show me how to set up my email on my tablet."

And there was the "I'm harmless" claim Roman had been anticipating since he had realized who she was.

The conversation moved on to contacts and wedding arrangements. Iced coffees replaced the white wine everyone had sipped with lunch. Huxley said something about the dock and took Ingrid to inspect it.

Melodie made no move to follow, choosing instead to shift forward slightly and remove her sweater, revealing a matching sleeveless top that clung lovingly to her breasts as she twisted to drape the sweater over the back of her chair.

"I didn't expect it to be this warm. It's fall at home. Quite wet and chilly." She sat straight and, as if she felt the chill across the Atlantic, her nipples rose against the pale lemon of her top.

A base male fantasy of baring those breasts formed in his mind. He saw pink tips resembling cherries melting off scoops of ice cream. He wasn't a breast man per se, but the languid image of caressing and licking the swells, working his way to the sweet, shiny niblet at the peak, was so tangible he had to part his thighs to accommodate the pool of erotic heat that poured into his groin.

At the same time he realized conversation had stopped. She was very still.

He lazily brought his gaze up and realized she'd caught him blatantly ogling her. A strange jolt hit him like an electrical charge, deep in his gut and far stronger than a zing of static. It was like a full current that reverberated in his chest, making his heart skip a beat and his abdomen tighten.

Her blue eyes held his, fathomless and not the least offended. In fact, her reaction to his masculine interest was arousal. He'd seen it in the tightening of her nipples and read it now in the confused shimmer of excitement and indecision expanding her pupils. Her lashes quivered, eyes shiny, and the tip of her tongue wet her lips.

The pull behind his thighs became more insistent. He wondered if he had ever experienced a more carnal moment.

She swallowed and jerked her gaze from his as though it was a physical wrench of muscle from bone.

He mentally berated himself for letting her see his interest, highly irritated by how easily she had got to him. It was time to drop the ax.

"Does, um, he come around the office much?" she asked, gaze scanning restlessly toward the water. "Are you used to their displays?"

"Who?" he almost growled, then remembered two other people were here. Ingrid and Huxley. They held hands and bumped shoulders as they staggered, love drunk, across the sand.

Roman was behaving almost as inebriated, forgetting they were even here, manufacturing lurid fantasies of possessing a woman too lethal to imbibe. He tried to shrug away the strongest wave of sexual attraction he'd ever felt toward a woman and almost wondered if she'd slipped him something.

"He might, but I don't," he replied belatedly, forcing his mind back to the conversation. "The whole point in being on the cutting edge of technology is to use it." He chinned upward to his office, rebaiting his hook. "I often telecommute."

"And Ingrid is your avatar in New York?" she guessed.

That took him by surprise. He almost chuckled, then caught himself, dismayed by how easily she kept disarming him. He eyed her, searching for the source of her power. "I hadn't looked at it that way. I suppose she is."

"Working from home always seemed so ideal to me," she mused, propping her chin on her hand. "But now I'm doing it, I find I'm becoming a workaholic, never letting it go. I keep sitting down for one more thing and losing another two hours."

"You live alone, then," he said, picking up on what he thought she wanted him to deduce. It shouldn't please him to hear she was single. She was nothing to him, certainly not a woman he'd bed. Not in these circumstances. Perhaps his libido found her leggy build stimulating. That faint scent of citrus and roses emanating from her skin was pure seduction, but as much as he hated her family and wanted revenge, he wouldn't stoop to grudge sex. He didn't intend to touch her.

She could go ahead and offer herself, though. Rejecting her advances would make for a delightful twist. He wondered if she'd take this game of hers that far, and decided he would make it easy for her to humiliate herself.

A pulse of expectancy tugged at him.

This was a chess match, not a flirtation, he reminded himself.

"I do," she answered, fingertips grazing the pearls at her throat where he thought he saw her pulse fibrillating. Her glance went to the house. He suspected she was mentally recalling whether she'd seen evidence of a paramour in there. She hadn't. He kept his companions out of his private space.

"Me, too," he provided.

Melodie's flushed cheeks darkened with a deeper blush as she cut a glance toward him, perhaps trying to work out whether his remark was a signal of attraction.

There was no use pretending otherwise. She'd already caught him lusting, so he let her see that, yes, something in him found her appealing. He didn't understand how it could happen when he held her in such contempt, but he rather enjoyed the fact that she was so disconcerted by her own response as she read his interest. Her reaction was too visceral to be fake, which was probably why he was aroused by it.

It was a bad case of misguided chemistry. She certainly wasn't desirable to his rational mind, but maybe it was the risk of the situation that he found compelling. He'd developed a taste for plundering in his early years. Not of women. He was actually very cautious with how he approached relationships, but he loved finessing his way past defenses, exposing closely guarded secrets. He liked to prove he could. It filled him with enormous satisfaction.

"Where is home?" he asked. He'd read the answer yesterday, but he liked seeing how his attention put her in a state of conflicted sexual awareness.

"Virginia," she answered, smile not sticking. "For now. I'm considering a move to New York, though."

"Don't bother," he said instinctively, then closed his mouth in distaste at reacting so revealingly. "It's a perfectly livable city, but I don't care for it," he said in explanation. "More than my share of unpleasant memories," he added, to see if she'd pick up that the filthiest ones involved her family. Others were so heartbreaking he pushed them to the furthest reaches of his mind.

She only murmured, "I feel like that about Virginia."

Her tone exactly reflected his feelings, as though she'd opened the curtain and stepped inside the narrow space where he stored his soul. It was so disturbing he bristled, but she didn't seem to notice.

Her wrinkled brow relaxed and she forced a cheerful smile. "I need a fresh start. And you've inspired me now with your talk of telecommuting. Tell me how you manage it. Ingrid said you're a global company, so I assume you travel a lot? I expect I will, too, as I become more established. What are the pitfalls and best practices?"

She was very smooth in her way of bringing the conversation back to his business. He had to admire her for her dogged stealth.

"The happy couple is returning," he noted, avoiding answering by directing her attention to where Ingrid and Huxley had stopped at the far end of the pool, admiring the view of the beach.

Ingrid glanced at him, and he inferred that a consultation was requested.

He stood and held Melodie's chair, getting another eyeful of her breasts, not intentionally, but he was a man and they were right there.

Her sultry cloud of scent filled his nostrils, imprinting him with the image of marble and turquoise and sunlight off dishes so he would never forget this moment of standing here, her lithe frame straightening before him. She had a slender waist and hips he longed to grip so he could press forward, bend her to his will, cover and possess. He had to school himself against setting a proprietary hand on her back as they moved to where the bride and groom were debating logistics.

· What the hell was it about her?

She moved with remarkable grace, he noted. Not so much skinny as long limbed. A thoroughbred. Not a mutt like he was. If he didn't have so much contempt for her bloodline, he might have questioned whether he was good enough for her.

Instead, he was the one with ethics while her sort wore an air of superiority that was only a surface veneer of respectability provided by old money. Perhaps she wasn't overt about thinking herself better than those around her, not the way her father had been, and perhaps she didn't act entitled, but she was among her own with Ingrid and Huxley. She took it for granted she was accepted. He couldn't help but appreciate that confidence.

"Would the guests moor here overnight?" Huxley asked.

"That's up to Mr. Killian," Melodie deferred, turning to him.

"Roman, please," he said drily. She could use his first name until he made his position clear, which would be about five minutes from now. "There's a shoal to be wary of," he said to Huxley, stepping forward so he could point.

He was fully aware of Melodie's proximity to his own. He had no intention of bumping her, though, and actually reached out absently to ensure he didn't.

Melodie was the one who recoiled in surprise, taking a hasty step backward.

He caught the movement out of the corner of his eye, heard her squeak of shock and snatched again, more deliberately.

She was already tipping backward. He missed her, tried again. Their fingertips brushed, but he failed to catch her. Her face pulled into a cringe as she fell backward into the deep end of the pool. Roman stepped back from the splash and stared at her one shoe caught in the grate.

CHAPTER THREE

ONCE MELODIE REALIZED her fall was inevitable, she let it happen, only splaying out her arms and holding her breath. Above her, through the rippled water, three blurry faces stared. Roman was throwing off his jacket and looking as if he might dive in.

She let herself sink, waiting until her foot tapped the bottom, then kicked herself back to the surface.

What an idiotic thing to do!

But that damned Roman had been throwing her for a complete loop, being all masculine and sexy, sending mixed messages of lust and disapproval, hovering next to her like a raptor, smelling tangy and male. She'd been standing next to him, admiring his build, thinking his voice was too hypnotic, when he'd reached toward her as if he knew she was there, as if he was a lover searching for the hand of his mate.

Her reaction had been startled fear that she'd betray how thoroughly he was affecting her if he touched her. She'd jerked back and…

"Pah!" she spat as she came up for air. "You might want to change the design of that grate before the wedding. Either that or we advise all the women to skip the stilettoes and wear flip-flops."

Ingrid and Huxley laughed unreservedly. Roman wore a more severe look.

It wasn't easy to tread water in a narrow skirt. Her second shoe came off as she kicked toward the edge.

Roman squatted as she reached for the lip of the pool. His strong hand grasped her forearm, dragging her closer whether she wanted his help or not. His other hand got hold of her opposite arm and he pulled her up and out of the pool as though she was a teensy ballerina, not a five-foot-ten mermaid pushing a hundred and thirty pounds. *Soaking wet*, she added with a private cringe.

Water sluiced off her, and she rather wished he had let her take stock before landing her in front of him, dripping and plastered with wet clothes, not a single thing left to the imagination. Her makeup had to be running and— Okay, good. Her pearls were still here, but seriously. She felt absurd.

She crossed her arms to hide the way her nipples hardened and risked a quick sweep of her gaze around the faces goggling at her. Ingrid was still snickering, hand cupped over her mouth while her eyes danced with laughter.

"What on earth, Mel?" she asked.

"You left your shoe on the bottom, Cinderella," Huxley teased, moving to where a large net lay against the low garden wall.

"I can't believe I did that," Melodie grumbled, mortified but able to laugh at herself. It was so ludicrous.

Roman didn't seem to think it was funny, though. He was staring at her so hard her wet clothes should have been nuked off her body.

"May I have a towel?" she prompted.

"Of course." He snapped into motion.

"Oh! I have a bathing suit you can wear," Ingrid exclaimed. "I bought it yesterday and left it in my bag." She disappeared into the house and Melodie shook her head. It was far too late for swimwear.

She followed Roman into the nearby cabana where he

turned with a towel in his hand. His gaze raked down her again, making her acutely aware of how her clothes were suctioned to her like a second skin. She plucked at her knit top, which only stretched the neckline and ruined it.

Roman came forward, shaking out the towel and slinging it around her. He was so tall it was no problem at all for him to get it around her.

Her heart did another somersault and his musky scent stole through the air of chlorine as his wide chest filled her vision. Weakness attacked her.

"I—" It would be silly to apologize. She hadn't fallen on purpose, but he looked so thunderous. "Thank you" was all she could manage as he drew the edges of the towel to where her waiting fingers brushed his.

"When you sank like that, I thought I was going to have to come in after you."

"It was quite refreshing, to be honest. I needed to cool off."

She shouldn't have said that. The sexual tension she was fighting became something they both had to acknowledge, like it was a real thing holding them in its vortex.

She found herself staring at his mouth, anticipating its feel against hers. Kisses were about as far as she went these days after losing her virginity for all the wrong reasons. Even kisses, however, always seemed to fall short of the hype. She always felt as though she was going through the motions, not really losing herself to the experience. If she couldn't get caught up in that much, there was no use going further, she'd decided.

But she remained ever hopeful that she'd find a man who made things different. Today, at least, she *wanted* to be kissed. Deep longing filled her, making her ache to know how it would feel to kiss the man before her.

Distantly she was aware of his hand grasping her upper arm. He stepped closer. His head tilted.

She should have been startled, but it felt so natural. She dampened her lips. Parted them. And gasped when he branded her with the heat of his mouth.

So hot, so smooth and commanding, instantly hungry. Claiming her like a desert warrior stealing her for his pleasure. His hand splayed in a firm pressure behind her tailbone, bringing her imperiously into the wall of his muscled frame.

Heat burned through her wet clothing, sealing them tight with only the friction of dampened fabric between them.

He kissed her as though he meant it. As though he was making sure she'd never forget this moment. As though she was his and he was ensuring she knew it.

She kissed him back with the same passion, not thinking of anything beyond exploring this new pleasure. Letting him have her because what he was doing to her was fresh and exciting and incredible. His kiss made her feel desired. His tongue touched hers and shivers of delight stung her skin. A flood of arousal seared between her thighs, urged her to lean into him and let a moan of pleasure fill her throat.

"Here you are—oh!" Ingrid said on a breathless burst, then laughed with embarrassed hysteria.

Roman jerked back, keeping one hand on Melodie's arm to steady her. His firm grip hadn't hurt her, but his touch left a tingling impression. She massaged the spot, trying to dispel the odd vibration while she noted the front of his clothing wore her moist imprint.

"I'll come back," Ingrid offered, grin mischievous.

"No," Roman blurted, brushing past Ingrid as he moved swiftly out of the cabana.

Ingrid, nearly doubled over she was laughing so hard, she stepped and pulled the curtain across. *"O. M. G,"* she said with exaggerated significance, eyes huge.

Melodie dropped her burning face into her damp hands, eyes closed in mortification. "I don't know how that happened," she groaned.

"Oh, please," Ingrid chortled. "He's Roman Killian. You should see what the office looks like when it's announced he'll be in. It's like a red-carpet event, there are so many women wearing push-up bras and designer labels. I'm not the least bit surprised you—pun intended—*fell* for him."

"No, I haven't..." Melodie tried to protest, but her bones were still weak, and if Roman had walked back in and told her to come with him, she would have gone without a second thought.

"Don't bother," Ingrid instructed with a shake of her head. "If I hadn't been crushing on Huxley my entire life, *I* would have fallen for Roman. He's gorgeous. What intrigues me, though," Ingrid lowered her voice to murmur, sidling closer with a little wiggle of excitement across her shoulders, "is the way *he* is falling for *you*."

Melodie shook her head. "You're mistaken—"

"He can't take his eyes off you," Ingrid insisted, enjoyment gleaming in her eyes as she gave Melodie's drowned-rat state a good once-over. "To be fair, I don't see him with women very often. I think he's the sort who compartmentalizes. Work. Play. Know what I mean?" Ingrid made little stalls with her hands. "But when I have seen him with a date, he keeps up that aloof facade of his, never planting one on them as if he can't wait for everyone else to leave. And they're always blonde and stacked. Kittenish. Not really striking me as his intellectual equal."

"I fell into the pool, Ingrid. Hardly a sign of great intelligence," Melodie argued, heart galloping at the idea that Roman had been unable to resist kissing her.

She was *not* the type to provoke men to passion. Most of them thought she was too tall and wiry. Her half brother had done a number on her as a child, tearing her self-esteem to shreds in a way she'd only been able to rebuild once she had left home, so she still considered herself an ugly duckling who'd arrived at goose, not swan.

That dented self-esteem, along with her mother's need of her, had kept her from a serious pursuit of love, but she longed for a deep connection with the opposite sex. With her mother gone, there was more than just a hole in her daily schedule. She felt her single status very keenly. The sight of couples and families made her feel very lonely. She wanted someone to share her life with. Not the facade of a shared life that her parents had had, but the sort of deep, abiding love that Ingrid and Huxley had.

She opened the towel and wrapped it like a turban on her head, throwing off self-pitying thoughts as she peeled away her wet clothes.

Ingrid pulled the tags off the bathing suit and something else that she held up for inspection. "Look. Huxley bought a shirt. You can borrow this, too."

Any relief Melodie felt evaporated a moment later. Ingrid was decidedly smaller than she was. The bikini would be microscopic even on her client. On Melodie, it was downright lewd.

Ingrid was not deterred. She dropped Huxley's sleeveless white shirt over Melodie's head. "It's a bit risqué, but nothing I wouldn't wear poolside or to the beach."

Or in the bedroom to incite her fiancé?

Melodie looked at the thin fabric hanging from narrow straps over her shoulders to scoop low across her breasts and waft in an indecently high hem across her thighs, barely covering her bottom. Even on the beach, this outfit would be nothing less than bait. With the pearls resembling puka shells around her neck, she looked like a surfer groupie trolling for a vacation hookup.

Unfastening the necklace, she muttered, "I can't believe this has happened. I look so unprofessional."

"It's fine. Better than fine. Your legs should be licensed as a deadly weapon," Ingrid said with a meaningful lift of her brows. "Let's see if Roman likes them," she added with a wicked grin, gathering up Melodie's wet clothes and zipping outside with them, leaving the curtain to the cabana open.

Melodie hesitated, not wanting to be so encouraged by what Ingrid had said about Roman's interest. She really wasn't very experienced with men. Aside from her insecurities, a lot of the reason was exactly what she'd told Roman: she was a workaholic. She'd been supporting herself a long time, spending what little extra time she had visiting her mother, advocating for her. The few men she'd been loosely involved with had been nice enough, just not the type to inspire her to make room in her life for them.

Not that she expected Roman to want a place in her life! Quite the opposite. He struck her as a man who expected his women to be self-sufficient and sophisticated. Which she definitely wasn't—not when it came to relationships. She might not be an actual virgin, but she was a one-time wonder, still not sure what had possessed her to go through with it the first time.

Well, realistically, she knew that immaturity and helpless fury had driven her. She'd wanted to strike back at Anton and had wound up hurting herself and a man who hadn't deserved to be used. Anton's *friend*, a young man Anton had been using so he could party on his family's yacht, had had a crush on Melodie. She'd reveled in the opportunity to show Anton that not only did his friends find her attractive after all, but she had the power to influence them. She'd made the boy turn down Anton's demand to sail in favor of taking her for a private cruise. She went through with the lovemaking she'd promised him, but it had been awkward and disappointing. He'd realized she didn't truly care for him and had been quite devastated.

The entire experience had turned into a lesson in being kind to others and true to oneself, which she had tried to follow ever since.

Today, the truth was she might not know Roman enough to care deeply about him, but she was fiercely attracted to him. She wanted to sleep with him. Really wanted that more than she'd ever imagined possible.

With an impatient noise, she reached for the damp towel and slung it around her waist, needing the shred of added protection as she went out to face him.

He wasn't there, which made her heart sink in an alarming way.

"He went up to change," Huxley said, jerking his head toward the balcony, adding with a smirk, "Probably having a cold shower, too."

Ingrid finished hanging Melodie's wet clothing across the back of the chairs and said to Huxley, "If we're going to test those jet skis you reserved, we'd better run. You can get a cab, can't you, Mel? We're going the opposite direction to the hotel. We'll see you tomorrow at the meeting with the hotel manager about the room block."

Could she *be* more obvious? Melodie liked Ingrid, but at this moment she wanted to push *her* into the pool. *Don't leave me alone with him.*

But the customer was always right, she reminded herself.

Scanning her gaze across the table, she looked for her phone and realized all she had was her credit card in the pocket of her sweater—which was dry, at least. Thank goodness she had *that* much.

"Sure," Melodie said with a stiff smile, as if she was still wearing her conservative suit and had this situation fully under control.

"Bye!" Ingrid blew a kiss, grabbed her fiancé's sleeve and hauled him away.

Blushing with embarrassed annoyance, Melodie contemplated whether to head into the kitchen and ask the chef to call her a cab or stick around to see if Roman wanted to finish kissing the daylights out of her.

Okay, her hormones cried excitedly.

She had to get out of the sun. She was blistering.

Moving to the bottom of the outside stairs, she wavered, but told herself she couldn't leave without at least saying goodbye.

Yes, wanting to see him again is all about good manners, she mocked herself.

She climbed with trepidation, heart pounding as though she was descending the basement stairs in a thriller movie. So silly. He wasn't going to attack her. That kiss had been a surprise, but invited and totally mutual. She had wallowed in it.

The part of her that wanted it to happen again and maybe go further was what scared the daylights out of her. She wasn't that girl. She wasn't blasé about intimacy. She wasn't desperate or angry or deluding herself into love at first sight.

She was just really, really enticed by everything about him.

As she reached the top of the stairs, she grew cautious, feeling like a burglar, afraid she'd catch him indisposed.

"Roman?" she tried.

A very deliberate noise sounded, like someone striking a single key on a keyboard, hard. "Yes," he said from his office.

"I'm afraid I have to ask you to call me a cab." She tried to act casual as she moved forward. "I didn't bring my phone and…"

She came even with the open doors of the office and discovered him standing before his clear screens. He had changed, dispensing with a shirt altogether, and now wore only a pair of drawstring linen pants that hung with rakish sexiness off his hips, accentuating his smooth, powerful back and the curve of his buttocks.

"I'd ask Ingrid for hers, but she and Huxley just left…" She could hardly speak. Her throat had gone dry.

He turned. His flat abs and nicely developed chest fixated her. Animal attraction gripped her.

Why? She didn't understand it, and lifted her gaze to his, trying to work out where this attack of sexual craving was coming from.

He was scanning down her low neckline, taking in the outline of tiny triangles that barely covered her nipples beneath the translucent cotton, eyeballing the towel that she gripped around her hips.

His Adam's apple worked. "Why are you here, Melodie?" His tone was graveled with intolerance and something almost erotic. Desire?

"I— What do you mean?"

"Here, in my home." He joined her on the balcony, confrontational and ominous, arms and shoulders tanned and powerful, bare feet planted firmly. "Why are you here?"

"The wedding," she stated, nerves strummed by the suspicion in his tone.

"Be honest."

"What do you mean? I didn't *plan* this," she said, waving at her borrowed garb, suddenly realizing how it could look. But she hadn't made this happen. She wasn't using it as an excuse to stick around and throw herself at him. Not really. Okay, maybe she was throwing herself at him a little, but—

Oh, good grief. Could this get any worse?

"I didn't bump you," he bit out, eyes narrowing. "I didn't even touch you."

"No, I know. I was just…nervous," she stammered, attacked by the same hit of discomfiture that had made her avoid him by the pool. She'd instinctively known his touch would have a devastating effect on her. She'd leaped back from his reaching hand as though he could have burned her. He *had* burned her. When he'd kissed her in the cabana, the contact had seared all the way to her soul.

"Nervous," he charged, brows elevating as if he'd caught her out. "Why?"

Because he was a force, not a man. Her reaction to him was so strong it petrified her.

"You're different," she hazarded, but couldn't explain it even to herself.

"How?"

Boy, he was like an extension of his technology with those robotic commands for more information.

She crossed her arms, annoyed, but Ingrid's words were ringing in her ears. Was he reacting to her and feeling as out of sorts by this situation as she was?

The thought brought a soaring of buoyancy that she quickly tried to tame. A million things were running through her head, all her thoughts coming back to the fact that she was finally meeting a man who made her feel alive. She was interested and excited. Running away like a teenage girl too shy to speak to him would be silly. She'd kick herself forever if she did that. They were grown-ups. She was, by nature, an honest person.

"I find you attractive," she admitted, and immediately blushed. It was as if she'd deliberately stepped onto a gangplank high over the concrete. Her footing seemed wobbly and threatened to drop her into a hard fall.

"Do you," he disparaged.

His tone peeled a layer off her composure. She told herself she was being mature and didn't have enough invested to have anything to lose, but her self-respect grew thin and strained. *Bug eyes. Don't talk to my friends. They all think you're ugly anyway.*

At the same time, she put herself into Roman's shoes and thought she knew the source of his cynicism. "If you think I'm making some kind of awkward play for the rich guy, that's not true."

"You'd think I was just as attractive if I lived in a cardboard shack in a back alley?" he scoffed, arms folding and chin coming up with arrogant challenge.

Dear Lord, he was attractive. Like a Greek god with all that burnished skin over toned muscle, his aura one of superiority and might.

She almost blurted out how she'd walked away from the sort of wealth and education that would have made any job unnecessary for the rest of her life. If he only knew how much contempt she reserved for powerful men and how sorry she felt for the women who loved them...

But all that was behind her, and this moment was only about her and him. Who they were in this moment.

"I might," she allowed with a weak shrug. This was a physical thing. She suspected no matter where she had encountered him, she would still be unable to control her response to him.

"You don't even know me," Roman derided. "Why—?" He bit off the word, looking out to the water, gripped by an angry frustration that went beyond his response to her. He closed his hand on the rail, trying to retain his grip on the situation.

But his gaze tracked unerringly back to Melodie. The low neckline of her shirt accentuated her slender neck and delicate collarbone, offering a teasing glimpse of the upper swells of her breasts. Her damp hair fell in waves around her bare face. She had the sensual innocence of a maiden from a primitive jungle culture, pure temptation in her open regard, Eve-like in her patience for him to succumb to the desire drumming through him. The message was subliminal and as irresistible as a siren's.

Come to me.

All he could think was, *This is a damned sight more than attraction.* He was blind with lust, trying to hang on to a cool head while his body still felt the writhe of hers nudging against his erection. She'd inflamed him with their kiss, promising untold pleasure, appealing straight to the basest part of him and completely undermining his capacity for logical thought.

Thank God Ingrid had interrupted them. He was disgusted with himself for kissing her in the first place, let alone allowing her response to ignite his own. The moment he'd walked away from her, he'd begun grasping for rationalizations to explain how he'd reacted so uncontrollably. Maybe he had it wrong. Maybe she wasn't Gautier's daughter. Maybe her presence here wasn't by design.

But he'd reviewed everything and it was all too neat. Her mother hadn't been in society in years, yet her funeral had been a who's who of the Eastern Seaboard. Melodie had not only started her new wedding business the minute she had put her mother to rest, but had immediately curried favor with an old family friend who *happened* to be the mother of his PA. The timing was *auspicious* indeed. And her fall into the pool, orchestrated so beautifully, allowing her to linger in his home while her clothes dried, was equally suspicious.

Not only that, since yesterday he'd learned that Gautier Enterprises was bleeding red ink by the gallon. And he'd turned up additional photos showing Melodie under her father's wing, all of them beautifully stoic in the face of her mother's death. Most significantly, sly moves were happening behind the scenes. Roman's customers were being offered exorbitant discounts if they signed exclusively with Gautier. False promises were being made about the performance of the most recent Gautier product, and dishonest warnings were circulating about Roman's.

A fresh rush of hatred had encompassed him a moment ago as he'd looked at a photo of her with her father. Grim anger coiled through him that Melodie had anything to do with the man. He wanted her to be real, not a weapon her father was wielding. Not a willing foot soldier against him.

And he hated himself for being susceptible to her. He'd fallen for Anton's lies once and was edging dangerously close to being taken in by Melodie's. It was intolerable.

He'd learned all her weak points, though. Her father might have insulated himself very thoroughly, but she was wide-open. All his plans were in motion. With a tap of a key, he had ensured Ingrid would pick up his email insisting she fire Melodie, and with another ensured Melodie would have no home to go back to in Virginia. The rest of the false front she'd built would collapse like a row of dominoes over the next hours and days.

All while she continued to look at him with those Bambi eyes soft with invitation, a hint of irreverent humor in her smile.

"How well do you usually know the women you're attracted to when you first meet them?" Melodie asked, pulling him back to the present moment.

Touché. He snorted, privately admitting that physical attraction was typically the reason he set out to learn a woman's name. Ironically, he had learned more about Melodie before he'd kissed her than he'd ever learned about most women he'd slept with.

Of course, he'd been more attracted to Melodie at first glance than he'd ever been before. He'd only become more intrigued as each minute had passed. And now, despite everything he knew, despite already taking steps to crush her plans, he could barely take his eyes off her breasts, rising and falling in a shaken tremble that was utterly fascinating.

The basest male in him wanted to kiss her again. Feel her under him. Be inside her and see how high the flames would fan.

"Do you think I'm not struggling with this, too? I don't kiss strangers. I don't…" She offered a helpless palm, averting her face so he only saw a look of confusion and longing in the profile she turned to the water.

The rest of her was pure temptation, nipples peaking in excitement beneath the tiny red bikini top. Her legs went on forever and his hand itched to find the skin beneath the drape of that oversize, yet completely inadequate, shirt. He was hardening at the thought.

"I just keep wondering how else you get to know someone except by spending time with them?" Her gaze came back to his, earnest and unsure.

He shook his head, amazed by how good an actress she was, relieved on some level that she wasn't genuine because he would have to do some serious soul-searching before involving himself with such a multifaceted yet sincere woman. He wasn't cut out for relationships with a future. That was why he was careful how and when he fell into the loose ones he did enjoy.

Fortunately she was a huckster peddling a shell of such relationships, amazing him with her tenacity and smooth attempts to manipulate him, her mouth trembling in a struggle to smile as she offered a hesitant, "Of course, if it's not a mutual thing, I'll…"

She took a few steps closer, gaze drifting to the patio below, lashes lowering and brow pulling together in a wince of rejection.

He didn't move. How could she be this good? How could he be feeling like this? He didn't want anything to do with her, but he wanted to understand why he was this easily taken in so he could guard against such things further down the road.

"What do you really want from me, Melodie?" he asked in his deadliest tone, willing her to come clean.

"Just, um… Honestly?" She blinked up at him, practically virginal with her defenseless gaze, her mouth working to find words. "For you to kiss me again," she said, her voice a thin husk. "To see if…" She licked her lips, leaving an expectant silence.

"Come and get it, then," he said gruffly, trying to scoff, telling himself he was only seeing the extent she'd go to in this industrial espionage of hers, letting her demean herself when he had every intention of rejecting her.

But it didn't happen that way.

She absorbed his command with a small flinch, then lifted her chin as though gathering her courage. As she stepped up to him, her hands opened on his rib cage in a feathery tickle that made his entire body jerk in reaction. His nipples hurt, they pulled so tight. She was tall enough that when she lifted on tiptoes, her mouth easily met his.

She pressed pillowy lips to his. He told himself to shove her back and tell her—

The rocking of her mouth parted his lips. He caught the first damp taste of her and his tongue shot out instinctively, greedily plunging into her mouth the way he wanted to plunge into her body. He closed his arms around her, pulled her into him with a strength he barely remembered to temper, and slanted his mouth to take full possession of hers.

She opened to him, arched and pressed into him and moaned capitulation.

Rational thought evaporated in a groan of craving.

CHAPTER FOUR

MELODIE HAD JUST wanted to see, that was all. See if he really did make her feel like this. See if something special existed between them.

But, oh, things raced out of control quickly. As their lips met and the kiss took hold, she stopped thinking, only vaguely aware that no man had ever run his hands over her skin like this. Such strong hands. Such an amazing feeling to be petted and shaped, firm fingers digging in as he pinned her tightly to his naked chest, then explored her with a touch like velvet.

Her body's reaction was a study in biology, skin growing so sensitive his touch was almost abrasive, yet inciting at the same time. She could feel the scrape of his chest hair through the light shirt she wore, could feel the burn of his body heat, and even though she could barely stand the conflagration, she wanted to be closer and closer still. Her arms went around his neck so she was belly to belly with him, loins to—

He was hard.

His hands cupped her buttocks and his teeth closed on her nape, making her bones turn to sand while she rubbed instinctively against that hard ridge. Something deeper than desire, a craven need, punched like a blow right there, where she felt him against her most private flesh. The ache was hurtful and demanding. Nothing like she had ever felt. Never had sensations overwhelmed her like this. It was stunning, absorbing, erasing all thoughts except primal want. *Please. More. Now.*

Her fingers went into his hair. She was pure reflex, wanting his mouth over hers, wanting to open and give and take.

He smothered her with his passionate, hungry kiss, hands smoothing up the contracting muscles in her belly to cup her breasts, making her sob with relief at the pressure of his touch on those tender, aching orbs. The cups of the bathing suit went askew and then he had her bare breasts in his palms, massaging, fondling, rubbing at her nipples so streaks of white-hot arousal shot straight into her loins.

She whimpered, seeking pressure where desire was pooling like thick lava. She didn't know how to tell him, only knew that his skin was as taut as a drum under her searching hands, his tongue erotic as he played with hers. A distant part of her wondered how this was happening, but another part didn't care, only wanted him to keep touching her, keep playing with her nipples, keep stirring and stimulating her.

His hand went to her hip and eased the bathing suit down. He stepped back to look as the bottoms dropped around her ankles. Watching his own hand, he slid his touch to the front of her thigh, up to her belly, then down, fingers combing, pressing—

"Oh!" she gasped, never having felt her body respond like this. Sharp and wicked and wanton sensations prickled through her as he sought with a fingertip and toyed with her, pulling her in for another kiss with a hand behind her neck, utterly devastating her with the waves of pleasure he was rocketing through her.

She caressed him with restless hands, wanting to touch everywhere at once, wanting to fill her palms with him, wanting to excite him the way he was doing to her. She no sooner cupped his hard shaft through linen, though, and his hand bumped hers, ceasing to caress her so he could release his drawstring.

His pants fell and he stepped out of them, completely naked. He was ferociously aroused, dark and thick and ready. She hadn't got a proper glimpse of her first lover, and Roman wiped all thoughts of the past from her mind. He fascinated her.

She wasn't frightened. No hint of hesitation struck. She was pure eagerness and excitement as she took in his nude frame, so perfect he was like a statue sculpted by a master, formidable and flawless, rampant and ferociously masculine.

Catching her up hard against his front, he lifted her as he moved, muscles shifting under her hands as he held her nose to nose, feet off the ground and dangling. His mouth nipped at hers, inciting her to kiss him back. She curled her arms around his neck, ran her tongue over his bottom lip, then drew on it, sucking flagrantly, liking the way his hands hardened on her. He took the few steps to his bed where he followed her to the mattress, spreading her legs as he came down over her.

Yes, she thought. It was the only word in her head. Her body was in a state of undeniable demand. Her entire being yearned for the feel of Roman's hard muscles and his weight and *yes*. The feel of his aroused flesh rubbed against hers, parting and arousing, teasing and dampening. Seeking.

Her arms cradled his head, her mouth pulled at his parted lips, licking and panting as he breathed raggedly along with her, breaths mingling, their gasps and growls carnal and unfettered.

With a blind, startled shake of his head, he drew back. "I didn't—"

"Don't stop," she cried, arching to offer herself where

she could feel him ready to penetrate, needing him inside her. She was so aroused she would die, actually die, if he didn't keep pressing *right there.* "Please, Roman, please."

He groaned and the insistent pressure increased. Her tight flesh gave way, parting and accepting.

Oh. It had been a long time and this was... Burning. Intimate. So much more like she'd always wanted it to be. His length pushed in, filling her, making her hold still to savor, wanting all of him...

With a growl, he opened his mouth against her neck, drawing a love bite up to the surface of her skin. She practically levitated off the bed, pressing up into him, surrendering utterly to the experience. His tongue licked against the artery pounding in her throat and he shuddered as his body came flush against hers, pressing tight, possessing her to the limits of their joined flesh.

She closed her trembling legs around his hips, astonished, beyond aroused. Mindless. She was pure sensation, her only dim thought that she was happy it was like this. Pure, abject passion infused the moment.

He lifted his head and looked at her, eyes fogged with passion. Something clouded his gaze, as if he was becoming aware of how fast they'd arrived at this point.

She didn't care about that. It was supposed to be like this. Animalistic, but with both of them caught up in overwhelming desire. She licked her lips.

His gaze followed the signal and his head bent.

They were lost again. Kissing deeply. Her body eased its tight grasp on his, inviting him to move. He did, muscles trembling, and his excitement fueled hers. She stroked his back and rubbed her thighs against his sides and lifted her hips to accept the return of his, seeking pressure where she ached for it most.

He made a feral noise and moved with more deliberation, making her gasp at the sensation of friction and something that strummed the very heart of her. It was the most instantly addictive feeling she'd ever encountered. She made a noise of female ardor and encouraged him with primal arches and a grind of her hips. The more he moved, the more reality fell away. All she cared about was the next thrust and the next.

More. Now. Please. *Please.*

They writhed in ecstatic struggle, fighting to hold on to the moment, lascivious sounds filling the air as the intensity grew, as he moved faster, as climax approached with merciless demand.

The paroxysm struck her suddenly, holding her in a hard grip, mouth open in a silent scream. Sensations detonated then reverberated through her, rocking her to her core.

Roman's arms locked straight, a ragged cry of triumph tearing through the air as his hips sealed to hers and pulses of heat met her clasping orgasm, strengthening and prolonging her pleasure.

They were wholly attuned, joined in body and involvement. It wasn't happening to him or her. *They* were the experience.

With broken cries, they collapsed into weakness, sweaty and wrung out, panting and shaking. Tears of deep emotion leaked to dampen Melodie's lashes as she kept her eyes clenched shut, so shaken by the wildness of her actions she could barely face what they'd just done.

That had been…

She didn't have words.

That was—

Roman lifted off Melodie and pushed clumsily to his feet, arms weak, knees shaking. The friction of leaving her was a pleasurable stroke that turned to the chill of loss. He had to turn away to keep from falling under her spell all over again.

No condom. He turned away, aghast at his carelessness. He never forgot, never lost his head. He liked sex, but he was always, *always* aware of protection.

He'd started to pull away as he felt her naked flesh against his pulsing erection. She was the one who'd yanked him back into the act, begging. Offering herself with such abandon he'd discarded all cares but getting inside her.

He shot a wary look her way, genuinely shaken by the way she'd slithered past his shields.

She'd rolled onto her side, but was still diagonal on the bed, knees together now, shirt pulled low to hide her nudity, head pillowed on her curled arm. Her big eyes blinked in sensual shock as she offered him a tentative smile.

"I've always wanted to be swept away by passion." Her languid tone was a caress and an invitation, as alluring as a drug to an addict. She made him want to join her, to lock out the world and let her become everything he needed.

Which was probably what she had planned. First, dull his senses with the kind of sex that reset the bar. Then lower his guard so he'd let her wander his home so she could, what? Dig through his files while he slept?

He had *not* meant to touch her. He hated himself for being weak enough to do so. He'd been on the verge of coming downstairs to spell out exactly how he was taking his revenge, but she'd come to him and coldcocked him with seduction.

A mix of emotions rose in him: contempt for both of them, fury, disappointment, a kind of defeat that took him back to a time when he'd been completely powerless... He *hated* feeling these things, especially all at once. With ruthless discipline, he shut himself down, refusing to be drawn by her sultry afterglow. Women were as vulnerable after sex as they were during, but he closed himself off to that, too.

Melodie must have read something in his look. Her lashes quivered and one hand tugged her shirttail down a little more. "Maybe it's always like that for you," she murmured self-consciously.

"It is," he lied flatly, unable to stomach how he'd let lust, for *her*, sweep him completely beyond himself. "I know who you are," he continued, before her flinch of defenselessness could have an impact on him. He strode across to gather his pants and stamped his feet into them, straightening to tie them into place with jerky movements. "You're wasting your time."

"What…? What do you mean?" She tucked her legs to the side as she sat up, brow furrowing.

"Charmaine Parnell-Gautier," he pronounced without inflection, as though they were exchanging information over a boardroom table. "I know your father and brother sent you here. Whatever you thought you could do to me isn't working. I'm three steps ahead of all of you." He picked up her discarded bikini bottom and brought it to the bed, placing it near her knee. "It's time for you to leave."

Her plump lips parted and her skin went so pale he thought she might faint. His heart lurched with alarm.

But she gathered herself quickly, drew a shaken breath and straightened her spine, shoulders going back.

"You think my father sent me here?"

"I know he did."

"You're wrong." Tilting her head at him in an admonishing stare, she looked him right in the eye. "My birth certificate says Garner Gautier is my father, but I don't have anything to do with him." Bitterness flashed in her expression. "I'm not surprised you might have a bone to pick with him. He buys friends and makes enemies, but whatever he's done to you has nothing to do with me."

Wow, he thought distantly. She certainly knew how to shuffle her hand and play a new card. He was supposed to be reassured, he imagined, by her pretending they had a common adversary.

"What he did was steal my work and lose me my home. I might believe you had nothing to do with his crimes if I hadn't spent yesterday afternoon reviewing recent photos of you two together."

Her lip curled in revulsion. She shook her head. "That's not what—"

"Melodie," he interrupted coldly. "This isn't a conversation. I don't *care* what you have to say. I'm simply telling you that your idea to use my PA to infiltrate my home has failed."

"I'm not *infiltrating*! I'm planning her wedding—"

"No. You're not," he informed, oddly empty of feeling as he served up the next slice of his revenge. This should feel good, but it just made him bitter. "I've instructed Ingrid to fire you. If she wants to hold her wedding here, which she does, she will find another planner. One who actually does this sort of thing for a living."

Melodie couldn't believe what she was hearing. Clammy fear was pulsing through her, killing her afterglow and beginning to make her feel dirty and cheap. She was sitting here half-naked, a very personal tenderness reminding her of what they'd been doing a few short minutes ago.

Snatching up the bathing-suit bottom, she tucked her feet into it and worked it up her legs, giving Roman her back as she pulled it into place. Her skin felt flayed under his regard, her inner self yanked into the open, kicked and spat on.

It was such a shock her mind could hardly make sense of it. All she knew was that this had something to do with her father and Anton. She knew all too well what a bitter taste they left in one's mouth. She clung to reason with her fingernails, tried to regain her poise and some semblance of control over this crazed situation.

She didn't sleep with strangers. She didn't—

Think, Melodie.

"You can't fire me," she said firmly. "I have a contract." She reached through the neckline of the shirt to straighten the bikini top. Where was her power suit when she needed it?

"Do *not* charge any cancellation fees," he warned. "If you try to recover any costs from this trip, if you so much as contact Ingrid to plead your case, I will make this worse than a job loss and eviction. Now go home, tell your father you failed and never come after me again."

"Stop," she insisted, spinning to confront him with an upraised hand, barely able to process what he was saying— *eviction*? She knew the cold fury and bloodlust that came of dealing with her father and half brother. Better than he ever would. She just needed to make him realize they were on the same side. "Roman, listen. I have *nothing* to do with him or Anton. Firing me will not impact them at all."

"It's time to leave," he said with quiet frost.

"They're not even going to know," she asserted, hearing the crack of growing emotion in her voice and clawing hard to keep her cool. It was really hard when voices in the back of her head were saying, *They're still doing it. They're still able to hurt you.* "What you're doing impacts me, not them."

"You're all one and the same." The Gautier lack of mercy left a virulent flatness behind his eyes. Broader understanding began to hit. He really thought she was some kind of spy. That she had been put up to this by her father and brother.

Oh, she vaguely knew what her brother did for a living. She'd never understood *how*. He was the furthest thing from a techno-genius, and now pieces were falling together. Of course Anton would have stolen the product that had filled his bank account. Of course her father would have covered for him and profited along with him.

"I don't know how to convince you, but you're wrong. Before you go through with all this, stop. Think about what you're doing. Give me a chance to explain."

"There's no stopping. It's done," he said matter-of-factly.

She swallowed, barely breathing, not wanting to believe him.

"You've already told Ingrid—"

"I emailed her before you reached the top of the stairs."

She shook her head, absorbing the magnitude of losing this contract. This wedding was supposed to put her on the map. She was finally starting a real job. A career she could feel excitement about. No more juggling two or three minimum-wage jobs at makeup counters or bistros. Her aspirations of finally moving into a decent apartment, maybe traveling because she wasn't tied down by her mother and debt, dimmed and doused like a candlewick gutting out, leaving only a wisp of smoke to sting her nostrils.

"You can't do this," she insisted numbly. Her mind leaped to wondering if she could start over somewhere, but as he'd pointed out, there was an investment in starting up a business like this. Without Ingrid's payment, she was in a very deep hole. Then there was the loss of Ingrid's circle of contacts. Starting over meant starting at the bottom, not stepping into a tony crowd with money and taste. "You're destroying my life," she informed him, heart beginning to tremble in her chest.

"Be sure to tell your father exactly how it feels."

He wasn't going to hear her on the lack of communication between her and Garner. She wouldn't bother mentioning it again. This *was* happening. She could see his resolve and, if dealing with her father had taught her nothing else, she had learned to accept that there was evil in this world. The best you could do was mitigate the damage.

Exactly what *was* the damage?

"What…?" She was afraid to ask. "What did you say about eviction?"

He folded his arms, feet planted firmly. "I've made an offer to the owner of your building, one he can't refuse. It's on condition that your unit be made available immediately."

Fury closed her fists into painful knots. "You can't *do* that."

He didn't react beyond saying, "Your things are being removed as we speak."

"To where?" she cried.

"The nearest Dumpster?" he offered with a pitiless shrug.

"You—" Her voice caught and realization began to squeeze her in its icy fingers. Fine quakes accosted her. She shook her head in convulsive denial as the buildup of emotion threatened to break the walls of her control. One thought formed and clung like a teardrop to a lash. "You're having my mother thrown in the Dumpster. Is that what you're saying? What the hell kind of man *are* you? There are *laws*."

His brows jerked together, the first sign of emotion since they'd been writhing with passion. "What do you mean?"

"My mother's ashes are in my apartment. You can't just throw someone away like that. You can't even—" Oh, what the hell did a man like him care about how hard it was to make the arrangements for scattering ashes?

Anxiety brought tears to her eyes, and she dashed them away, furious that she was breaking down, but this was the last straw. Losing things, starting over, having nowhere to live… Those were all problems she'd overcome before. Defiling her mother's remains was more than she could withstand. Her breath hissed in her pinched nostrils while her mind raced through all the hours of travel it would take to get back to Virginia to save her.

"I'll make a call," he said.

Because the wheels were already in motion.

It hit her that he'd been making these arrangements yesterday, long before he'd kissed her in the cabana. He had set up all these horrible things, consigned her mother to the Dumpster, then had sex with her. She recoiled as she realized he'd already been filled with hatred and thoughts of revenge as he'd carried her to this bed.

Her revulsion must have shown. He reacted with a dark flinch.

"I will," he assured her, glancing around as though he was looking for the nearest phone.

"You'll make a call," she repeated as she edged toward hysteria. "You're just full of consideration, aren't you, *lover*," she spat. The word tasted like bile.

"Do you want me to do it or not?" His gaze flashed back to hers with warning.

She was ready to take him apart with her bare hands and he must have known it. He tensed with readiness, stance shifting as he balanced his weight on his planted feet, darkly watchful. His lethal air should have terrified her, but she was pulsing with the sort of protective instincts that drove people to lash out in a blind rage. Her mother's well-being throbbed in her brain, urging her to injure and incapacitate in order to save. She wanted to hurt him. Badly. So badly.

Don't, a voice whispered in her head. *Don't be like them.*

"As if I'd trust you," she managed, voice wavering, whole body beginning to rack with furious shakes. "*I* will make a call," she said raggedly, knocking her breastbone with her knuckles. "I'll keep her safe. I'm the only one who ever has. The only reason I went back there was for her," she cried, throwing the truth at him like a grenade. "I swore I'd never set foot in that house again, but my father wasn't going to let me have her ashes unless I put on a state funeral and gave him those damned photos you're so convinced prove I'm here on his behalf. You think you're the only person they've ever hurt, Roman? Don't be so arrogant. You're not that special!"

She spun toward the door.

"Melodie," he ground out. "I'll call to make sure—"

"My friends call me Melodie. You can call me Charmaine. Like they do. Because you're just like them."

She went through the interior of the house. It was faster and allowed her to avoid going anywhere near him as she made her exit. She ran down the hall, blind to anything but a blur of yellowed marble and red carpet, barely keeping her footing on the stairs before she shot out the front door.

She heard her name again, but didn't look back. The paving stones were hot on her bare feet, burning her soles, but she barely felt the scorch and cut of the pebbles. Her only thought was that she needed to get away from him. Needed to get to her mother.

CHAPTER FIVE

THREE WEEKS LATER, Roman was in New York, conscience still smarting from everything that had happened with Melodie. Her final words—*you're just like them*—kept ringing in his head, growing louder as time progressed, cutting like a rope that grew tighter the more he struggled against it.

Initially, he'd thought she was merely twisting things around as she'd seen her plans falling apart. He'd had very little pity for her in those first postcoital moments, too angry with himself to hear that he might have computed things wrong.

The bit about her mother's ashes had bothered him, though. He had nothing of his own mother except vague, poignant memories of a woman who had seemed broken and defeated, voice filled with regret as she promised to get him back. Given how hard she'd tried to turn her life around, he'd felt doubly cheated when she had died before she was able to regain custody. The fact he'd only been informed of her death as an afterthought had been insult to injury.

He quickly turned away from those painful memories, frustrated that he couldn't seem to keep his mind plugged into work. It had always been his escape from brooding and he needed it more than ever.

Yet he found himself rising and stepping away from his desk to look over his view of Central Park. At least his eviction plans hadn't actually put the ashes in danger. As Melodie had pointed out, there *were* laws. His ability to have her things removed required thirty days' notice. She'd arrived home and cleared out within days, according to the building manager. Her mother's ashes had been safe the entire time, and Melodie had taken them with her when she'd left.

Twelve years ago, he *had* been thrown out of his home overnight, losing everything. The locks had been changed while he had hitchhiked from Virginia to New York, still nursing broken ribs and two black eyes after confronting Anton at his father's campaign office. His meager possessions had been gone when the super had let him into his apartment, not that he'd cared about anything except his custom-built computer. Taking that had been pure malice. They'd already had the files. They'd wanted to set him back, quite literally disarm him, and it had worked.

Roman hadn't dared go to the police. Not after Garner's threats of charging him with hacking. Roman had that prior conviction and no money to hire a lawyer. No time to wait for the wheels of justice to turn. Survival had been his goal.

Living on the streets, really understanding what his mother had been up against, he'd not only come to understand and forgive her, but he'd even considered a form of prostitution himself. The temptation had been high to sell his skills to the highest bidder and embrace a life of crime. Honest work hadn't been paying off.

Somehow, though, he'd found himself outside Charles's house—the security specialist who had helped him all those years ago. He'd walked as though he was being pulled toward a beacon, arriving without understanding why or how his feet had carried him that direction. Charles hadn't been there. He'd been in a home, suffering dementia. But his wife, Brenda, had let him in.

Until then, as a product of the foster system, Roman hadn't really believed things such as friendship and kindness and loyalty were real. He'd seen Charles's singling him out as a mercenary move, a specialist developing a skilled apprentice for his own benefit. Anton had befriended him to exploit him, as well. That was how it was done, Roman had thought. Nothing personal. People used people. That was how life worked.

But as Charles's wife had taken him in for no other reason than because Charles had always spoken fondly of him, Roman had begun to comprehend what one person could mean to another. Not that he took advantage of her. No, he had carried his weight, taking out the garbage and giving her what he could for groceries and rent every week.

She hadn't needed his money, though. She wasn't rich, but she was comfortable. She had grown children she saw often, so she wasn't lonely. The house had been well alarmed in a good neighborhood. She hadn't needed his protection. She'd had no legal obligation to help him.

She'd done it because she had a generous heart.

It had baffled him.

He still wondered what he might have resorted to if she hadn't taken him in for bacon and eggs. Told him to shower and provided him with clean clothes. If she hadn't listened to his story and believed him.

He'd been wary, not allowing her to be as motherly as she had wanted to be. Almost his entire life to that point had been a reliance on strangers. He hadn't wanted to go back to that kind of setup, but her unconditional caring had been a glimpse of what he had missed in losing his own mom. Parents, good ones, were a precious commodity.

So the thought of Melodie's mother's ashes being mistreated still bothered him, even though nothing terrible had come to pass. It had been more than the basic indecency of such a thing. He simply wasn't that cruel.

Meanwhile, the claim Melodie had made about how she'd come to have those ashes had shaken his assumptions about her and her family. He had needed to know more, to understand if what she had claimed about her estrangement from her father could be true. He'd made a number of calls over the ensuing days, first talking to her building manager at length.

Melodie, it seemed, was a perfect tenant who paid on time, lived quietly and took care of minor repairs herself. In fact, until the recent passing of her mother, she'd spent most of her days out of her apartment, working or visiting her mother at the clinic.

When Roman had looked more closely at her finances, he'd learned that she'd been living simply for years. Her income was low, especially for the daughter of a senator who received dividends from a global software company. For six years she had worked in a variety of part-time and minimum-wage jobs, only taking on debt to improve her mother's care and then to start her wedding planning business.

He'd spoken to Ingrid's mother, too, learning more about Melodie's mother than Melodie herself, but even that had been an eye-opener. Patience Parnell had been a fragile sort at college. She'd been given to tears and depression over the tiniest slight. She'd quit school when a modeling agency had scouted her, but after the initial boost to her self-esteem, that sort of work had ground her down. She'd left that career to marry a rich widower, expecting to be a homemaker and help him raise his son. Instead, she'd been his trophy wife, constantly on display as he set his aspirations on Washington. The demands of networking, campaigning and entertaining had grown too much for her. She never really recovered from postpartum depression after having Melodie. She'd checked into a sanitarium six years ago and, it was whispered, had checked out under her own terms.

When she had been diagnosed with breast cancer, she had refused treatment, letting it take her life in a type of natural suicide.

Every time he thought about it, he saw Melodie before him in that ridiculous outfit. Her anguish had been so real as she'd said, *I'll keep her safe. I'm the only one who ever has.*

That crack in her control was the thing that niggled most. She had been such a coolheaded fighter up to that point. He'd seen it in the way she'd doggedly tried to argue with him. At any other time he would have admired such a quick, clear ability to reason her way out of conflict. Hell, he probably would have tried to hire her. People who could step past emotion to straighten out a tense situation were gold.

All he'd seen at the time, however, was an attack. A cold-blooded one. His mind had been so skewed by his experience with her father and brother he'd stayed on the offensive, refusing to hear her, especially because she'd been so levelheaded in her defense. He'd read her wrong because, until those last moments, she hadn't flinched or broken down.

That strength in her had thrown him, making him see her as an adversary. Now all he could think about was how it would feel to put all one's energy into fighting for someone, for your *mother*, and lose her to a lack of will to live.

He swallowed, pushing stiff fists into his pockets, knuckles coming up against the string of pearls he should have returned to Melodie by now. He kept thinking she might contact him, but, in her shoes, would *he* want to talk to him?

If there was a good enough reason, he thought she would.

The beads rubbed mercilessly against his knuckles, the way a certain question kept rolling around in his mind, rubbing and aggravating.

Did no condom mean no birth control?

A lead blanket descended on him each time he recalled his fleeting moment of sobriety, as he had recognized the mistake he was about to make.

He was a man of logic. He didn't believe in giving in to feelings. He still couldn't understand how he had, especially with his view of Melodie as dark as it had been. He'd been appalled in those first seconds afterward for so much as touching her.

Yet it had been the most profound sexual experience of his life.

Had it been the same for her? Had their physical attraction been real? *Please, Roman, please.* His entire body clenched with tension and his breath drew in and held, savoring the memory of skin and musky scents and hot, wet welcome pouring over him like a bath. Behind his closed eyes, another question, the most burning question, glowed brightly.

Was she pregnant?

Beggars can't be choosers. It was a truth Melodie had learned to live with the day she'd come home six years ago to discover her father had badgered her mother into a hospital she couldn't leave.

She's an embarrassment, he'd said.

He was the embarrassment, Melodie had informed him. Terrible words had followed, ending with her nursing a bruised cheek, a sore scalp and a wrenched shoulder while she'd begged through choked-back tears for permission to see her mother. He'd forced her to stay silent on his abusive behavior if she wanted so much as a phone call.

After striking that deal, Melodie had walked out, going to a friend's house and never returning. Her privileged life had ended. She'd learned the hard way how to make ends meet, taking whatever job she could find to survive.

Of course, there was one job she had refused to stoop to, but today might be the day she completely swallowed her pride. They'd noticed at her temp office job that she had a flare for organization. They wanted to offer her a permanent position with a politician's campaign team. Become a handler. A political gofer. *Barf.*

But the money was significantly better than entry-level clerk wages.

And her mother's wish to have her ashes sprinkled in the Seine was weighing on her.

So Melodie begrudgingly put on a proper tweed skirt and jacket over a black turtleneck, put her hair in a French roll and closed the door on her new apartment far earlier than necessary so even if she missed her first bus, she wouldn't be late for her interview.

This was an old building, bordering on disrepair, and it smelled musty, but the price was right and all the locks worked.

As she walked down the stairs, she told herself to be thankful she had anything at all. After a lifetime of watching her mother struggle against negative thoughts and spirals of depression, Melodie had learned not to dwell on regrets or could-have-beens. She accepted her less-than-ideal circumstances philosophically and set goals for a better situation, confident she would get to where she wanted to be eventually. This apartment and taking a job she didn't want was merely a step in the process.

This was also the *last* time she started from scratch, she

assured herself, grateful her mother hadn't lived to see her fall on her face this way.

Mom. Pearls. France.

Her hand went to her collar, didn't find the necklace, and her heart sank into the pit of her stomach.

She tried not to think of France, but Roman crept into her thoughts day and night, taunting her with how horribly she'd misjudged him.

She blamed her sunny ideals. All her life she had wanted to believe deep emotional connections were possible, even though her mother's yearning for a better love from her father had been futile. And even though, among the loose friendships Melodie had made over the years, she'd seen more heartbreaks than success stories.

Ingrid and Huxley had fed her vision, though. Every once in a while, she came across a couple she wished she could emulate: the people who communicated with a glance and did sweet things for each other, just because.

The only way she'd coped with her barren early years had been by promising herself that real, true love would come to her eventually.

She'd mistaken a sexual reaction for a signal of mental and emotional compatibility where Roman was concerned. Maybe she wasn't as delicate as her mother had always been, but grief had been taking its toll. A month past her out-of-character encounter with Roman and she could see how susceptible she'd been that day. Ingrid's joy in her coming nuptials had created impatience for a life partner in Melodie. She'd seen the possibility of a future in a kiss from a superficially attractive man.

Relationships, she decided, could wait until both her finances *and* her heart were back on their feet. The thought allowed her to feel resilient as she reached the ground floor. She was capable of meeting challenges head-on with equanimity. She would take this job and rebuild her life.

After striding across the lobby, she pushed open the glass door onto the street.

The bluster of a nor'easter yanked it out of her hands.

Actually, it was a man. He filled the space, blocked her exit. He wore a suit and an overcoat. His dark hair glistened with rain. He was clean shaven and green eyed like a dragon. Heart-stoppingly gorgeous.

Roman Killian.

Melodie was still in Virginia, but had moved to Richmond.

The moment that detail had been reported to Roman, he'd booked a flight. The dry, musty interior of her apartment building, with its ugly red-and-silver wallpaper, closed around him as he stepped into the foyer, forcing her back several steps into the wall of mailboxes. He barely took in his surroundings. He was too busy studying her.

She looked…thin. A stab of worry hit him as he considered what that could mean for an unborn baby. Her face was wan, too, beneath her makeup. She wore a smart suit beneath an open coat, but her eyes swallowed her face. Her pale lips parted with shock. Whatever she held dropped from her grip with a muffled thump.

It was just her purse, but he shot forward in instinctive chivalry.

She snatched it before he could, jerking upright to stare down on him.

It was the oddest moment of juxtaposition. *She* was the one living in a low-end ZIP code in a modest suburb of the city. *He* appeared on list of Fortune 500 CEOs as one of the richest men in the world. His suit was tailored, his handkerchief silk.

Yet Melodie stood above him like a well-born lady. Which she was.

He knelt like a peasant. A scab on the complexion of society.

Which he was.

He held her gaze as he rose, shedding any traces of inferiority. Refusing to wear such a label. Not anymore. The struggle to get here had been too long and too hard.

Her eyes grew more blue and deep and shadowed as he straightened to his full height. He found himself resisting the urge to smile as they stood face-to-face. He'd forgotten she was so tall. She met his eyes with only the barest lift of her chin. And she impacted upon him with nothing more than turmoil and silence.

The same fascination accosted him that he'd suffered in France. He was instantly ensnared. If anything, her pull was stronger. Now he knew what it felt like to kiss her and touch her, to possess her and release all of himself into her. The power she had over him was deeply unsettling. Through air coated in layers of old carpet and must, his nostrils sought and found the hint of roses and oranges.

"What are you doing here?" she asked.

That sweetly ambling voice of hers made him want to sit back and relax. "We need to talk."

"I'm busy," she said flatly, thumbing the face of her phone to check the time. "I have an interview." She started to move around him, but he held out his hand.

It was enough to stop her. She very pointedly held herself back from accidentally brushing his arm.

Her aversion stung.

"I have to catch a bus," she said stiffly.

Seeing her in this low-end building, using public transport, gave his conscience another yank. He had another reason for being here besides the possibility of pregnancy. He needed to know for sure. Was she really estranged from her father? Had he really crushed an innocent beneath his heel that day?

"I have your things in my car," he said, "I'll drive you wherever you need to go."

"Mom's pearls?" Her averted gaze flew to his, round and anxious. "Why didn't you bring them in?"

"I saw you through the window as I was getting out. I thought—" That she might somehow escape him if he didn't act fast to catch her here in the foyer. His actions had been pure reflex.

She figured out what he'd almost revealed. "We have nothing to say to each other, Roman," she said tonelessly. "Just go out and get them. I'd like them back."

"We do have to talk," he asserted firmly, watching her for signs of evasion. When she only gave a firm shake of her head, refusing to look at him, he reminded her, "I didn't use anything that day."

Her expression blanked before comprehension dawned in a dark flood of color. Her jaw fell open, appalled. "I'm not pregnant!" she cried.

Someone down the hall opened a door and peeked out.

Melodie was scarlet with embarrassed anger. Her dismayed blue eyes glared into his as she folded her arms defensively, mouth pouted in humiliation. "I'm not."

"Are you sure?" he challenged.

"Of course I am. But I'm stunned that you've tracked me down to ask. I assumed you'd been careless on purpose. When it comes to ruining a woman's life, leaving her with an unplanned pregnancy is about as effective as it gets."

That bludgeoned hard enough to knock him back a step.

"I wouldn't do that." He was deeply offended she would think him capable of such a coldhearted form of revenge. When she only lifted disinterested brows, he insisted, "I wouldn't. I know too well what it's like to *be* an unplanned baby. I'm here to take care of my child if I have one. Do I?"

"No," Melodie insisted, forcing herself to meet his gaze even though it was very hard. She was telling the truth, but she didn't want to see his sincerity or have empathy and understand him. She only wanted to put him and her grave error behind her.

But his being here, asking the question, affected her. She'd been relieved when things had cycled along as normal. Of course she'd been relieved. Yet a small part of her had suffered a wistful moment. A baby would have been a disaster, but it would have been family. Real family. The kind she could love.

Holding out a hand, she said, "Can you just give me my mother's necklace?"

"There's definitely no baby."

"Definitely."

He absorbed that with barely a twitch of his stoic expression before he jerked his head and held the door for her.

Dear Lord, he was handsome with those long, clean-shaven cheeks set off by his turned up collar, his mouth pursed in dismay, his short thick hair tossing in the bluster of wind that grabbed at them.

The fierce breeze yanked her bound hair and shot up her skirt to bite at her skin. She clenched her teeth and beelined for the limo at the curb.

He opened the back door himself. "What's the address of where you're going?"

"Don't do me any favors, Roman. I'll just take the necklace and go."

"You're refusing my help out of spite?"

"I'm protecting what's left of my self-respect." Her knees knocked as the blustering cold penetrated mercilessly. Teeth chattering, she held out her hand. "Pearls?"

"They're right there. Get in. I have more to say."

"To quote *you*, I don't *care*."

With an air of arrogant patience, he closed another button on his coat and set his back to the wind, adopting a stance of willingness to wait for the spring thaw.

"You won't just hand them to me. You're determined

to make me miss my job interview. Look around. Getting me fired did nothing to my father," she charged.

"I know that I misjudged you," he snapped back. "But your father and brother are on the attack against me. That's not up for dispute. It's reality. And it's not common knowledge that you've lived apart from them all these years. Given the way things looked in the funeral photos, it was an easy mistake to make."

"I know," she said with the same impatience. She could understand and almost forgive that part. She had plenty of unexpressed anger of her own toward her father and brother. "And I have no problem believing they stole from you."

His brows went up a smidgen. "Not many would take my word for it."

"Anton isn't capable of writing his own email, let alone launching a high-tech start-up. I've always wondered how he managed it." She smiled bitterly. "And I have a lot of experience with how low they can sink."

His gaze sharpened and she dropped her own, shielding herself, unprepared to let him delve into all the anguish and fury roiling inside her.

"So get in."

"No."

"For God's sake, why not?"

"Because I don't trust you!"

His head went back and his expression grew carved and stoic. "I'm not going to touch you. I didn't mean to sleep with you that day."

"Oh, that's funny," she choked, trying to end that topic before it went any further. She was mortified he'd brought it up.

"It's the truth," he shot back, his energy like a living thing that whipped and raced on the tail of the wind, lashing her with its force. He was tense. Very tense as he confronted her, as if he was willing her to believe him. It was weirdly fascinating.

She tore her gaze away, not wanting to get caught up in trying to decipher the truth from his lies. Not wanting to hear excuses and let down her guard. He'd already gotten past her defenses too easily, setting her back so she was as naked and defenseless as she'd been that day. It wasn't him she mistrusted, but herself.

She ought to be able to shut him out the way she had with her father and Anton. Roman meant nothing to her. Less than nothing. As bitter as she was toward her father and half brother, she went days, weeks even, without thinking of them, but no such luck with Roman. He was top of her mind every day, ambushing her with memories of kisses and caresses and wrenching pleasure.

She swallowed, not wanting the recollections to surface now.

Her blood warmed anyway. Her senses heightened, making her aware of his scent, masculine and sharp, beneath the sweet smell of rain and the comforting notes of damp wool. Clothing didn't make a man, but everything about his appearance amplified his stark masculinity. His cheekbones were proud and chiseled, his nose a blade, his lips twitching almost into a closed-mouth kiss as he prepared to speak.

"I slept with you in spite of who you are, not because of it," he said in a growl.

"Had a staggering crash in your standards, did you?" Insult blindsided her as she absorbed that he was saying she'd been willing and he had merely taken advantage. Any man would. "At least when I thought you seduced me for revenge, it was personal. I honestly thought I couldn't feel worse about that day. Thanks, Roman. You're a real guy."

"And you're twisting me into a far more vicious bastard than I am."

She stared at him, astonished. "You made *hatred* to me." The words swelled in her throat. She clenched her jaw, trying to hold back convulsive shivers, trying to hold on to control and not allow emotion to rise up and sting her eyes. "At least I had some respect for you that afternoon, before you started ruining my life."

"Would you get in the damned car?"

She realized people were walking by, staring. Overhearing.

She was freezing, and warm air radiated from the interior. With a sob of annoyed misery, she threw herself into the backseat.

He followed and slammed the door, adjusting the vents so hot gushes of air poured directly onto her.

She didn't thank him, even though her legs were stinging and her fingers were numb. She attacked the box with her name on it, spilling her mother's necklace into her lap. Picking it up, she pressed the treasured beads to her lips.

"I only meant to do to you what they did to me, which was cut short your career and leave you with bills to pay," Roman said.

She dropped her hands. "But you accidentally slept with me, even though you hated me," she charged, going hot again. Bristling with temper.

"Yes," he asserted, as if that proved some kind of point beyond the fact he was a conscienceless womanizer.

"To humiliate me," she confirmed in a jagged voice, looking over at him in time to see guilt flash across his expression before he controlled it.

"I thought you were throwing yourself at me for their purposes. It looked as if you were trying to trick me into letting you stay in my house. I let you come on to me so I could turn you down," he admitted.

"But you went through with it," she said, returning to that deep sense of bitterness that had burned through her with every step of her journey back to the hotel that day, as she'd absorbed that what had looked like a white knight had actually been the same blackened soul that the men in her family possessed. "How do people like you sleep at night? That's what I want to know."

"Do *not* lump me in with them, Melodie," he fired back, temper riled enough to darken his expression and press her into her seat. "Do you see them chasing you down the East Coast to ask about consequences? I am *not* just like them." His jaw worked. "I'll be the first to admit I'm not a good man, definitely not a great one, but I'm *not* as immoral as they are."

The way she'd set him on the same reprehensible shelf as the Gautier men ate at him. She could see it. That should have been more satisfying, but it just made her feel small.

"Sleeping with you just happened," he muttered.

"Because I threw myself at you," she provided, feeling the sting press forward from the backs of her eyes to blur her vision. "Because you couldn't resist me." *Spider arms. Freak.*

She narrowed her eyes, turning her face away as she willed Anton's voice to silence and willed her tears to dry before they squeezed past her lashes and fell.

"Yes."

She hated Roman in that moment. Really hated him. Because he sounded so begrudging as he said it. Not smooth and charming and manipulative. Resentful. He sounded as confounded by his reaction as she was by hers. That made him sound truthful even though she was convinced he had to be lying.

"I know I'm not beautiful. At best, I'm striking," she said, straining to keep emotion from her voice. "I'm certainly not the type who inspires lust, so give it a rest. You wanted to hurt me. Which you did."

"I'm not here to hurt you again," he ground out, flinching as though she'd slapped him. "I can't take back what I did. If I could…" he began tightly, emotions so compressed she couldn't read anything in his tone but intensity.

He *would* take it back? Her heart clenched in a surprisingly strong contraction of agony.

Of course she would take it back, too, she assured herself, even as their heights of pleasure danced through her consciousness, reminded her how rare and singular the experience had been. He'd ruined her for accepting anything less, if he wanted the truth, which left her feeling bleak and hopeless.

"You told me that day that you were attracted to me," he said.

"Don't throw that in my face," she cried, recoiling from being mocked.

"I was attracted, too. More than I knew how to handle. That's why I slept with you. Not out of revenge. Not to humiliate you."

She swallowed, wavering toward believing him, but it strained credulity. "It wasn't love at first sight, Roman. I saw the way you looked at me the day I arrived. You weren't interested."

"I didn't let my interest show. There's a difference."

She had to turn her nose to the window then, hope rising too quickly. Did she have no sense of self-preservation? Believing in him had only gotten her a giant helping of heartache the last time.

But he was very contained, not giving away much, very good at keeping his thoughts and feelings well hidden. Maybe he had been attracted.

Even if he had been, so what?

With a troubled sigh, she realized she was crushing the pearls in her clenched hands. Her fingers were warm enough to work now. She reached to close the strand around her throat.

Wool slid against leather and Roman was in her space, fingers brushing hers.

With an alarm that came more from a jolt of excitement than fear, she released the pearls and let him take over, angling herself so he could finish quickly. Her skin tightened all over her body as his knuckles brushed the tiny, upswept hairs at the back of her head. Beneath her layers of clothing her nipples tightened into sharp peaks and her blood grew hot, radiating heat outward to dispel any lingering chill for the rest of time.

The moment he was done she shifted away from his disturbing touch, adjusting the weight of the necklace so it felt right, and flashed a nervous glance his way.

He was watching her intently. "I felt it, too. There's something in our chemistry."

"I don't know what you're talking about," she dismissed with an unsettled shake of her head. If the traffic hadn't been so busy, she would have pushed out her side of the car. "I need to get to my job interview. Let me out."

"Don't start lying to me now, Melodie. Not when we're clearing the air." He didn't move.

Her heart began to pound with a trapped bird sort of panic. "Look," she said, tugging the hem of her skirt down her knee. Electricity seemed to crackle between them like fingers of lightning. "I know I gave you the impression I'm easy. I'm not. So don't start with your moves."

"Moves," he repeated on a dry chuckle. "Like how I seduced you that day? *You* kissed *me*."

"Don't remind me!" she cried.

"I will remind you," he said, leaning into her. "And I'll even be honest enough to admit I lied to you that day. I said it's always like that for me, but who has an encounter like that *ever* in their lifetime?"

Melodie shot her gaze to his. He was so close and disturbing. His brow was pulled into a perturbed line, his skin taut with challenge and something else. Discomfort, maybe, with how much he was admitting.

Between one breath and the next the shared memory of their wild coming together filled the tiny space behind these tinted windows.

She couldn't look away from his rain-forest eyes. He pinned her in place with nothing but a tiny shift of his attention to her mouth.

Her heart began to race and her blood felt as though it zigzagged in her veins. Her breasts flooded with heat, growing heavy and achy, the tips tight with reaction.

Desire clouded his irises.

A fog of longing smothered her consciousness, making sensible thought slippery and vague. She found herself looking at his mouth. In her dreams those lips plundered hers. She always woke with one question uppermost in her mind: Had it really been that good?

His lips parted as he came closer.

She opened with instinctive welcome.

They made contact and intense relief washed through her as a great thirst was finally slaked. His hand came to the side of her face, open and tender. She tilted into his touch, feeling moved and cherished as he cradled her head and gently but thoroughly devoured her.

She drew on him with greedy abandon, forgetting everything except that he filled a vast need in her. There were no words, just a craving that both ceased and grew as they locked mouths and touched tongues. His body closed in, pressed. He overwhelmed her as he wrapped his arms fully around her.

She moaned, pleasure blooming in her like a supernova. She instantly ached for more intimate contact with him.

His arms tightened, gathering her to draw her with him as he sat back, pulling her into his lap.

The shift was enough of a jolt to make her pull back

and realize where they were, how her knees had fallen on either side of his thighs, skirt riding up. She was losing all contact with reality. Again.

Then what?

"This can't happen," she gasped.

She pushed off him, throwing herself awkwardly onto the seat opposite and glaring back at him. She felt like a mouse that might have freed herself from the cat's mouth, but only until he wanted to clamp down on her again.

"Not here, no. Come to my hotel with me," he said, voice sandpapery and exquisitely inviting.

"For what?" she cried.

"Don't be dense," he growled. "We're an incredible combination. You can feel the power of it as well as I can."

"You've really perfected this technique of yours, haven't you?" she choked. "Listen, you might sleep with people you loathe, but I don't. I won't sleep with a man I hate."

He snapped his head back.

Her conscience prickled. She didn't hate him. There was too much empathy and understanding in her for such a heartless emotion.

"Well, that's that. Isn't it?" He thrust himself from the car, holding the door open for her.

Icy wind flew in to accost her, scraping her legs and stabbing through her clothes as she rose from the cozy interior to the ferocity of winter, entire body shaking, heart fragile.

"Goodbye, Roman," she said, feeling as if she was losing something as precious as her mother's pearls.

"Melodie."

Not goodbye, she noted, but his tone still sounded final and made her unutterably sad. Clutching the edges of her jacket closed, she walked to the bus stop on heavy feet.

CHAPTER SIX

ROMAN WENT BACK to his house in France where he could live in his own personal exile and ruminate, but despite only being here once, Melodie infused the place.

He never should have gone after her. If it hadn't been for the possibility of a baby, he wouldn't have, but there was no way he could have let a child of his grow up the way he had—not just poor and alone, but with a million questions and a million facets of rejection glittering into the furthest corners of its psyche. The one time he'd asked his mother about his father, she'd said, "He was a rich man who said he loved me, but I guess he didn't because he didn't come back."

He was a rich man, one who was very careful not to use those words and provoke false hope. He'd always hated his father for being a liar while secretly fearing he was just like the man: incapable of real love. He wasn't particularly likable. He knew that. Foster care had taught him to hold back, be cautious, not expect that he was anything but a burden to be tolerated. He came in too late with any sign of caring, long after he'd been written off as stunted. This was why he didn't pursue serious relationships with women or even have close friendships.

But he didn't usually provoke people to hatred. It maddened him that Melodie felt that way. He shouldn't have kissed her, he knew that, but the attraction between them had still been there. She'd responded to his touch.

Yet she reviled him too much to let things progress.

While he could think of nothing but touching her again. Grazing the warmth of her neck with his fingertips had been the height of eroticism. Kissing her again had inflamed him.

The fact that she was driving him insane, mentally and physically, told him it was time to cut ties altogether. It was time to forget her and move on with his life.

Melodie had always read her horoscope, trusted in karma and hoped fate really did have a plan for her. For the sake of her sanity she clung to the belief that good things happened to good people if they stuck in there long enough. The Gautier men were masters of cynicism, but she was different. And she wouldn't crumble under the weight of the dark side like her mother had, taking the first path out of life that was offered. She would fight and prevail.

Then Roman Killian had happened.

He'd not only shown her that she couldn't trust her own instincts and judgment, he'd provoked bitterness and pessimism in her. A depressing attitude lingered in her long after her encounter with him in his limo, an aimless feeling of "what's the point?"

That wasn't like her, but she couldn't seem to shake the mood. Her only hope was that fulfilling her mother's wish for her remains to float down the Seine would help her find closure and move on. Accomplishing that was the reason she had sold her soul and taken the job campaigning with Trenton Sadler.

And, since fate had a sense of humor, that seemed to demand she face Roman Killian again.

As coincidences went, winding up at a New York gala he was attending was a kick in the teeth from the karmic gods, but what had she done to make the planets align against her so maliciously?

Maybe it was just a fluke. She *was* traveling in higher circles these days, literally traveling, finally seeing New York if only from a hotel window. Her new employer was actively seeking corporate introductions, happy to be seen hobnobbing with lobbyists and special-interest groups.

He was exactly like her father, and she'd made her deal with Trenton Sadler like a blues guitarist shaking hands with Satan at the crossroads. He didn't know she was a senator's daughter. No, he thought she was simply a surprise talent he'd rescued from a temp agency, one who'd dabbled in catering and event planning. But Melodie was pulling out every maneuver she'd ever learned at Daddy's knee. Trenton loved her for it.

She didn't care for him at all, hated the work because it had everything to do with political-party advancement and nothing to do with the needs of the people, but she was good at it, and the compensation was more than a livable wage. And Trenton had promised her a bonus if he got the nomination he was after. It would be enough to square up her line of credit and fund her trip to Paris.

That was the only reason she was living out of a suitcase along with the rest of Trenton's handlers, renting black strapless evening gowns and pressing palms while conjuring a vapid smile. Tonight she'd lost track of whether they were buying or selling, whether this was a fund-raiser or a charity auction or a grand opening. All she knew was that she was in another hotel ballroom. She felt as if she'd come full circle, accomplishing nothing with her life, when she glanced toward the entrance and saw *him*.

Her heart gave a lurch.

Roman Killian had the uncanny ability to make whatever he wore fall into the background so all she noticed was the magnificence of the man. His head was tilted down to a beautiful blonde by his side, but with a disconcerting suddenness he jerked his head up and scanned the room.

Melodie watched with morbid fascination, thinking she was imagining what she was seeing, but as she watched, Roman cataloged the crowd like a robotic laser shone from his eyes. The blonde continued speaking, but he didn't seem to notice. His visage slowly rotated toward Melodie, as though he was computing every face in the room until—

He stopped when he spotted her.

She was almost knocked back a step. All of her froze except her pulse, which galloped like a spooked horse, kicking and squealing. His hair was extra rakish tonight, suggesting that the woman's fingers had ruffled it. His jaw looked hard and polished. His expression was completely unreadable as he kept his gaze fixed on her.

"Who is that?" Trenton asked beside her, rattling her out of her stasis.

"Roman Killian." Her throat was dry. Her entire being went numb as Roman flicked his gaze to Trenton and came back to her before he turned his attention to the blonde, his expression inscrutable.

"Tech-Sec Industries?" Trenton asked, forcing Melodie to bring her mind back from a limo and a kiss that had been every bit as profound and memorable as the ones in France and twice as much of a letdown afterward. "Why didn't you tell me you had a connection like that?"

"I don't," she said huskily. "We've only met once. Twice." *Three times.* "We're not friends," she assured him.

"Sure about that?" Trenton asked, giving her the kind of male once-over he'd started sending her way this trip. She had watched him flirt openly with more than one impressionable young supporter in his office, despite having a wife who kept the home fires burning. He hadn't gone out of his way to hit on Melodie, though, preferring to bark orders for coffee and sandwiches in her direction. Being the only female traveling with the group seemed to have elevated her to a target, however.

"I'm sure," she affirmed, recalling her last words to Roman, which had been most unfriendly. She tried to clear the catch from her throat as she added, "I should leave, or I might become a liability."

"No," he said with a thoughtful glance at the way Roman had joined a group near the bar, but had positioned himself so Melodie was in his line of sight. "Introduce us. Be as nice as you have to be to get him on my side. I want his support."

We don't always get what we want, Melodie wanted to say.

"He wasn't on the list," she reminded him. Mrs. Sadler had stayed home for this whirlwind junket. The rest of the team had stayed in their rooms and Melodie was standing in as Trenton's date, something he seemed to think gave him the right to hands-on access. She'd been finding ways to sidestep, but she had her assignment when it came to ensuring the right connections were made. Roman Killian wasn't one of the names in the room they had to touch base with, though.

In fact, if she'd known he'd be attending, she would have wormed her way out of this evening altogether. Mentally reviewing the guest list, she recalled a Swedish actress had been on it. Roman must be her plus one. Why his being involved with someone should cause a pinch near her heart, Melodie had no idea, but she didn't want to get close enough to see how deep his involvement with the stacked blonde went.

Trenton didn't care about her needs, though. "Introduce us," he repeated firmly.

Paris, she thought.

"If you like." She gathered her courage and found a stiff smile.

It took time to work through the crowded ballroom. They had to stop midway to listen to a speech about the refurbishment of this iconic hotel, one of New York's first skyscrapers. Applause happened, balloons fell, dancing started.

Melodie tried to pretend she wasn't in an intricate waltz with Roman, one in which she took two steps forward and sidestepped one. She was aware of his every shift and turn as he and his date worked the room. When he took the actress to the dance floor, Melodie told herself she only noticed because he was Trenton's quarry. They were gaining on him.

He came off the dance floor feet away from where she stood with Trenton, practically an invitation to approach. The tray of champagne appeared to have been their goal. Roman took two and turned his back on Melodie as he handed a flute to the blonde, but the opportunity was at hand.

Melodie felt his nearness like the heat off a blaze. Anticipation began to buzz in her. She neutralized her nerves by setting a light touch on Trenton's arm to break into his current conversation.

"I believe our opening has arrived," she told him, smiling a goodbye at the navy general and his wife as Trenton covered her hand, insisting she maintain the contact while they crossed the small distance to where Roman and his girlfriend were sipping their drinks.

Roman looked at her, and it was the same sweep of her feet out from under her as ever. All the air seemed to leave her body under the impact of his cool, green gaze and she had to gather her composure just to speak.

"Mr. Killian. What a surprise to bump into you here. I don't think you know Trenton Sadler—"

"I've seen the ads," Roman said, flicking a cynical twitch of his lips at Trenton as they shook hands. "This is Greta Sorensen."

"I've seen some of your films. I love romantic comedies," Melodie said, sincere for the first time all evening.

"I'm filming one now. That's why I'm here in New York," Greta said in her prettily accented English.

"And she has to be at work very early tomorrow morning," Roman said. "So we were just leaving. Good night." It was quite a snub, one that made Greta's eyes widen slightly before she turned it into a smoky look of anticipation aimed straight at Roman.

"I'll assume that brush-off was meant for you, not me," Trenton said tightly as Roman steered Greta toward the exit.

"I told you we weren't friends." Melodie reeled from the rebuff, her entire body stinging as though she'd been lashed front and back. Something in her ought to have been worried about how this would impact her job, but all she could think was that the encounter had made her incredibly sad. Especially if he was in a rush to make love to his date before she got her unnecessary beauty sleep. Lucky Greta.

"You didn't exactly try to kiss and make up, did you?" Trenton charged.

Ah, the temperament of the politically hungry. Melodie ignored his tone, swallowed back a disturbing thickness in her throat and adopted her own implacable smile as she nudged Trenton toward a paunchy older gentleman. Work. Paris. She would not speculate on what Roman was doing with that Swedish sex kitten.

Nor would she wonder what her life would look like right now if she'd allowed Roman to take her back to his hotel room that day four months ago. Had she been tempted? On a physical level, absolutely. Even now, she regularly woke up damp with perspiration, deeply aroused, remnants of sexually explicit dreams lingering behind her clenched eyes.

Why did he have to torture her this way?

A man who could set aside revulsion toward a woman and bed her anyway was obviously incapable of the sort of love and respect she had always wanted. He'd battered her heart so thoroughly she doubted she'd ever recover.

Which made her furious with him all over again.

Firm hands descended on her waist from behind.

She gasped under a jolt of electricity, nerve endings flaring hotly, immediately aware who was touching her. She covered his hands, trying to remove them, but he only held on more possessively.

Trenton broke off midspiel and glanced at her, brows going up as he recognized who stood behind her. "I thought you were taking your date home?" he said.

"She's staying on the eleventh floor. Dance with me, Melodie."

No. She couldn't breathe to speak.

"Good idea," Trenton said, piercing her with a significant "be nice" look.

Numbly she let Roman guide her onto the dance floor. Actually, she wasn't numb. She was so sensitive every touch and smell and sound overwhelmed her. She couldn't pick out the beat in the music or tell whether his hands were hot or her skin was flushing in reaction to his hold on her. Her throat hurt where her pulse thrummed. Her limbs felt clumsy as she set one hand on his shoulder and the other hand in his.

"Why—?" she tried, but her voice didn't want to work. She wasn't sure what she was asking anyway. So many questions crowded up from the hollow space between her knotted stomach and her tight lungs she couldn't make sense of a single one.

"Are you sleeping with him?" he asked with seeming disinterest. "He's married, you know."

She snorted, disdainful words choking past the locked

gate of her collarbone. "I'm aware, and no. He's my boss. What happened to Greta? Turn you down?"

"I don't sleep with clients, but she wanted to make an appearance." His touch on her changed, fingers closing more firmly over hers. His hand weighed more heavily at her waist. A hint of dry humor glinted in his eye. "Now that we've got that out of the way…"

"I don't care," she tried, but came up against her own dishonesty as quickly as his smirk flashed and disappeared.

"No. Of course not. You hate me. Why are you dancing with me, then?"

"I was told to be nice to you." Offering a lethal mimic of Greta's smoky look, she warned, "Do *not* get me fired, Roman. I *will* kill you."

"He's a sycophant."

"So am I," she retorted, squirming inwardly at being caught out as one of Trenton's minions. "It pays the bills."

Roman's mouth tightened briefly before he allowed, "You're good at working a room. I've been watching you."

Melodie tingled with awareness at the idea of his watching her, covering her reaction with a blasé "Mom always needed a wing woman at these sorts of things. When it was her turn to host, I made all the arrangements. Ingrid's wedding really would have come off beautifully under my hand, you know. How are the arrangements coming along?"

"I have no idea. She's training her replacement and that's enough comedy for my tastes."

"Because weddings are a joke? Falling in love is for the weak and pathetic? I'm beginning to agree with you, Roman. Which makes me hate you all the more," she added with a quiet burst of ferocity.

He spun her off the dance floor and behind a mirrored column.

"I tried to apologize to you that day," he reminded hotly.

"You tried to pick me up," she threw back, scraped raw all over again.

Four months had passed since their last meeting and Roman had managed to convince himself he'd forgotten her. The moment he had entered the room, however, a preternatural sense had sparked awake in him. He'd known she was here.

Then he'd spied her, toffee hair swept up to reveal her long neck and those deliciously modest pearls. Her shoulders were bared by her dress. The rest of her gown had hardly impacted upon him as he'd taken in the statue-still bust her head and shoulders made staring back at him.

She still hated him, he'd seen immediately, judging by her lack of a smile.

Then he'd seen her date touch her arm and something had snapped awake in him, an emotion that was blade sharp and ferocious. He suspected it was jealousy, because for a moment he'd been blind. All the hairs had lifted on his body and his blood had pumped in anticipation as he had prepared to shove through the crowd to get to her.

Sense had prevailed, albeit very weakly. He hadn't been able to dump his date fast enough and get back to Melodie once she'd opened the borders and spoken to him. Now her scent filled his nostrils and his muscles twitched to clamp his arms around her. He was primed to throw her over his shoulder and steal her from the room while fighting off rivals.

He was damned close to doing so. The bitter look she gave him was filled with acid and ate away at what control he had.

"Do you think I wouldn't control this if I could? That I don't hate *you* for affecting *me* like this?" He threw the words at her.

Her head flung back as if he'd slapped her.

"No, it doesn't feel very good, does it?" he gritted out, skin threatening to split under the pressure of containing himself. "It's not me doing this to you, Melodie. It's *us*. I'm this close to having you against this damned wall with the entire room watching. It's that powerful."

"Even though you hate me." She turned her face to the side, eyes glistening.

"What do you want me to say? That I love you?" The word caught like a barbed hook on the way out, snagging in his chest and the back of his throat. It wasn't a word he even understood beyond its bastardized use. *I love this car. I love crème brulée.*

"I wouldn't believe you if you did, but I want the man I sleep with to say it," she said with a break of anguish in her voice. "I want to feel it. It's the only thing that's kept me going all those years, believing I'd make better choices with men than my mother did. I'm so lonely I want to cry, but I can't bring myself to believe any of you anymore." Her lips trembled. "You *broke* me, Roman. That's why I hate you."

He sucked in a breath that felt like razor blades.

"I hate being this person. I hate being skeptical and negative," she went on, skimming trembling fingertips beneath her eyes. "I hate using words like *hate*." She sent a quick, desperate glance toward the exit. "I need to go to the ladies' room."

Because she was falling apart.

He thought he might. *Hell.*

Catching her arm, he used his height and confidence to muscle through the crowd to where a bellman was checking names at the door. "You have something for me. Roman Killian."

"Of course. Right here, sir." The bellman handed over a small folder with a number on the inside cover. It contained Roman's room key and the credit card he'd handed to a member of staff on his way back into the ballroom after dropping off Greta with a handshake.

He hadn't intended to book a room here until he'd seen Melodie.

Melodie gave a muted sniff and turned toward a sign pointing out the facilities, but he drew her across the atrium toward the elevators.

"I can't leave," she said, accepting Roman's handkerchief as he hustled her along. Then she paused to lean into her smudged reflection in an etched panel. "Actually, I should go to my room to fix my makeup."

The elevator doors opened and he pressed her into the car.

"Six," she said.

He ignored that and pressed the P.

"Roman—" She started to poke 6.

He stopped her. "We're going to talk, Melodie. Clear the air once and for all."

"There's no point," she insisted, voice husky and fatalistic. "You're right. We do goad each other and bring out the worst. That means we should stay as far away from each other as possible."

Her words spiked into him, making him fearful to draw breath, knowing it would burn. "Do you really think that?"

A rush of emotion welled in her eyes and made her clamp her lips together. She dropped her gaze.

"I didn't listen to you that first day. We might not have damaged each other so badly if I had. This time we get it all on the table. Neither of us can move forward until we do."

"I damaged you?" she asked with disbelief. "How?"

"You made me question whether I'm a worthy human being."

CHAPTER SEVEN

MELODIE FLINCHED AT being called out for hurting him, astonished that she could.

And disturbed. It meant they really were bad for each other. So how could she drop her anger and embrace the idea they could sort things out? Anger was safe. Listening and understanding would only make her feel guilty and vulnerable. Trusting Roman would mean abandoning her defensive animosity, and that scared her. It would leave her with nothing to hold him off.

He still scared her, she admitted privately. Still caused a reaction in her that was stronger than logic. Whether it was fury or passion, she'd never dealt with such intense feelings. The closest she'd come had been the fire that had burned inside her while fighting with her father over her mother's care. Those emotions had made sense, though. They'd been born of deep loyalty and love...

She cut short looking for similarities. Roman was a stranger. They'd only met a handful of times, and even she, with her Pollyanna ideals, suspected love at first sight was a myth. If it did exist it wouldn't feel like this. As if a man she barely knew was a god with the power to smite her in a blink.

As they entered the penthouse, he went to the bar while she took in the well-appointed suite with its view of the New York skyline, its Old English furniture and its softly glowing vintage lamps draped in shimmering crystal beads.

"Scotch? Or wine?" he asked, holding up a bottle.

"I can't stay long." She glanced at the time on her phone, ignored a text from one of the aides asking how things were going and dropped the device back into her clutch, sighing heavily. "What is there to say anyway? I was feeling very low about my mother's death when we met. I wanted to meet someone, to feel alive. I let myself think there was more potential between us than there was. I shouldn't have slept with you, but I did. It gave you the wrong impression about how I conduct myself."

He brought her a glass of white wine, the glass frosted by the chill of the liquid. His expression was cool and unreadable. She sipped, wetting her dry tongue and soothing her burning throat, trying to collect herself while the strange energy that emanated off him took her apart at the seams.

"Did you hear me that day in the car? I didn't make *hatred* to you. There was nothing in my mind at that moment except the pleasure we were giving each other."

"Don't," she said, brushing a wisp of hair behind her ear and using the motion to hide her flinch of self-consciousness.

"We have to be frank. I don't like it any more than you do." He brought his glass of neat scotch up to his lips but paused and lowered it again. "I don't chase women for sport, Melodie. It's important to me that you believe that. I'm lousy in a relationship, but not because I treat women like sex providers. If I hadn't had a reason to kick you out that day, you would have been in my bed until *you* tired of *me*."

"Does that happen?" she asked with a faint attempt at levity. It was supposed to be a swipe at the man she assumed him to be: a gorgeous playboy with enough money to hold any woman's interest.

"I'm emotionally inaccessible," he said with a pained

smile, as if it was a tragic but proved fact. "And the sex has never been like it is with us." He spoke as though it was something happening in the now, and indicated the invisible strands that pulled her toward him and, if he was to be believed, drew him just as inexorably.

She shifted away from the disturbing aura of sexual tension that grew between them so easily, feeling terribly weak. She would understand this gross sense of helplessness if she had given her heart to him. As a child yearning for love and approval from Garner and Anton, she'd walked around as spineless as her mother, taking each slight to heart. Eventually, living in the real world, she'd suffered fewer attacks, and most of them from people she cared little about. Her inner defenses had rallied and strengthened.

Now, after a handful of encounters with Roman, a man who should mean nothing to her, she was more emotionally sensitive than ever, responding to every word he said as if it was her own inner voice. It was disconcerting.

She eyed him, unsettled by his talk of feeling the same irrevocable pull. "I don't understand how it can be like this if we don't love each other."

"I've never understood how love enters into sex at all." He tilted his glass to watch the liquid move in the square bottom of his glass. "I've always thought pleasure was the point. Don't look like that," he chided gently, glancing up to catch what was probably a wounded expression on her face. "I didn't say that to mock you. I'm being honest."

She ducked her head. "It still hurts. You didn't even think I was attractive, Roman. It wasn't until the second day that you started to act as though you were interested, and that was after you knew who I was."

"I told you in Virginia, just because I didn't let it show doesn't mean I wasn't attracted. I'm not interested in serious relationships, Melodie. By that I mean marriage, kids, a lifetime commitment... I'm not cut out for that. You looked like the kind who is. So you're right, at that first meeting I made sure to keep my interest hidden to avoid going down a dead-end road. Then you smiled for the pictures and..." He frowned, took a sip of scotch and curled his lip in self-deprecation. "The truth is I was captivated. I couldn't hide how I was reacting when you came back the next day. I stopped trying. You're very beautiful."

She shook her head, not comfortable hearing that ever, but especially from him. Especially now. "Roman, I'm trying to believe you. I need to make sense of all this, but we have to be honest if—"

"Your mother was in magazines," he cut in with a baffled look. "You resemble her. How could you not know how pretty you are?"

Anton. She didn't say it. She wanted to be completely over him and his ugly criticisms.

"Mom was always described as *unusual* or *arresting*. She was just really emotive in front of a camera, unable to hide what she was feeling."

"And you're the same. Your true self comes through, and that woman is lovely, Melodie. I should have paid attention to that, not the fact that you happen to share the name Gautier," he added in a mutter aimed at the bottom of his glass.

She took a few swift footsteps away. He made her feel positively defenseless. She did everything in her power not to react, even though she wanted to flinch, while her pulse tripped in alarm and insecurity attacked her. She had worked so hard to get over all the self-doubts instilled by her upbringing. If there was any benefit to her mother's hospitalization, it had been the secondhand counseling she'd received. She may not have battled the same physiological depression her mother had fought, but her early years had been exactly the same steady erosion of her self-esteem that her mother had faced.

Now Roman was saying he could see past all the small shields she'd managed to assemble for herself. It was terrifying. She stood in silence, trying to pretend he held no such power while she waited to see where and how he'd use his power to advantage.

"I don't *want* the ability to hurt you, Melodie," he said finally. "I'm emotionally detached by conscious decision, but I can't stay indifferent around you. *You*," he said with a significant tone. "No one else gets under my skin this way."

She almost found a shred of humor in his vexed tone. She could relate. The truth was she didn't want the power to hurt him, either.

"I don't understand why we're like this," she said. "We don't *know* each other."

"Don't we?" He set down his drink and pushed his bunched fists into his pockets. His shoulders went back and his profile was a sharp silhouette against the black windows. "Who holds a woman's ashes hostage so her daughter has to put her grief on display? It's as bad as stealing a young man's only hope for a future by threatening to expose his one mistake in the past."

Melodie swallowed, acknowledging that he probably did understand her at a very deep level. "Did Anton contribute *anything* to that software program that built his fortune?"

"His name." Roman's expression lost its warmth, hardening. "He was doing me the favor of attaching himself to it. I was desperate enough to give up fifty percent for that. After a sound beating, I agreed to a hundred."

Melodie gasped, feeling his words like a wrecking ball hitting her chest. But she supposed any man who could shake a woman until she begged for mercy could beat a man to a pulp.

"After Mom's funeral they were never going to be in

my life again. The job with Ingrid was a fresh start, finally a potential career. I couldn't have traveled for work while Mom was alive. She needed to see me every day. We needed each other," she corrected, setting down her own glass and purse on a side table to hug herself.

"Dad always had final say in her care, so he was always this dark presence that kept me on edge. Then, finally, even though it was only her ashes, she *was* in my care. I saw myself drawing a line under my childhood but…" She shrugged, accosted by vulnerability again, but it wasn't as hard this time. She was beginning to feel safe making her confession to him. "You were supposed to be the redemption, Roman. You were supposed to prove that not all men are the same. You let me down. You proved that they can still hurt me. That all the brutality and ugliness they put into the world is still able to bounce back and hit me."

"Melodie, I didn't *know*."

"I know," she acknowledged with a jerky nod. "Anton has a daughter out there from a college girlfriend. I check in on her, send her money sometimes. He doesn't care. You cared enough to show up and ask if you had a baby on the way. I knew that day in the limo that you weren't really like them. I just…"

"Still hate me."

"I'm trying to, Roman. If I don't, then you'll—"

"What?" he prompted quickly, demeanor changing.

He knew. She blushed and had to look away.

A muted noise sounded, and they both looked to the clutch where she'd set it next to her glass. Her mobile vibrated inside it.

"Trenton is wondering where I am," she guessed, then made a face, feeling as though she was with a friend after all, she supposed, because she found herself saying a very uncharitable, "I should text back that I'm *being nice* to you."

The banked sexual awareness between them flared like the catch of a match.

"That wasn't—" she hurried to say.

"I know." He sounded as though he was laughing at her, making her shoot a scowl his direction. "I'm not going to make another unwelcome pass, Melodie. No matter how much I want to."

Which was a pass in itself, she noted drily, but managed to say, "Good." Even though she was suddenly reluctant to accept that. Her mind was expanding with one ballooning thought. What would it be like now, when they'd set aside the misjudgments and animosity?

"I should go," she said briskly. Before she lost her mind.

"I'll walk you down."

"You don't have to." She picked up her clutch and headed toward the door.

He pocketed his room key off the bar and followed her. "Better if we both reappear without looking flushed and disheveled."

"Right." Flushed. Disheveled. Skin damp and whole body tingling in the aftermath of orgasm. That would be bad. "Yes," she affirmed. "You're probably right."

"Only probably? Don't give me an opening, Melodie. I will take it," he said.

They stood at the door, his hand on the latch, his white shirt and black jacket filling her vision.

"An opening for what?" She was playing dumb, not like her at all.

His mouth lifted at one corner, knowing. "I said I wouldn't make an unwelcome pass," he said, then touched her chin, gently forcing her to tilt up her face until she couldn't avoid his eyes. "If this is not welcome, say so now."

His touch was bringing her to life in ways she had thought were manifestations of an overactive imagination.

"I keep wondering—"

He covered her mouth and she knew. They were every bit as volatile as before. They stepped into the kiss with synchronicity, her arms going over his shoulders, his hands sliding to her lower back, pulling her hips into his. In heels she was eye level with his mouth, and they both moaned with pleasure at how perfectly they fit together.

The buzz sounded again from inside her purse.

They broke away.

She threw the clutch toward the sofa, missing. It hit the floor and slid while they stepped into tight contact again, lips meeting without hesitation or clumsiness. Her same distant thoughts of how and why penetrated, but she honestly didn't care. *He* was the man who did this to her. She couldn't turn away now that it had started. And there was no evidence of his trying to slow things down as his fingertips dug into her buttocks and he rotated to press her into the door.

Oh, the weight of him felt good!

Pushing into his thighs with her own, she incited where he was already hard.

He ground back, making a growling noise as he drew back just enough to smooth the fine hairs from her neck, then nipped and nibbled his way to her bare shoulder. The action was both tender and feral, as though he was asserting his dominance but with gentle care, demanding her capitulation in the exposure of her throat to him, rewarding her with caresses that trickled delicious fire through her whole body.

Threading fingers into his hair, she moaned his name, helpless to the onslaught of pleasure. Weak against the masculine power that didn't need muscle to overwhelm her.

"Feel what you're doing to me," he said, lifting his head

and dragging her hand to his neck. Beneath her palm his artery pulsed in hard, rapid pumps.

"Mine's going to explode, too," she said, drawing his hand to her chest, where her heart raced in such a rapid tattoo it alarmed her.

He slid his palm lower, cupping her breast, watching as he plumped the swell and circled the tip with his thumb, nipple tight and straining against silk.

Showers of delight glittered through her. She slid her hand to the back of his head and urged him to kiss her again.

He did, once, hard, then lifted his head. "I want to do it right." He clasped her hand, drew it from his hair so he could kiss her wrist. "I want to take our time and do it because we make each other feel so damned good. Stay with me."

It meant trusting him. Trusting that afterward he wouldn't throw her out and ruin her life.

Her stupid purse hummed, making her look past his shoulder with an anguished noise. When she tried to step away from him, he resisted letting her go. For one long second his muscles locked in refusal. Then he sucked in a breath and stepped back, hands up with frustrated surrender, shoulders hitting the wall next to the door as he accepted her rejection with a stoic face and a knock of his head into the wall behind him.

Paris, she thought. And, *Be nice*.

Looking back at Roman, at the way he'd lowered his eyelids to hide his thoughts but couldn't disguise the way his mouth had gone flat with dismay, she shrugged off doubts and skepticism. All she could think was *I want him*.

She walked over to kick her purse so it skittered under the sofa, then looked over her shoulder at him.

He came off the wall, alert.

Swallowing, she reached behind to begin lowering the zipper on her dress.

As it loosened across her bust, his breath hissed and his chest swelled. He came across to help.

She wanted to smile, but her gown puddled on the floor around her spiked heels. She hesitated, wearing only her bra and thong underpants, the vulnerability of the moment striking her with a sudden chill.

The way he looked at her bolstered her courage, though. His gaze ate her up while he shed his jacket, then pulled at his bow tie.

"Condom?" she managed to ask, trying to hang on to some shred of sense.

His expression blanked, hinted at panic, then he reached to pick up his jacket and swiftly went through the pockets, coming up with his wallet. Showing her the two foil packets he removed, he pushed them into his pants' pocket, dropped his jacket and chinned toward the opposite side of the room.

"Bedroom," he said in a graveled husk. "Or I'll have you over the back of this sofa. You make me insane, Melodie."

Yet he looked completely in control. It strained her trust, made her wonder for a bleak second if she was being reckless again. But the idea that she might have some kind of ability to provoke him was incredibly exciting.

She let her hips roll in a wicked sway as she walked ahead of him, providing what she supposed was a lurid view of her buttocks atop her long legs, but the thought made her feel sexy and desirable for the first time. With another twist of her arms behind her, she shed her bra as she went, leaving it on the floor, not turning around, smiling at the idea of teasing him.

"You're enjoying this," he accused, not sounding the least bit displeased as he came up behind her next to the bed and caught her back against him, one firm, confident hand capturing her breast as if he owned it.

It was both comforting and deeply provoking, especially when he gave her breast a firm caress and nearly buckled her knees with the catch of her nipple in a light pinch. She leaned into him weakly, legs shaking as he fondled more deliberately, playing with her nipple until she had to cover his hand to slow him down. It was getting too intense too quickly.

"Roman," she whispered, part protest, part plea.

"I want it to be so good for you that you know without a doubt that it's only about this, Melodie." His other hand slid to the front of her lace undies, fingertips slipping under without hesitation, cupping, massaging, working with gentle but insistent pressure to part and find her slick center.

Gasping, she wriggled back from his hot touch only to feel the thick ridge of his erection against her buttocks. She stilled with surprise.

"Yes, you're arousing me as much as I'm arousing you." His caress became deliberate, flagrant, pressing her into the thrust of his clothed hips against her backside as he drove her relentlessly toward orgasm.

Her head fell back against his shoulder while he took full advantage of her capitulation, biting the side of her neck.

"I want us to be together," she gasped, trying to still his hands on her, growing completely overwhelmed.

He lifted his mouth from sucking a mark onto her neck and said, "We will be. I'm going to lose it any second." His voice grated roughly, as stimulating as his touch. "Look," he said, shifting her slightly and there they were, caught in flagrante delicto in the mirror, his hands possessing her, his expression over her shoulder so filled with masculine intent she would have been alarmed, except then he strummed her again.

And told her how sexy she was, how badly he wanted her, how this was only the first of many so let him watch. Give him this because he needed to see he could make her feel good—

She cried out, embarrassed by the sight of herself losing control, so weakened by the buffet of climax she was wholly dependent on his support as he made it play out for her in lingering strokes that caused pulses of fading delight.

When she hung in his arms, he pressed hot, dry kisses and sexy compliments to her damp temple, finally turning her into his embrace so he could kiss her properly.

She belonged to him then. He utterly and completely owned her, and she didn't care. If misgivings surfaced, she brushed them away before she could identify them, too busy cradling his face so she could kiss him, telling him with her lips and body how incredible he made her feel.

He was hard, so hard all over. Absolutely primed with arousal, chest like sun-warmed bronze as she opened his shirt and caressed his hot, hard muscles. When she kissed her way across his chest, lightly brushing his beaded nipples with her fingertips, he threw back his head and groaned at the ceiling.

His reaction wasn't fake. What man as contained as he was would let her see the blind passion in his gaze as he cupped her cheeks and kissed the life out of her? What man that aroused would strip them both, then take his time pressing her to the bed?

What man wanting only to use a woman for his pleasure would kiss his way past her navel and ensure she was as ready as he was?

Sweeping her arms as though she was making angels in the satin sheets, she encouraged him with lusty moans, abandoning herself to the heaven of his tantalizing play. "Roman, I'm so close," she gasped.

He turned his mouth into her thigh, biting the twitching muscle there, drunk on her scent and taste, wishing he could hold out to finish her like this and arouse her again, but wanting her with him when he lost it inside her.

With a growl of strained control he slid up the silken length of her, pausing for light bites of her gorgeous breasts, eyes nearly rolling into the back of his skull as she framed his hips with her bent knees, offering herself. It was all he could do to fumble a condom into place.

The barest few words could be found in the miasma of his consciousness—*heat, softness, roses, citrus, wet, welcome. Melodie.*

She arched as he entered her, taking all of him in one slick thrust that sent a streak of sensation down his spine, flexing his shoulders and yanking his stomach muscles into a hot knot of masculine energy. His thoughts grew even more base. *Thrust, own.* She panted and clutched at him, opened her mouth to his kiss and licked at his tongue without inhibition.

The animal in him took over, protective enough to ensure he didn't hurt her, but driven by instinct to imprint himself indelibly. He returned to her again and again, his tension and level of stimulation so high he was blind and deaf to everything but her wordless expressions of yearning and need. He wanted everything she was. *Everything.*

"Give it to me. All of it," he ground out, needing her complete surrender to passion before he could give in to it himself.

Tossing her head, she cried out jaggedly, trembling beneath him, nails scraping down his upper arms as she bucked. Then it happened for her. He felt her release and his own struck like a hammer. He drove into her pulsing center and held himself there as they both were clenched in the paroxysm of orgasm.

Time stood still. Nothing mattered except this pleasure. No one existed but him and Melodie and this state of ecstasy.

Roman rolled away, forcing Melodie back to awareness of the room, how intimate they'd just been, that she was supposed to be working…

She covered her eyes with her forearm, not ready to face any of it.

The ring of the phone on the bedside table jarred into the silence. Roman came up on his elbow, damp skin brushing hers as he leaned across her, lifted the receiver and promptly dropped it back into its cradle.

Melodie peeked at him from under her arm. "Booty call from your Swedish friend?"

"For you, I imagine. I only booked the room an hour ago. No one I know would think to look for me here." Continuing to loom over her, he slid his leg across hers, pinning her erotically to the mattress as he picked up the receiver again and punched a number before bringing it to his ear. "Put my phone on Do Not Disturb," he ordered, then lowered the phone to ask Melodie, "Do you want anything?"

"I should go," she said, shifting restlessly under the weight of his leg.

Holding eye contact with her, he said into the phone, "We'll need a pair of overnight kits, toothbrushes and—" He paused to listen, then said, "Perfect. Thank you." He hung up. "The drawer in the bathroom likely has everything a couple might need, including more condoms."

"They said that?"

"It was implied."

"Did *I* imply that we needed more? Because I think I said I should go."

"Exactly. *Should.* Not that you were intending to."

"I begin to see why women tire of *you*," she said in a pert undertone. "Apparently you don't tire at all."

His grin flashed as he settled more of his weight on her and began searching her hair for pins. "Look, I'm no expert, but I'm thinking this hairdo of yours is *not* going back to the ballroom. So you might as well stay."

She should have taken her own hair apart, but instead she turned her head on the pillow to allow him to find the rest of the pins while she played delicate fingers across his collarbone and down to his biceps, where he braced himself on his forearm.

This was nice, she thought. It was the sort of sweet moment that *should* happen after lovemaking. If only...

"Why the sigh?" he asked, making her aware she'd released one. The last of her hairpins went onto the night table and he slid lower so they were eye to eye. "Regrets?" His tone held a fresh note of reserve.

"No," she said halfheartedly, then more sincerely, "No, this was..." Nice? Hardly. It had been basic and regressive. The blatant way he'd watched her come apart in the mirror, then devoted himself to her pleasure before stamping her with guttural thrusts rushed back at her. The burn of a self-conscious flush crept into her throat and face. "I'm embarrassed, if you want the truth. I don't fall into bed with men. I don't behave like this at all. Ever."

"Except with me," he said, as though making the statement of a closing argument.

"Except with you," she agreed softly, shifting her head so she felt his forearm under her cheek and had her lips against the smooth skin inside his biceps. He tasted faintly salty against her openmouthed kiss and smelled dark and masculine as she drew another fatalistic sigh.

"I'm not intuitive, Melodie, but you don't sound happy about that."

"Because even if I stay the night, I still have to leave in the morning. I'll never feel like this again and that's depressing."

"You don't have to leave."

"I do. We're flying to, um, gosh, I'm losing track." She looked to the headboard as though it had the answer. "Hartford, maybe. Leaving really early."

"You don't sound as if you enjoy this job. Quit."

"I can't. If I finish my contract and Trenton gets his nomination, I get a bonus." As she brought her chin back down, she adjusted the pearls so they weren't strangling her. "Before you think I'm all about the money, it's for Mom. She always wanted to go back to Paris. I promised her I'd sprinkle her ashes in the Seine."

"I'll take you," he offered smoothly.

"Please don't ruin this by suggesting I become your mistress," she admonished, both tempted and slighted. She'd thought they'd acted as equals here.

"I have companions, not mistresses," he corrected, pulling back and letting his hand fall on her stomach, but at a subliminal level, he'd pulled *way* back. "I don't buy women."

"Really. You don't support your lovers? Buy them clothes or jewelry? Take them on trips?" she asked skeptically.

"I meet their needs while they're with me, yes, and sometimes that extends to after we've stopped seeing each other. But it's not an exchange for sex."

"You're just that generous?"

"I try to be."

He sounded truthful, if stiffly reserved. Insulted?

"Well, I only have to get through the fall with this job and then I can look for something else. So I will," she said.

His lips twitched with dismay. "I don't like that answer," he informed her. "Quit now and look for something when it suits you."

Yes, she was a fool to think they were equals. Here was the rich tycoon who got what he wanted without regard for other people's wishes.

Proceeding delicately because she didn't want to ruin this fragile accord they'd managed to find, she said, "Roman, my mother put her fate in the hands of a powerful man, then birthed me into the same situation. It didn't work out well for either of us. I need my independence so I don't feel trapped or obligated."

"I'm not trying to trap you," he said with a scowl. "You could leave anytime."

"Then, I'll leave in the morning," she said gently.

He swore. "Walked into that one, didn't I?" He set his teeth. A muscle pulsed in his jaw. "I suppose I'll have to use other methods of persuasion." His gaze tracked back to hers and the heat in his eyes made her heart leap with panic.

"Don't!" She pressed her hands to his chest, holding him off as he started to tuck her beneath him.

He went motionless, only his head coming up slightly as he dragged his gaze from her nudity beneath him to the conflict that must be evident in her eyes.

"I'm not going to hurt you, Melodie," he said, brows coming together with concern.

"I think you might," she said, feeling her lips start to tremble. "You scare me, Roman. The way you make me feel. Please. If tonight is about making peace, please don't use my weakness against me."

He absorbed that in silence, only a small tick in his cheek letting her know he'd heard and was processing. Finally his mouth flattened in annoyance. "You're telling me I have to help you resist what we both want? *That* will hurt you, Melodie. I don't want to do that."

She didn't know much about computers, but she knew what circular logic was, and that was a big bunch of it right there. At the same time, her hands moved restlessly on him, smoothing his tight skin to his shoulders, pressing with involuntary invitation for him to lower onto her and kiss her.

They stole one brief kiss. Another. She could feel him hardening and opened her legs so he could settle properly between her thighs.

"I'm not going to deny you," he warned, smoothing her loose hair back from her face. "I'm going to give you everything you ask for. I'll stay just this side of barbaric as I ravish the hell out of you. If you can bring yourself to leave after that, I'll let you go."

Her heart trembled in her chest. Words stayed locked in her throat. All she could do was reach between them to guide him, telling him what she wanted. He teased her for a few moments, letting her feel his naked length against the growing ache in her loins, kissing her deeply until she was writhing with need beneath him. Then he covered himself and thrust, both of them catching ragged breaths as the agony of anticipation ceased and the perfection of joining commenced.

He was a man of his word; however, he dragged a pillow under her bottom so he could service her as thoroughly as possible, leaving her near weeping from the power of her release. Then he drew away, still hard, and proceeded to coax her down the road of sexual play all over again. He found all her erogenous zones and took his time stimulating her until she was ready for a firmer touch. A more insistent pull on her breast with his lips, a more erotic caress that he watched, soothing her when she tried to close her legs, claiming it was too immodest.

He gently dominated her then, rolling her so her stomach was on the pillow and covering her, but not taking her. He just stroked her with his body in a mimic of what they both wanted.

"Hurt?" he asked in a rasp. "I want everything in you, Melodie. Every last scream, but I won't take them. You have to give them to me."

She was sobbing, so aroused she was trembling. Shifting, coming up on her knees, she drew him to where she wanted him and clenched her fists in the sheets as he caressed her while he thrust. It was elemental and primitive, both of them stripped down to the very core. All her romantic notions of how men and women should come together dissolved in a flood of carnal hunger, decorum gone, both of them filling the room with erotic noises.

When they hit the peak, his fingers bit into her hips, locking them together as she cried, "Deeper, harder, yes, *yes*." He bucked and she gave up a long cry of gratified fulfillment.

CHAPTER EIGHT

ROMAN SWORE, SNAPPING Melodie from a doze.

"What's wrong?" she asked sleepily.

"Can't you hear it? Does he think he owns you?"

She lifted her head off his chest, where the steady thump of his heartbeat had lulled her. She heard the distant hum of her phone vibrating in the other room. Glancing at the clock, she said, "He's probably worried I'll miss the flight."

Roman's arm tightened on her.

She rolled onto him, growing addicted to the feel of his body against her own, loving the freedom to be like this: more than familiar or intimate. Close.

Nuzzling her nose into the fine hairs at his breastbone, she hid the dampness that rose behind her eyes as she drank in his scent, murmuring, "I have to leave soon. Not *should*," she clarified. "Have to."

"I heard you," he grumbled, massaging her scalp through the thick fall of her hair. "I still want you to stay."

"I'm glad," she said with a crooked smile, thinking of the way he'd thrown her out the first time. The remembrance didn't hurt as badly now. She had this incredible memory to replace it. "But I think in the long run we'd wind up in conflict. I do want love and marriage and kids, Roman. You were right about that."

His caress gentled to a light comb of his fingers through her hair. He didn't say anything. Didn't try to convince her he was a changed man, that they had a future. The silence caught at her tender heart, telling her she was making the right decision.

"But I could shower here," she suggested, lifting her head to offer a sultry look through tangled lashes, a smile pouted with invitation. "Rather than in my own room, alone."

"Deal."

Roman was jealous. He wasn't just annoyed on Melodie's behalf that her boss thought he had first call on her time. He was illogically threatened and nursing an uncomfortable state of rebuff as he walked away from her closed hotel room door and forced himself back to the elevator and his own room.

Emotions.

He eschewed them at every opportunity. Hope, happiness, pride. Those were all harbingers of a fall to come. That was what he'd learned through a very hard childhood. Better to focus on sensory pleasures and external goals that had a hope of being accomplished than seek some sort of inner fulfillment.

Melodie was right in saying they would run into conflict in the long run. She might act tough, but she was very sensitive, and he would wind up hurting her with his active attempts to feel nothing.

Which was exactly what he tried to do after walking her downstairs and returning to his empty suite. He was exhausted from lack of sleep, muscles aching from their night of marathon lovemaking, but he wasn't interested in crawling back into their wrecked bed. It looked too cold and empty. Unwelcoming.

Finding his scotch from the night before, he sipped it. It wasn't yet six and he hadn't slept, so that meant it was still last night, right?

One night. Since when did he feel depressed about any

woman leaving, whether it was within hours of their coming together or months?

Forget her, he insisted, thumbing across the screen on his phone to check his emails. Just as quickly he swept that screen aside and flicked to Melodie's contact card. Her number was still there. It hadn't accidentally been erased. Checking was completely juvenile, but asking her for it had been even more adolescent. He didn't chase women. He wouldn't call her. He had just wanted to know if she was willing to give it to him.

He wished he'd taken another shot of her this morning, clean faced and wearing a hotel robe, ball gown slung over her arm as she'd slowly closed the hotel room door on him. Her expression had been soft with sensual memory, her smile sweet and wistful.

How the hell did he even know what wistful looked like?

It looked like wanting what you couldn't have, he supposed, which was something he understood all too well. His childhood had been nonstop wishing. As an adult, he'd learned to get what he wanted or stop wanting it, very seldom coming up against a situation such as this.

I do want love and marriage and kids, she'd said. He turned that over in his mind, thinking how determined he'd been to find her in Virginia and take care of any child they might have conceived. There hadn't been any hesitation in him on that score, but what would things look like now if she had been pregnant? Would they be married?

He supposed there were conditions under which he would seek a lifetime commitment, but those conditions weren't *love*. His chest started to feel tight just thinking about opening himself up to that depth of emotion.

Damn it! Why the hell couldn't she have simply forgotten her pearls again and given him an excuse to call?

She'd taken them off at one point, but had asked for his help after her shower to put them back on.

He wandered the suite, scanning for forgotten items, finding only the hotel toothbrush she'd left in a glass next to the sink. Leaning in the bathroom doorway, staring at himself wearing his tuxedo pants and the shirt he'd been too lazy to close all the way, eyes dark with sleeplessness, shoulders slumped in defeat, Roman faced the fact he wasn't going to forget her. Ever.

Which tightened the vice in his chest a few more notches.

You don't tell me what you're thinking. He heard female voices complain from the past. *You go through the motions, but I don't feel like you really care.*

He cared. Cautiously. When it came to Melodie, he cared quite a bit. She was too sweet a person to deserve the battering of the Gautier gauntlet. He wanted to protect her from them, and he didn't care for this new, overbearing boss of hers one bit, either. He should have given her his number, told her to call anytime. For any reason.

Not bothering to overthink it, he dialed her number to tell her exactly that.

A male voice answered.

"Sadler?" Roman guessed, even though it didn't sound like him.

"This is his aide. Who's calling?"

"I'm looking for Melodie. It's Roman Killian."

A muffled conversation, then a voice he recognized. "Killian," Sadler said. "Melodie is no longer with us."

The worst emotion, the one she seemed to bring out in him most and which weighed the heaviest—guilt—descended on him. "You fired her," he deduced instantly. "For spending the night with me."

"I need my employees to be accessible at all times," Sadler said.

"But you told her to be nice to me," Roman said with

false conciliation. The man was lucky the sounds of traffic and car doors were coming through behind him, or Roman would be hunting him down in this hotel right now.

"Sluts become a liability," Sadler said. "You know that."

Roman closed his eyes, fighting the fire of rage that roared alive in him. Too intense. It had the power to murder. "I think you fired her because she wasn't nice to *you*. You're going to be very sorry *you* were not nicer to *her*."

Roman ended the call and strode out of his room, straight to Melodie's.

She didn't answer his knock, so he took the stairs down to the registration desk, asking them to ring her room.

"She's checked out, sir."

He bit back cursing aloud, his fist so tight on the marble desktop he could have shattered the stone with a single pound. She was probably in a taxi heading to the airport and back to Virginia—

Wait. A woman sat in the lobby restaurant wearing a fitted business suit. She had her shiny brown-gold hair pulled into a clip at her nape. Coffee steamed next to the tablet she had propped before her.

She was going to splash that coffee into his face, he thought, but went straight over anyway.

Roman threw his disheveled form into the chair opposite her. He'd showered with her, still smelled faintly of hotel soap, but he hadn't bothered shaving and, Lord, he was sexy with that stubble and hair that had dried uncombed. His shirt was still a deep, open V down his chest, the sleeves rolled back to his elbows. He was every woman's walking fantasy.

And he wore the most thunderous expression.

"Really?" he demanded. "I got you fired again. Really."

"It's like a gift, isn't it?" she said, thinking she ought to be more furious, but the relief was too profound. "Trenton phoned you to tell you? God, that's just like him. He waited until I was down here, you know. So he could do it in front of everyone. He didn't expect me to call him a hypocrite. Nice and loud, too. They all do it. I guarantee you all the other aides were picking up women in the bar while I was working the ballroom with him last night, but just because I'm a woman, I'm a slut. Men are such pigs."

As Roman turned his face away, his expression falling into weary lines, she found herself feeling sorry for him.

"Present company excluded, of course," she said.

He shook his head as if he couldn't believe what had happened. "I didn't mean to do this."

"You didn't," she said wearily. She was the one who had stayed in the penthouse with him, putting her physical gratification above her job, but she didn't get a chance to say so. The waitress arrived with her breakfast special.

"I'll have one of those," Roman said.

"Take mine," Melodie replied, snagging the fruit cup off the plate and nodding for the waitress to put the rest in front of Roman. "But he needs his own coffee."

He nodded agreement to the waitress, then looked at the plate of eggs and hash browns before him as if he couldn't face it. "You're giving me your breakfast? After I got you fired?"

"I had a voucher, but this was all I really wanted." She gently stirred the fresh berries into the yogurt beneath.

"How are you this forgiving? Because I want to slash the guy's tires. I want to slash my own," he added with self-disgust.

She shrugged. "I guess because I'd do it again," she said, hearing the poignant rasp in her voice as she recalled their night together.

"Would you?" He lowered his cutlery as he pinned her with a green stare as brilliant as the heart of a flame.

"I meant…" Wow. This wasn't going to be easy. He only

had to look at her. Focusing on chasing a blueberry with the tip of her spoon, she said, "I mean that, given the chance, I wouldn't have made a different decision last night. But the decision I made this morning still stands, Roman."

"Why?" he challenged immediately. "You don't have a job to go back to."

"I'm aware," she said tersely, glancing at the tablet that had gone black, but had conjured a handful of weak prospects a few seconds ago. "Rent is covered for next month, at least," she muttered. "But everything else is going to be a challenge."

Paris was out of the question for the foreseeable future.

"Melodie, you have to let me help you."

She shook her head. "I'll manage. I'm just bummed about Paris. I feel as if I'm letting Mom down." When her mother had refused treatment, had declined in such slow pain, the promise of Paris had been the only thing Melodie had been able to offer as comfort.

He reached across to take her wrist, thumb caressing the back of her hand. "Let me take you."

"Roman..." She turned her hand so she was gripping his fingers. "I *can't*."

"You can. You just don't want to." He pulled his hand away, jaw thrust out belligerently. He took up his fork with an air of impatience.

She acknowledged he was right with a jerk of her shoulder, wondering how he'd managed to make her feel guilty.

They ate in silence, breaking it only to thank the waitress when she cleared their plates.

Melodie took her last swallow of coffee, but struggled to get it down without choking as she realized this really was it. The end.

"Will you do something for me?" he asked, not letting on what was going on behind his aloof expression.

"Will you come up and let me show you something in my room?"

"Etchings?" she guessed facetiously. "I really should get to the airport. I'll be flying standby, so…"

"Please." He stood and shouldered her travel bag.

"You can't just tell me what it is?" She followed him to the elevator where she studied his enigmatic expression the whole way to the top floor. "You're being very mysterious," she said when he slid his key card into the reader.

"I'm really not," he said with a disparaging smirk, leaving her bag just inside the door. Moving to the bedroom, he jerked his chin at the bed.

"What?" She stood beside him to look at the rumpled sheets and indented pillows.

"We're both exhausted." He turned his head to give her a somnolent look. "Let's not make any decisions right now. I'm not asking for sex. I just can't think when I'm this tired. I become very one track, and all I know is that I want you there." He pointed at the bed.

"You really aren't mysterious, are you?" she said, struck by a wave of emotion that maybe came from tiredness, but also from what sounded like an oddly revealing statement from him.

She *was* tired. Stupid Trenton had waited for her to check out before cutting her loose, so she couldn't go back to her room and her own bed. She'd already been dreading the wait at the airport, trying to stay awake to hear if she'd been given a flight… It all began to look too overwhelming to face when there was a comfortable bed right there and a man peeling his shirt from his powerful chest.

She opened the button on her jacket, glanced at him with a small scold.

He said, "Thank you," in a quiet voice that was strangely soothing. She removed her jacket, gave it a shake, then folded it and laid it over the back of a chair. The rest of her clothes went neatly folded onto the seat. She kept on her underpants, but shed her bra, never comfortable sleeping in one. Instead, she picked up his shirt from where he'd dropped it on the floor and slid her arms into it.

"Do you mind?"

"Not a bit."

Closing a couple of buttons, she rounded the bed as he got in the other side. He held up the covers and she slid in beside him, feeling his arms close around her very comfortingly. Their bare legs braided together, and his lips nuzzled her hairline before he stole the clip from her hair and tossed it off the side of the bed.

Feeling secure and warm, Melodie let out a deep sigh. Roman's arms grew heavier on her, and that was all she remembered.

She woke to feel his erection straining the front of his shorts and pressing into her stomach. He was still asleep, but she couldn't help tracing the shape of him, already feeling liquid heat pooling between her legs in anticipation.

With a long inhale, Roman rolled onto his back, eyes opening to catch her gaze. They flashed with surprise and immediate desire.

"Come here," he said in a sleep-rasped voice, lifting his hips to push his boxers down and off before drawing her to straddle his thighs.

She removed her underwear and leaned for the condom herself before straddling his hips and covering him.

His hand came to the back of her neck and urged her down for a kiss. They rocked in ever-deepening caresses, wriggling and adjusting until he was penetrating, making her moan with indulgence. For a long time they barely moved, just kissed and enjoyed the sensation of being joined. She sat up to throw off his shirt and he starfished his hands over her breasts, letting her lean into his grip as she searched for a rhythm that made them both happy. It was good, so good, and lasted for a deliciously long time.

He was the one who said, "I'm going to explode," and slid his hand to her hip, thumb dipping inward to circle and incite.

The sharp sensation made her buck and seek more, so she moved urgently, flying them to a swift and sudden culmination that ended with him rolling her beneath him and kissing her deeply while the aftershocks played out.

Then came the reckoning. She didn't know how to leave after that. It had been too good.

He rolled away to dispose of the condom and she asked, "What time is it?" It came off sounding as though she had a train to catch. Funny, he'd made it sound as though a solid sleep would help her think more clearly, but she was more conflicted than ever now.

"Two." He rolled back and caught her hand, bringing her fingertip to the gentle bite of his teeth. "Our body clocks are going to be a real mess when we get to France."

"Nice try." She smiled, admiring his confidence. "But I'm not quite ready to head to Paris yet. There are a lot of hoops to jump through when you want to transport ashes. I've been wading through bureaucracy for months."

"I'll make a call," he said, weaving their fingers together.

"To whom?" she demanded. "It's not easy, you know."

He dismissed that with a snort. "I'm an approved government supplier in both America and France. I have contacts."

"I wouldn't say no to a call," she conceded. "Anything that could streamline that side of things would be a huge favor, but, Roman—"

"Listen," he said in a grave tone. "I didn't have the chance to do anything for my mother when she died. If there was a service, I wasn't invited. I want to do this."

She blinked, surprised. "Why not? What happened?"

He fell onto his back, untangled their fingers to tuck his fist beneath the pillow under his head. For a moment she thought he wasn't going to answer. She couldn't read a thing on his face and, as the silence lengthened, she felt as though she'd transgressed. He was spurning her, and it left her feeling bereft.

"If you don't want to talk about it—"

"I don't," he said. "But I should. If I want you to stay, you have to know who I am. I was nine when she died. I had already been in foster care for a few years. She…" His face worked, fighting for control. "She had resorted to prostitution to feed me. Ironically, that's why she lost me. She was just doing it until I was in school. I remember her telling me everything would be better once I started school and she got a real job, not that I really understood what she was doing. That came later, but…"

Shock closed cold fingers around Melodie's heart.

"Then I was taken from her, so she did get a job, except it was a terrible one in a sweatshop. There was a fire. I realize there wouldn't have been a body for me to see, but they didn't even tell me when it happened. It took weeks. I kept asking if I could call and there would be all these muttered conversations, and finally they told me she was in heaven. It took years to find out heaven is actually Hart Island, where the poor and homeless are buried in mass, unmarked graves. There hadn't been any money for a service, so there wasn't one."

"Oh, Roman, I'm so sorry." She set a comforting hand on his chest.

He caught it. For a moment she thought he was going to reject her touch, but after a few seconds, his hand flexed on hers and he swallowed. "Every time I talked to her, I asked her when she was going to come get me." His voice had thickened. "She took that stupid job for me."

She opened her mouth, but only a burn of anguish came in, searing her lungs. Settling over him, she pressed her face into his neck and offered the only comfort she could.

Roman stiffened as Melodie blanketed him in compassion. It was almost cloying, making his old grief too fresh and unbearable. He wanted to push her away, push all of it away, but after a second her scent penetrated to the most primitive part of his brain. Things he associated with her, such as softness and forgiveness and pleasure, pulled him back from falling into the dark emotions that talking about his mother had opened up.

Jerkily he closed his arm around Melodie's slender frame, sealing her silken nudity against his own bare skin.

They lay like that a long time. It was strange. He wanted to roll into her and forget all of it with the pursuit of physical gratification, but he wanted to stay like this, too. Still and calm, in quiet harmony.

Maybe they dozed, because the buzz of his phone on vibrate made Roman jerk in surprise. Since he'd pretty much been off the grid for nearly twenty-four hours, he sat up to find his pants and looked at the screen. Melodie's number flashed back at him.

"Looks like you're calling me," he told her, answering with "Sadler?"

"His aide again, Mr. Killian. We're wondering, is Melodie with you?"

"She is." He glanced at her.

She sighed and gathered the sheet across her breasts as she sat up and held out a resigned hand.

Roman kept the phone.

"May I speak to her?" the aide asked in a tone of tested patience.

"No," Roman said. "Lose this number. I don't want to hear from you again."

"Wait! Ask her to call us. We're looking for a file and can't find—"

"No," Roman repeated firmly. "Remind Sadler that I told him he'd regret not being nicer to her. Let him know that I'll be making some calls to his biggest corporate sponsors, too. Melodie can give me that list, I'm sure."

"We're prepared to reinstate her," the aide rushed to say.

"I'm not going to tell her you said that. And if you even think about making her life difficult because of this, you're going to find out exactly how vindictive I can be. Am I making myself clear?"

After a beat of silence, the aide said tightly, "Let me pass this over to Trenton."

"Don't bother." Roman ended with a cheerful yet filthy suggestion for the bunch of them and stabbed a button to end the call.

Melodie tucked her chin, admonishing him, "I heard them offer me my job back."

"And you didn't speak up."

She sighed, knees coming up so she could hug them, then set her chin on them. "Do you really want to help me with Mom? Like, would it help you?"

He dropped his gaze from the earnest softness in hers. He was still pulsing with the sort of discontent that came from smashing your own thumb with a hammer, sorry that he'd told her something so personal. It was the kind of intimate detail he never, ever gave up about himself. Especially if it was going to make someone look at him like that.

So did he expect that going through a memorial of some kind with her mother would *help* him? No. It would stir up this turmoil inside him that he'd spent years sublimating. Was he willing to put himself through it to keep Melodie with him?

Bizarrely, the answer was yes.

"Let me make that call," he said.

CHAPTER NINE

THREE DAYS LATER Roman flew Melodie by private jet to Paris. They discovered that rivers and streams were off-limits for scattering ashes, but found a special remembrance garden where they were able to spend a reflective hour settling Patience into the state of peace that had eluded her in her living years.

"Thank you," Melodie said, reaching across the back of the limo to take Roman's hand as they left the gated cemetery. She was hollowed out, eyelids stinging and swollen from crying, throat still scratchy, but she felt at ease for the first time in years. Maybe since the first time she had fully realized what sort of tortured existence her mother had led. "I couldn't rest until I'd given her that. Nothing can hurt her now. This means a lot to me. Thank you."

"You're welcome." His distant, faintly wooden response might have struck her as disinterested if she hadn't seen him struggle several times during the small ceremony she'd arranged. She remembered him calling himself emotionally inaccessible, and he certainly kept his cards close to his chest, but he wasn't indifferent. As he'd cradled her against him when they'd been left alone to say their good-byes, she suspected he'd offered a much-delayed farewell to his own mother.

Not that she would intrude to ask.

Instead, she twisted her head on the seat to look at him. "When you told me you try to meet the needs of your companions, did you ever see yourself doing something like this?"

That caught him by surprise, making him laugh. "No," he pronounced drily, faint grin lingering.

"Well, I appreciate your making an exception," she teased, leaning across to kiss his cheek.

He cupped the back of her head, keeping her close for a few short, sweet kisses on her lips.

"Where are we going now?" she drew back to ask. They'd flown overnight, arriving about six in the morning Virginia time, and had come straight to the cemetery for a midday ceremony. She wasn't sure if she was tired or hungry or what.

"What do you want to do?" he asked easily.

"I'm not sure." The sky had been low when they'd landed, but was brightening by the minute, and she kept seeing trees in blossom against rain-washed stone, tulips and cafés and smiling couples. "Could we walk around the city a bit?"

"Of course." He had a word with the driver and they pulled over a moment later.

For the next two hours they wandered aimlessly past flower stalls and into shops for pastries. When she paused to examine the price tag on a newsboy cap in olive green with a cute floral band wrapped into a smart little buckle, he plopped it on her head and held out his credit card to the proprietress.

"I was only thinking about it," she said, adjusting it in the mirror after the tag had been removed.

"It suits you."

"Well, thank you," she said cautiously. Accepting a gift from him was a slippery slope. She was already indebted to him for the flight, and he hadn't been satisfied with making this a weekend trip, stating he had business to take care of later in the week.

Since they were staying at his apartment and he wasn't footing the bill on a hotel, she had acquiesced. She fully intended to cook for him while they were here, but when she mentioned picking up a few groceries, he said, "I made reservations. For an early sitting since I knew we'd be tired. I've been steering us toward the club. It's only another block over. We should change, though. I was going to leave you next door and walk across to the men's shop."

"Next door" was a boutique where the saleswomen greeted "Monsieur Killian" by name. One even pressed her cheek to his and said something warm in French that made Melodie's toes curl in dismay. When he mentioned where they were going, the women began pulling out black cocktail dresses that didn't have price tags *at all*.

"Roman," Melodie started to protest.

"Take your time. I'll come back when I'm finished and they'll pour me a drink while I wait over there." He nodded to a small but luxurious lounge area. "I know the drill."

"Because you've done this before?" she guessed.

He heard the edge in her tone. His own cooled. "I have. Although never to this specific jazz club. They have a female blues singer there. You said your mother used to listen to French blues. I thought you'd enjoy it."

Which sounded very thoughtful of him, but…

"I'd like to take you on a proper date, Melodie," he added. "We haven't had one yet."

Yes, they had, but he didn't stick around to hear her argue that dinner and a movie in Virginia was a perfectly acceptable date. Another night, she had cooked for him and he'd run out for a bottle of wine, bringing back flowers, as well.

"Mademoiselle?" the boutique owner prompted.

In the end, after their afternoon of walking, Melodie found herself grateful for a reason to sit down and sip a fortifying glass of champagne and freshly squeezed orange juice while dresses were brought to her for consideration. Crackers appeared with foie gras and caviar, salty and delicious.

As for the dresses, the sleek, modern designs with cutouts and daring necklines were beautiful, but Melodie's eye kept tracking back to something a bit more modest with a hint of flounce. The bodice was silk organza, fitted in the front and disappearing behind her shoulders into a backless pair of straps. The skirt was short and narrow, but had a fuller sheer overlay that added femininity and swung sassily. Beaded detailing at the waist gave the dress more of a figure-eight figure than her stalk-like build usually had.

The saleswomen made several admiring remarks about her *jambes* after she tried it on with a pair of deceptively simple black high heels with detailing down the tall, wickedly sharp heel. One suggested if she lost six or eight kilos, she could find work in Paris as a model.

"Kilos," Melodie repeated. "Those are bigger than pounds, right?" *Fifteen pounds? Really?*

They weren't being catty, though. They were actually very nice. Maybe Roman paid them to be, but Melodie still felt pampered and relaxed by the time she had her hair styled to cloud around her face and her eyes smokily made up so the blue of her irises popped.

Then a funny attack of nerves hit her as she walked out to greet Roman. Even as a teenager living off her generous allowance, she had never taken this much care with her appearance. Anton had always made her believe it was futile to try. She'd resigned herself to never affecting boys and had rarely wanted so badly to impress a man.

Roman was looking at his phone, a drink on the side table next to him, his arm stretched out to rest along the back of the sofa. His new white shirt fit him just this side of bursting its seams, hugging his muscles and pulling across his chest. The collar was turned up and his hair had been given a professional ruffle. He hadn't shaved since just before they landed and the shadow on his cheeks and jaw gave him a rakish air.

He sat with his ankle crooked up to rest on his knee, straining the fabric of his black pants, which were tailored to showcase his toned thighs. Argyle socks peeked between the cuff of his pants and his shiny shoes.

He was so casually hot she had to stop to catch her breath.

Then he looked up and stole her breath all over again.

Only his eyes moved as they leisurely traveled from her hair in its big, loose curls, to the glossy pink lips she tried not to ruin by pressing them together instead of licking them, to the ever-present pearls against her collarbone. Her shoulders twitched and her breasts prickled as she felt his gaze caress her there, then her stomach sucked in and her intimate muscles clenched when he stroked her bare legs with his gaze.

"Turn around," he commanded huskily.

Swallowing, she suppressed the feminist in her that scolded her for letting herself be objectified, arguing that this was different. This was...

She turned her back, her entire body coming alive under the awareness that she had his complete attention. When she turned again to see him, he was rising in an easy flex of his strong frame. He came toward her, and she reminded herself, *Breathe, idiot, breathe.*

"You're beautiful," he murmured, lips grazing her brow as she dipped her chin self-consciously. His hands settled on her bare arms in a light, tantalizing caress while the starchy smell of new clothes came off him along with a fresh sample of cologne and his own masculine notes.

"I feel beautiful," she said. It wasn't just the dress and the makeup. It was the way he reacted to her every min-

ute of every day. He complimented her whether she was
coiffed and made-up or disheveled and wearing a house-
coat. Today was simply the day she embraced his words as
true. "I do," she said sincerely. "Now. Thank you."

"How could you ever doubt it?" he scoffed lightly.

She debated, not wanting to spoil the moment, but she
wanted him to understand how much confidence he gave
her.

"You already know my upbringing wasn't the best.
Anton hated that Dad had remarried and it didn't matter
that I was his half sister. No matter what I wore or said,
he put me down. It's taken a long time to get past it. But
since I have so much more respect for your opinion than
his," she said ruefully, "I *must* be beautiful."

His expression had grown sober as he'd listened, then
he gently caressed her cheek. "There will be a correction,
Melodie. Rest assured I'm taking note, and the extent of
their crimes will not go unpunished."

"Don't— I didn't say that so you'd stoop to their level."

"I know. And I won't. But I'm not as forgiving as you
are. Mark my words, when the time is right they'll receive
their reckoning. But let's not spoil our evening thinking
about them." He tugged her into his big frame.

Her hands went to his waist and splayed, taking in heat
and firm, taut man. She could get used to leaning on him.
Easily. Far too easily.

"Ready to go?" he asked, breath faintly scented with
scotch.

"I don't know how far I can walk in these shoes," she
said, lifting a foot so he could see the wicked spike.

"The car's outside."

The boutique owner carried out Melodie's things in a
bag and handed them to the chauffeur while Roman helped
her into the backseat.

Moments later he helped her out again and they entered

a nightclub lit only by candles and subtly recessed indigo bulbs. Glowing white tablecloths draped tiny tables surrounded by comfortable chairs. The glassware sparkled and the servers wore tuxedos. The place was already full, but they were shown to a reserved table in an elevated alcove that allowed them some privacy yet offered a perfect view of the stage.

The meal was served in a series of courses between sets, the food excellent, while the chanteuse created a warmly nostalgic mood that allowed Melodie to envision her mother as a young model in Paris, briefly happy.

Roman leaned his arm on the back of her chair and played with her hair. She set her hand on his thigh and wondered if this was a dream. They even danced, although it was more a prelude to what would come later. Like every other couple, they plastered themselves to each other and swayed lazily, using the music as an excuse to arouse each other.

Weakly tilting her head back so she could see him, she didn't have to say a word.

"I'm ready, too," he said hungrily, and tightened his arms on her so she could feel how hard he was. "I'll call for the car."

She was past the point of trying to understand it. Between New York and Virginia, they'd been making love every time they found a shred of privacy. She was shocked by how constant their desire was, but she'd stopped fighting it. She was only grateful the distance to his apartment was short.

Expecting a high-rise, she was surprised when the car halted outside an art gallery. A bright glow came through the windows and a chic crowd mingled inside.

"Are we going in?" she asked as they stepped onto the sidewalk.

"My flat is upstairs." He walked her to a steel door next to the gallery entrance, slid open a panel and peeked inside.

The door cracked open. Inside was a small closet for coats and shoes, then a flight of stairs to an open-plan bachelor apartment. No sound from the crowd below penetrated, and the lighting was all indirect and moody.

Melodie took in exposed brickwork, high ceilings and elegant white furniture in a lounge containing ferns and colorful throws. A butcher-block island with copper cookware suspended above it separated the kitchen and its stainless-steel appliances from the rest of the apartment. Floating stairs led to a bedroom in a loft. The bedding looked sumptuous with its rich colors and tasseled pillows. Beneath the loft was a cozy library with bookshelves and a pretty antique desk that was probably strong enough to hold a laptop, but was more for looks than serviceability.

"This is not your apartment," she said decidedly.

"Why do you say that? My iris is the one that opens the door. And the housekeeper's," he allowed. "She comes in once a week. Which reminds me. Open."

He came toward her with his phone, holding it before one of her eyes, which widened in stern outrage.

"This is your love nest," she accused as he clicked.

He didn't respond to that immediately, taking his time tapping the screen before tucking his phone in his shirt pocket. "You saw how I slid open the reader. It's painless. No flash or anything. Just look into it and the door will open."

She folded her arms. "You're not going to admit you bring women here?"

"I have an office here in Paris," he said. "With accommodations attached. Very utilitarian. If I'm here strictly for work, I usually stay there."

"But if you have a companion, you tuck her up here."

"If it bothers you that you're not the only woman who

has stayed with me here, we can get a hotel." He showed no emotion, completely matter-of-fact about it.

"It bothers me that you're maneuvering me into being your *companion*," she said. "This is nice," she hurried to add, sweeping her hands to indicate the gorgeous outfit she wore and the beautiful flat. "But I can't let you take over, Roman. I can't—"

"Is that what it is? Melodie," he cut in with gentle firmness. He came forward to take her flinging hand in both of his. "The first day we met you said there was only one way to get to know a person, and that was by spending time with them. I want to spend time with you."

"I'd like to get to know you better, too, but—"

"I can't sit in Virginia waiting for you to find a job that will keep you out all day. Listen, I understand not wanting to rely on people. I'm a foster kid. I was always a guest, always a burden. I hated that feeling. But now I'm someone who can pay and pay back. I want you to let me."

He was taking all her arguments, defusing them and setting them aside like empty milk bottles.

"It seems wrong," she mumbled weakly.

"You're not taking advantage of me. This is my decision. Do you really want to go back to Virginia?" he asked, playing dirty by drawing her against him so she was surrounded by all things Roman: his warm strength and the animal scent that went straight into her brain and shorted it out. A streaking sensation of kindled desire followed the brush of his lips from her temple down her cheek to her nape.

"No," she allowed, throwing back her head so he could nibble the sensitive skin in a way that softened her knees. "But you're not playing fair," she complained.

"And if you stay I will play unfair to you as often as you want me to," he promised, biting lightly into her earlobe. "Would you like that?"

A shiver of acute need chased through her.

"Yes," she admitted.

"Here? Or somewhere else?"

She almost hated him in that moment, wishing she had the strength to insist on going somewhere that he hadn't taken other women when he obviously had the capacity to hold off and she didn't.

"Here," she moaned weakly, chasing his mouth with her own.

"Good," he growled. "Because I can't wait."

They didn't even make it up the stairs, christening his Turkish rug instead.

CHAPTER TEN

THE WEEK IN Paris passed in a pleasant blur of lovemaking and walking tours of the old part of the city. And, when Roman had time to join her, they window-shopped and he bought her whatever she showed the least bit of interest in. He was too generous, buying her a new outfit for every dinner, cocktail party or gala cruise on the Seine. If he didn't buy her something while they were out, he brought her flowers or, this morning, a fancy new mobile phone.

"Roman, I can't."

She was starting to feel as though all the spoiling was his way of compensating for the fact he didn't offer much of himself. He was the most attentive lover she could ask for, but when it came to anything really personal, he was very adept at turning the conversation in another direction.

"You're doing me a favor. It's a prototype. It needs to be tested." He showed her how to log feedback for anything that didn't work to her satisfaction. "If they don't notify you of an update that fixes it within twenty-four hours, tell me. I'll follow up. Look, it has a GPS so I can track you down wherever you are and join you."

"Or you could call me and ask," she supplied with a chipper smile. "What about a cover? I don't want to break it."

"It's unbreakable and waterproof. If it's not, my suppliers will answer for it." He went on with nerdy enthusiasm about its space-age alloys and special screen, the airtight design and its ability to be compressed into a diamond if dropped under a steamroller. "If you lose it, we can track it to within a meter, but try not to lose it. I might misplace my temper if you do. And if you sell it, do not settle for less than a quarter of a million euros or I will be highly insulted."

"Roman!" she cried. "I can't walk around with a phone worth that kind of money! And who is likely to buy a phone that costs that much?" she asked with sudden puzzlement. "Have you thought this through?"

"Your half brother would easily pay that much for this phone," he stated flatly, then quirked a brow as he added pithily, "When it goes to market it will retail for a few hundred dollars, competing with the rest of the smartphones. At the moment, however, the technology is fresh and incredibly secure to use. Far better than anything else currently available. My competitors would be extremely interested in breaking it down before it's released."

"And you're trusting me with it?" she asked with awe, hugging the hard shape to her breast. She swallowed back a rush of emotion, moved to tears. "I mean, the way we met…"

"I trust you, Melodie," he said, sounding sincere.

She melted inside. Of all the gifts he could have given her, his trust was the most touching. It cracked the last of her resistance against letting him support her. She wanted rather desperately to stay with him and see where this relationship could go.

That afternoon she used the credit card he'd given her for the first time—in a lingerie shop. She figured the purchase was really for him, and he was highly appreciative when she modeled it for him later.

And since they were getting along so beautifully, when she sprawled atop him, her lacy underthings askew, and he said, "I have to be in Germany on Tuesday," she lifted her head and said, "Do you mind if I charge a suitcase to the card? You've bought me too many outfits. They won't all fit in mine."

"I told you what your limit was. Charge anything you like to it." He tucked a wisp of her hair behind her ear. "But leave a few things here for when we come back."

"When will that be?" she asked with surprise.

"I don't know. Probably not until after the summer. I have some meetings in Italy next month and I thought we could spend some time on my yacht after that, but eventually we'll come back here."

After the summer. The words sent a funny, exciting sensation into the pit of her belly. Maybe they did have a future.

Roman was in a perfect place. Of all the women he'd dated over the years, few had been such a good match for him on every level as Melodie. Definitely the sex was better than any man had a right to, sometimes playful, sometimes erotic, always intensely satisfying. Professionally, he couldn't ask for a better partner by his side. She not only sparkled like a sapphire, lighting up a room, but she knew how to strike exactly the right balance of warmth with boundaries. Aside from the sparest of details such as where they might have eaten dinner or which part of a city they were staying in, she shared nothing of their private life with anyone.

When they were alone she was equally capable of being a charming, amusing companion, yet always respected his retreat after questions such as, "Do you know anything about your father?" and "What were the foster homes like? Were you safe there?"

No, he didn't know anything about his father. No, he hadn't always been safe. There'd been good ones and bad ones, the most important thing being that they had been impermanent. Buying the house in France, along with being a status symbol, was also his way of creating a proper home for himself. A place he could and always would return to. Why France? He liked the climate.

He didn't know why he couldn't simply say that to her. Because he had long ago programmed himself to keep such things private, he supposed.

And she seemed okay with the status quo, so he didn't see any need to change.

Until she had an issue with her phone and he wound up being called in to help troubleshoot. That was when he learned Melodie not only had been looking for work in Virginia, but also had even looked up one-way flight details for a week from now.

The blood seemed to drain out from his toes, leaving him staring at a screen that didn't make sense while his agile mind froze, needing a reboot. For a few long minutes he wasn't even sure he was breathing. All he could think was *She can't leave.*

Despite his attempts to keep his feelings for her light, he was struck by how much she was coming to mean to him. It made his joints grate like sandpaper as he rose and went to find her where she was reading her tablet next to the pool off his penthouse here in Rome.

He set down her phone on the table beside her, lowered himself onto the side of the lounger alongside hers and confronted reality in the way he'd learned to do. "You're thinking of leaving?"

Surprise flashed in her blue gaze before she glanced at her phone and said, "You looked at my browsing history?"

"For the search-engine problems you were having. I wasn't trying to spy." He betrayed no hint of defensiveness. All his feelings were firmly buried in the sealed vault behind the barred door, in the bottom of the abandoned building that was his mortal coil. "The job board came up."

She tucked her chin downward, half sheepish, half admonishing. "I'm not used to being idle, Roman. It's making me a little crazy, doing nothing. I enjoyed Berlin and obviously Rome has an amazing history…" She frowned at the view of the Coliseum amid the rest of the red-tile rooftops across the city. "But it's not really as if I'm on vacation. Not with you anyway. You're working. I thought I might be able to find something that I could do remotely."

Okay. He could see that, but "Why the flight, then?"

"Oh, that was for a friend. She's been traveling around Europe and thought she might be able to join us here for a few days if she could change her flight home."

The relief was so great in him he almost slumped forward, but he was highly experienced at not betraying his reactions. He only nodded. "You're not planning on leaving, then."

"No." She searched his gaze and, he was quite sure, found little of his thoughts. "Not unless you want me to," she added hesitantly.

"I don't." He could see the uncertainty in her, the need for reassurance. He felt a discord in himself, too, as if they'd had a conflict and even though it had been easily ironed out, something more was needed. Still, he only rose and said, "How do you feel about organizing the launch party for the phone? Marketing is already working on the timeline, but planning the event would be very much within your forte. Would you like that?"

"If you would like me to do it, then, sure."

"I'll inform them now." He walked away, knowing he should have taken more steps to close the gap between them, but it had taken everything in him to face the possible dissolution of their arrangement. The spring of emotion at their staying together was too raw and concentrated to work through anywhere but in complete solitude.

Melodie nursed a let-down feeling until that night when she and Roman went to bed, practically acting like an old married couple in the way they brushed teeth and undressed, crawled in under the covers and snuggled close for a kiss good-night.

Their good-night kisses almost always turned into lovemaking, but tonight it turned into something that went beyond it. Roman was so hard, so urgent, he pressed into her almost before she was ready, making her flinch a little at the sting.

He groaned an apology and seemed to gather his control at that point, ensuring her pleasure again and again while he possessed her, imprinting her with his scent and touch and branding kisses to the point where she nearly wept with joy and fulfillment.

Later, in the sultry dark, pinned against him by arms that had closed tightly around her, she rubbed her cheek against his chest.

"I wish you would tell me what you're thinking and feeling," she murmured.

A long pause, then: "I know."

Part of her suspected he *had* told her exactly what was going on inside him, but what if she was interpreting things wrong?

Two days later Roman and Melodie moved onto his yacht, sailing toward Sardinia with the intention of visiting both that island and Corsica before making their way to his home near Cannes. At least now he was working from his office on board, inviting her to interrupt him at any time. They were closer physically if not emotionally.

She told herself they just needed time. If she had any

doubts about him, she just had to look at his actions rather than wait for words. Her life really couldn't get much better than it currently was.

"Is there any way to improve the camera features on the phone?" she asked him one evening over dinner, feeling like a spoiled brat since, really, the camera was already quite good. But she'd resurrected a hobby she'd enjoyed as a teenager and handed over her phone so he could see the shots she'd taken thus far. "It's better than any other phone out there, I know. And part of me enjoys the challenge of getting what I want despite its limitations, but there are some things I'd like to try that just aren't here— What's wrong?"

"Nothing. These shots are very good. I tend to think of you being a natural in front of the camera. I didn't realize you had such talent behind one."

"I don't. It's just something to keep me busy," she dismissed.

The next day a high-end digital camera showed up with a dozen lenses and other pieces of equipment.

Melodie didn't even bother scolding him. She was too delighted.

She was happy. Happier than she'd ever been, so she ignored how tenuous things felt, not wanting to cause ripples.

Which was why the call from her father a few days later nearly had her dropping her brand-new camera onto the deck. When her phone rang she was so distracted with trying to work out one of the high-tech menu options, she picked up the call very absently, expecting Roman was being too lazy to come and find her from his office.

"Charmaine," her father said, and she managed to catch the camera with her thighs and drop herself into a cushioned chair. Her stomach curdled. She hated that name. It was his mother's name, and she'd been a horrible woman, bullying Melodie's mother in a hundred ways, not the least of which being her insistence of being the namesake of her granddaughter.

"What—?" she asked faintly, unable to compute. "How did you get this number?"

"That doesn't matter. The fact you have a new lover is the important piece here."

Her fingers were going numb, her mind racing. "It's none of your business."

"Oh, I assure you it's very much our business. Something we're going to turn to our advantage."

"How?" she choked. "By stealing from him again? There is nothing you can do to make me do *anything* for you." Hysteria edged into her tone. "You have nothing to offer me. Nothing to hold over me." A distant memory came to her of Roman using a certain phrase. "Lose this number," she spat. "I don't ever want to hear from you again." She drew her arm back, ready to throw her beloved phone into the sea.

A hand caught hers from behind, nearly making her jump out of her skin.

Roman.

Oh, God.

She knew instantly by his grim expression that even if he hadn't heard everything that had been said, he knew who she was talking to. He would believe she'd betrayed him and this would all be over, everything they had—

He pried the phone from her vice-like grip and ended the call, then moved so he stood facing her.

"I didn't call him," she stammered out quickly, beginning to shake. "I don't even know how he got the number." Her vision blurred as she grew convinced he was about to reject her. It was like seeing the car coming, yet having her feet stuck in cement. "I'm sorry," she started to babble. "I didn't know what to do—"

"Melodie," he said firmly. "You did the right thing." He

set aside her phone and squatted in front of her, stilling her trembling hands as she tried to keep the camera in her lap. "Aside from the part where you nearly gave my prototype a burial at sea. Although it might have been a fun exercise using the signal to retrieve it."

"Don't make jokes," she said, fighting tears, clinging to his hands with cold fingers. "Maybe it was my neighbor, the one getting my mail and watering my plants," she sniffed, brain starting to work as she realized Roman wasn't going to throw her overboard. She swiped at the wetness tracking to the corner of her mouth. "She doesn't know anything about my relationship with him. If he got hold of her, she probably would have thought it was okay to give him my number. Roman, I'm so sorry. I don't want him badgering us, making trouble—"

"He won't," he assured her, sounding so confident, the tears simply wouldn't stay put behind her lashes.

She laughed bitterly. "I don't think of you as a naive man, but surely you realize that he'll do awful things now, try to get between us. Why didn't I see this coming?"

"Melodie," he chided, cupping the side of her face and brushing a thumb beneath her overflowing eye. "I'll have the number changed. You won't hear from him again. Now please stop crying. I don't like seeing you upset by him."

"He'll keep trying!" she insisted.

"Let him try. I won't let him near you. Believe me." So commanding.

"How could you possibly stop him?" she asked, accosted by the kind of hopelessness she'd thought she'd managed to escape for good, that feeling that a dark lord could leap out of the shadows to rake her through the coals of hell at any moment. "I don't know why I didn't see that being with you, of all people, would make him—" She would have to break up with him if she expected to find any sort of peace.

Roman scowled, silently regarding her for a long, frustrated minute, before his brows lifted and a smile ghosted across his lips. "I'll call our new friend, Nic Marcussen."

"What for? No. Please don't! He already thinks I'm an idiot!" Day two with her new camera, she'd trained her lens on the dolphins dancing against the media mogul's bow, completely unaware she was also snapping shots of his family. Apparently he was extremely protective of his children and had insisted on boarding Roman's yacht ten minutes later, stealing Melodie's memory card and returning it minus several of her best shots.

Roman had not been pleased, but more because he could see how upset Melodie was, not because she'd got him off on the wrong foot with one of the world's most powerful men. They'd actually wound up having drinks later when they'd both anchored in the same cove. Nic's wife was a peach, but Melodie still felt as if she'd grossly invaded their privacy. It had been a good lesson in requesting permission before clicking the shutter.

"He never paid you for the shots he appropriated."

"I didn't want him to!" When Nic had offered to pay her the scale rate for news photos, she'd been horrified, wanting to erase the whole mortifying experience. "It was too much anyway. I'm just an amateur."

Roman gave her a patronizing look. "Your amateur shots are better than many professionals', and you know it. And if you'd accepted his payment, you would be a professional yourself. Come with me."

She dragged her feet as she followed him into his office and watched as he called Nic on his tablet. "Melodie needs a favor," Roman said. "Are you aware that her father is Garner Gautier? Have you heard of him?"

"On occasion," Nic said with reserve.

"Sounds as though you know what kind of man he is.

Melodie is thinking of writing a memoir about her child-hood. Quite a tell-all."

"No, I'm not!" she cried, shaking her head vehemently.

"You're offering me exclusive rights to this memoir?" Nic asked.

Both men ignored her protests, talking over her.

"That's right," Roman continued.

"Roman, no!" Melodie insisted. "I don't want to profit from my family's dirty laundry. My mother's memory doesn't need that kind of smearing and neither do I. *No*."

"I could give Gautier a call, ask him if he'd like to con-tribute his side of things?" Nic suggested.

"You see where I'm going with this. I knew this was the right call to make."

Melodie didn't. "Both of you, stop. I really don't want all that to come out. There would be paparazzi, a complete media circus…"

Roman clasped a reassuring hand on her arm. "It's never going to come out, Melodie."

"Gautier is going to pay back your advance to me so I will kill the book before it's written," Nic explained. "And that figure would be…?"

"Not a penny less than three million. Five would be better," Roman said.

"That's blackmail," Melodie gasped, pulling from his grip to cross her arms.

"It's a message," Roman insisted. "He doesn't have to pay, but he'll understand the potential consequences if he comes near you again. If he does pay, well, think of all the programs that money could beef up at your mother's clinic."

"It's still bribery," she stated, but she was warming to this outlandish idea.

"And since Nic taking your photos was larceny…"

"By all means, let me redeem myself," Nic said drily.

And that was that. They left it with Nic, and Melodie spent the afternoon quietly reeling. Later that night, when she felt an urgent wave of attraction, as though she couldn't get enough of Roman, he accommodated her very tenderly, overpowering her to slow her down, whispering, "It's okay, Melodie. It's okay."

She wasn't so sure. For a short while she'd been terrified she would lose him. It had been the most painfully lonely vision of her future she could imagine.

But she didn't lose him. One week on the Med turned into two, then three. Roman worked every day and Melodie filled her time with photography, joining amateur forums online for tips and critiques, thinking of starting a blog just to have a reason to share her best shots.

It was an incredibly easy existence after so many years of hardship. She didn't know how to handle it and it bothered her sometimes, made her think she wasn't trying hard enough or wasn't paying her dues. Rather than relaxing into confidence that they were a solid couple, she grew more and more anxious that something would tear them apart.

Maybe if he showed more emotion, she found herself thinking as she stood at the rail, photographing their approach to his beachside home. But despite weeks of close proximity, she really didn't know Roman much better than she had the first time she'd arrived at this elegant home.

"I just told Ingrid you're my date for her wedding tomorrow," he said as he joined her.

Talk about leaving things to the last minute. Melodie lowered the camera. "What did she say?"

He shrugged negligently, not surprising her a bit when that was the sum total of his reply.

She sighed and lifted the camera again. "I suppose I should be grateful you didn't just appear with me by your side without any explanation at all," she groused.

"Our being together wasn't any of her business until now."

"Is that really why you waited this long to say anything?" she asked.

"What do you mean?"

She pretended to change the menu options on the back of the camera, but really just clicked through the settings. "I can't help thinking you weren't sure if we'd still be together, so you skipped mentioning it until you knew for sure that we would be."

"And now you're picking a fight to put that in jeopardy?"

"No," she grumbled.

"I'm a private man, Melodie. You know that."

This time when she sighed, it was much heavier, laden with impatience. "I am aware, yes. I'd love to know why talking is so hard for you, but wouldn't dare ask."

Silence.

Misgivings rolled in like fog, making her feel chilled, as if her breaths were wet and thick.

"I'm sorry," she said, sincere, but even she could hear the tone she was taking. Frustration flattened the apology. "I really don't want to pick a fight. I was just feeling…" *Insecure.* She didn't want to admit it.

"You're hardly the first woman to become annoyed with me," he allowed.

"Oh, good. Compare me to the rest of your *companions.* That'll smooth things over. What's that white thing out there?" she asked, swiftly changing topics to avoid a bigger fight. "Is that the water doing that? Churning up or something?"

"It's a rip current," he said testily, taking a step toward the rail. He glanced from the water to the interior of the yacht, as if he couldn't decide whether he wanted to stick around and work out the niggle between them or escape it.

Melodie chose to pretend it hadn't happened at all, only saying, "That explains why it was so hard getting back to the hotel when I first came here. There was a rock... You can't see it now. I guess the tide is higher, but I had to sit and catch my breath. I was so sorry I didn't have a camera, though—"

"Wait, what are you talking about? You swam in that current? When?" He turned into robot Roman, the one who shot out questions, extracting information like a laser scalpel, green eyes piercing into hers.

"That day. The last time I was here." Maybe that was why she was picking a fight. The tension of coming back to this place was adding to the uncertainty she felt in their relationship.

"There are signs that say No Swimming."

"I know, but I was hot and tired and my feet hurt. I wasn't wearing shoes. Swimming across the bay looked shorter than walking all the way around, so—"

"I sent a cab, Melodie! I told them to find you on the road and assumed they did. Are you seriously telling me you swam in that?" He pointed toward the streak of white foam.

"I swam across it. Not in it. I'm not stupid."

"I beg to differ!" His voice went up. "People die in this area every year. Stupid tourists who think they're strong enough to— *What the hell were you thinking?*"

"That I wanted to get back to the hotel." She'd seen Roman angry before, especially that first day, but nothing like this. He wasn't just irritated. There was a quality beneath his flush of rage that hinted at desperation. She could see him fighting for control, visibly struggling, but his temper exploded out of him anyway.

"You could have died!" he shouted. The curses that followed weren't exactly aimed at her, but they had enough color to take her aback.

She stared, wide-eyed in astonishment as he paced away a few feet, looked across the water, slammed another look her direction that was so outraged it should have knocked her overboard, then smacked his fist onto the rail.

"Don't you *ever* do anything so reckless again. Do you hear me? No matter how sad you are about losing your mother or how angry you are at me, you do *not* act as if your life means nothing. You're smarter than that. You're—" He pressed his finger and thumb into his eye sockets, shoulders bowing for a moment. "The world needs more people like you. Don't act as though you're disposable."

He threw himself away from the rail and disappeared into the interior of the yacht.

Melodie realized that the weight on her neck was her camera. Her hands had gone lax at her sides. Thank goodness she always kept it tethered or it would be on the bottom of the sea by now.

She swallowed, stunned by the depth of emotion that had just detonated out of Roman in a way she could never have expected. It took her a few minutes to recover from her shock, but she finally did and went to find him.

He was in his office, door firmly locked against intrusion.

CHAPTER ELEVEN

ROMAN FELT LIKE an idiot—one of his least favorite feelings. Although he'd already been standing there feeling it before he'd behaved like a mother hen on steroids.

Melodie had been right. A part of him had been convinced she wouldn't last until the wedding, that his aloof persona would drive her away and he'd be without a date at all when the big day happened.

Instead, she'd become such an integral part of his world he feared he couldn't live without her. As she'd made her facetious little remarks today, he'd heard the hurt beneath. Maybe other women had been as injured by his reserve, but he hadn't felt an answering pinch in the same way. He hadn't hated himself quite as much for causing suffering. He hadn't considered explaining that being nothing more than a file all your life, having your personal details handed from one person to the next, as if privacy was for other people, not you, had left a mark.

Maybe if those details hadn't made it from the confidentiality of a folder into the mouths of his foster home siblings, he could have withstood it, but the foster parents had always managed to gossip somewhere along the line and the kids had always wound up overhearing. Then the hierarchy of judgment would start. Kids who were abused were rescues. Kids such as him, whose parents were deemed reprehensible, were tarred as worthless.

Oddly, with Melodie he already knew she wouldn't

make those same judgments. But it was the very fact that she wouldn't, and would more likely try to comfort him, that made it seem an even more painful prospect to open up to her.

So he'd stood there trying to see a way out of the corner he'd painted himself into when she'd distracted him by telling him what she'd done after leaving him that day. After she'd fled like a Victorian maiden ravished by the local duke. Hot, tired, emotionally distressed, she'd done something so irresponsible he could hardly think of it.

Every summer the local news reported on at least one or two deaths in that current. The fact the tide had kept the water low was likely the only thing that had kept her from being a headline and statistic. His blood ran icy thinking of it.

The vibration of the engine stilled. They were at the dock outside his home. No more hiding. He pulled out his earbuds, ceasing to pretend he was working, and gathered himself to face Melodie. Hell, the entire crew had probably heard him tear a strip off her and would stare at him.

He wasn't entirely sorry. She *had* been heedless of very real danger, but he was angry with himself, too, for raising his voice. She was sensitive, her thoughts and feelings so easy to read he couldn't help but trust her.

But he was furious with himself for letting emotion get the best of him. He'd ceased trying to figure out why she prompted such strong feelings in him. All he could do was work to control and hide them.

He cursed under his breath, ran a hand over his face to clear his expression and unlocked the door.

It wouldn't have surprised him to find Melodie packing to leave him, and she *was* in his cabin loosely gathering some things that she'd piled on the bed, but she'd stopped to look at her camera. Her hair hung in a loose curtain off one side of her bent head, her lips were pouted into concentration, her thumb working the controls while the rest of her slender height was still.

He couldn't count the number of times he'd found her like this since he'd bought the thing for her. She loved it, and Roman got a kick of amusement and pleasure every time he saw how much she enjoyed it. Her photos were excellent and she was always fooling around with the settings, reviewing what she'd done, trying to improve. He did the same with his own work and liked seeing her pursue something that gave her so much satisfaction.

"I was worried that you were dragging your feet about telling Ingrid because you weren't sure if you really wanted me here," she murmured without looking up, reminding him that the radar between them worked both ways. He rarely sneaked up on her without getting a smile of greeting before he was in touching distance.

No smile today. She didn't even look at him.

"I couldn't assume you'd want to be here, not after the way I treated you the first time we were in this house together." He had barely admitted that to himself and didn't like saying it aloud. He didn't want to remind her. She might agree and leave.

Then, even though it made him feel as obvious as a boy picking flowers, he gave her what he thought she needed to hear.

"And I have never invited any woman here, except you and Ingrid that day. I suppose it sounds ridiculous that I had to think about it when you've already been here, but I wanted to be sure I was making the right choice, bringing you into my home." It had been a remarkably easy decision, in fact. So easy he'd forced himself to mull it over, refusing to commit until the last minute despite his gut clamoring for her to become a fixture there.

She finally looked up, her blue gaze surprised and vulnerable, searched his in a way that made him deeply uncomfortable because he feared he didn't have whatever it was she was hoping to find. He had to look away first, which was a terribly revealing thing to do, but he couldn't take her scrutiny.

She set her camera on the bed before coming across to him, expression solemn. When she cupped the side of his face, his first instinct was to tense with resistance. She ignored his rebuff and lifted on tiptoes to set her lips against the corner of his mouth.

"Thank you for telling me that," she said, breath warm against his lips and chin.

As her scent filled his nostrils and she started to lower to flat feet, his arms went around her of their own accord. He felt her start, then soften to accept the convulsive tightening of his arms around her.

Words, stupid words, crowded his throat, but he couldn't put them in any sort of order that made sense. He couldn't figure out which ones were safe to say and which ones would hurt and damage and lower her opinion of him. He could only frown at the carpet over her shoulder and drink in her scent, cheek to cheek with her.

Somewhere beyond the door, one of the crew said something about luggage. Footsteps approached and Roman and Melodie stepped apart.

An hour later, when the crew had dispersed to beach-based pursuits and the house was theirs alone, he caught up to Melodie in his master bedroom. She was in the walk-in closet, hanging a dress she'd obviously decided would be suitable for the wedding tomorrow.

He turned her toward him again, unable to keep from kissing her. He wanted her. Needed to make love to her. Not with the passion and lust of their first time, but with this well of tender cherishing overflowing within him. Soft feelings like gratitude and deep admiration filled him so thoroughly he had to pour them onto her, to somehow communicate how deeply he regarded her.

It was so intense they could only lie in silence afterward, bodies tangled, damp skin glued as if only a fragile cell wall kept them from conjoining into one being. He should have been disturbed by the magnitude of the moment, but he was oddly reassured. They fell asleep with the filmy white curtains shifting in the light breeze, the swish of low waves hypnotic and lulling.

The next morning Ingrid aimed a very pointed look at Melodie the moment she entered the house. The day already had got off to an extremely busy start with people arriving every five minutes. The wedding planners hired to replace Melodie were a male-female duo who were competent enough, but wound up with so many questions Melodie might as well have been the one organizing it all.

She had quietly appointed herself in charge rather than pressing Roman into that position. If *she* asked him whether a tent should be moved twelve feet, he gave the matter serious consideration. If anyone else asked him for an opinion, he gave them a look that suggested they take a long walk off his short dock.

So Melodie was running interference—even when she wound up in the guest room with his former PA, the bride-to-be.

"How—?" Ingrid blurted as she opened a small suitcase that was all makeup, hairbrushes, curling irons and body glitter.

"There was a misunderstanding. We worked it out," Melodie said with a circumspect smile, not pretending she didn't know what Ingrid was asking.

"Oh, Melodie," Ingrid said with a pitiful shake of her head. "You've turned out just like him. Are you really not going to give me any of the details?"

"Maybe another time," she lied. "When you're not so busy. Surely you have better things to do today? The salon people have taken over the sitting room. Let me get a round of mimosas for you and the bridal party. I'll meet you in there."

The day came together beautifully. When Ingrid came down the stairs she was a vision, making the entire guest list gasp in unison. Lilies floated in the pool, carpet lining her route alongside it, but she still sent a wink toward Melodie as she made it past the hazard without mishap. She met Huxley under the archway set up for the occasion, and their vows and deep connection brought tears to Melodie's eyes.

Tears of happiness, but sad ones, too. That kind of everlasting commitment to another person was her dream, but she wasn't holding her breath that it would ever really happen. Roman cared for her. She was convinced of that much after his freak-out over her swim in the rip current, but he didn't feel anything like what Ingrid and Huxley shared. Not the kind of love that demanded to be locked in for a lifetime.

She distracted herself by playing back-up photographer, surprised when she heard a masculine and intimate "Hey, beautiful."

Looking up with a smile already in her eyes, she found herself confronted with Roman's phone. It clicked and he lowered it.

"Did you seriously just take my photo?"

"I did. And don't you dare aim yours at me. Put it down and come dance with me."

"Since you asked so nicely," she teased, wrinkling her nose at him, but pouting a little that he was dodging a photo. He was in a tuxedo. That was always a good look for him.

She loved dancing with him, though. They were a perfect match height-wise, and he led with smooth assurance. "Are you a natural? Or did you take lessons?" she found herself asking.

A pause, then, "Lessons seemed a wise investment once I began attending formal events."

She let that fact absorb, along with the knowledge that Roman hadn't hesitated very long at all before answering a personal question. Perhaps they were making progress.

"Are you enjoying this formal occasion? You were rather pithy about weddings the first time we talked."

"No," he answered, his reply so prompt she flashed a glance upward at him.

A pang of disappointment struck. He still found weddings a waste of time, then.

"I wish they'd all go home so I could have you to myself," he said. "You really do look incredible. That shade of blue is definitely your color, and those shoes are coming to bed with us."

She laughed, enjoying his suggestive remark and the reassurance that it wasn't the wedding putting that dismayed edge in his voice.

"Whatever possessed you to invite four hundred people into your home if you hate weddings so much?" she asked.

He didn't answer and she sighed inwardly, thinking they'd lost that fragile strand of communication twining them together. It was always like this, and it created a lot of despair in her.

"I'm embarrassed to tell you," he said so quietly she almost didn't hear him.

She tried not to betray how surprised she was, just murmured, "Why? It's a very nice thing to do."

"If it was for Ingrid's sake, it would be, but I wanted people—her sort of people—to see me as their equal. Now they're here, I can't be bothered speaking to them. I'd rather dance with you." His mouth quirked in self-derision.

The importance of status was never lost on someone with a family in politics, but Melodie heard something else in his tone. Humbleness. *Her sort of people.*

"You are their equal," she informed him with quiet sincerity.

"I told you what kind of mother I had."

"One who made sacrifices for her child. Trust me. You do not own the patent on scandal or tragedy. I would think a man who makes his living running background checks would be fully aware of that."

Roman had to hand it to her. Each time he gathered his courage and revealed a moment of personal angst, she came through, reminding him that he had every reason to stand tall.

They made the rounds after that, branching out from the bride's and groom's immediate family, whom they'd already met, to circulate among the other guests. Melodie fairly sparkled, she was so bright and delightful. He even found himself laughing when she described her fall into the pool that first day, only excusing them when someone joked that Roman had pushed her so he could perform mouth-to-mouth.

"I'm sorry," Melodie murmured as he steered her toward the bar.

"It's not your fault," he said. "The guy is drunk." And it was juvenile of him to feel insulted and mocked, but he didn't want anyone to think he treated women roughly. He was past throwing punches over that sort of thing, but he didn't listen to it. As for being so smitten with Melodie he would behave like a dolt in a romantic comedy, well, he wasn't about to stand around for that accusation, either.

In all honesty, the whole day was a bit of a trial for Roman on that score, constantly demanding that he examine his feelings and intentions toward her. In fact, he had watched Huxley gaze at Ingrid in a way that wasn't far off from what he was beginning to feel toward Melodie. She was precious and beautiful and captivating to him, but he couldn't bring himself to tell her or allow others to see that in him.

"I'm going to take a few more photos," she murmured, touching his arm as she stepped away.

He nodded, aware he could call her back, that she probably wanted him to, but letting her go anyway. He didn't wear his emotions on his sleeve. He didn't even know how to put on the coat.

CHAPTER TWELVE

MELODIE UNDERSTOOD NOW. She wasn't tired of Roman, but a woman could take only so much uncertainty. She kept telling herself to live in the moment, enjoy what they had, that taking it day by day was fine. She didn't delude herself that there was another man out there who had all Roman's qualities plus an open heart, a desire for commitment and a burning need for children. The man she was with was definitely as perfect as she could expect.

But not knowing how long she and Roman would last made her anxious. She was always looking for the end so she could anticipate it, soften the blow. She could easily see why his other companions had made it happen just to get the suspense over with.

She didn't want to leave him, though. She loved him.

Loved him, loved him, loved him.

And if she judged him on his actions, he cared quite deeply for her. At least that was what she thought he was communicating. So when she received a job offer, Melodie was torn.

Under any other circumstance she would have been beyond elated by the contents of the email, but it meant leaving Roman for a few days. That made it a bit of a test of their relationship. On the other hand, it gave her the fallback position she needed if they were destined to break up.

The prospect of confronting exactly how tenuous their

relationship was kept her silent on the topic for several days, until she *had* to make a decision or lose the opportunity altogether.

She brought it up over breakfast in the sunroom she adored.

"It's an Italian couple. Well, the wife is Canadian. They're friends with the Marcussens and saw the photos I'd taken of the family. They asked if I'd come to their home on Lake Como and take some candid shots of them with their children. It would have to be next week," she said, trying not to betray how nervous she was.

Roman set aside his tablet and sat back in his chair. He wore his usual morning attire of pajama pants, so he was all bare-chested and manly. She wore the silk robe he'd bought her in Paris. A morning breeze wafted in, dewy and tanged by the lemon grove. The low, quiet murmur of waves on the shore was the only sound for a long moment.

"I have to be in New York." No inflection. No real reaction beyond exchanging information.

"I know. That's why I'm talking to you about it. I keep trying to say no, and they keep offering me more money. They'll pay for my flight, put me up. They're very determined, but it has to be next week or it won't happen at all."

"Do you want to do it?"

She lifted a shoulder, genuinely conflicted. Roman could call her his companion all he wanted, but she knew she was his mistress. As idyllic as it should have felt to let him support her, she had spent a lot of years becoming self-reliant. She might not *need* a job right now, but she *wanted* one, and being a photographer was a dream career for her, something she'd barely imagined she could pursue as a hobby, let alone anything more. If she could establish herself at this level, it could be a proper way to make a living.

"It's a really good opportunity," she managed to say.

"You told me I could be a professional if I took money for my photos, and this couple seems to think I'm good enough. I guess there is a part of me that wants to try."

Nothing showed on his face. Only his green eyes flickered as he cataloged every nuance of her expression, making her feel more self-conscious by the second. Was she fooling herself? Was she really not that good?

Did it bother him at all that she was talking about leaving? That she wouldn't be at his beck and call?

"This could turn into a career for you," he said.

"I keep thinking it could, yes." She glanced at the hands in her lap that were knotting her belt, trying to disguise the disappointment that he hadn't first leaped to how it would affect him. *Them.* "I don't have any illusions," she continued, doing the work for him so he'd see the broader picture. "I realize I'd be chasing commissions and have to do a lot of traveling."

She flicked a look up at him.

Still nothing. Her heart felt pinched in a vice that slowly closed as she squeezed out what she thought needed to be said.

"That's something I always wanted to do. Travel." It was his cue to say, "We already travel." He didn't.

"Running your own business isn't a picnic, I know," she continued. "I don't even know where I'd pay taxes or if I need a work visa, but…"

"You'd regret it if you didn't try," he summed up. He was very still, very watchful, but didn't express any regret on his side. This was purely her decision, he seemed to be saying.

"I think I would, yes." She said the words steadily enough, but her heart was listing in her chest. Sinking.

He nodded. "Then, you should do whatever you need to. I have every confidence that you could be very successful if you give it your all. I won't hold you back."

His words were like the slide of a guillotine, hissing and thunking. She'd known this moment would happen, but the shock still reverberated through her. It was over. She had wanted him to fight for her, but he was making it easy for her to leave him. She nodded, head loose on her shoulders. "I'll go email them."

She rose, feeling weightless and uncoordinated. Despite the warmth of the morning, her skin pimpled with cold. Her fingers were nerveless and her essence stayed at the table while the shell of her body moved away.

The separation of soul and self was so painful she couldn't even react. Couldn't cry.

When Roman made love to her that night she shuddered in ecstasy but couldn't talk afterward. Couldn't face the emptiness of her future, even though emptiness was the only option open to her.

If she had thought there was a chance for them, she might have forgone taking the job and stayed with him, but Roman wasn't like her. He enjoyed female company, loved sex, cared to a point, but he didn't love her back.

And maybe, if she hadn't seen firsthand how emotional and financial dependence had gutted her mother's self-esteem, Melodie might have settled for one-sided love. But she couldn't do that to herself.

So she held back her tears until, a handful of days later, Roman left for New York and she caught a flight to Italy. They pretended they'd see each other soon, but she knew this was the beginning of the end. Better to make the break a clean one.

Before Melodie had even finished her work in Italy and sent her thank-you note to the Marcussens for referring her, she received a request from each of Nic's three siblings asking her to do similar jobs for them. Without hesitation she accepted the commissions. She found herself in Athens by the end of that week, Paris the next and over to New York at the end of the month.

Roman was gone from that city by then, having been called to a supplier's factory in China. Their face-to-face wireless connections had turned into texts and emails and became more sporadic. She had thought—hoped—Roman would make the effort to track her down or invite her to meet him somewhere, but her schedule was constantly filling and he was making no effort to ask her to come back to him.

Their temporary separation had obviously clarified itself into the natural end to their arrangement. It felt like an amputation. She pined and longed and yearned. Fortunately, though, she was so busy she could only break down at night before she went to sleep alone and dreamed she was with him again.

At least she was creating a decent life for herself. As word spread, a studio in New York reached out to her. It was extremely well respected, had all the print facilities and lined up gigs for its photographers. Quite unexpectedly, Melodie had a home base in the city she'd always wanted to inhabit. All her preparations for the wedding-planning business came in handy now as she reworked them for her new photography business. Practically overnight she was supporting herself.

Roman greased the wheels, of course. She realized that after a few weeks, when one of the studio owners dropped a remark about how he'd come to hear of her. The sublease on her one-room flat was equally a convenient find, but she chose not to fight Roman on it. She suspected he was trying to make up for flattening her first attempt at a proper career. She let him help her. It was a kindness that went both ways.

But she missed him with every breath in her body, every minute of every day.

Roman was stunned. It took him weeks to fully absorb that Melodie had left him. One day he was waking to the shift of silken limbs against him, the next he was walking around like a bomb-blast victim, shell-shocked and unable to make sense of the empty landscape around him.

He kept going back to that moment when she'd told him she had a job offer. He had felt everything in him draining away then. He'd seen himself about to lose everything and he hadn't known how to stop it. It was like being nine years old again, completely powerless to change what was happening to him.

He couldn't stand in the way of Melodie taking a job she wanted, though. He'd already caused her to lose her livelihood twice. And she genuinely loved photography. How could he blurt out that the idea of her leaving him made him physically sick?

Which was the real crux of the matter, he knew. He hadn't had the courage even to face how deep the cut went as she was carved out of his life. The bleeding never seemed to let up. He barely slept, having no desire to crawl into an empty bed, and when he woke he saw no point in rising. His company was dominating the financial pages. The demise of Gautier Enterprises was a done deal. They were declaring bankruptcy while rumors of corruption dogged its board. He couldn't care less.

His schedule had finally pulled him to New York, where he knew Melodie now had a flat, but she wasn't even in the city. He followed her social-media accounts, and she was posting from Spain.

A blip on the reader of his office door announced his

PA, Colette. He liked her well enough now that she was up to speed. Ingrid had always been cheerfully efficient, and Colette was equally strong on details and light in mood, not that anything really penetrated anymore. If he had felt like a puppet before, someone who moved through life without feeling, now he felt like a ghost. Even simple sensory pleasures such as a good meal or a piece of music were lost on him.

The worst part was he had fought deep emotions for so long he ought to have been an expert at suppressing them. The things he was feeling now were too big, however. Too dark and heavy and all pervading. There was no escaping the barbed and piercing pain that squeezed him in its coil.

He was in hell.

"Lunch," Colette said, holding up a white bag, snapping him from what he realized had become a blank stare. "Thanks for buying this round. Everyone is really grateful."

He shrugged. Colette had started a Friday lunch thing that seemed to boost morale and communication. She'd invited him to join them, but Roman had declined, preferring to brood in here alone.

He would always be alone.

He should have asked Melodie to stay.

But he couldn't. Not when she deserved so much more than he was able to offer her.

Colette left, and he moved with robotic detachment, pulling out the carton and finding Chinese markings on its side. He wasn't hungry for anything, he realized, least of all cheap noodles and overly sauced, chewy meat.

But he supposed he should eat.

Fishing for the chopsticks, he wound up touching something that he recognized and almost didn't want to see, but he pulled it out and looked at it anyway: a fortune cookie.

He'd met Melodie many months ago, had spent countless hours with her since, and still he could remember their first conversation. She'd been so disappointed in him, so brightly engaging with her optimism in the way she described marriage, while he'd called weddings a shell for a useless piece of paper.

Before he realized what he was doing to do, rage broke through his shields and he smashed the cookie, pulverizing it in its cellophane wrapper. The white fortune with its pink ink peeked through beige shrapnel.

Swearing, wondering how the hell his control had deserted him so thoroughly, he opened the package and shook out the crumbs until he could pick out the tiny strip of paper.

"Patience will be rewarded sooner or later."

Had he really hoped for actual guidance? Fortune cookies were stupid.

Weddings and marriage and lifetime commitments were equally useless things to place faith in. Just like women were.

Moving to the window, Roman rubbed a knuckle against his brow, chest tight. Was that what he really thought? That women were faithless? Because his mother had died before she could get him back? Because every woman he'd remotely cared about had left?

Had he given any of them a reason to stay?

The fact was, his father had been the one to abandon his mother. What did it say about Roman that he hadn't even tried to keep Melodie in his life? Did there have to be a child at risk for *him* to take a risk? What made anyone fight to keep someone in their life?

On impulse, he turned to the phone and dialed a number he knew by heart, but rarely called. The woman who answered was the only woman he'd ever known who'd completely devoted herself to one man, despite the fact he'd left her—involuntarily, but definitely left her—years ago.

"Brenda? It's Roman. Can I buy you lunch?"

A surprised pause, then, "Why don't you come over here? I'll make you grilled cheese."

Grilled cheese and tomato soup. Hardly the fine dining he'd grown used to, but Roman was ridiculously comforted by the simple meal when he sat down in Brenda's kitchen an hour later in what had been his only real home, and even then only for a year.

Brenda, so motherly it had been almost unbearable when he'd lived here, poured him a glass of milk, still attempting to nurture him. He hated milk. Always had, probably because he'd drunk it sour more times than not.

"This is a really lovely surprise, Roman." She stopped there, didn't ask him why he was here, even though her curiosity was evident in the long silence after she spoke. But she understood him and respected his boundaries. He'd always appreciated that about her.

So even though he felt like a world-class idiot, he opened his chest and set his heart on the table, self-deprecatingly stating, "I'm having girl trouble, Brenda."

"And you came to me? I'm touched, Roman. I truly am. Tell me about her."

He stalled. How could he possibly describe Melodie and all she'd come to mean to him? Her smiles, her quiet toughness, her fierce resiliency and her soft, soft heart.

"I just want to know…what makes people stick around? Is there something I can say that would make her come back? For good? Because I'm not good with words and…"

She wasn't laughing at him. Her graying head was bent a little as she patiently watched him struggle.

"Charles doesn't recognize you anymore, but you're with him as much as you can be. What keeps you faithful?" he asked.

She flinched, then smiled crookedly. "*He* does."

Roman narrowed his eyes, trying to understand.

Brenda lowered her gaze to stir her soup. "I've always kept Charles's confidences, but I can see you need to hear some of them. He told me once, not long after he hired you, that he saw something of himself in you. That always made me sad because I knew what he'd been through as a child. His mother had a boyfriend who was very cruel to him. Very, very cruel." Her voice hollowed. "I know he didn't even tell me all of it, but what he did tell me…" She shook her head. "I don't know how people can be like that to another human being."

Roman's view of his first employer, a man who'd been athletic and smart and gruffly wise—seemingly impervious—shifted. He grew angry on his friend's behalf. He wanted to go back in time and defend this person he'd suddenly discovered he not only respected and admired, but cared about very much.

"It wasn't easy in our early days. He simply didn't want to talk. I completely understand that coping strategy. I don't want to talk about how difficult it is to put the man I love in a home and watch his health decline. To see him every day but never see recognition in his eyes." She welled up and dabbed a napkin to her trembling lips, recovering her composure after a moment. "Some things are just too painful to speak about."

"Brenda, what can I do?" he said, reaching out impulsively. It wasn't like him at all, but he'd gotten into the habit of touching Melodie when she was upset, trying to comfort, and his affection for Brenda ran as deep.

"You've done all that can be done. Research," she said with a fatalistic lift of her shoulder. "Hopefully in the future it won't come to this for other spouses and families. But what I'm trying to say is that I understand how futile it feels to speak about things that can't be changed."

He nodded. That was it exactly. Why bother telling Melodie that he'd once nearly been raped, that he had a cigar burn scar under his elbow or how alone he'd felt after his mother had died? What point would it serve?

"But talking helps," Brenda said quietly, adding with an apologetic smile, "Talking is important, Roman. Especially to a woman. Charles showed me in a million ways that he loved me, but until he said the words, I wasn't sure. And once he'd said it, once we'd devoted ourselves to each other, I knew that nothing could separate us. His illness makes it impossible for him to show me he still loves me, but I know he does. It would break his heart if I stopped believing it… But I wouldn't know how much he loved me if he hadn't told me before his illness started affecting him."

Roman winced from that peek into the intimacy of his friends' marriage. And he cringed from the idea of laying his heart on the line so blatantly. What if Melodie didn't want his love? Yes, he knew she wanted the whole package, but what if she'd left because she'd rather someone else offered it?

They finished eating in silence, but afterward he took out his phone and showed Brenda his gallery of Melodie photos, from springtime in Paris to her languid smiles on his yacht to the dreamy beauty of two days before she'd left him, when he'd caught her on the beach, taking a break from using her own camera to lift her face to the sun.

"Is there a reason you're sitting in an old lady's kitchen rather than chasing this woman down?" Brenda asked. "A picture is worth a thousand words, and there are a million 'I love yous' in each of those photos."

His heart lurched. He stood, smirking to hide how desperately he hoped she was right. Touching her shoulder, he wavered, then gave in to impulse and bent to kiss her cheek. Then, because he was starting to understand how this worked, he said, "Your generosity has always meant the world to me, Brenda. You're like a second mother to me. I wish I'd let you treat me like your son."

It was a terrible risk that paid off immediately.

"Oh, my boy." She patted his hand and turned her face to kiss his knuckles. "There's still time to let me. Invite me to your wedding."

CHAPTER THIRTEEN

MELODIE WONDERED IF there was anything quite so beautiful as an Indian wedding. She'd covered a few nuptials by now, including an Arab one that had been so over-the-top with luxury she'd been fairly sure she'd been transported to another planet. This one in London, where both families lived, had a celebratory quality that was as solid and fascinating as the abundant gold weighing down the bride. The colors, dear Lord, the colors. And when it came to capturing the joy of family and children—something that was becoming her forte—there was nothing so perfect as the natural warmth of two Indian families coming together through a love match.

Maybe it was the cultural shift that made her appreciate this wedding more than the Spanish heiress's last week. That one had made it too easy for to see herself in the gown and Roman in the morning coat. It had left her crying hard through the night. She couldn't think of it now. She'd start crying again.

Roman was gone. Life had to go on.

She forced her mind back to arranging the groom's family, with his parents and abundance of siblings, their spouses and children, along with his new bride. One of the four-year-olds in the party had pretty much given up on this exercise, so Melodie had to snap fast.

"No, please, keep looking at the camera," she called when half of the arrangement turned their heads to take note of something across the room. Beautiful, happy people abounded at weddings, but when the groups got this big, it was like herding cats to get them all to do one thing.

They weren't cooperating. The distraction of the growing reception was too much. The groom actually stepped away to meet someone working through the crowd. The rest of the group broke up. Melodie silently whimpered, then felt a tingle that she usually only felt when—

She gasped and spun around at the exact moment she heard, "I need to speak to your photographer."

Roman. So tall, so commanding. So inappropriately dressed in a T-shirt and jeans, a brown leather jacket thrown on over it.

"What are you doing here?" she asked, voice squeaking with astonishment. Her body actually hurt from the sting of excitement that shot through her veins.

"I want to talk to you."

"How did you even find me?" She'd been called in last minute on this one, flying to London first thing this morning.

"Your office. They owed me for referring you in the first place. I didn't realize you'd be working." He gave the anxious bride a friendly nod. "I don't know why it didn't occur to me. Weddings are evening events, so the odds were good, I suppose. But I won't get you fired." He turned to the groom, handed over his card and said something about a free security system for a home or office if he was allowed to borrow Melodie for a few minutes.

"Can we go somewhere?" he said to Melodie, taking her arm and looking over the heads in the crowd, starting to usher her from the ballroom toward the interior of the hotel.

"Where? No," she added quickly when he signaled to a

server in a uniform. "No hotel room. You know what will happen and I *will* get fired."

He acknowledged that with a cant of his head and a quirk of his lips. "Promising," he remarked under his breath, changing direction toward a door to the balcony.

"Also, I'm not pregnant, if that's why you're here," she blurted, unable to think of another reason.

He opened his mouth, paused, then said, "We'll come back to that one."

Would they? Her heart was already going a mile a minute, and now it threatened to leave her body altogether.

He drew her away from the wedding guests milling on the balcony and moved toward the outdoor café that was shut down for the evening, sectioned off at the far side. He scissored his legs over the low glass rail that separated the area while she moved into the shadows and opened the gate, letting herself in. They circled around a trellis and moved to where they could see the Thames cutting through the sparkle of city lights.

And there her world stopped, because it was all she could do to hold back a choke of tears, she was so happy to see him and so devastated at the same time. Did he have any idea how difficult it would be to say goodbye again?

It was up to her to talk, though, she supposed, and searched for her voice, wanting to know why he really was here.

He surprised her by saying abruptly, "It wasn't just the way your father and brother treated me." The words dropped into the empty air off the top of the hotel. His hands gripped the rail and he didn't look at her. "It was the same message again and again my whole life. My needs weren't important. My feelings didn't matter. No one cared, so what was the point in showing or asking or wanting? It was far easier to become self-sufficient and not talk to anyone."

It was such an odd yet intimate statement, she could only stare up at him, shocked and rather suspecting he'd been rehearsing the words, waiting to get them off his chest.

Her hand went to his and he quickly turned his palm up to grasp her fingers, making her blood sing. The pressure was so tight it was just this side of painful, warning her that for all the detachment he was affecting, this was very hard for him. But still he was trying. Reaching out. Asking to be understood.

"I learned to shut myself off, too," she offered. "When I was surrounded by people who watched to see what was important to me so they could use it against me. I would never try to hurt you like that, Roman. I hope you believe that."

"I do. That's why…" In the dark, she saw him struggle to retain his stoic expression.

When he didn't continue and the only sound became the music that grew louder as doors were opened off the ballroom, she covered his grip in a signal to ease up his hold. "Roman, why are you here?" she asked, pushing the words past the catch in her throat.

"I never saw any point in marriage," he said, continuing to squish her fingers while she went lax in his grip, not wanting to hear the tiny sparks of her dream snuffed out for good.

"Then I realized that if you were my wife, and you knew I expected you to come back after each job, maybe you would."

"Oh, my God," she whispered, feeling as if this tight grip of theirs was the only thing keeping her from plummeting off the building.

"I want to love you, Melodie, but I don't know if I know how. I quit feeling anything years ago to save myself pain. I fought what I feel for you as hard as I could, but I can't *not* feel something for you. And I don't know whether it's enough. Is it love? I don't know. I just know it's…good. When I think of you, when I touch you, the way I feel is so damned good. Sweet and hopeful and warm—all the things you are. I lose all that when you're not with me. It's just hollow emptiness and I can't stand it. It *hurts*. Every day. I want the good feeling back. I want *you* back."

Her head spun. Her heart soared on a roller coaster, climbing and dipping and spiraling so she didn't know which way was up.

"All the way here a voice in my head kept telling me you wouldn't forgive me for letting you go in the first place. I was afraid I'd broken you again, that you'd stopped believing in men and love and the sort of life you deserve. But…" He reached his free hand into his shirt pocket and came up with something small.

A shiny black pearl nestled against a shiny white one in a platinum setting surrounded by glittering diamonds. She was sure she was going to faint at that point. Or she was dreaming and would wake up. Could this possibly be real?

"How's that for optimism?" he said. "The minute I saw it, I thought of you." He started to kneel.

"Oh, Roman, no!"

He froze. "You don't—?"

She felt his recoil at the perceived rejection and threw herself against his stiff body. "No, I mean, yes! I want to marry you. I love you. You don't have to go down on one knee!"

His breath rushed out and his arms tightened on her. "Sweetheart. This is one of the few romantic gestures I could possibly figure out on my own. Let me do it." He gently set her back a step, a half grin catching at the corner of his mouth as he went down on one knee. "Saved me some suspense, at least. Will you marry me, Melodie Parnell?"

He offered the ring and she found her throat too locked to speak again. All she could do was nod and hold out her shaking hand. He threaded the ring onto her finger and she fell on him, letting him catch her on his hard thigh and squeeze her to his brawny chest with viselike arms so tight she could barely breathe except to gasp, "Yes."

"And you love me? Because if you're not sure—"

"I do," she said, sniffing back emotional tears that refused to stay behind her eyes. "Believe me, I've tried not to, but I love you so much I feel as if I'm dying without you. I *was* angry you let me go," she admitted. "But since you came after me, I'll forgive you."

"So softhearted," he murmured, brushing his lips against her temple. "I'm sorry I didn't tell you that day that your leaving was the worst possible thing you could ever do to me. I didn't know how to stop you. I couldn't find the words and, damn it, Melodie. I had destroyed your livelihood twice. I know how much you love photography. How could I refuse to let you try to make a career of it?"

"I do love photography. Just not as much as I love you," she pouted, clinging to his neck as he lifted her and moved them both into a chair, her on his lap, legs dangling over the arm. She couldn't get close enough. Each cell in her body plumped a little more with each breath, like a succulent absorbing the water it needed to survive.

He breathed a laugh against her hairline. "You have no idea how much I like hearing you say that."

"That I love you? I do!" She hugged him again. "But I don't want to quit working," she rushed to say. "Not altogether. Just, you know, I won't let it come between us again."

"That's okay. I would never ask you to give up something you enjoy so much. But, yes, if you could ease up, maybe take fewer clients so we can have more time together, I'd like that a lot. Charge more," he advised loftily.

"A lot more. Slow down those offers and make it worth our while for you to leave our bed."

She snorted, wanting to be in bed with him right now. He wanted that, too. She could feel him hard against her hip and wriggled to let him know they were on the same page. That part hadn't changed one teensy bit, and she missed him *so much*.

He stilled her with firm hands. "Darling, you know where that's going to lead. I'll be arrested along with getting you fired."

"Might be worth it," she teased, nipping at his jaw.

"Might be," he agreed, running possessive hands over her. "But maybe it's a good thing that I don't have the option of letting my body do the talking right now. It's not easy for me to open up. For you, for us, I want to try, though. No one has ever affected me the way you do, Melodie. From the first moment... Hell, I am the last person to believe in love at first sight or soul mates, but no one means as much to me as you do."

She swallowed and ducked her forehead under his jaw, too moved to speak.

"I want to change, to be whatever it is you need in a man, but it will be hard. Bear with me. That's all I'm asking," he said, cradling the back of her head in his big hand. "And maybe, after we've given ourselves some time, if you want..." He swallowed, then cleared his throat. "We could talk about a baby. If you want."

She tightened her arms around his neck and shuddered as a sob of joy took her.

"Don't cry. I said only if you want," he rushed to repeat.

"I'm happy!" she choked. "You're giving me everything I ever wanted. I can't help crying."

"Oh," he said ruefully, cuddling her closer. "Okay." He took a deep, emotive breath that shook her on his chest. "I want to make you happy."

"You do," she assured him. "Just by being with me. I love you."

"Is that how it works? Because it's the same for me," he said, tilting his head and tipping hers so they could look into each other's eyes. "I was missing you as though a piece of me was gone. Then, the minute I saw you today, everything was right. I need you in my life to make it worth living. That must be love, right?"

"I'm sure of it," she agreed, pressing her smile to his.

EPILOGUE

MELODIE STEPPED OUT to the glitter of evening sunlight bouncing off the sea. As she reached the top of the stairs, the silk of her gown poured like milk off the first step.

She paused to gather it, sending a smile to her groom where he waited at the bottom.

Roman wore a black tuxedo with a cream-colored waistcoat and a silk tie in the same color. It was the perfect level of formality for their small wedding and, as usual, it didn't matter what he wore. He projected masculine beauty no matter what.

He leaped up the steps to take her bouquet and offer his free hand, ensuring she was steady as she made her way down. No father of the bride to give her away. She hadn't even considered it, thankful that her "memoir" and her brother's financial and legal troubles had kept both her father and Anton out of their lives for good.

No, Roman was walking with her to their understated altar. He hadn't wanted to wait for her to come to him on the beach. *The whole point of marriage is to do things together, isn't it?* he'd said as they were making the plans.

So she'd been allowed to kick him out of their bedroom while she put on her gown, but that was it. They'd even slept together last night, making love and murmuring their "I love yous" afterward just as they did every night. He said it again now, as they started to walk.

Her heart swelled, moved every time he spoke those particular words, but feeling them especially today.

"I love you, too," she breathed.

Floating candles barely moved as they passed the pool, flames burning steadily. Overhead, the sky was deepening from a pink glow to a devoted red. Potted flowers perfumed the warm air, giving her a vague déjà vu feeling, as if she remembered this moment from another life.

They reached the beach and the carpet where their guests stood waiting. It was a small wedding with only a few of her friends from Virginia and two colleagues from New York. Roman had invited a handful of people including Ingrid and Huxley—they were standing up for them—and Brenda, who smiled and dabbed her eyes as they arrived in front of the justice of the peace. Brenda had been pulling double duty as both mother of the bride and groom. Very soon, Melodie thought with secretive joy, she would also play honorary grandmother.

"Why don't we start trying?" Roman had said one night soon after they'd set a date.

They hadn't rushed their wedding plans, partly to give themselves time. He hadn't cracked open like an egg the moment they'd become engaged, and it had often been a two-steps-forward-one-step-back process. "Can we talk about it later?" was one of his favorite responses, but he rarely made her wait more than a day or two before he found whatever words he needed to explain his thoughts or feelings.

A baby was a huge decision, though. "Are you sure?" she'd asked, so anxious to start a family she could hardly function, but it had to be right for both of them or it could set them back. She knew that.

"It's all I think about," he'd admitted sheepishly. "I've been thinking about it since we got engaged. I'm more than sure. I'm impatient."

She'd laughed and they'd tried.

And earlier she'd done more than put on a gown in the short hour of privacy he'd given her. She'd taken a test. She was bursting with anticipation, eager to give him their wedding gift.

But she had to say her vows first. He knew something was up. They read each other very well these days, and his gaze sharpened, delving into hers, smiling at how widely she was grinning as they exchanged rings and clasped hands, binding themselves together with more than promises and a piece of paper. More than a new life even.

Love bound them, the kind of eternal connection that no one could put asunder.

"I do," she said when it was time. Then "I love you," hearing it back again in his sure timbre, just before they kissed. And when her lips were against his ear, she whispered, "We're having a baby."

She felt the shock go through him. He drew back and cupped her face. His expression was awed and dumbfounded, easily interpreted as he tried to assimilate this information while a huge beam of pride and excitement lit his face, no reservations and nothing held back. He shook his head, bemused and pleased. "I thought we were celebrating how happy we've been so far, but there's lots more to come after today, isn't there?"

"You're starting to sound like an optimist," she teased.

"That was confidence, sweetheart. I don't hope. I know." He stopped her laugh with a kiss.

* * * * *

AFTER THEIR VOWS

MICHELLE REID

CHAPTER ONE

'WHAT do you want me to do about it?'

Seated behind his desk, engrossed in the business report spread open in front of him, Roque de Calvhos responded impassively, 'You do nothing.'

Mark Lander continued to hover like a man in a quandary, frowning behind his spectacles because doing nothing was not an option his employer could afford to take.

'She could make trouble,' he dared to offer, all too aware that the younger man did not take kindly to interference into decisions he made about his private life.

Roque de Calvhos was a chip off the old block when it came to a cut-throat mentality. When Eduardo de Calvhos had become ill and died suddenly three years ago, no one had expected his notorious playboy son to calmly stride in here and start making his presence felt, with far-sweeping decisions most people had believed were a precursor to the quick demise of de Calvhos power.

They now knew better. What Roque had done with the huge network of diverse companies which made up the de Calvhos business empire had put his father's colossal success in the shade. Now obsequious respect shadowed the thirty-two-year-old's every elegant footstep. If the financial industry could give out such awards, Roque de Calvhos would have sprouted wings. He was also remarkably good-looking, insufferably laid-back, and so impossible to read that there were still some fools out there who dared to underestimate him—only to learn the hard way what a huge mistake they had made.

His estranged wife was not one of those people. 'At the moment she is citing irreconcilable differences. Think about it, Roque,' Mark advised. 'Angie is basically letting you off the hook here.'

Giving up on the report, Roque sat back in his chair to look up at the older man. Eyes as black as the neatly groomed hair on his head revealed nothing as he studied the lawyer's concerned face.

'You are about to remind me that my wife signed no pre-nup,' Roque predicted. 'Take it from me, Mark, Angie is not greedy. I trust her not to attempt to skin me alive, okay?'

'That depends on what you mean by skinning you alive,' his lawyer responded dryly. 'That she doesn't want your money? Okay, I will agree with you that Angie does not want your money, or she would have been demanding a large cut of it long before now. I would, however, be willing to lay odds that she does not feel the same way about skinning you of your honour and pride. She wants this divorce, Roque.' Mark stated it firmly. 'If the only way she can get it is by playing dirty then you have to consider if you are going to like her citing adultery on your part to get what she wants. If she does decide to go down that route there is just no way we will be able to keep it out of the public arena, and you know as well as I do the old can of worms she will be opening if that happens.'

Roque set his teeth together in frustration behind the moulded shape of his lips because he knew that Mark was right. *The Playboy and the Two Supermodels...* headlines were bound to start up again. Last time, the slick, character-slaying stories had run for weeks, trawling out his cavalier playboy past and quoting phrases about leopards and spots.

He released a sigh, hating it that Mark was right.

Taking that sigh as an indication that he could go on, Mark Lander took in a deep breath and went for broke. 'Angie has hard evidence that you slept with Nadia Sanchez. The stupid woman gave her the evidence herself because she wanted to break up your marriage.'

'She succeeded,' Roque confirmed flatly.

'You were damn lucky back then that Angie decided to keep silent about the affair in an effort to save her own face.'

There was a lot more to Angie's motivations than mere saving face, Roque mused, using the luxuriant swoop of his eyelashes to shade his eyes so that the lawyer could not read his thoughts. Angie was hurting. Angie was nursing the worst kind of broken heart a woman could nurse. Angie blamed him and hated him for causing it.

Angie had also caused a minor sensation when she'd walked away from her modelling career and hadn't been seen again for months. He'd had teams of trackers out looking for her all over Europe without one of them managing to flush her out. He'd hounded her kid brother, hoping that Alex would relent and tell him where Angie was. The then eighteen-year-old had told him nothing and enjoyed watching him suffer. When Angie had eventually turned up again, she'd strolled blithely into CGM Management and asked her old boss Carla for an ordinary office job. Now she fronted the desk at the famous modelling agency, and not once in the whole lousy year of their separation had she acknowledged that he was even alive.

Now she was coming at him with a divorce petition, as if she expected him to jump on it with glee. Roque shaded his eyes by another millimetre, the dark iris glittering calculatingly behind the guard of his eyelashes as he considered the unfinished business he had with his very hurt, very English, runaway wife.

The kind of business which involved Angie crawling on her knees and begging him to take her back. His pride and his badly bruised ego demanded it. And unfortunately for Angie he had the perfect tool with which to make it happen—he was thinking of a matter Mark knew nothing about, which he'd been keeping a close, watchful eye on.

'No divorce,' he announced, making the lawyer start in surprise as he sat forward and returned his attention to the business report.

'So you're just going to ignore it?' Mark said in disbelief.

'I will deal with it,' he promised, 'but in my own time and way.'

Not liking the sound of that, Mark shifted his stance. 'I think it would be—safer to keep this impersonal and go the legal route.'

'"*A esperança é a última que morre,*"' Roque murmured, unaware that he had slipped into his own language until after he'd quoted the old Portuguese proverb with a dryness only he understood.

'Hope is the last one to die,' he translated silently, for no other reason than it felt good to know he had that much faith in Angie coming round to his way of thinking.

Though he had no similar faith in Angie's thieving rat of a kid brother, he tagged on.

After Mark had finally given up on trying to change his mind and left him alone, Roque sat for a few minutes, considering what his next move should be, before he pulled a drawer open in his desk and removed a manila file. A few minutes after that he rang for his car to be brought round to the front of the building, rose up to his full and intimidating six feet three inches of hard muscled height, and strode with his usual casual grace for the door.

'Cambridge,' he instructed his driver, then relaxed back and closed his eyes to contemplate netting a small fish to use as bait to reel in the bigger fish.

The atmosphere in Angie's small kitchen hit strangulation levels. 'You've done *what*?' she choked out in dismay.

Sitting hunched over on a kitchen chair, her brother mumbled 'You heard me.'

Oh, she'd heard him, okay, but that did not mean she wanted to believe what he'd said!

Angie pushed her tumbling mane of fiery hair back from her brow and drew in a breath. When she'd arrived home from work this evening to find Alex already waiting for her, she'd been too pleased to see him to question why he'd made the journey up from Cambridge midweek, with no prior warning that he was planning to pay her a visit. Now she wanted to kick herself for not sensing trouble straight away.

'So, let me just try and get this straight,' she said, fighting to keep her voice level. 'Instead of attending to your studies you've been spending your time gambling on the internet?'

'Playing the stockmarket isn't gambling,' Alex objected.

'What do you call it, then?' Angie challenged.

'Speculating.'

'That's just gambling by another name, Alex!' Angie instantly fired back, 'Stop trying to pretty it up.'

'I wasn't!' he denied. 'Everyone else at uni is doing it! You can make a fortune right now if you know how to play it right.'

'I don't give a damn what everyone else is doing. I only care about you and what you've been doing,' Angie fed back. 'And if you've been making your fortune speculating on the markets, why are you sitting there telling me that you're in debt?'

Like a cornered young stag, her nineteen-year-old brother reared upright. Six feet of long, lanky male, with spiky brown hair and vivid green eyes shot through with burning defence. He threw himself across the room to go and stand glaring out of the window, his hands pushed into the pockets of his zipped-up grey fleece.

The tension in him buzzed. Wrapping her arms around her middle, Angie gave him a minute to get a hold of himself before she pressed quietly, 'I think it's time you told me just how bad it is.'

'You're not going to like it.'

She'd just bet that she wasn't. Angie abhorred debt.

She was *scared* of it. Had been that way from the tender age of seventeen, when their parents had been killed in a car accident, leaving her and her then thirteen-year-old brother to find out the hard way how their privileged lifestyle had been mortgaged to the hilt. What bit was left after probate had finished liquidating their few assets had been barely enough to pay her brother's boarding school fees for the next year. She'd been forced to walk away from her own private education and take two jobs a day in an effort to survive. And she'd worked and scrimped and carefully hoarded every spare penny she'd earned so that she did not fall into debt. If it had not been for a chance meeting with the owner of a top modelling agency she dreaded to think where she and Alex would have ended up.

By then she'd been burning both ends of the candle for twelve long, miserable months, serving behind one of the beauty counters in a London department store by day, and serving tables in a busy City restaurant by night, before going home to her miserable bedsit to sleep like one exhausted and then getting up to repeat the same routine again the next day.

Then Carla Gail happened to come to her counter to buy perfume. Carla had spotted something marketable in Angie's reed-thin figure—exaggerated in those days because she hadn't been getting enough to eat—her emerald-green eyes, and the bright auburn hair set against her dramatically pale skin. Without really knowing how it had happened she'd found herself propelled into the unnatural world of high fashion, earning the kind of money that could still catch her breath when she thought about it.

Within months she was the model everyone wanted

on their catwalk or on the front cover of their magazines. She'd spent the next three years following the fashion drum around the world. She'd stood for hours while designers fitted their creations to her long slender figure, or posed in front of cameras for glossy fashion shoots— and she had willingly accepted every single second of it, coveting the money she earned so she could keep Alex safe in his boarding school environment.

Her proudest achievement, in Angie's view, had been ensuring that Alex never missed out on a single thing his more privileged schoolfriends enjoyed doing. When he'd won a place at Cambridge she'd felt as pleased and as proud as any parent could, and she'd done it all without once being tempted to take on debt.

'It's all right for you.' Her brother broke into her reverie. 'You're used to having money to play with, but I've never had any for myself.'

'I give you an allowance, Alex, and I've never denied you a single thing you've asked for over and above that!'

'It was the asking that stuck in my throat.'

Tightening her arms across her body in an effort to crush the pangs of hurt she experienced at that totally unfair response, it took Angie a few seconds before she could dare let herself speak.

'Come on,' she urged heavily then. 'Just get it over with and spit out how much it is we're discussing, here.'

With a growling husk of reluctance Alex quoted a figure which blanched the colour out of Angie's face.

'You're joking,' she whispered.

'I wish.' He laughed thickly.

'Fifty—did you just say *fifty* thousand?'

Turning around, Alex flushed. 'You don't have to beat me over the head with it.'

Oh, but she did! 'How the heck did you get the credit to spend *fifty* thousand on speculation, for goodness' sake?'

Silence came charging back at her as they stood with the width of the kitchen between them, Angie taut as a bowstring now, with her arms rod-straight at her sides, and her brother with his chin resting on his chest.

'Answer me, Alex,' she breathed unsteadily.

'Roque,' he growled.

Roque—?

For a horrible second Angie felt so light-headed she thought she was actually going to faint. She tried for a breath and didn't quite make it. 'Are—are you telling me that—*Roque* has been encouraging you to play the stockmarkets?'

'Of course he hasn't!' her brother flung back in disgust. 'I wouldn't take his advice if he did. I hate him—you know that. After what he did to you, I—'

'Then what are you saying?' Angie sliced through what he wanted to say, 'Because I'm really confused here as to why you've even brought his name into this!'

Alex scuffed a floor tile with a trainer-shod foot. 'I used one of your credit cards.'

'But I don't use credit cards!'

She had the usual cash debit cards everyone needed to survive these days, but never, ever had Angie dared to own a credit card—because a credit card tempted you to go into debt, and debt was...

'The one that Roque gave to you.'

Angie blinked. The one that Roque gave to her... The credit card attached to Roque's bottomless financial resources that she had never used, though the card still languished in this apartment somewhere, like a—

'I came across it in your bedside drawer last time I was here and...'

She sucked in a painfully sharp breath. 'You went through my private things?'

'Oh, hell,' her brother groaned, shifting his long body in a squirm of regret. 'I'm sorry!' he cried. 'I don't know what came over me! I just—needed some money, and I didn't want to have to ask you for it, so I went looking to see if you'd any spare cash hanging around the flat. I saw the card lying there in your bedside drawer, and before I knew what I was doing I'd picked it up! It had *his* fancy name splashed all over it—the great and glorious *De Calvhos Bank*!' he rasped out, revealing the depth of his dislike for a man he had never tried to get along with. 'At first I meant to cut it into little pieces and post them back to him with a – message. Then I thought, why not see if I can use it to hit him where it will hurt him the most? It was really easy...'

Angie stopped listening at *easy*. She was so sure that she was going to really faint away this time that she reached for a chair and sat down on it, lifting up a set of icy fingers to cover her trembling mouth.

Roque—dear God. Closing her eyes, she gave a helpless shake of her head. 'I don't want to believe you could do this to me,' she whispered against her cold fingers.

'What do you want me to say?' her brother choked out. 'I did a stupid thing, and now I'm sorry I did— but he was supposed to take care of you, Angie! You *deserved* to be taken care of for a change. Instead he cheated on you with Nadia Sanchez and—well, now look at you.'

She flicked her startled eyes open, 'Wh-what's wrong with me?'

Alex let loose with a short laugh, as if she'd made a stupid joke. 'You used to have the kind of career most girls only dream about, Angie. I couldn't look around without seeing you plastered on a billboard or a magazine somewhere. You were famous—fabulous. My friends used to envy me for having such a gorgeous sister. They'd fight each other for a chance to meet you. Then Roque came along turned you inside out. You stopped modelling because *Roque didn't like it*—'

'That's not true—'

'Yes, it is!' His face was hot with anger now. 'He was a selfish, arrogant, superior swine who wanted to rule over you like a tyrant. He didn't like your job commitments—your commitment to *me*.'

There was a bit too much truth in that part for Angie to argue with it. Roque *had* demanded her exclusive attention. In fact Roque had been demanding all round—her attention, first call on her loyalty, the full extent of her desire for him focused on him between the sheets...

'Now you work at a lousy reception job for the same modelling agency that used to roll out the red carpet every time you walked into it. And you struggle to make ends meet again while *he* flies the world in his private jet, and I daren't ask you for an extra penny any more without feeling as guilty as sin. Roque owed me big-time for what he did to you, Angie, and you just let him get away with it—as if—'

'He owes *me*, not you!' Angie flared in response to all of that. 'Roque was *my* mistake, not your mistake, Alex. He never did a single thing to you!'

'Are you kidding?' her brother flared back. 'He robbed me of the sister I used to be proud of and left me with the empty shell I'm looking at now! Where's your natural vibrancy gone, Angie? Your stylish sparkle? *He* took them.' He answered his own bitter question. 'If Roque had not married you and then cheated on you, you would not be floating through life looking like the stuffing has been knocked out of you. You would still be flying way up there at the top of your profession, raking in the money, and I would not have needed to use his credit card to play the markets because *you* would have financed me!'

Of everything he had just thrown at her in that last bitter flood, the part making its biggest impact on Angie was seeing the truth about the brother she so totally adored staring her hard in the face. In her endless efforts to make his life as comfortable as she could possibly make it for him she had created a monster. A bone-selfish, petulant man-child who thought it was okay to steal someone else's money if it got him what he wanted.

What was it Roque had said during one of their fights about her brother? 'You are in danger of creating a life-wasting lout if you don't stop it.'

Well, that damning prediction had come true with a vengeance, Angie saw—only to toss that aside again with a stubborn shake of her head. For what gave Roque the right to criticise the way she'd handled a rebellious teenager when his own privileged upbringing had given him everything he wanted at the nod of his handsome dark head?

Alex had been only seventeen when she'd first met Roque, still attending boarding school and reliant on her for everything. Falling in love had not been an option she could afford to let happen—yet she'd been unable to stop herself from falling for Roque. And what Roque wanted Roque got, by sheer single-minded force of will—which in Angie's view put him and Alex in the same selfish club. Between the two of them they had demanded so much from her that sometimes she'd felt stretched so taut in two different directions she'd thought she might actually snap in two.

On one side of her she'd had the brother who'd become such a handful to deal with, skipping lessons to go out on the town with his friends and constantly getting into scrapes, which meant she'd had to travel down to his school in Hampshire to deal with the inevitable fall-out. Then there'd been Roque on the other side, angry with her for pandering to her brother's every whim.

But at least she'd felt vindicated when Alex won a place at Cambridge. He hadn't achieved that by spending every night out on the town. And he'd settled into university life over the last year without giving her very much grief.

Then she shook her head—because Alex *hadn't* settled down at all, had he? He'd just hidden it from her that he was still doing exactly what he wanted to do—even if that meant sneaking around her flat and stealing credit cards to pay for his excesses.

'I hate him,' Alex said, with no idea what his sister was thinking. 'It would've served him right if I'd gone on a real bender and completely cleaned him out. I should've bought a yacht or two, or a private plane like his to fly myself around in, instead of sitting in my room at uni spending his rotten money before he found out it was me doing the—'

Alex snapped his mouth shut, leaving the rest of what he had been going to say to slam around the room like a clap of thunder.

Angie shot to her feet.

'Finish that,' she shook out.

Biting out a curse, her brother lifted a hand and grabbed the back of his neck. 'Roque came to see me on campus today,' he confessed. 'He called me a weak, thieving wimp and threatened to break my neck if I didn't—' He stopped, clearly deciding to swallow down the rest of the insults Roque must have thrown at him. 'The bottom line is,' he went on huskily, 'he wants his money back, and he told me that if I don't give it to him he's going to take the matter to the police.'

The police—? Angie sat down again.

'Now I'm scared, because I don't think he was bluffing. In fact I know that he wasn't.'

So did Angie. Roque did not make threats unless he was prepared to carry them through—as she'd discovered in the hardest way there was.

Bitterness suddenly grabbed at her insides, burning a hole in her ability to hold back from recalling that final showdown, when she and Roque had stood toe to toe like mortal enemies instead of loving husband and wife.

'*I am warning you, Angie, go chasing off to your brother's aid this time and I will find someone else to take your place tonight.*'

She'd gone. He'd found Nadia. Marriage over.

Pulling back from where those memories wanted to suck her, Angie sat back in the chair. 'So, how does he expect you to pay him back?' she asked heavily, already suspecting what was coming before her brother loped over to the table and produced something from the back pocket of his jeans.

'He said to give you this…'

He was holding out a business card, which he set down on the table in front of Angie. Looking down at it, she saw '*Roque Agostinho de Calvhos,*' printed in elegant black script below the de Calvhos family crest, which crowned just about everything in Roque's world— from his high-end international investment empire to some of the finest vineyards in his native Portugal and vast tracts of inherited land in Brazil.

'He wrote something on the back,' her brother indicated awkwardly.

Reaching out, Angie flipped the card over with a set of ice-cold fingers. '*Eight o'clock. The apartment. Don't be late,*' Roque had scrawled there.

If she'd had it in her Angie would have scratched out a dry, mocking laugh.

The underscored *don't* was the ultimate command from a man who'd grown very intimate with her most besetting sin—an innate lack of good time-keeping. She'd kept him waiting at airports and restaurants. She'd kept him kicking his heels in their apartment while she rushed around like a headless chicken, getting ready to go out. She caught a sudden sharp glimpse of him waiting for her, looking tall, dark and fabulously turned out for a night at the theatre, lounging stretched out in a chair with his eyes closed, his silky black eyelashes resting against his high-sculpted cheekbones, his wide, full and sensual mouth wearing the look of long-suffering patience he could pull off with such excruciating effect.

He'd lost all patience with her, and perhaps she'd deserved it, Angie acknowledged—but enough to send him into the arms of another woman?

And not just any woman, his *ex* woman.

'Will you go and see him?'

Having to blink to bring herself back from where she had gone off to, Angie swallowed thickly and gave a nod of her head.

'Thanks.' Her brother heaved in a long breath. 'I knew you wouldn't let me down.'

So did Roque, thought Angie.

'Look…' Alex shuffled his feet. 'It's already seven o'clock, so I'll go now, sh-shall I? So you can—get ready…'

Desperate to escape now he'd done what he'd come here to do, Alex was already heading for the door when Angie stopped him.

'The credit card?' she prompted. 'Where is it?'

She watched his shoulders give a wincing twitch. 'Roque took it.'

'Good,' Angie murmured, and watched him flinch again as her meaning struck home.

Alex now knew he had lost her trust in him. Her home had always been his home—he had his own bedroom here, his own key. He'd had the same things at the apartment she'd shared with Roque. He was family. You should be able to trust family.

As if he knew what she was thinking, Alex twisted round to aim her a glancing look of remorse. 'I really—really am sorry, Angie,' he husked out painfully. 'I'm sorry for all of it—but especially for dropping this part on to you.'

He'd done that because he had no other option. He'd

done it because she'd always been there to fight his battles for him.

'I promise you on my life I won't ever do anything like this again.'

Looking up at him, Angie saw their father's hair and nose and their mother's eyes and mouth. The aching urge to just get up and go over there to hug him, reassure him that everything was going to be okay, almost got the better of her. But for the first time since she'd taken responsibility for him she controlled the urge.

'I'll call you later,' was all she said, and after a few more seconds of helpless hovering he turned and slunk away, leaving her alone with Roque's business card and that oh-so brief message to stare at.

Eight o'clock. The apartment. Don't be late.

Angie felt a pang of wry appreciation for his slick, short way of getting his message across. She wasn't a fool. She knew the divorce papers would have landed on Mark Lander's desk today, and this was Roque's response to them—with her brother sent along to deliver it and add a bit of clout.

A lot of clout, she extended.

Eight o'clock. The apartment. Don't be late...

Angie drew in a deep, fortifying breath. Well, she could do that, she told herself, aware that she really didn't have a choice. However, she would not be turning up in the role of a wimpy victim Roque was expecting to see, she determined grimly as she rose to her feet. Her brother might see her as a pathetic creature with all the stuffing knocked out of her, but she was not and would never be that feeble! She'd spent too many years fighting her own battles to let fear of what Roque could do to Alex grind her to a quivering pulp now.

On that bracing reminder, Angie tossed her hair back over her narrow shoulders and stepped across the kitchen to catch up her bag. A minute later she was standing in her hall, dragging on her coat as she followed her brother out of the door.

CHAPTER TWO

FRESH from the shower, Roque took a call from the lobby informing him that his wife had arrived in the building with a flicker of surprise.

She was half an hour early.

A deliberate ploy on her part aimed to back-foot him, or was she just running scared? he mused curiously as he rubbed his wet hair with a towel. He was under no illusion that she had rushed over here because she was eager to see him. Only two things fired up Angie enough to make her expose any hint of weakness like this—her brother and money.

If he left out the other thing she always fired up for, which was him. His hands and his mouth on her body, her complete lack of self-control when it came to the pleasure he could inflict on her smooth silken flesh. She knew it too, which was why she had spent the last twelve months avoiding all contact with him.

Or it was one of the reasons, he amended with a frown as he strode into his dressing room and came out again a minute later, still flipping shut the last few buttons on a pale blue shirt across the deeply tanned contours of his taut stomach.

He heard the warning ping telling him that the lift

was arriving as he put a comb through his still damp hair. He headed out of the bedroom onto the elegant spread of the mezzanine landing which looked down on the spacious luxury of open-plan living backed by panoramic views of London's skyline and his long, graceful stride took him down the stairway and across an expanse of rich dark teak wood flooring to the squared opening that led to the inner foyer which housed his private lift.

His confidence that he had Angie exactly where he wanted her was absolute. He did not even question that belief. Angie might prefer to run in the opposite direction but she could not, because the chains of loyalty to her brother were too heavy and too tight. In a few seconds she was going to step out of the lift into his waiting clutches, having dragged herself and those chains across London to get here. An hour after that she would be back in his bed, where she belonged, chains and all, he promised himself.

With that very satisfying moment to look forward to, Roque propped a shoulder up against the wall beside him, slid his hands into the pockets of his black silk trousers and watched as the lift doors slid open, revealing to him the wife he had not set eyes on in almost a year.

Slender and tall, dressed from neck to feet in dramatically unrelieved black, with her flame-bright hair spun in fiery tendrils around her once famous, extraordinarily beautiful, green-eyed, passionate-mouthed face.

Sensation shot across the gap towards him, generated by the highly charged mix of burning acrimony, icy defensiveness and a transparent spark of sexual alertness that hit Roque with a hot stab of tingling provocation low down in his pelvis.

Angie just froze for a second, momentarily stunned by the shock of actually looking at him in the flesh.

She had spent the time it had taken the lift to bring her up twenty floors of luxury living charging up her defences in preparation for this moment, but as she stood staring across the gap separating them she was discovering she had no control whatsoever over the sudden accelerated punch of her heartbeat or the aching thickness that had taken a stranglehold on her throat.

And she knew the reason why she was suffering like this. For almost twelve long months she'd blocked Roque out as if he wasn't a real person. If she'd thought about him at all it had been from within a thick fog. She was good at blocking out things she did not want to look at—had been doing it for most of her adult life. But this was bad, she recognised as her breathing stalled altogether. She had to fight hard to stop her feelings from showing on her face. She'd expected to feel nothing. She'd wanted him to leave her cold. It was almost grotesque to discover that far from feeling nothing she was feeling everything. The old fierce, unstoppable attraction, the sexual excitement stirring up her blood. Even the desperate, aching clutch of hurt was a feeling. It just wasn't fair.

He was so tall he was intimidating, and that was saying something when she was no small thing herself. And the way he was standing across the lobby, backed by warm accent colours of brick-red and aubergine, framed by the soft lighting, he could have easily passed for a brooding, dark male model posing for a glossy photo shoot. His raven-black hair was wearing a luxurious damp sheen to it, and the smooth gloss of his olive-toned skin highlighted the kind of cheekbones any male model would pay with their souls to possess.

As if someone was working her by remote control, she just couldn't stop her eyes from drifting down his supremely elegant stance. His wide shoulders and long, powerful torso were encased in fine pale blue shirting, the top two buttons left undone to reveal a tantalising hint of the warm brown skin lurking beneath. Her mouth ran dry as she looked at that dark golden triangle. She tried not to give in and moisten her lips with the tip of her tongue. Dragging her gaze lower, she saw his hands were lost inside the silk lined pockets of his smooth black trousers—trousers that lovingly skimmed his taut narrow hips and his long, long powerful legs.

As her senses came alive like crazed vandals she knew what she was experiencing was all her own stupid fault.

She should not have blocked him out so thoroughly. Familiarity bred contempt. She should have made herself remember him in fine detail at least twice a day. She should have listed his assets—and he had a lot of them—then eventually she would have started finding a million faults. She'd witnessed this happen so many times in her line of business. One day you were right up there with the best of them, the next you'd suddenly grown a bigger nose, or your smile was no longer as alluring as they'd thought it was and your legs were too fat.

So where did she look to hunt down Roque's physical faults? she asked herself.

'Well, is everything still where it should be?'

The soft, slightly husky accented prompt brought

her eyes flickering back to his face. His half-hidden eyes were as black as midnight; a half-smile curved his wide, passionate mouth. The same half-smile she had been drawn towards from the first time she'd looked at him. The same hot, breathless sensation filled her now as powerfully as it had done back then.

Only this time it hurt to feel like that. This time she saw that beautiful mouth giving pleasure to another woman's mouth. She saw those deep, dark long-lashed eyes warming for someone else.

Roque watched as she stiffened up like a slender column of concrete. He watched the darkened shimmer in her beautiful eyes fade to hurt, then chill to ice.

Something grabbed hold of his loins like a strongly clenched fist and anger flared deep in his chest. He wanted to go over there and grab hold of her by her tension-packed narrow shoulders and give her a damn good shake.

As if she knew what he was thinking defiance sparked—always that sharp, stinging sizzle of defiance came shooting back at him from this woman, if they were in the middle of a fight or making love. He watched her cute, almost pointed chin lift upwards, the way she pinched in the delicate corners of the beautiful mouth. Even the way she tossed her head back, sending the glorious weight of loose silky red spirals trembling back from her face, was a form of defiance.

'I have absolutely nothing to say to you, Roque,' she told him.

Roque allowed his lips to twist out a mocking smile, 'No, I could sense that talking was not in your mind when you looked me over, *meu querida*.'

Annoyed with herself for giving him the weapons to

fire off that taunting shot, Angie stepped out of the lift and into the lobby, which fed all those extra services this vast-sized apartment enjoyed—like the full-size swimming pool and the all-purpose gym, the glass-covered garden that had always reminded her of an exotic hothouse where she'd once done a shoot at Kew.

Angie walked towards him, glazing him out of focus and determined to keep him like that. He did not move a single muscle as she approached. Angie gauged the gap in the arch to one side of him to make sure she had enough room to pass through it without needing him to move out of her path.

She knew exactly where she was heading, so she made the long lines of dark teak flooring her runway. It was like falling off a bike, she discovered. Once you got back on the rest came naturally—even down to blocking her audience out.

Roque followed the long graceful glide of her body as she walked towards him. He knew what she was doing. He'd been handed this kind of treatment before. Angie could be irritatingly focused when she wanted to be, infuriatingly stubborn and tough. Once he had dared to believe he was marrying a sweet and innocently naive lost creature. A lonely child trapped inside a woman's body because she'd never given herself the chance to properly grow up and taste life. He'd soon learnt that the stubborn child in Angie had a grip of steel. The simple truth of it was she didn't want to be anything other than what she was.

Except in his bed, he reminded himself. In his bed, in his arms, she lost the will to fight him on every level—and so fast it was like watching driftwood catching light.

On that grim reminder as to where he intended this evening to end up, Roque allowed his gaze to drift over her again. She was wearing a short black raincoat, tightly cinched to her waist, and her amazing long legs were sheathed in matt black. She had on a pair of flat black ballet shoes that did nothing to diminish her elegant height, and a bright green bag he had not noticed before swung from one shoulder—one of those extravagantly sized bags that were the fashion right now, which she kept crushed to her side with a taut elbow as she walked.

The temptation to reach out and take it from her as she levelled with him curled his fingers into a light fist. The urge to pull her to a stop by placing his hands on her shoulders and then spin her around to make her acknowledge him properly stung like an itch he could not scratch. But he was curious as to what she thought she was up to, arriving early and then just walking past him as if she was the one of them in control here.

So, instead of spoiling her frankly impressive entrance, he turned to follow in her wake.

Angie cut a weaving line through the different cleverly designed living areas. She did not glance at the fabulous view to be enjoyed through the wall-to-wall windows. She did not glance up at the mezzanine gallery where the bedroom suites were situated. She was heading for the only room down here to have a solid door guarding it.

Roque's study.

Her soft mouth set like a clamp as she turned the handle and pushed the door open, then felt an aching squeeze of emotion challenge her composure as she took the first step into what she'd always thought of as his domain.

Everything in this room was as tastefully designed as the rest of this vast place, but in here was Roque's personal stamp. A telltale glimpse at the deeply serious side to his complex personality displayed in the rows of lovingly collected first edition books lining the rows of shelving, and the heavy black leather recliner on which he liked to stretch out to read.

The only television set in the whole apartment rested wafer-thin and flat against a wall of burnt orange. Beneath it spread all the technology required to make it and his complex music system feed sound throughout the whole apartment. Then, of course, the usual computer and communication equipment had a place, as you would expect of a man as internationally structured as him.

But the desk—the big, hand-carved antique desk made of rich dark colonial rosewood he'd had shipped here from his family estate—stood dead centre of everything, making a major statement about his proud Portuguese roots. He could spend hours sitting at that desk, working with a concentration Angie had used to find unfathomably sexy. The cut of his wide shoulders as he leant forward, the sheen of light across his bent head, and his strong, handsome features etched by a depth of concentration that she...

Angie sucked in a breath, not wanting to go there. Not wanting to recall anything intimate about their time spent here together or the fact that there were times when they'd actually existed here in peace.

Yet, right on the back of that desire not to remember, she saw herself, curled up in his recliner with her cheek supported on a cushion she'd filched from a living room sofa, slender white fingers idly twirling a ringlet of hair while she read one of her own meagre assortment of books.

Contentment… Her throat began to hurt. Bare pink toes curling and uncurling in time with the music playing softly in the background. A glass of wine and a snack within lazy reaching distance and her handsome dark man pooled in the desk light only a couple of metres away.

Her eyes dared to glaze with moisture for a second. Then she winked it away, drew in a breath, and made herself walk over to the desk.

She heard Roque pause in the doorway. The silence between them buzzed. He was curious, she knew that, waiting to discover what had brought her in here before he made any kind of comment.

But that was Roque—a master of strategic timing, Angie thought dryly as she set her bag down on the top of his desk, then began rummaging inside its capacious depths with a frowning ferocity that helped to keep her focused.

'Okay, I will bite,' he drawled lazily. 'What are you doing?'

'You should have known to lay off my brother,' Angie responded. 'You know you don't have a single leg to stand on by threatening him with the police, because that credit card was mine.'

'Linked to my personal bank account,' he confirmed, moving closer.

'Then you only have yourself to blame if you don't like what I did with it. A wiser man would have cancelled it the same day I walked out.'

'Strange,' Roque said, 'but I had this rather touching image of you cutting it into little pieces and then depositing the bits—ceremonially, of course—into some fiery hot furnace.'

Angie paused over what she was doing to wonder why she hadn't thought of doing exactly that, instead of shutting the card away in a drawer.

'Well, I didn't,' she said, 'and now you know why I didn't.'

He arrived at her side to settle the lean cut of his hips against the edge of the desk. 'Are you telling me that you gave your brother permission to squander my money?'

Refusing to so much as glance at him, Angie returned to hunting through the assortment of things she kept in her bag while she fought a fierce battle with herself over giving him the honest answer or—

'Yes,' she forced out.

'Liar.' He sighed in disappointment. 'We both know that you would rather pluck out your fingernails than hand over a credit card to your greedy brother.' Reaching up, he gently brushed a twisting length of hair back from her smooth cheek. 'You are one of those rare creations—an honest person, Angie,' he murmured, grimacing when she flinched away from his touch. 'I recall a time when you even made me drive you back into the centre of Lisbon because some shop assistant had overpaid you ten euros in your change. How many people do you think bother to do that, *meu querida*? Even honest people?'

Fingers closing around her chequebook, Angie drew it out of her bag, 'You move in the wrong circles,' she countered. 'You want to try working in a shop—then you would know how that poor assistant would have had to make up the shortfall from her own purse if I hadn't made the effort to take it back.'

'However, as you informed me at the time, I am too rich to know how the real world works.'

'Look…' She turned her face to spear him a fierce look. 'I was the one that played the stockmarkets, okay?'

Eyes of a disturbingly fathomless black held hers steady. 'That makes it two lies you've told me.'

Angie tugged in a breath. 'I decided it was time I made you pay for the months of hell I endured being your stupid blind wife.'

'Blind?' he echoed musingly, indecently long eyelashes lowering slightly. 'Mmm,' he confirmed, 'very blind.'

Angie looked away from him, feeling hot suddenly, and agitated when she'd been so determined to feel nothing at all. Pushing her bag to one side, she spied Roque's fountain pen lying on his blotter and reached for it. Aware that he was watching her every move, she opened the chequebook and bent over it to write.

What happened next threw her totally. In her own way she had been so fixed on what she intended to do that she had not given a thought as to how Roque might react. So his hand suddenly arriving to grasp her wrist, long brown fingers closing like a clamp and then tightening their grip, surprised her into uttering a sharp squeaking gasp.

'Drop the pen,' he gritted.

Angie's fingers tightened in direct objection to his command. 'I was just—'

'I know what you were doing,' he cut in thinly. 'And I, as you see, am stopping you. So drop the pen, Angie.'

When she still refused to comply, the air left his lungs on a hiss. In a smooth snaking move he had completely surrounded her with his hard body as he rose up to swing in behind her, his other hand reaching out to snatch the pen from her, then tossing it away in contempt across the desk.

'Y-you—'

'Shut up,' he growled.

Still holding her wrist imprisoned, he picked up her chequebook next, so he could read what she'd managed to write. Another hiss of anger shot from him, making Angie quiver, because his warm breath had seared across her already burning cheek.

She gave a yank of her wrist and managed to free it, then spun around to glare at him. 'I'm not into cavemen!'

'My apologies.' He took a step back.

Her heart was thumping heavily and her breathing was clipped short. There was a terrible quiver going on inside her and— 'Then what was all that about?' she shook out.

Roque was still frowning at her hurried scribble, all hint of lazy humour wiped clean from his face. He threw out a few tart lucid curses, tossed the chequebook back down on the desk, then spun on his heel to pace away from her like a big prowling cat spoiling for a good fight.

Jerking up her hand to rub at her wrist where it still burned and tingled, Angie watched him warily, still feeling shaken and really uncertain of her ground now—

because she had seen Roque angry before but never like this.

'Twenty damn thousand,' she heard him mutter, as if the sum was an insult.

'It's all I have right now!' she cried out. 'I mean to pay you the rest when—when I can. I just need—'

'It is not your debt, Angie!' He swung round on her forcefully.

Green eyes shimmered, 'What does it matter to you so long as you get your money back?'

Roque scowled, his black satin eyebrows fusing together across the bridge of his long, thin flaring nose. 'I did not allow for this,' he muttered.

'Allow for what?' Angie demanded in bewilderment. 'That I might still have some money of my own left?'

'And this is it?' The look he seared her brought her lips together with a tingling tremor of a snap. 'Twenty lousy thousand is all you have left from your modelling days? Where has the rest gone, Angie?' He strode back towards her in a way that sent her sinking backwards against the desk, but all he did was stop in front of her. 'You were earning big money when I met you. The kind of money even your high-maintenance brother could not spend, given the chance.'

Angie moved a narrow shoulder. 'I b-bought my f-flat—'

'Cash?' he fired at her.

Having found her dry lips had stuck together, Angie nodded.

'Cash…' Roque made a sound of disgust. 'Only you would hand over that amount of money in *cash*!'

'At least I did not go into debt, like most people do.' She defended her strict principles.

Like a man unsure what he wanted to do next, Roque swung away again—only to swing straight back, catching Angie out so that she blinked.

'No, you don't have a clue what it is like to go into debt, do you? Which is why you believed you could stroll in here like a holier-than-thou prima donna and calmly hand me an instalment on your stupid brother's debt and it would make everything all right!'

'I am not playing the prima donna!' Angie protested.

His expressive eyebrows rose to a sardonic arch. 'Enter the betrayed wife, with her beautiful chin held up high and her sensational green eyes turned to ice. *"I have nothing to say to you, Roque."*' He gave a wincingly good mimic of her cool boarding school accent, bringing an uncomfortable flush to Angie's cheeks. 'I was then treated to that fabulous supermodel walk through the apartment, the long sexy glide and the sizzling fire hair aimed to hook me into following you like a panting puppy dog—'

'A puppy dog?' She was glad to get her teeth into something. 'You were never anyone's panting puppy dog, Roque. You came into this world a fully grown, womanising wolf!'

In a totally unexpected turn of mood, a shaft of pure amusement spread across his face, and he bared his perfectly even flashing white teeth, then uttered a low, sexy growl in response.

Angie received that growl with a burst of indignant fury which set her eyes sparking and her slender body tensing away from the desk.

The sting Roque felt hit his loins was hot. She was going to launch a physical attack on him. He could read her like an open book. When he flipped the mood over between them like this she never could resist rising to the bait. Every muscle he possessed went on alert, ready to catch her when she attacked. The inside of his mouth moistened in anticipation, his lips filling with warm pulsing blood.

He watched her take a step towards him, sensational in anger, so beautiful to look at, and so much his woman he—

Then he saw her remember, watched her eyes darken and her flushed cheeks wash white. In an abrupt movement she spun back round to face the desk again.

Disappointment grabbed at every alerted instinct inside him and closed them all down into a single tight clench. Once, just once, he had called her bluff when she'd firmly put her brother between them. If he'd ever wondered what it was like to stumble into a deep black hole of his own damn making then he'd found out that long and miserable night.

Anger and guilt rolled around Roque's chest in equal measures, followed by a bitterness that thankfully overshadowed the other two feelings—because the devil if he was going to apologise, he told himself harshly. The devil if he was going to explain himself or the motives of that foolish bitch Nadia now, when it was twelve months too late.

And this was about Angie's brother, he reminded himself grimly. Alex—the spoiled, weak, thieving lout.

Stubborn to the last drop of her hot swirling blood, Angie opened up the chequebook, then stretched across the desk to recover the pen. With a firm scrawl she laid her signature in the appropriate place.

Angelina de Calvhos... She stared at it, vowing fiercely that it was going to be the very last time she would *ever* sign that name.

Then he was right there behind her again like some grim dark power force, reaching for the chequebook again, taking it from her resistant fingers yet again. This time he took it with him as he strode around the desk. With a finality that made Angie choke out a gasp, he opened a drawer and dropped the book into it, then closed the drawer again with a resolute snap.

Tall, dark, supremely in control of himself, he then lifted his proud dark head. 'I think we will begin this again from a more formal perspective,' he intoned coolly.

Angie snapped her arms across her body to contain the way it wanted to shiver in the sudden chill. 'Please don't hurt my brother,' she begged.

CHAPTER THREE

LIKE a man hewn from stone, Roque showed no reaction whatsoever to her quivering climb-down.

'He is a thief.' He stated it brutally. 'He stole your identity and committed credit card theft! And he did it with a complete disregard to the amount of money he was stealing from me. How can you, Angie, of all people, want to defend him for doing that?'

She'd winced all the way through his cold judgement of Alex, but still it did not change a thing she felt. 'He's my brother,' she whispered.

And there it was, Roque recognised, the unconditional love she had a right to expect her brother to return in equal measures. But somehow she did not seem to understand that.

'I can pay you back the full amount he st...spent,' she insisted, with only that small but telling fault in the middle. 'I will just need a little time to get it.'

'By selling your flat and making yourself homeless?' Roque was not impressed.

Neither was Angie. She flared him a scornful look, 'My flat is worth more than fifty thousand pounds, Roque,' she informed him. 'And you already have twenty thousand sitting in that chequebook you've just stolen from me and put in that drawer!'

Fifty... Roque had stopped listening at *fifty*. His lean face carefully without expression, he added *lying wimp* to his brother-in-law's steadily mounting list of sins.

'I'll—I'll go back to modelling,' she explained quickly. 'I'm still in demand, and Carla keeps on trying to get me to change my mind, so I could earn the rest in—in—'

The way Roque flung himself across to the plate glass window behind the desk and thrust his hands in his pockets made Angie's voice slither to a strangled stop. It wasn't so much that he'd turned his back on what she'd been saying but the way he had done it which filled her with dread.

When he wanted to, Roque could become chillingly unreachable. And he felt no love for Alex at all. In his view her brother was the main reason why their marriage had fallen apart. He'd refused to understand that in taking on the parental mantle for her brother she had a duty to see her responsibilities to Alex through—even when they intruded an awful lot on their marriage.

It was just the way things had to be. Teenagers by reputation were rebellious and pushy and difficult. And, okay, so Alex had played up to Roque's often stinging criticism of him, she conceded, but even that did not change the unalterable fact that standing between the two of them had made her marriage a year-long exhausting fight.

'Please listen to me...' Angie lowered her stubborn guard because she knew that she had to, her voice trembling as she did so. 'I can—'

'No.' He turned around again, and the moment she

looked into his face she felt a wave of sick apprehension riddle her stomach. 'Not this time, Angie. This time you are going to listen to *me*.'

He strode back to the desk and opened the drawer again. With a graceful flick of his long fingers he produced a folder which he set down on the desk. '*Angie*', it said, in his own sharp scrawl on the label. That was all—just '*Angie*'—yet seeing her name written there made Angie feel slightly sick.

Opening the dossier and flicking through the pages until he found what he was looking for, Roque then spun the whole thing round and sent it sliding across the desk, so it came to a neat stop in front of her.

Mouth so dry now it felt as if she'd been eating sand, her eyelashes fluttered, and she looked down and began to read. Her heart started to thump as she tallied up the column of figures on the right hand side of a long list of transactions going back months and months. It was only when she saw confirmation of the horrifying total at the bottom of the third page that she finally—finally—blanched.

Roque was silent. He just stood there and let her discover how deeply her brother had thrown her into debt to him. She could not even look at him. Horror and shame sent her trembling fingers flicking back and forth through the pages in the vague hope that she'd mis-tallied the figures—then it suddenly dawned on her.

'*Angie*'...

She looked up. 'You thought it was me, didn't you?' she breathed unsteadily.

'At first.' Roque nodded. 'I thought you were trying

to force a response out of me, so I decided to play along and see how far...'

His voice tailed off to an expressive grimace, leaving Angie to fill in the bit he'd left out. Forever the strategist, she thought bleakly.

'So you could have nipped Alex's stupidity in the bud a whole lot sooner?' Angie concluded thickly. 'Thanks for nothing, Roque.'

'It was not mere stupidity, Angie. It was theft!' Roque thrust out the hard distinction. 'And when did you ever allow me any say over what your brother did?' he added harshly. 'I was the interloper in my own marriage. If I uttered a complaint you went off the deep end. If I offered advice you threw it back in my face. Well, this time it will be different.' Reaching over, he drew the dossier back to his side of the desk. 'This time I will have control of what this represents, Angie, and you are going to have to swallow your frankly annoying stubbornness and deal with that.'

The way he stabbed a long finger at the damning bank statements made Angie blink and her eyes started to sting. 'But—but you know I will get you the money,' she choked in confusion. 'Why are you making such a meal out of this?'

'Because,' Roque stated, 'it is not your debt.'

'But it is!' she insisted. '*My* credit card! *My* name on the bills! I know you can't have a leg to stand on. I just need time to check that out with a lawyer or something, but—'

'Or we could bring in the police and let them decide.'

'Or I could change my divorce plea.' Angie went in for the kill, because she had nothing else left to fight him with. 'And go for half of everything you own, citing your adultery with Nadia!'

Roque heaved in a breath.

'Go for it,' he invited, his fabulous bone structure hard as nails now, 'and I will have your brother arrested. Make no mistake about it. This is called a stalemate, Angie, in case you have not yet worked it out.'

What it was, Angie thought, was Roque throwing down the gauntlet between them. He might as well have slapped her with it, hard in the face!

Dropping the pen, she stepped back from the desk with a jerk. 'So why have you brought me here if you are not prepared to negotiate with me?' she demanded in a hurt, bewildered voice.

Her long, slender frame so taut that it trembled, her hands clenched into white-knuckled fists at her sides, she might sound bewildered and hurt, but she still had enough spirit left in her to fling back her head, Roque noted dryly as, within the circle of light from the over-head desk light, he watched her shimmer like a fire-cracker about to go off.

Without needing to think about his answer, he went with his instincts and strode around that light pool until he was standing directly in front of her—towering over her as intimidating as hell.

'I brought you here for this,' he murmured ever so succinctly, lifting up one of his long-fingered hands to rest it warm against her throat.

'Don't you dare!' she seethed, knowing what was coming.

Oh, he dared. Angie tried to push him away, but Roque had that covered. He planted his other hand on the base of her spine and drew her inexorably against him.

Anticipation as to what was about to happen sent fiery sparks showering down over Angie's flesh. Everything about him was big and hard and familiar, like making contact with something precious she'd lost.

'I hate you,' she whispered in a last ditch attempt to save herself.

He just hit her with one of his mocking smiles because he knew—oh, how well he knew—what she was really fighting.

Then he wasn't smiling. He was parting his lips and bringing them down into burning contact with hers. She stiffened her whole body and trembled in her determination to feel nothing. She tried—tried not to give any kind of response. But then he made that slow, sensuous glide with his tongue across her lips, and on the back of an unforgivable shiver of pleasure she surrendered. She surrendered like a fool with no brain and let her lips fall apart in an invitation he accepted with the hot, stabbing thrust of his tongue.

She drowned in that kiss for a full thirty seconds. She let him drive her wild as the natural firecracker living inside her went off with passionate force. It spun her back into a world she had tried so hard not to remember—the feel of him, the glorious taste, the urgent trampling heat of desire he could create inside her so quickly, which flung her from icy with hatred to hot with desire without a gap in between. Her fingers clawed up his shirt-front, making him shudder as her nails raked flesh covered only by the thinness of his shirt, then wince when they dug like talons into the back of his neck.

Roque jerked his head up. *'Gatinho,'* he muttered.

The little cat inside Angie purred with angry triumph,

then went for the kill with a lethal precision he really should have been ready for. She sank her teeth into his full and pulsing sexy lower lip. With a grinding growl of reaction he bent her into such an acute arch that she cried out. The next thing she knew he was kissing her so deeply she lost the ability to do anything else but cling. Her heart went crazy, another anxious, helpless moan sounded deep in her throat, and her breasts were crushed against his chest now, their dusky pink tips stirring and tightening to sensitive pinpricks. If it hadn't been for her coat he would have felt them. As it was he just kissed her until she gave back with a melting urgency she was thoroughly ashamed of even while she couldn't stop herself from doing it.

Roque drew back his head and looked down into the dazed shimmer of her eyes, then at her full, hot, pulsing mouth. With a sensual arrogance he lowered his head again to slide his tongue across its quivering width. Angie released a helpless little whimper. He repeated the stroke and finished it with a deeply erotic tangling with her tongue before he lifted up his head again.

Smouldering dark eyes burned a cruelly implacable look down at her, 'This,' he said, ever so softly, 'is your only negotiating chip, *minha doce*. Take it or leave it.'

Then, with a coolness that stunned Angie into a deep freeze, he put her away from him, stepped around her, and strode for the door.

Reeling around to watch him go, every inch of his long, powerful body in such perfect harmony, Angie cringed inside with the flaming heat of her own humiliation for being so weak as to let him do this to her.

'To listen to you anyone would think you were lily-white and perfect,' she flung after him shakily. 'But you were unfaithful to me, Roque. Does that count for anything with you?'

Roque stilled on the threshold, the breadth of his shoulders revealing only the slightest hint of a tense twitch. 'It counted for something twelve months ago, when you deserved an explanation and redress from me but refused both. Now it is too late. I will give you neither. So take my advice and get over it, Angie. This is a different time, with different issues. Get a grip and move on.'

Get a grip and move on…?

Angie released a strangled little laugh that made those shoulders hunch a second time as he continued out of the room.

'Get a grip and move on' from the sight of the man you loved heart and soul wrapped in the arms of another woman? Not in this lifetime—or even in the next life, come to that. He'd broken her heart. He'd wrecked her ability to believe in herself.

The first time she'd met Roque had been at a London fashion shoot. Tall, dark, just too gorgeous to be real. She'd automatically assumed he was one of the brooding male models turning up for the shoot. It was a few minutes later when Nadia Sanchez, an exotic dark Brazilian model, went to wind herself around him and she realised that he must be the latest lover Nadia had been going on about like a fluttery love-sick bird.

'Don't you know who he is?' another model had whispered. 'That's Roque de Calvhos, the most gorgeous, sexiest, richest playboy bachelor out there!'

And he'd been staring directly at Angie as if Nadia wasn't standing there, showering his handsome face with kisses. Roque had lost his chance to make an impact on her right there and then. She had no time for smooth, self-obsessed love-rats who thought nothing of eyeing up other women while his current lover poured adoration over him with an enthusiasm he obviously believed he deserved. And anyway, she'd already had too many other things to think about without adding the unexpected problem of the swift, unwanted hot flare of attraction she'd suffered as her eyes had made contact with his.

So she'd turned her back on him and hadn't let herself glance that way again until she was sure he had left, with Nadia still clinging to him, blissfully unaware that she'd just been insulted by the very man she was no doubt about to go to bed with.

Within hours she'd made herself forget all about him. So when he'd called her at her hotel that same evening and introduced himself it had taken her several seconds to connect with the name.

'I would like to take you to dinner,' he expressed, in a dark accented voice that oozed with the sensual self-confidence that she was about to jump on his neck with gratitude and delight.

She told him bluntly where to stick his invitation and cut the connection. When the flowers arrived ten minutes later she returned them with a note.

Let's get a couple of things straight, Mr Calvhos. I don't go out with love-rats and I don't cheat on my colleagues. Take my name and number out of your little black book and don't contact me again.

'*De* Calvhos,' he corrected lazily by telephone the next day. 'And little black books became obsolete with the arrival of the BlackBerry.'

'And I'm running late for my flight to New York,' she responded, before cutting him off once more.

She'd done the full fashion circuit and was right here in London before they met up again. She and Nadia had not crossed paths since the last London shoot, so when the other model arrived for London Fashion Week Angie was already on her guard, expecting Roque to appear at any moment. She spotted him front of house, sitting next to Carla, and she seethed all the way down the runway and back up it again—because she could feel his dark eyes lazily undressing her from the flimsy scrap of multi-coloured silk she was wearing as if he had the right. But what really disturbed her was the thought that she'd probably been undressed like that a thousand times before without ever noticing.

Making the clothes look fabulously sexy and alluring was her job. Full-stop. She didn't want to feel Roque's eyes doing that to her. She didn't want to know she could be susceptible to any man's glance.

After the show he arrived backstage with Carla on his arm. Smooth and sleek, and infuriatingly sure of himself, he used the only person Angie could call a friend to assure a formal introduction between the two of them. When he wanted them to, Roque's charmingly polite manners could melt an iceberg. Shame it was spoiled by Nadia, who came to wind herself around his other arm like a slinky dark sex kitten with a hot siren's smile.

Angie was actually happy to have her mobile phone burst into life, with her brother's headmaster on the other end of it informing her Alex had been taken to hospital after a brawl with another pupil had knocked him out. She made hurried excuses and rushed out of the reception, her attention fixed on finding a taxi that would take her to Hampshire.

Roque appeared at her side as she was begging a black cab driver to make the journey. 'Come on.' He took hold of her arm. 'My car is parked over here. I will take you.'

The beginning of the end of her resistance to him, Angie thought now with a bitter wry smile. The breath-taking patience with which he'd dealt with her prickly hostility even as she'd let him drive her all the way to the hospital local to Alex's school. The way he'd waited patiently while she'd checked that her brother was not at death's door and dealt with his censorious headmaster because her brother had apparently started the brawl.

Limp as a rag by the time they'd started the journey back to London again, and in snappish mood, she'd reminded him that he'd left Nadia standing back in London.

'Nadia and I have not been an item since I first saw you,' he'd stated coolly. Then, with a deliberate change of subject, 'Tell me about your parents. Why are they not here to deal with your brother?'

And that had been it. For some reason Angie still could not figure that quietly serious question had ended her objections to him. For the first time since she'd taken responsibility for Alex she'd found herself pouring it all out on that car journey back to London. By the time he'd seen her safely inside her Chelsea apartment she had already been halfway infatuated by his quiet manner and his seriously disturbing charm.

Angie sighed, narrow shoulders hunching inside her coat as she slumped down onto the edge of Roque's desk and stared down her long legs at her flat-shoed feet. Within a week he had been her lover. Within three months he'd asked her to marry him. Within a year all her rose-tinted dreams had lain broken—more than broken—*shattered* by a sequence of nightmarish events she still found impossible to think about, though the hurt they'd inflicted refused to hide away with the thoughts.

'Take off the coat.'

Lifting up her head, Angie was not quick enough to cover up those feelings her memories brought back. She hurt. She *hurt*. And he was lounging there, at ease in the doorway, arms folded across his shirt-front, eyes slightly narrowed, watching her steadily.

In charge.

She dragged her eyes away from him. 'When I look at you I see Nadia,' she told him bleakly.

'When I look at you I see a blind, stubborn woman,' he drawled back. 'Stop fighting me, Angie,' he then said flatly. 'Your year-long sulking time is up. Accept it.'

Sulking? He dared to think she was merely *sulking*?

'I just don't want to be in your life any more!' Hating that she was revealing even this one small glimpse of vulnerability to him, Angie shot away from the desk.

'But you will be in my life again,' Roque returned, smooth as glass, 'because, *meu querida*, baby brother expects you to do whatever it is I want you to do.'

He was challenging her to deny it. To call his bluff. In one dark corner of her agonised feelings Angie even suspected that he wanted her to walk away.

Power games, she recognised. Not with her this time, but with Alex. He wanted her to leave her brother to face up to his crimes for himself.

'I don't even understand why you want me back.' She was genuinely mystified by that. 'It's not as if you enjoyed living with me the first time around.'

His mouth gave a twitch. 'You had your good moments.'

Angie uttered a low husky laugh. 'You can get good sex anywhere, Roque, and without having to put up with the hassle of a pain-in-the-neck wife breathing all over your guilty conscience.'

'I don't have a guilty conscience.'

'Well, you should have!' she flared. 'You took Nadia to bed. You had great sex with her. The newspapers were *full* of how good it was. So don't you *dare* stand there and admit to me that you don't feel guilty about it when it was me they ridiculed because I could not keep my husband happy!'

'Well, did you—keep me happy?'

Seeing the arched eyebrows which accompanied his calm counter-charge, Angie saw no hint—not even a glimpse of a hint—of regret in his hard, handsome face.

She pulled in a breath, feeling an unwanted pressure building up in her chest. No, she had not kept Roque happy. But when had he bothered to make an effort to make *her* happy?

He'd complained about her job commitments. He'd complained about Alex. Every decision she'd had to make about her brother he had opposed. When she'd tried to make him understand her point of view he'd grown impatient with her and walked off. Sometimes she'd felt so lonely and confused she'd hidden in the bathroom and wept.

'I'm hungry,' he said. 'Are you going or staying?'

He was thinking about food while she was killing herself with their miserable past? Angie folded her arms and did not answer. A burning resentment sizzled in her blood. The silence stretched—she stretched it—until Roque decided to make it snap.

'Are you going or staying?' he repeated.

'Staying!' Angie burst out with a whip-cracking fury that should have brought the walls tumbling down around them both.

Roque winced as he pushed away from the door-frame and strode further into the room. The air between them crackled and fizzed with the echoing effects of her burst of fury. Angie was actually breathing fast in the aftermath, but without saying another word Roque just reached for her arms, calmly unfolded them, then set about untying the belt on her coat.

'You would not become this agitated if you were not such a control freak,' he opined, with all the diplomacy of a superior being talking down to a mulish child.

Raising her eyes to send him a swift acid glance she hoped would sear off a layer of his golden skin, she noticed the swelling in the centre of his lower lip and was suddenly overtaken by remorse. By the look of it she had a horrible feeling she had actually drawn blood.

'I'm—sorry,' she husked. 'About the...' She lifted a finger as if to touch his lip, then curled the projecting finger into her fist, dropped her hand again and made do with a shrug.

As if he wanted to make her suffer, he ran the tip of his tongue over the swelling with such lazy sensuality Angie felt as if she was suddenly drowning in static.

'I *really* hate you,' she choked, as if the declaration was going to make the feeling go away.

It didn't.

Sliding a hand inside her coat, he laid the flat of his palm against the base of her long, supple spine, then used his long fingers to exert pressure to ease her up from the desk. She arrived a short whisper away from the hard-packed warmth of his body and her inner sizzle just got worse. Like a silly, breathless, tense little whippet she dropped her eyes from his mouth to stare at the triangle of tanned skin left exposed by the open collar of his shirt and let him ease her coat from her shoulders, then toss it across the desk. Tears were pressing at her. Her heart felt like a huge aching lump in her chest.

'I won't have sex with you.' As if she was mesmerised by that golden-brown triangle of skin, her declaration had arrived on the back of her wanting to lean and press her lips against it then stretch up to do the same to his beautiful bruised lip.

He caught hold of her hand and said absolutely nothing. What Roque could do with silence should be bottled and sold, Angie decided, as she wimped out of fighting to get her hand back and let him lead her across the room.

He knew why she'd just blurted out her last comment. He knew she'd never been able to stand close to him without wanting to devour him alive. Roque was her one confessed weakness. Not his mind, not his wealth, not his gorgeous looks, nor even the warm and exciting charm he could turn on occasionally.

No, she lusted after his body, full-stop.

But she didn't love him any more, she told herself. She didn't.

She let him trail her behind him across the wide open space that made up the seating area of soft black leather sofas set around a black marble wall-fire, currently licking with flames behind a plate of glass. It was dark outside now. London was twinkling. He brought her into the spacious kitchen bay, where Angie picked up on the delicious aroma of something spicy for the first time.

She'd eaten nothing since a snatched lunch consisting of an apple and a yogurt, so her nostrils flared hungrily and her stomach gave a timely growl.

Propping her up against one of the shiny black kitchen units, Roque turned away to cross over to a giant-sized cooking range. Angie frowned, curious, because of all the things Roque was infuriatingly good at, cooking wasn't one of them. He could manage to put together a grilled bacon sandwich if he absolutely had to, or throw some salad between two slices of bread, but cooking—real cooking, the likes of which was giving off the delicious aromas she was picking up—came under the heading of 'Professional Chefs' or an assortment of favoured good restaurants as far as Roque was concerned.

Had he changed his mind and brought staff in here to take care of him? Mrs Grant came in daily, to keep the apartment in order, but she had never been expected to cook. Still frowning, Angie watched the under-cupboard lighting reflect down onto his long brown fingers as he lifted the lid off a pan of what looked like simmering pasta.

'You made that?' She could not stop herself from asking the question.

'From a packet,' he admitted, 'with precise instructions printed on it. The rest came ready-cooked in cartons from Gino's.' He named a local Italian bistro they'd used to eat at often. 'Gino refused to provide his fresh pasta for me to ruin.'

Flipping open the door to the microwave, he removed a sealed carton and almost burnt his fingers in the process. With a cursing *ouch*, he dropped the hot carton down on the granite counter. Fighting with herself not to do it, in the end Angie sighed and walked forward to pick up a teatowel, then silently shoved him out of the way.

A few minutes later Gino's best savoury sauce had been blended with steaming pasta, and a mound of succulently spicy meatballs was heaped on the top. Refusing to glance at Roque, who now leant casually against the counter-top content to watch her finish what he had started, Angie picked up the serving dish and turned to transport it to the small dining table set in front of one of the floor-to-ceiling windows next to the kitchen. There was another table in the more formal dining area—a grand-looking antique imported from his native Portugal, like the desk, but it had rarely been used by them unless they'd had guests for dinner, which hadn't been often because their time schedules always...

Angie stopped that train of thinking before it eroded this temporary calm they seemed to have reached without her knowing how they had done it.

The small table was already set for two, which almost—almost—brought a smile to her lips, because setting a table was one of the few domestic chores Roque could undertake. Or *would* undertake, she amended as she set the dish down in the middle of the table.

'Exquisite,' he murmured.

'Of course it is. Gino made it,' Angie said as she straightened up.

'*Meu Deus*, I was not referring to the food,' he husked, bringing her gaze swinging round and up to his face.

CHAPTER FOUR

ANGIE felt suddenly as if she was suffocating. A sizzle of self-awareness imprisoned her breath. He was looking at what she was wearing, his too-dark eyes coming alive with a glow which highlighted their true rich brown colour as he swept them down over her black mini-skirt splashed with emerald-green dots teamed with a flimsy black chiffon top.

A low drumbeat of tension began to throb between them as Roque followed the way the skirt clung to her tiny waist and fell in soft gathers three-quarters of the way up her lengthy thighs. Without the matt black tights the skirt would be indecent. With the tights what that tiny skirt did for the length of her legs was nothing short of sensational. What the flimsy top did for the high, firm rounded breasts he could see moving behind the gauzy fabric was, however, a different thing entirely, and his reaction was striking directly at the raw, macho and possessive heart of him.

He knew she worked on the front desk at CGM Management. He knew by the timing that she must have rushed like mad to get over here as quickly as she had. But the thought of his wife tripping around CGM's vast white marble reception area all day wearing this outfit ignited his primitive side. Her hair was a shiny mass of silky red spirals clinging to her narrow shoulders; her legs went on for ever inside those matt black tights. If she had walked in here stark naked she could not have turned him on as hard and as fast as this outfit was doing right now. He wanted to lift her up so she could wrap those long legs around him. His wanted to sink his head down and suck on those twin peaks he could see pressing invitingly against the lace outline of the top.

She was his. She belonged to him. His long, tall, sexy bride who'd almost got away from him. He wanted to haul her upstairs and stamp his claim on her so thoroughly she would never want to get away from him again.

'Stop it,' she choked.

'Stop what?' he growled in hungry response.

That, Angie wanted to say as that hungry growl made itself felt in the stinging tips of her breasts and the clamouring juncture of her thighs.

'Do you want to eat this food or not?' She turned away again, and caught the sound of his exhaled breath.

'At least the big green bag suddenly makes sense,' he murmured, a trifle whimsically.

Refusing to take that whimsy on, she said, 'It came with the outfit,' pulling out a chair for herself and sitting down on it quickly when Roque made a move to do the polite thing and hold the chair for her. 'And it's an old one,' she added—because it was the truth. 'I bought it last year, after I…'

The rest of what she had been about to say just froze into a lump in her throat. Angie dipped her head down, appalled with herself for almost blurting out what she had.

A silence developed—a thick one, with aching undertones that contracted the walls of her chest. The lowest point of her life, she thought bleakly. Even lower than the moment she'd discovered that Roque had cheated on her.

'Where did you go when you hid away from me?' The quiet question arrived from across the table, and she looked up to find Roque had sat down at the table without her even realising it.

'Nowhere.' Dropping her eyes from his again, she attempted an indifferent shrug while making a play of smoothing the folds of her skirt.

'I looked for you,' he said almost roughly. 'I looked for you everywhere, but you just seemed to disappear off the face of the earth.'

'When—when you have a relatively well-known face you have to disappear off the face of the earth if you don't want to be found,' Angie pointed out, with what she hoped was a cool dryness aimed to cover up what she was really feeling.

Roque grimaced as he served food onto their plates. 'A convent, perhaps?' he suggested. Then, 'No,' he mused thoughtfully. 'I had all the convents checked out. Same with the hotels...*all* holistic retreats. I began scraping the barrel when I started checking the hospitals—but I suppose that you find it highly satisfying to know you worried me like— What?' he demanded sharply when Angie turned white.

Staring at the plate of steaming food sitting in front of her, Angie felt her stomach contract. Her legs were tingling with an urgent need to get up and run away from what he'd said. She did not want to remember her three long months of self-imposed isolation—or the other month she'd spent confined to a hospital bed.

Across the table Roque was frowning, tracking back over what he had said that could have put that terrible expression on her face.

'Angie—'

'I don't want to talk about it.' Reaching out blindly, she picked up her wine glass—only to find it was empty when she raised it to her lips.

Smothering an urge to growl in frustration, Roque picked up the wine bottle and stretched across the table to take her glass from her, so he could fill it up.

By then Angie had dared to look at him. She saw the controlled volcano he was grimly keeping banked down because she refused to open up to him, and wished, for a split second, that he wasn't her enemy.

'Thanks,' she mumbled when he offered back the wine glass. A delicate sip or two later and the tense clutch of nausea had eased its grip on her stomach.

She picked up her knife and fork and made herself eat, taking tiny mouthfuls which tasted divine but were still difficult to swallow. Roque did the same. When, seemingly, they'd both had enough of pretending they were enjoying the meal, he sat back with a sigh, and Angie leapt on the moment by standing up and reaching across the table to pick up his plate.

Once again he took her by complete surprise, grabbing hold of her wrist.

'What now?' she demanded, watching another frown descend over his face.

'Your rings,' he said. 'You are not wearing your rings.'

'Of course I'm not.' She snatched her wrist back. 'I

took them off when you stopped being a faithful husband to me and...'

Her snappy voice trailed away to a strangled nothing when it suddenly hit her what they were actually talking about, and she just froze to a breathless effigy where she stood.

Her rings.

'Oh, my God.' Her mind went into total freefall.
Her rings!

If her brother could calmly lift a credit card from her bedside drawer and swan off to use it, then what about the other things she'd stuffed in the drawer with it?

Moving on legs which felt vaguely fluffy now, she stepped away from the table and ran across the apartment into Roque's study. A few seconds later she was rushing back out again, with her bag swinging from her fingers while she struggled to drag on her coat.

'Where do you think you're going?' Roque demanded.

Angie hovered halfway between the lobby and the table, where he now stood looking like an angry black cloud about to pour down on her head.

'I...need to go back to my flat.' Knowing she must look as white as a sheet, because she felt as if she did, she moistened her dry trembling mouth. 'I think I l-left something on—the cooker. I...'

Lying didn't come easy to her, and by his face Roque knew she was lying through her chattering white teeth. But she didn't dare say out loud what she was thinking. She didn't dare bring her brother's name back into this.

'I'll come back,' she promised, and started moving

again, quickly, like a prisoner trying for escape. 'When—when I've—'

'I'm coming with you.'

'No!' Taut as a stretch of wire, the refusal almost scraped the lining off her throat. 'I can grab a cab—' She hit the lift's call button. 'You don't have to—'

Roque's hand on the base of her spine propelled into the lift carriage, 'Stop taking me for a fool, Angie,' he bit out as he sent them sinking down. 'Whatever it is that just spooked you, I want to know about it.'

'Nothing has spooked me! I just remembered I might have left a pan on the cooker!'

'Liar,' he rasped, and that was it as far as he was concerned.

The lift doors slid open onto the basement car park. He guided her to his midnight-blue Porsche and saw her inside it with such grim precision Angie had to scramble inelegantly to fold in her long legs.

She dared a swift glance up at his hard profile. 'I might not have done.' She decided she'd better cover herself, ready for the moment when her lie was exposed. 'I'm just not sure. But I have to go and—'

'Shut up.' Roque shut the door.

By the time he joined her his temper was on such a fine trigger Angie decided to take his advice.

They drove across London in absolute silence, Angie growing more tense and anxious the closer they came to her flat. She was out of the car before Roque had even stopped it, scrambling in her bag for her keys while she hurried to get the door open before he arrived. In her tiny hallway it took only two strides for her to reach her bedroom. Trembling lips pressed together, she walked over to her bedside cabinet and slid open the drawer, then just stood looking down at its contents through eyes that stung.

All kinds of small things were scattered in the drawer. She had not seen or thought about them in months. But it was a small box her fingers reached for, and with a heavy thump playing havoc with her heartbeat she pulled in a taut breath, then flipped open the lid.

Two rings winked back at her. One an intricately woven rich yellow gold wedding ring Roque had had to have altered to make it fit the narrowness of her finger. It was a family heirloom, passed down the line through the de Calvhos brides for too many centuries for her to dare to count. The same with the betrothal ring, with its fabulously rare pink diamond gleaming like a lustrous living thing from a bed of exquisite white diamonds.

She'd meant to return the rings to Roque when she'd returned to London, but she'd pushed them into this drawer along with the credit card and promptly forgotten about them.

Wanted to forget about them.

Needed to forget about them.

Though now, as she stared at these priceless and irreplaceable pieces from the de Calvhos jewellery stock, guilt made a fierce grab at her conscience for the way she had just tossed them into this drawer as if they were worth nothing.

Her brother had missed the jackpot when he'd left the rings behind, she thought helplessly, for the pink diamond alone would have paid off his debts, with an obscene amount left over for him to squander further.

A spike of hot bloody anger held Roque still in the doorway. It wasn't because of the rings. The rings were still there—he could see them sparkling in the box from here. It was having to witness Angie's fear that her brother had taken them that was infuriating him.

Without saying a word, he walked forward, then bent to ease the ring box out of her grasp. She flinched when he snapped the box shut and closed it inside his clenched fist.

'Okay.' He sounded harsh, but couldn't help it. 'Now we are here, you can pack a bag before we leave again.'

'He—he didn't do it, Roque,' Angie whispered.

'What the hell difference does that make?' he exploded, without knowing he was going to do that either. 'You believed he was capable of stealing your rings from you, Angie! You are sitting there like that, fighting back the tears, because you are so relieved that he did not! Now, pack a damn bag!'

'Don't shout at me!' Angie sprang to her feet and glared at him.

'Do you need me to spell it out to you before you recognise what's going on here?' he rasped. 'The rings do not matter. The credit card he took matters! If we let him get away with what he has done, what do you think he's going to take next? Or, worse, who is he going to steal from to finance his gambling habit?'

'It's not gambling!' Angie heard herself repeat Alex's own defence from a hazy place filled with horror and self-disgust. 'Y-you speculate on the markets all the time, Roque, and I've never heard you call it gambling.'

'I do not steal from other people to do it. I do not drag my family down to a level where they are forced to defend me like you are doing now—just to save his face!'

Guilty as charged, Angie quivered out a pained, shaken breath. 'He's all I've got and I love him.'

It came out so bleak and so broken that Roque swung away in a lithe, angry movement to glare at the nearest wall with a burning desire to throw his clenched fist at it!

And he knew why he felt like that. Hell, did he know.

'Where is his love for you, Angie?' He swung back to her, grinding his teeth together when he watched her flinch. 'He walks all over you—because you let him. How long do you think the rings would have remained in that drawer if what he's been doing with the credit card had not been exposed? Do you think he did not notice the ring box?' he pushed on relentlessly, even as she dropped weakly back onto the bed.

'He resisted the rings because the credit card was easier. He has more nous than you, *meu querida*, because I think he worked it out that selling the famous de Calvhos diamond would bring him more trouble than it was worth. And what the *hell* were you doing, tossing such a valuable object into a drawer as if it was a cheap piece of junk?'

'I know.' On an agonised groan she lifted up a hand to cover her face. 'I'm very sorry.'

Roque released a growl like an angry and frustrated snarling animal. The atmosphere in the room hit incendiary levels because he did not want her apology—he wanted—

Ramming the ring box into his pocket, he reached down and lifted her back to her feet. 'Okay,' he said, 'this is what is going to happen.' He gave her a gentle shake in case she wasn't listening to him. 'You are going to pack a bag and come back home with me.'

The *home* bit sent her lips parting and her chest rising on an intake of air, ready to object.

'Then,' he continued uncompromisingly, 'there is going to be a new order of things in our marriage, where I take full control of your brother and you willingly hand that control over to me.'

'If you hurt Alex in any way I will never forgive you!' Angie instantly choked out.

'I don't want to hurt him. I want to teach him how to be a man before it's too damn late!'

When she blinked, as if he'd shocked the hell out of her, Roque made himself tug in a controlling breath.

'I will tell you something, Angie,' he continued, less harshly. 'I think Alex craves to be taught that lesson. I saw the need burning in his eyes when we faced up to each other today. He hates me, but he would love to be me—why do you think he chose to gamble on the stockmarkets in this current financial climate, when only the hardy dare touch it? I am his role model. The only successful male role model he's had any real contact with. He would have loved to have thrown the credit card and a stack of profited money at me and then told me to go to hell today.'

'Instead you sent him to m-me, with his tail between his legs.'

'Exactly where his tail deserved to be,' Roque delivered without a hint of regret. 'It was his first lesson in facing up to his actions.'

To her own surprise, Angie let out a strangled snatch of a laugh. 'You would not be saying that if you'd heard what he had to say about you.'

'I'm a big boy. I can take his insults.'

'At a price.' Angie slipped out of his grasp and moved away from him.

As if someone had cued the precise moment it was to happen, her phone starting ringing. Turning back to the bed, where she'd dropped her bag when she'd come in here, Angie hunted through it and came out with her mobile phone.

'It's Alex.' She knew that it would be. 'I promised to—'

'Don't answer it.'

About to connect with the call, Angie lifted her head up in shock. 'But he—'

'Let him stew.'

There was a stony cool in the way Roque said that which sent a chill chasing down Angie's back. Her fingertip hovered over the appropriate button on the phone, but her gaze clung to Roque's grim, hard and inflexible expression while she battled with a desire to defy his instruction and the helpless knowledge that he was right.

As if Roque had planned this whole wretched scene, a police car's siren whined past her bedroom window as it sped down the street. In her hand her phone sang out its insistent melody, and her mouth began to tremble, her eyes began to sting.

On a hiss of impatience, as if he wasn't happy at all about what he was going to do next, Roque reached out and took the phone from her. 'I will talk to him.'

Was that supposed to make her feel better? 'Please, Roque.' Angie burst into speech. 'Don't—'

'Pack that bag.' He turned with her phone and strode out of her bedroom.

Left standing there, Angie listened as the ringing stopped, then Roque's deep, smooth-accented voice murmured with excruciating casualness, '*Boa tarde*, Alex. Your sister is busy right now. Can I be of help?' before the bedroom door swung shut.

She packed an overnight bag with the mindless inefficiency of someone who did not care what she packed. She did not pack more than she needed for an overnight stay—refused to. Refused to think beyond this one horrible night.

By the time she'd hauled the holdall strap over her shoulder and scooped up her green bag, Roque was striding back into the bedroom again with the long, loose-limbed grace of a man in control of everything—even his body. Angie sizzled with the desire to take a swing at him with the heaviest bag and knock the over-confident devil off his self-assured plinth.

'Ready to leave?'

Pressing her lips together, she said nothing, knowing if she opened her mouth at all she would be begging him to tell her what he'd said to her brother—and she refused to give him the satisfaction of seeing how completely she felt she was dancing to his tune.

He reached out to lift her holdall off her shoulder, then really surprised her by offering her back her mobile phone.

'Don't you want to put it in your desk drawer alongside my chequebook?' she asked him tartly.

'Don't put ideas in my head.'

Angie snatched the phone from him and plunged it to the bottom of the green bag. Roque did not bother to tell her he had switched it off before handing it back. Switched-off phones did not hand out temptation to use them, and he wasn't comfortably sure he had eased her brother's panic.

He offered up information. 'I have set up a meeting with Alex for tomorrow.'

Bright head tilted down, Angie cinched the belt even tighter to her tiny waist, as if the coat was a piece of armour she could use to protect herself from him.

No chance, Roque thought. 'What happens at the meeting depends entirely on you,' he added, soft and goading as a sharp fingernail being drawn down the skin of her back.

Shoving past him, she walked into the hallway, leaving him to grimace as he followed her outside. They drove back to his apartment in sizzling silence and entered it in silence. By then the time had gone way beyond midnight, and Angie felt as if she was about to drop where she stood. Turning around and almost bumping into Roque, because he was so close behind her, she kept her eyes firmly lowered from his hard, handsome face while she took her holdall from him.

'Goodnight,' she said, then walked off towards the stairs.

Once again Roque said nothing, and she dragged that nothing with her all the way up the staircase onto the mezzanine above. She'd already said her piece about their sleeping arrangements, she reminded herself stubbornly. It did not need repeating.

She did not look down to where she knew he stood, watching her every single step of the way. She refused to give the ever-present tears she could feel pushing at the back of her throat room to vent. She chose a bedroom as far away from their old shared bedroom as she could possibly put herself. Dropping her bags down on the chaise at the end of the bed, she unzipped the holdall, fished out a set of hastily packed pink silk pyjamas and her soap bag, then headed for the bathroom.

Ten minutes later she was crawling beneath a fluffy white duvet with her mind turned into a stubborn blank.

Ten minutes after that Roque trod silently into the same bedroom and came to stand looking down at her, a wry, slightly regretful expression on his face.

She was just a curled-up mound beneath the duvet, topped by a glossy mass of copper curls spread out behind her on the pillow, and she was well and truly out for the count. Watching the gentle rise and fall of her breathing, he wondered what kind of rat would want to disturb her from such a deep slumber.

This rat, he answered his own question. There was no way he was going to ease up on Angie in this new order of things he had mapped out.

Drawing his hands out of the pockets of his bathrobe, he bent down and gently scooped her and the duvet up into his arms. She stirred with a complaining sigh which sent him still for a second, his arms tensing in readiness for a fight. But she just settled more comfortably into his shoulder, and he got his first good look at her sleeping face. A rush of feeling sank down through his torso as he gazed at her softly parted lips. The urge to dip his head and claim that mouth almost got the better of him—until he grimly curbed the urge and turned instead to head out of the room.

Angie felt as if she was floating. She felt warm and comfy and safe. She turned her head so she could nuzzle the pillow, and dreamed she was nuzzling Roque's warm throat.

That dream again, she thought with a sigh, and then dreamed up the soft hiss that Roque always used to let her know he was becoming aroused. One day, she vowed, she would find someone else to dream about who would wipe Roque de Calvhos clean out of her head.

Then she shivered as her floating body touched down onto something cool and the duvet was summarily stripped away, bringing her awake with a start. Her eyes flew open, hot and gritty. She threw a sleepily confused glance down the length of the bed, where the duvet now lay neatly folded beneath her feet. Bewildered as to how it had got there, Angie stretched down to grab it. She had just managed to haul it up to her chin when a sound sent her head twisting on the pillow to discover that Roque was standing right there beside the bed, calmly stripping off a navy blue robe.

Heart banging against her ribs, 'What do you think you are doing in here?' she tossed at him.

CHAPTER FIVE

'COMING to bed,' Roque murmured impassively.

Angie clutched the duvet all the tighter. 'Not with me, you're not!'

His response was to cast the robe aside with the casual grace of silent intent. He was wearing nothing beneath it, not a single solitary stitch, and was so absolutely carelessly at home with his naked beauty he just stood there and let her look her fill.

Angie's mouth dried up. The helpless need to reacquaint herself with every familiar contour sent her eyes drinking in every glossy square inch. The satin bronze power in his wide shoulders. The sleek bulging biceps in his upper arms. She made a sweeping scan of the steel-plate formation of his hair-peppered torso down to the corded bowl of his narrow hips to where he didn't even care that he was displaying the rampant fullness of his arousal. A fire lit down deep in her belly, and she wriggled her bottom and clutched more tightly on the duvet.

'Y-you agreed,' she whispered.

'I agreed to nothing,' he denied, flipping up the duvet with the clear intention of climbing beneath it.

Angie whipped across to the other side of the bed

like a sidewinder. It was as she did so that she noticed the other duvet, lying in a fluffy mound of white on the floor, and belatedly took in her surroundings.

'You moved me!' she gasped.

'You sleep where I sleep.' Stretching out beside her, he yawned widely, then spread out an arm to douse the light. 'Now, be quiet and go to sleep. I'm shattered.'

He was shattered? Angie had not been awake past ten o'clock for months, and her head was spinning with exhaustion. Throwing herself around to glare at him while he made himself comfortable, she considered climbing back out of the bed again, then changed her mind. She was so tired her legs felt as if they'd been pinned to the mattress by lead weights. She could barely keep her gritty eyes open, and she had a dull, aching thump happening in her head. And if she did get up she knew he would only bring her back again.

On a sound of disgust, she yanked a pillow out from beneath her head and rammed it down the middle of the bed. 'If your skin so much as touches my skin, even accidentally while you sleep, I will give you another thick lip,' she threatened, thumping her remaining pillow before dropping her head down on it.

A stunning silence followed that declaration. Angie shut her eyes tight and built fabulous images behind her closed eyelids of her suddenly gaining super-human strength and knocking out the over-muscled, over-endowed brute. It was such a very satisfying fantasy that she kept it running over and over, in the hopes that she would dream about it all night.

Then Roque dared to laugh. 'One touch from me and you would break up into hot little pieces.' His taunting drawl came across the pillow.

'In your dreams,' Angie mumbled.

'You never could resist me,' he insisted. 'You are like this iced-in little flame on the outside, but on the inside you've always been so hot for me it's like an extra pulse-beat, throbbing incessantly in your blood. I only have to look at you and you're dead meat, Angie. I am your sexual master—always have been.'

That self-promoting statement brought her lurching into a sitting position, pushing her tangled hair back from her face. 'Well, you conceited swine,' she heaved out. 'Do you really believe that you are the only man to ever make me feel like that?' She turned her head to look down at him through the darkness. 'You do, don't you?' She caught the mocking glint in his eyes. 'You genuinely believe that because you were my first lover I couldn't possibly want to make love with any other man. Well, I have news for you, Roque. I moved on—just like you did.'

The glinting eyes took on a dangerous aspect. Lying through her teeth had never come easy to Angie, but, gosh, it was worth it to see that glint.

'And you can quit looking at me like that,' she told him.

'Like what?' he questioned softly.

Angie felt a sudden need to anchor the duvet tight around her chest. 'Like I'm talking dirty,' she enlightened him, then added a scornful little laugh. 'Yet you're the one with the serial sexual record. No wonder you have such a bad playboy image. You earned it recording notches on your bedpost of which I was only one.'

'Is that so?' he breathed, barely distinctly.

In full aggrieved flow now, Angie nodded her tumbled head before throwing herself back against the pillow. 'Exclusive you are *not.*'

'So you decided to follow my example and take a few lovers or your own? Is that what you are telling me?'

Even through the darkness Angie could read the level of threat contained in his tone well enough to fling herself onto her side, as far away from him as she could get.

'I would need to be taking sex-enhancing drugs to follow *your* example.' She thumped her remaining pillow again and then resettled her head. 'All I'm saying is don't put yourself on a sexual pedestal of my making. I've been around now. I've known better and worse lovers than you, so—'

He moved so fast that even though she had been half expecting it he still drew a choky cry from her at the speed with which she found herself pinned flat on her back.

'Better than me?' he scythed out.

'Well…hello, Mr Ego,' Angie drawled as his angry breath warmed her face.

His glinting eyes narrowed. 'Tell me you are lying to me.'

Angie arched perfectly formed dusky brown eyebrows and said nothing.

'You are out for revenge. You are trying to score points.'

'Not finding it nice to have your prowess compared with others, *querido*?'

Roque shifted against her, and somehow managed to make her legs part enough to accommodate the pressure of his hips.

It was okay, Angie assured herself. The duvet was

between them. He still wasn't touching her skin. His warmth seeped through the barrier, though, as did the lurking evidence of his hard male potency pressing against the soft apex of her legs. He was supporting his weight on his forearms. Hard-muscled biceps shone in the dimness, displaying a physical strength that echoed the power built into his chest. And his long fingers hovered a small centimetre away from her cheeks, teasing her with the threat of capturing her face, so the skin there prickled and tingled in readiness.

And she was hot, feeling stifled by the duvet and by the heat coming from him. Eyes as black as jet held onto her defiant green ones, showing enough of a glitter to tell her he was not at all happy with the way this particular battle had taken shape. Now he was waiting for her to say something else foolish, so he could react.

But what he really wanted her to do was to confess that she'd been lying.

'You're heavy,' she told him.

'You love to feel my weight bearing down on you,' he came back, soft as air. 'You like to feel overwhelmed by me so you can have an excuse to let go of everything. Did your other lovers not recognise this?'

Angie moistened her lips, dried by his warm breath, and didn't answer.

'Frustrating for you, was it, *minha doce*, not having your special needs catered for?' he goaded, shifting that oh-so sexy mouth even closer to hers. 'In your desire to knock me off my pedestal were you driven to closing your eyes and opening your legs for these many new lovers?'

'Don't be so disgusting,' she mumbled absently, engrossed in watching his lips move.

That wide, passionate mouth stretched. 'I could have you crawling all over me in seconds,' Roque taunted. 'Before you could draw in a single breath you would be making those soft, anxious whimpers of pleasure while you tasted me. Ice-cool Angie you were *not* in my bed, *querida*. You were a sexy, slinky, greedy little wanton with only one goal in mind: having me deep inside you and driving you out of your head.'

Angie's eyes were almost closed. She was trying so hard not to let his huskily delivered taunts spark a response from her. But her body was not playing. Her body was stirring up every sense she possessed.

As if he knew it, Roque shifted on her slightly, and the tips of her breasts stung as they sprang into tight, tingling pinpricks of feeling against the tautly stretched duvet. Gently but surely he pressed his hips downwards, and the greater contact with her thighs made them start to pulse. And still his fingers continued to hover a hair's breadth from her cheeks. Still his mouth maintained that tiny tantalising gap above hers.

'Come on, Angie, say something,' he encouraged. 'Describe how these many lovers matched up to me.'

Mutely, Angie shook her head.

Roque sucked some air. '*Were* there any other lovers?'

'You deserve there to have been a thousand other lovers!' she burst out, without knowing she was going to say it.

And that was it—the moment she lost it. The anguished force of her response sent her lips brushing against his, and sparks flew as the volcano of feeling burning inside her just blew its top. She dragged an arm free of the duvet so she could punch him. Roque muttered something as he ducked his head, then captured her mouth with a full-on, hot, driving kiss. With a whimper like those he had just described, Angie hit out at him again, and kept on hitting him—and kissed him back like a wild, reckless wanton.

But she was sobbing while she kissed him. She was writhing and gasping and still hating him. He crushed her into the mattress and scorched her with the ferocity of his own burning passion, until her hands went from punching him to clutching at his hair instead, her hot angry tongue spearing urgently between his lips.

Shattered by her own surrender, Angie found she could not contain what she'd let loose. It was as if twelve long months of grievous hurt just tumbled out of her. She felt wild with pleasure, and furiously angry at the same time. Hot, needle-sharp pricks of excitement set her fingers anxiously kneading his scalp. She could feel the heavy beat of his heart through the duvet and her limbs were melting. The thickness of his arousal was a blatant pleasure force he used to encourage her thighs even wider apart.

When he raised his head she found she was panting like a sprinter. His ridiculously dark eyes leapt with burning flames, his deep chest heaving, his teeth gleaming white in the darkness between his hot pulsing lips.

'Were there any other lovers?' he repeated the question.

Wanting that mouth back on her mouth—needing it there— 'No,' she squeezed out.

He threw himself away from her, rolling back across to the other side of the bed. Angie just lay there in a state of shocked numbness, stunned that he could just stop like that, but more appalled at how easily he had turned her into this shivering, quivering sensual wreck.

Then he really deepened her humiliation by picking up the pillow she'd shoved between them and repositioning her pathetic barrier as if it was himself he was trying protect now.

'Go to sleep,' he rasped, before he slid onto his side with his back towards her.

Angie rolled onto her side too, opening a gap between the two of them that made the silly barrier superfluous in a bed as big as this. Her eyes were burning with unshed tears, and she wondered if this was the point where she finally let them escape. She knew deep inside she had asked for everything Roque had just dealt out to her. She'd challenged his ego, poured scorn on his masculinity, and derided his prowess as a lover. Having satisfactorily reclaimed all three of those things, he was now content to fall asleep.

Taut as coiled wire, curled up in a ball, she pushed a hand up against her quivering lips and closed her eyes tightly, working very hard to make sure he did not feel the tremors shaking the bed. She would get up in a minute, she told herself. She would wait until the rotten, faithless, cruel brute had fallen asleep, then she would go back to the other bedroom and this time lock the door so he couldn't get in...

She dreamed of locked doors and the helpless constraints of imprisonment as if someone had locked her in. Anxious, restless, she had no idea that she was whispering little pleas into the darkness, begging to be set free. When she uttered a small sob, Roque gave up on lying there watching her, removed the pillow from between them, and gently drew her into the middle of the bed. She curled into him as if she was hunting for safety, and whispered his name against his throat.

Angie slept straight through until morning, when she came awake with a jittery start as if something or someone had woken her up. Remembering exactly where she was arrived half a second later, launching her into a sitting position as full recall of the night's events flooded into her head.

Pushing her hair back from her face, she swivelled a wary glance at the other side of the bed. It was empty. Relief quivered through her—followed by a burst of fury aimed entirely at herself, for falling asleep here when she'd meant to hot-foot it out of this bedroom and lock herself into the other one.

What time was it?

A glance at her watch sent her diving out of bed. She should have been walking into work as of *now*! Rushing out of the room and down the mezzanine landing to the other bedroom, she headed directly for the bathroom, and only thought about Roque's meeting with her brother when she was standing beneath the shower.

Had he already left?

Quickly drying herself, she grabbed the bathrobe hanging up behind the door and dragged it on as her bare feet took her back out onto the landing and down the stairs. Last night's dinner things had been cleared away, she saw as she crossed to the kitchen—then came to a thoroughly disconcerted halt.

A complete stranger stood elbow-deep in washing up suds—a long, tall, curvy-shaped stranger, with short floppy blonde hair, wearing jeans and bright pink sneakers to match her bright pink tight, stretchy top. When she turned around Angie saw she had big baby blue eyes and a lush heart-shaped mouth.

'Oh, good morning, Mrs de Calvhos.' The lush mouth broke into a melting smile. 'I'm Molly Stewart,' she introduced herself. 'I come in here each day to clean up.'

Roque employed a blonde bombshell as a daily cleaner? Suspicion as to Molly's real role here slunk like poison through Angie's blood. What had happened to old Mrs Grant?

'Do you know where my husband is?' Angie asked, stunned to hear herself use that possessive title as if she was sending out a warning to the blonde.

'He left about half an hour ago,' Molly Stewart told her. 'He said for me to let you sleep.' Picking up a towel, she began drying her hands on it. 'Can I get you some breakfast? Cereal and juice? Some toast and a pot of coffee or tea?'

'No—thank you,' Angie answered with polite cool. 'I'll—I'll just grab a bottle of water from the fridge.'

Why was she behaving so awfully? she asked herself. Because you don't like the thought of this sexy creature polishing Roque's floors and making his bed, Angie answered her own question, frowning as she crossed the kitchen towards the fridge, with the blonde watching her every step of the way.

It all felt just so weird—as if she was an intruder here. A one-night stand left behind to sort herself out while the great Latin lover disappeared out of the firing line of an awkward morning-after scene.

Then she wondered just how many one-night stands Molly the daily had greeted with offers of breakfast.

Had Molly Stewart been one of them? Was Roque into seducing the cleaning lady on her days off?

Not liking the ugly path her mind was taking her along, she tugged open the fridge door and selected a small bottle of water, then pushed the door shut again, turning to find Molly staring at her pensively, as if she had something she wanted to say.

'Your husband said I was to make sure you ate something, Mrs de Calvhos,' Molly murmured anxiously. 'In fact he was very specific—'

'That is not his decision to make,' Angie responded, with a snap she would have preferred had not been there. But she was struggling with hearing herself referred to as 'Mrs de Calvhos' now, because she didn't feel like a Mrs *anyone*. She didn't want to feel like a wife at all.

Especially so after last night's humiliating fiasco in Roque's bed.

Great will power you have, Angie, she thought grimly, then glanced up sharply as Molly suddenly rushed into speech.

'You're Angie Hastings, aren't you? Gosh, you're even more beautiful in the flesh than you look in the magazines.'

Thoroughly startled by this unexpected compliment, Angie just stared, and Molly started blushing as if she'd made some terrible gaffe. Angie suddenly saw how young she was—and actually kind of cute. Despite possessing the sexiest curves she'd seen in a long time, being in the industry Angie was in, Molly Stewart had a natural warmth about her that made Angie feel mean for being so cool with her.

'Let's start again,' she offered with a ruefully apologetic smile. 'I was surprised to find you here, and I'm cross with my…just cross,' she edited, unwilling to use that *husband* word again. 'I should have been at work by now, and—'

'I wish I had your hair,' Molly cut in breathlessly. 'The colour is fabulous…'

'Trust me, you don't.' Angie gave in and just laughed. 'It's hell to manage, and you can't hide the fact that you're a genuine ginger-head. Did my…?' There it was again—the word she didn't want to utter. Avoidance is futile, Angie, she told herself whimsically. 'Did my husband leave a message for me other than that I am supposed to eat?'

'Oh.' Molly jumped. 'He wrote you a note…' Walking across the kitchen, she picked up an envelope, then released a giggly laugh. 'He also said that if you tried to leave the apartment I was to barricade you in, but I don't think I was supposed to pass that detail on.'

Frowning again, because Angie was picking up on a definite air of friendly intimacy being passed around between Roque and Molly, she asked as casually as she could, 'How long have you worked here?'

'Since I started full-time at the London Business School, with the help of Mr de Calvhos's financial sponsorship,' Molly informed her with prompt honesty. 'I could not have studied full-time without his help, so I try to pay him back by keeping this apartment nice for him to come back to when he's in London… My grandmother used to work here before me, but she had to retire due to ill health.'

'Oh, I'm sorry. I hadn't heard that Mrs Grant was ill.'

'She's not any more.' Molly smiled as she handed an envelope to Angie. 'Mr de Calvhos paid for her to have private treatment and she's in fine health now. He's been very good to us. We are ever so grateful.'

Hating herself for wondering *how* grateful, Angie let the envelope claim her attention instead. Murmuring something about going back upstairs to dress, she took the envelope with her, and didn't open it until she was back in the guest bedroom.

'I have organised professionals to clear out your apartment, so I've taken the keys from your bag,' Roque had scrawled, without a care for the presumption he was displaying. 'Be sensible and don't try to contact your brother. Wait here for me. I will be back by lunch. R.'

Be good and stay put and wait for him like an obedient wife, in other words. Angie read between the lines of the final part of his missive, and instantly dived for her green bag, with the intention of fishing out her mobile phone to do exactly what he had told her *not* to do and call Alex.

It wasn't there.

He didn't trust her to do as he'd ordered, so he'd taken her phone as well as her keys!

Refusing—point-blank—to acknowledge that she had been about to add substance to his lack of trust in her, Angie stood seething with frustration for a few seconds. Then she remembered the time and took her frustration out on finding something to put on.

At least her holdall was still there, she saw. He hadn't gone as far as removing her clothes so she couldn't leave. Ten minutes later she was walking back down the stairs, looking hard-edged and street chic in drainpipe designer jeans and a purple top which should have clashed horribly with the green bag but somehow didn't. She'd scrunched her hair back from her face, and now wore a pair of high, chrome-heeled leather clogs on her feet.

Molly stared in awe at her as she strode towards the lobby. 'I wish I could look like that in ten minutes,' she sighed wistfully.

Try living and breathing the fashion industry for a few years, Angie thought ruefully. She'd learnt quickly that it was all in the execution.

She managed to grab a passing cab as she stepped out of the building. Fifteen minutes later she was striding into the glossy white reception area belong to CGM Management, ready to take up her duties a whole hour late, only to be met by the surprise sight of her employer calmly manning the front desk.

'You look as if you've spent a night on the tiles,' Carla Gail drawled by way of a greeting.

Carla was an ex-supermodel from the nineteen-eighties, still stunningly beautiful, with a long slender figure and wheat-blonde hair. Inside she was made out of cut crystal, with a business brain that scared most men into shivering shakes.

'Sorry I'm late,' Angie apologised, without bothering to respond to the critique. 'I overslept.'

'With anyone I know?' Carla posed curiously.

Angie lifted up her chin. 'You want me to publish a kiss and tell?'

'God, no,' her svelte blonde boss refused, 'Too boring, sweetie. And, knowing you as I do, it was probably the kid brother who put those worry bruises beneath your eyes. Get someone in Make-up to do something about them.'

Carla strode off then, leaving Angie to grimace at how close to the truth Carla's supposition had been.

A steady string of hopeful wannabe models arriving for interviews kept the morning busy. Angie was experienced enough to know at a glance which of them—if any—were going to be seen by someone higher than the lowliest ranking member of the team. She kept looking at her watch, wondering what Roque was saying to Alex. Several times she almost gave in and called her brother using the desk phone, but then someone else would walk through CGM's famous glass doors and the temptation would fade for another few minutes.

When lunchtime arrived, so did an increase in her stress levels. Had Roque arrived back at the apartment yet? Was he angry that she wasn't waiting for him there like a good girl? Had he murdered her brother, or just threatened to do it? Was Alex trying to call her on her mobile phone?

Carla strolled back into the foyer with a casual glide that said she was on her way out to lunch. She paused halfway across the shiny white foyer as her mobile phone leapt into life. Lucky Carla, Angie thought as her boss paused to speak to her caller, then flicked a strange glance at Angie before turning back the way she had come.

'Give me a minute to reach my office,' Angie heard her murmur as she strode by.

Business before food. Business before pleasure. That was Carla, Angie thought. Her personal life currently involved a low-ranking member of the British aristocracy who liked to keep his extra-marital affairs discreet. Which, when she thought about it, was why Carla had turned bored at the mention of kiss and tells. Carla would rather be boiled in oil than swap personal stuff with anyone. The only reason Angie knew about

Carla's lover was because she'd been having dinner at Carla's apartment one evening when the guy had turned up unexpectedly.

The hidden wheels and cogs of life, she mused cynically. She had yet to meet a married couple who could truly claim they had a strong, happy relationship—not in *her* social and business sphere anyway. Hotshot businessmen with vast wealth and huge responsibilities needed to vent their manic stress levels somewhere other than with the little wife.

She had watched it go on so many times during her modelling days. High-end mistresses attending catwalk shows with blank chequebooks provided by their indulgent lovers whose sadly blind wives would more often than not be at the self-same shows, with their own blank chequebook to use. It was the ugly underbelly of a beautiful world. A world she had vowed would never tempt her. Yet she'd fallen in love with and married such a man—a man who would turn into such a man when he got older, more jaded, and bored with playing happy families.

Had turned into one, Angie reminded herself, and he'd done it so fast that even she, with all her cynical views on marriage to rich men, had been left flailing like a landed fish, left to die a slow, suffocating death while the fisherman moved on to more appealing fishing grounds.

It wasn't the best bit of timing for CGM's plate glass doors to swing open and for Angie to glance up and see Roque striding in.

CHAPTER SIX

HE WAS wearing a grey pinstripe suit that draped his long, powerful frame as if it loved being there, and he looked—sensational. Tall, dark and tanned, with the kind of hard-angled, well-balanced features that just instinctively attracted women to him: the exotic curve of his cheekbones, the thin fleshless nose, the gorgeously sexy full, sensual mouth.

Her insides gave a telling little leap of soul-deep attraction, her eyes unwillingly gluing to the slightly sardonic gleam in his. And he was smiling.

But, worse than all of that put together, Angie could see him naked again, after his conceited pose beside the bed he had dumped her on last night. And this was a guy who liked snowboarding down the Alps or skydiving off them. This was a guy who swam umpteen laps of his swimming pool every day before breakfast and could pump iron without breaking into a sweat. So he had pecs, he had abs, he had big strong shoulders and bulging biceps, and a chest splashed with virile dark hair hidden beneath the fine cloth of his bright white shirt, and muscles that could take her breath away cording his long, powerful legs inside the smooth cloth of the pinstriped suit.

As he strode towards her a whole line of wannabes lost their boredom in favour of covetously lapping him up. Jealousy erupted. It was so horribly possessive Angie wanted to tell the wannabes to get their greedy eyes off him.

Mine, she heard some inner voice insist, and despised herself for feeling like that.

She shot to her feet. 'I want my keys and my phone back,' she hissed at Roque the moment he came to a stop at her desk. 'And if you've hurt my brother you are going to be sorry.'

The row of wannabes shifted on the shiny black leather chairs they were sitting on, their interest further piqued.

Roque lost his smile.

With the instincts of a natural-born predator cornering its spitting prey, he used his superior height to lean forward and stretch a long-fingered hand out across the desk to capture her chin.

'*Bom dia*, my beautiful green-eyed shrew,' he greeted her softly. 'May I advise you to keep your fight with me under wraps until we do not have an audience?'

The *shrew* part hit its mark, and Angie flushed. He was right. She was turning into a terrible shrew, all bitter and twisted and— 'You—'

He kissed her into silence. He just leant further across the width of her shiny black desktop and claimed her shrewish mouth.

A skitter of appreciatively amused gasps ran along the row of wannabes. Feeling the helpless softening of her lips, for a second Angie feared that she was going to start gasping too. By the time he drew away again her lips were warm and pulsing and her cheeks were on fire, and Roque was looking grimly satisfied because he'd felt her respond to him.

'Well, if this doesn't answer a lot of questions…' a cool voice drawled from somewhere just beyond Angie's hazy vision.

It was Carla, being as sardonic as she possibly could be.

'*Bom dia*, Carlina.' Straightening away from the desk, Roque greeted her smoothly, using Carla's full name even though he knew she disliked it. 'You look *atordoar*, as always.'

'I do hope that was a compliment, Roque,' Carla responded.

'What else?' Roque sent her one of his charismatic smiles.

Walking forward, Carla aimed a brief glance at the row of onlookers, which sent their heads dipping as if they'd been struck by a whip. Then Angie watched her boss hold out a hand for Roque to take.

It was only when Carla said, 'Shall we leave Angie to—cool down, and go through to my office?' that Angie realised with a start there was something happening here that she wasn't privy to.

'What—?'

'Ask Izzy to hold my calls, Angie,' the boss side of Carla interrupted what Angie had been about to say.

The two of them strode off, leaving Angie gaping after them. Roque didn't even spare her a second glance. It was obvious that Carla had been expecting him. More obvious now that the call Carla had taken here in the foyer a few minutes earlier must have been from Roque. She recalled the strange glance Carla had sent her before she'd walked back the way she had come.

And, whatever it was that Roque was up to now, Angie began to feel cornered. Was he sweet-talking Carla into sacking her? Was she about to become jobless as well as his reluctant wife again?

And what about her brother?

Making a quick decision which was really a surrender to something she'd been trying to stop herself from doing all morning, Angie picked up the desk phone and called her brother's mobile phone.

There was no answer. It didn't even go to voicemail. By the time Roque reappeared the wannabes had been led away into CGM's hallowed inner sanctum and Angie had turned from shrew into anxious-eyed mouse.

'Where is he, Roque?' She almost fell on him in her urgency to know the answer.

He caught her by her elbows. 'You called him?'

Angie nodded. 'He didn't answer.'

Something very close to grim satisfaction honed the naturally sensual curve of his mouth and Angie leapt on it. 'What have you done? Why isn't he answering his phone? Did you—?'

'Calm down,' Roque said, turning slightly, so she could see Carla standing just behind him, viewing their interaction through curious eyes. The last thing Roque needed right now was for Carla to jump back onto Angie's side of the fence after the work he'd just put in bringing her down on his side.

'*Adeus*, Carlina,' he bade her coolly, barely giving Angie time to snatch up her bag before he was ushering her towards the exit as fast as he could.

'I will expect to hear from you, Roque,' Carla fed after him like a threat.

'*Sim*. Soon,' he promised over his shoulder.

Outside the building, instead of his Porsche, a sleek chauffer-driven silver limo idled on double yellow lines five strides away. Even with her long legs Angie struggled to keep up with him as he covered the distance in three. Handing her into the rear seat, he joined her and closed the door. A second later they were slipping smoothly into London's nose-to-nose traffic.

'What's going on?' Angie twisted on the seat to spear a taut look at him. 'What have you been discussing with Carla? Have you just lost me my job? And where is my brother? You had better come clean fast, Roque, because you won't enjoy watching me fall into a screaming rage!'

'You are already there.' Turning his dark head, he scanned her taut features and bright eyes. 'If you had invested this much emotional energy into trying to make our marriage work we would not be in this present situation,' he clipped out in contempt.

'Well, that's great, coming from the man who took other women to bed,' Angie flung back.

He removed his eyes from her and said not a single word in his defence, and Angie slumped back against the soft leather upholstery. 'You're such a hypocrite.'

'Your brother still has his head attached to his neck,' he drawled, as cool as ice. 'He is not languishing in a police cell or cowering in a dark corner somewhere, scared that I have set a band of hitmen onto him.'

'Thank you,' Angie murmured, with excruciatingly well-mannered ill grace.

Then she glanced back at him, to find he was looking at her again. The skin banding her throat started to prickle, because the way he was looking at her somehow relayed his resentment for needing to look. Sparks flew between them—they always did. Hot sparks, angry sparks, sexually stimulating, breath-catching sparks.

'What was all that with Carla?' Angie mulishly persisted when his mood told her she should not.

'Business.'

And that was it? The dark glint in his eyes dared her to continue. The need to constantly take him on fizzed like a fever in her blood. It had something to do with not letting him claim the upper hand over her, for he was the kind of man who would eat her alive if she gave him the chance.

The car pulled up outside his apartment block. Angie frowned when Roque instructed the driver that they would need him again in a couple of hours.

'Why? Where are you going?' Having to rush to keep up with him again, Angie was forced to ask the questions to his back.

He stabbed the lift button and leant back against the casing like a surly boy in a very bad mood. 'Just shut up for two minutes, Angie,' he growled at her. 'I am still too angry with you to want to play fair right now.'

Widening her eyes, 'What have I done?' she cried out.

He didn't bother to answer. He just strode out of the lift like a man in search of escape.

Angie followed at a slower pace, confused, really unsure of her ground now, for she did not understand his mood. Molly the cleaner was no longer in evidence, she noticed. Everywhere looked polished and neat. Sliding her bag off her shoulder and depositing it on one of the sofas, she followed Roque as he made directly for his study. The way he threw the door open wide made her blink in anticipation of it hitting the cabinet she knew stood just behind it.

It didn't hit the cabinet, but she was still left with a wincing sensation as if it had. This was crazy, she thought. She didn't even know what he was angry about! And what had he been discussing with Carla? Why had her boss let her go with him without putting up an objection?

Tugging in a deep breath, she followed him, determined to get some answers even if it felt as if she was about to enter the lion's den. And her heart was hammering at the prospect of taking him on yet again, she noticed.

He was standing behind the desk with his dark head lowered as he flipped through the small stack of mail Molly must have placed there. Angie could not see his face, but she could feel the circle of grim reserve he had drawn around himself like an invisible line he was silently warning her not to cross.

Pressing her teeth down into her bottom lip, she made herself walk forward. 'Roque—'

'Smile for me, Angie,' he said.

'Wh-what?' She pulled to a nerve-crunching standstill.

'Smile for me.' He lifted his head up and speared her with a grim, cynical look. 'I smiled for you when I came to collect you this lunchtime. So—smile for me. You owe me one. Smile for me and say something pleasant.'

This was a joke. It had to be a joke. 'You're angry with me because I didn't return your smile?'

'It is called interacting,' Roque provided. 'You know—man to woman—woman to man. I smile;

you smile back. I say *bom dia*, Angie, you say hello, Roque.'

'This is mad.' She threw her hands up. 'All I'm trying to do is—'

'If you ask about your brother just one more time…' he exploded, with quite spectacular force.

'I wasn't going to!' she lied, only to blush and spoil it. 'What's got into you, for goodness' sake?'

He responded with an action that stalled Angie's ability to draw air into her lungs. He opened the drawer and withdrew her chequebook, then tossed it down on the desk. As she watched in blank silence her mobile phone arrived next, which he dropped onto the chequebook, followed by her keys, which he withdrew from his trouser pocket.

'Take them,' he invited, then slammed the drawer shut.

Angie couldn't move. A deep chill of foreboding was settling over her. He was going to give up on her. He'd changed his mind because he was already fed up with her shrewish attitude. She could feel the change of heart bouncing off the grim hardness of his long, elegant stance.

'Roque…please…' She didn't even care that she sounded pleading.

'Please, Angie?' he quizzed cynically. 'Now, there is a word I don't often hear you speak. Tell me, are you begging for your brother's sake or for your own sake?'

'I just don't understand what's the matter with you!' she cried. 'I thought we had an—an agreement, but the way you're giving off so many confusing signals I no longer know what I'm supposed to think!'

His dark eyes flared on a snap of anger. 'You remind me that we have an agreement, yet you've already defaulted on your side of it by taking yourself off to a different bedroom to sleep, then sticking a pillow down the middle of the bed when I carried you back to ours!'

Angie stared at him in gaping disbelief. 'You're in this mood because I refused to give you sex?'

'I could have had the sex if I'd been inclined to take it, Angie,' he drawled in grim derision, reminding her that *she* had not been the one who'd wanted to stop last night. 'I am not that big a slave to my libido,' he denied, implying that maybe she was. 'I accept that we both need time to—adjust to being together again.'

'Really?' Angie folded her arms and speared a look at him. 'Perhaps the blonde bombshell I met in the kitchen this morning keeps your libido less slavelike these days?' she struck back. 'Because all I recall from the last time we lived together is you wanting it wherever and whenever you could get it, and turning into a growling nasty bear when I said no—like you're doing now.'

'You never said no,' he countered. 'You grabbed with both hands and whatever other greedy part of your anatomy you could grab me with. When I mentioned the bed thing—' he rolled a long-fingered hand '—I was merely trying to point out that you have been defaulting on our agreement from the moment we agreed it. And who is the blonde bombshell?' he demanded curiously.

Feeling slightly ashamed that she'd brought Molly Stewart into this just to score points—though she was still uncertain as to whether the new cleaner *did* have other special duties—Angie stepped up to the desk.

'Thanks for my stuff.' She gathered up keys, phone and chequebook, then turned to leave.

'Where do you think you are going?' he sighed out.

'To make myself scarce while you decide what the heck it is we're supposed to be fighting about.'

'Well, don't make yourself too scarce. We are due to fly to Portugal in a couple of hours.'

Angie froze, then swung back round again. 'Portugal?' she echoed, as if he'd named a different planet.

'I live there,' Roque reminded her.

'Yes, but…' The ground suddenly felt shaky beneath Angie's feet.

'My London offices usually see me only one week a month.'

'Yes.' She knew that too. 'But…'

Roque looked at her and waited, drawing her hesitation out as if it was stretched on wires while her mind ran through the string of objections she wanted to utter before she discarded them one by one in case she fed his weird mood.

'I thought…' She stopped yet again, and her lips quivered on a shaky intake of air. 'There's my job—'

'Already sorted. Carlina has given you an extended leave of absence.'

So that was what their cosy meeting for two had been all about. Roque had convinced Carla to let her go, probably using the 'giving their marriage a second chance' excuse, and Carla had let him convince her without asking Angie what she wanted to do.

'You are not my mistress, Angie,' he inserted into the steadily thickening silence, so coolly she almost missed the relevance of the prod. 'In general mistresses stay put in one place while wives travel.'

Nadia suddenly stood between them like a raven-haired apparition, with a very smug smile on her beautiful face. Nadia was as exotically Brazilian as Roque was hot-blooded Portuguese. They even spoke the same language, which meant they could converse with each without anyone around them knowing what they said.

And Nadia travelled… As Angie had once travelled… Nadia followed the fashion drum wherever it led her, and if that happened to be the same port of call Roque was in then so much the better—did he think she was dumb?

'Well, I don't travel any more,' she said.

'You will go where I say you will go.' Roque flatly countered that. 'I let you off the hook too much the last time we were together. I let you dictate where and when I was allowed to be with my own wife. This time you will do the compromising, *querida*—and remember, please, before you start yelling at me, that your brother's present situation is depending on your absolute acceptance of that.'

A ragged laugh was torn from Angie. 'I don't even know what his situation is, since you haven't bothered to tell me.'

Roque flicked out a grimace in acknowledgement of that.

'But if you think I'm going to just fly off to Portugal and leave Alex here alone to get into—' Belatedly realising what she'd been going to say, Angie choked the rest of that sentence back.

Too late, though, to stop Roque from finishing it. 'Alex will not be left alone here in England to get into more trouble for the simple reason he will not be in England at all.'

She was staring at him now, in the grip of total

stillness, so concentrated on what he was saying that she couldn't even draw in a breath.

'We went together to speak to his college dean this morning,' he went on to explain. 'Alex is taking a gap year from his studies, effective as of now.'

'S-so where is he going?' Angie breathed almost indistinctly.

'Brazil,' Roque relayed. 'To my ranch near Sao Paulo, to be exact.'

'Brazil...?' she whispered, as if he had not added the other details.

'He is going to learn all about ranching, cattle farming, living off the land—'

'Brazil?' Angie repeated one more time, her voice rising to a shrill pitch. 'You are sending my nineteen-year-old brother to the other end of the world for a whole year without my say-so?'

'Alex is over eighteen. He is allowed to make these decisions for himself.'

That wasn't the point. 'You mean it was your decision! What were his options—Brazil or a prison cell?'

'*Sim,*' he confirmed, without flickering a glossy black eyelash. 'He chose to work the next year, helping to pay back what he stole from me.'

The blunt use of the word *stole* had its effect on Angie, paling her face even further and closing up her throat. 'S-so where is he now?' she only just managed to utter.

'As of right now—?' With a smooth flick of a bright white shirt-cuff he exposed his gold wristwatch and gave his attention to it. 'Experiencing the comforts of first-class air travel somewhere over the Atlantic,' he answered. 'On his way to Sao Paulo...'

For a whole thirty seconds Angie couldn't seem to find a reaction. Pure shock was holding fast. She just stared at Roque, still standing there behind his desk like some lofty, unreachable lord and master, dark as the devil and cool as a long drink of iced water. He watched the emerald glow in her eyes slowly, slowly disappear, until the colour had turned pure bottomless black. Then she lowered her head to look down at her hands, still clutching her recovered possessions.

'You took my phone,' she mumbled.

Not understanding the relevance of the comment, Roque drew his eyebrows together in a frown.

She said it again, this time lifting those darkened eyes back to his. 'You took away my phone so I couldn't call him. You sent him away without allowing me to speak to him before he left... Why would you do that?'

For the first time since this had begun Roque's voice revealed a hint of roughness. 'I felt it would be easier on you if you had no input—'

'Easier on you, you mean.'

'Alex needs to face up to his responsibilities,' he persisted doggedly. 'He did this a lot faster believing that you were out of the loop.'

'You—you let him think I've turned my back on him?'

Roque released a sigh. 'Angie—we agreed that I would take control of your brother—'

'Just shut up about our stupid agreement!' She would have screeched all of that at him if her voice hadn't become muffled by the strangling blockage currently in control of her aching throat.

'We need a breathing space to work on our marriage

without your brother constantly tossing a spanner in the works!'

'But I don't *want* to work on our marriage!'

'Then why are you standing here?'

The hard challenge shimmered over the full length of her taut figure. He dared to stand there, seemingly expecting her to turn into the perfect amiable wife because he had taken control of her brother and her life?

'Why are you bothering to do this at all?' she fed right back at him.

Roque lowered his dark head. 'My family does not do divorce,' he answered smoothly.

Angie had to suck in a long hard breath to control the ever-pressing need to tumble into the kind of wild weeping jag she had not allowed herself to vent since—

No... Swallowing tautly, she told herself she was just not going to go there, staring down at the things clutched in her fingers and refusing to let them blur out of focus.

'So we must try harder to make a success of our marriage this time around...'

Still she made no response, but the telling sheen in her eyes held him captive. It was as if she was projecting an image of Nadia into the gap between them, and he let out a sigh.

'I want to try,' he added, in a roughened tone.

She blinked her long eyelashes and the sheen was gone—but not the hurt, he saw.

'To your standards or mine?' Without giving him a chance to answer that, she spun away from him. 'Just be clear, Roque, that the moment I stop caring about my brother will be the same moment you will lose control over me.'

She closed the door softly on her way out, making Roque wince as if she'd slammed it, then grimace because what she had said was true.

The complicated paradox of having a relationship with Angie, he mused ruefully. Her brother was always going to come first.

He raked out a laugh, wondering why he was giving himself all of this hassle when there were lots of women out there he could be enjoying a perfectly contented relationship with.

The answer was in the question. He did not want any other woman. He did not want perfect contentment in his life. He wanted a red-hot-tempered, red-haired shrew, with a fierce ability to love unconditionally—so long as your name was Alex, not Roque.

CHAPTER SEVEN

ROQUE turned the Range Rover in through the gates of the Quinta d'Agostinho, and drove into a tunnel of trees. Darkness swallowed them up in a moment, the spread of the car's headlights arcing eerily across the narrow strip of tarmac and into the surrounding undergrowth, washing the colour out of everything. The narrow driveway twisted and turned from there on, keeping them climbing steadily, as they had been doing since they'd left Lisbon behind.

For the *quinta* nestled in historic splendour on a lush green plateau near the peak of a forest-strewn hill. To see the house at all, unless from an eye-squinting far distance, you had to be in the air and flying over the top of his steep grey-tiled roofs.

As the tunnel of trees eventually thinned out, Angie shifted on her seat for the first time since they'd swapped Roque's plane for his sturdy four-wheel drive. She had visited this place only once before, which felt oddly unnatural now, when this was after all her husband's main home. Roque also owned an apartment in a beautifully converted sixteenth-century palace in the centre of Lisbon, which they'd used to use a lot. But this fabulous estate, with its rich dark forests and neatly tended formal gardens, was almost a stranger to her.

The last of the trees gave way to an elegant spread of sweeping lawns and flower-strewn shrubbery. Light suddenly bathed the car. As if inexorably drawn by it, Angie sat forward even further, to peer through the windscreen up at the house itself, standing within its own pool of welcoming warmth.

Lit for the master coming home, she thought, feeling breathless and vaguely threatened at the same time, though she did not understand why.

Great wealth, quintessential elegance and centuries of history stood right there, in the sugared apricot colour of its grand manor house walls. Angie glimpsed softly lit deep ground-floor terraces, and pretty arched upper balconies dressed in white-painted latticework, and the stone-built tower curving out from one corner as if stuck on as an afterthought. She caught a glimpse of the silky blue water in the swimming pool shimmering in its own beautifully tended bowl of a garden towards the far side of the house.

Then the car took a sweeping turn to the left, dipping them down and away from the front elevation towards the left-hand side of the house, where several open-arched, stone-columned garages came into view.

Roque stopped the car, switched off the engine and climbed out.

Angie stared balefully at his proud, handsome profile as he strode around the car bonnet on his way to open her door for her. He held out a hand to help her alight, which she accepted. They had been very polite to each other since they'd left London. Polite, distant, seemingly finally emptied of words.

She shivered as the cool evening air touched her skin, and still without saying a word Roque slid out of his jacket and dropped it onto her shoulders.

She supposed he was thinking she should have worn her coat, but when numb silence was the current order of things she didn't bother to say it out loud. She'd found a turquoise jersey shift dress lurking at the bottom of her holdall—one of those garments made of crease-free fabric that was so easy to pack—so she'd changed into it before they left and just stuffed everything else back into the bag—including her coat, along with her green bag.

Even in the mood she'd been in, not wanting to care about anything, the natural stylist in her could not let her walk around in a turquoise dress with a huge vivid green bag slung over her arm. So all those essentials women had to carry around with them everywhere they went now resided in a Harrods carrier bag she'd found at the bottom of a drawer. It now languished with the assortment of luggage that had appeared at this end of their flight.

'Your things,' Roque had deigned to offer in flat response to her puzzled frown.

Her 'things', all professionally gathered and packed into a brand new set of tan leather trunks and cases, were now stacked in the rear of the Range Rover. She had been moved, lock, stock and barrel, in other words. Evicted and expatriated with the swift efficiency of a man who was so at his best when he was in charge.

A little man wearing a white shirt and a soft black apron appeared like a magician at Roque's side, with a deferential bow and a smile. Turning his attention to the newcomer, Roque conversed with him for a minute or two, then turned back to Angie. '*Meu querida*, this is Antonio. He speaks no English, so please be kind.'

The *be kind* bit struck Angie like the plunge of knife. Why would she be anything else to any of the staff in Roque's employ? Did he really think that she was such a shrew she did not know how to behave herself? The idea that he did think that hurt.

Finding a smile, she offered it to Antonio with an outstretched hand. '*Boa tarde*, Antonio,' she greeted him, as warmly as she could.

'*Boa tarde, senhora.*' Antonio beamed a smile back at her, then went off into a rush of Portuguese which forced Angie to angle a helpless look up at Roque.

'He is welcoming you,' he explained.

'Oh.' She looked back at Antonio. 'I…thank you.'

'*Obrigado,*' Roque corrected.

'*Obrigado,*' Angie repeated obediently.

Antonio bowed again, before removing himself to the rear of the car, and she felt Roque's hand arrive in the centre of her back, lightly pressing her to walk towards the house. They entered it by a side entrance, but still the black and cream chequered floor and rich mahogany woodwork spoke of timeless elegance lovingly preserved. The house was more like an antique emporium. Nothing Angie rested her eyes on was less than a hundred years old. Walking down a long hallway with Roque a half-step behind her, she felt as if he grew in stature the further inward they were drawn.

Eventually the chequered floor opened out onto a vast crescent-shaped grand front entrance, with spectacular wood and marble twin staircases sweeping up the curving apricot-painted walls to the floor above.

A neatly dressed woman who to Angie looked

uncannily like Antonio awaited them. The resemblance was confirmed when Roque explained that this was Antonio's sister, Zetta. After he'd guided them through the same greeting ritual, he added a few brief instructions to Zetta.

It was only when his hand returned to the base of her spine to urge her towards the stairs that it began to hit Angie why they had come in through a side entrance.

Roque was making a very expressive point.

For the only other time he had brought her here had been as his new bride, and he had carried her in his arms through the front door. There had been no servants waiting to meet them, just the two of them and their soft laughter as he insisted on carrying all the way up the stairs.

This time there was to be no such romantic gesture—just a side entrance through which to gain access to the house, and the use of her own legs to carry her up the grand staircase. No soft laughter, no stolen kisses along the way.

Roque walked one step behind her and even the atmosphere felt cooler, making her tense fingers clutch the edges of his jacket more closely to her as she walked. And the silence between them grabbed at her heart and squeezed it. What had they lost? What had they done to all of that warm, soft, beautiful romantic love they'd brought into this house with them on their wedding night?

Reaching the point where the two stairways came together in a graceful sweep, Angie turned beneath the wide plaster archway which led through to the upper wings of the house. Without needing instruction she turned to the right, which led to the master apartments in this huge many-bedroomed place. Any idea of trying to escape to a different suite of rooms didn't even get an airing this time. It seemed pretty pointless to try it when she knew Roque would simply do what he'd done in London and gather her up and bring her here.

Anyway, she was all out of fight, tired and depressed, feeling hollowed out from the inside by old memories she wished she didn't have.

As they reached the door that barred the way further, Roque stepped forward to lean past her and do the polite thing with the door.

For a second she felt his arm brush her shoulder. For a second she felt his breath stir her hair. For a second she felt her senses leap and then tighten when he made a breath-catching pause. She could feel him wanting to say something, could feel his gaze on her half-lowered profile, as if he was willing her to turn her head and look at him.

Was he remembering the same things she was remembering? Her heart gave that same aching squeeze again, and the need to take a breath or suffocate in the heavy airlessness of their shared tension acted as a stimulus to a set of vibrations she wished she couldn't feel.

Then he was pushing the door inwards and she was free to move again, walking on legs that felt rubbery into a huge, beautifully appointed bedroom, with four long windows dressed in a bitter lemon-and-lime-coloured heavy silk brocade which matched the cover thrown over the huge central bed.

Angie didn't look at the bed. She didn't really focus on anything. She just slipped Roque's jacket off her taut shoulders and draped it over the back of a chair, then kept on going across an expanse of wooden floor strewn with beautiful rugs. She only came to a halt when she reached one of the windows, though it was much too dark outside to see anything through it.

'Antonio will bring up your luggage shortly.' Roque spoke at last.

Angie nodded.

'And Zetta is preparing a light supper,' he pushed on, sounding like a super-polite hotel concierge. 'As the hour is so late, I thought you might prefer to eat it up here.'

Angie nodded again, then added a courteous, 'Thank you.'

The long hiss of his breath ran straight down her spine. 'Angie—'

'I'll have a bath first, if that's okay,' she interrupted.

'Of course it is okay.' He'd started to sound irritated, but she didn't react—didn't want to react. She didn't want to fight with him any more. She felt cold and empty, as if she'd lost something precious.

Which she had, she acknowledged bleakly. Her freedom of choice.

She could almost feel him biting back the desire to say something else, but instead he turned and strode back out of the suite, the door closing into its housing with such a numbing softness it made her flinch.

Turning around, she crossed the bedroom and stepped beneath one of the plaster archways which stood either side of the huge, deeply carved bed. The archway opened up into a spacious, custom-designed dressing room she could have fitted the whole of her London flat inside. She crossed the floor to where she remembered the bathroom was situated, and by the time she'd run a bath in the huge porcelain tub, and indulged herself by soaking in it for ages, she began to feel more human again.

Wrapped in the velvet-smooth white bathrobe she'd found hanging behind the door, Angie padded out of the bathroom—only to pull to a stop in surprise when she discovered that while she'd been soaking in the bath her things had been unpacked and put away. Her suits, her dresses, tops and blouses all hung in co-ordinated neatness in the open-plan-style wardrobe spaces. Her assortment of shoes lined up in rows. Toiletries, cosmetics, perfumes were all carefully arranged on the wall-to-wall mirrored dressing table, and everything else was either neatly folded away or placed discreetly in the central island bank of drawers.

I've well and truly been moved in, she noted ruefully. Then padded out into the bedroom to find the promised supper spread out on a table by one of the windows. She discovered fresh, warm crusty bread, a baby tureen filled with a light aromatic soup, and a pot of tea with the distinctive scent of her favoured Earl Grey.

Left alone to enjoy her supper, she eventually let her attention drift towards the bed. A bed she had carefully avoided looking at until now, because it was the place she had spent her wedding night.

A night of warm and gentle teasing, then wild and hot rising passion as their hunger for each other closed them in. She'd learnt right there in that bed that there was a difference between being a lover and being a wife, as if the vows they'd exchanged had cast aside the mere physical, opening them up to a new and deeper intimacy that had overwhelmed them both.

He had loved her then. Angie was sure of it. And she had so loved him. They'd told each other so over and over during the long, dark and deeply passionate night in that bed.

A bed she would share with Roque again tonight—and goodness alone knew what else he intended them to share. It had already been prepared, with the lemon and lime cover stripped away and left neatly folded on the ottoman at the end of the bed, the crisp white bedding turned down.

Well, hello, honeymoon, she thought with a mockery she did not like to hear at work in her head. But there it was, mocking her rather than the situation, because their real honeymoon had spanned only that one night before her mobile phone had started ringing and she'd been rushing out of here to catch a flight back to London. Her brother had got himself into trouble again.

It was a wonder Roque had put up with it, she thought now, almost eighteen months after the event. The thought made Angie rise up from the table, tense again suddenly, restless, not liking it that she was seeing how putting her brother's needs before everything, even their honeymoon, must have felt to Roque.

Like an interloper in his own marriage. Angie winced as she recalled Roque saying that. It was no wonder they'd stopped loving and started fighting.

The suite door suddenly swung open and Roque strode in, still wearing the dark suit he had changed into before they'd left London, minus the jacket, of course, and now also minus his tie. Butterflies inside her stirred into life. He oozed streamlined grace and smooth, dark sophistication, exotic and earthy and unconditionally male. The bright white of his shirt highlighted the width of this shoulders and long lean torso. The absolute finest dark silk-wool mix draped his hips, his long, powerful thighs and legs.

But when she looked at his face she could see the polite shutters were still in place, joined now by a grim purpose that put Angie warily on her guard as he strode up to her, then held out his hand.

Her eyelashes flickering slightly, she studied his closed features for a second, then looked down to see he was holding out his mobile phone.

'Take it,' he instructed.

Not understanding why she needed to, Angie moistened lips and did nothing.

'It is your brother,' he said. 'I managed to catch him between stopovers.'

It was ironic that he should do this now, when the last person she wanted to think about was Alex.

'Roque—' she said with a husky jerk, wanting—needing—to say something to him but with no clue as to what the something was.

The grim set of Roque's mouth moved in a tense twitch as he took hold of her hand and placed the phone in it, then turned and strode away again, crossing the room to disappear into the other dressing room. Angie followed his tall, straight, purposeful stride through slightly blurred and helplessly confused swimming eyes.

'Are you there, Angie?'

It was only as her brother's impatient voice arrived in her ear that she realised she'd lifted the phone to it. 'Y-yes,' she confirmed, blinking fast. 'I'm here. Are you all right?'

'Of course I'm all right,' Alex responded. 'What do you think I am—a baby?'

Yes, thought Angie. 'No, but…'

'I can't tell you how great all of this is,' he rushed on excitedly. 'I'm flying first class—'

'Wh-where are you?' Angie asked him.

'Hell, I don't know.' He didn't sound as if he cared. 'Some VIP transit lounge somewhere. I didn't register where. We stopped to refuel. Did you know you can have a shower and a massage while you wait in these places? Just great how the other half live.'

'But—what about your studies, Alex? You can't just—'

'Oh, blow my studies,' he dismissed with absolute indifference. 'I can return to them any time. This is just the very best thing that's ever happened to me, Angie. Roque's been amazing. Who would've thought it of the guy? Did he tell you I'm going to ride with real gauchos and learn to rope cattle and stuff? I feel really guilty now for being such a bastard to him.'

The line crackled, and Angie heard her brother mutter something. 'I didn't catch that,' she said, squeezing the phone closer to her ear.

'I've got to go. We're being called to board. Listen to me, Angie,' he went on quickly, 'I'm sorry I messed everything up for you two.'

'You didn't—'

'Of course I did,' Alex sighed out. 'I meant to do it! I was so jealous of him I wanted to split the two of you up. But taking that money was way too low. I'm lucky I've still got my head attached to my neck.'

'Alex—'

'I just want to say I love you, sis, but it's time I started taking responsibility for myself.' The line crackled again, and kept on crackling. 'I'm fine…' she thought

she heard between the crackles. 'Do yourself a favour…
Roque…'

'Alex—?'

The crackles stopped and the line was dead. Angie
stood there, staring at the phone clutched in her tense
fingers. Her brother was enjoying himself. He was excited. And suddenly Roque had gone from being his
most hated enemy to his absolute very best friend. He
didn't mind being shipped off to the other end of the
world, away from her. In fact he sounded happy to be
given the space!

A sob broke from her. She didn't know where it came
from. A set of long fingers arrived to gently prise the
phone free from her grasp. And she was trembling,
Angie realised, quivering and shaking, with tears rolling down her cheeks.

'Take a couple of deep breaths,' Roque advised
quietly.

But Angie shook her head. She wanted to cry. Now
that she had given in to it, she wanted to sob her silly
aching heart out.

'You're suddenly his hero,' she said, on a choke that
could not make its mind up whether to be a sob or a
laugh.

She'd stood between the two of them like a boxing
referee, with arms outstretched to hold them apart while
they'd thrown verbal punches at each other. Now, out of
nowhere, they'd decided to call a truce. Why couldn't
they have tried to do it when it would have meant something to her?

Now Nadia stood between her and Roque like a smug,
smiling spectre. And not just Nadia, she thought as she
broke down on another sob.

She heard Roque release a sigh, then his arms came around her. There was a stiff reluctance in the way he drew her close. They were still at loggerheads, she remembered. Allowing her contact with her brother had not been done in the form of an olive branch.

'I apologise,' Roque said, and even that left him with distinct unwillingness. 'I accept I should not have withheld your right to reassure yourself that your brother was okay before he flew off. But he was already in the air and I knew I could not contact him for hours. I am a ruthless bastard when I go after something,' he ended flatly.

'I can't make my mind up if you've sent him to Brazil to make a man out of him or because you just want to put him as far away from you as you possibly can.'

'A bit of both,' Roque confessed with a dry slice of honesty. 'Here—use this…'

He handed her a clean napkin off the table. Taking it from him, Angie took the hint that she'd cried enough tears and made an effort to put a stop to them. 'It's me who should be saying sorry,' she mumbled into the napkin. 'I didn't mean to fall to pieces.'

'If you want my opinion it is something you should have done a long time ago.'

He was probably right. For hours, days, months—years—she'd been bottling it all up without knowing she was doing it. From the age of seventeen she had lived her life by walking a narrow path wearing blinkers on her emotions, because it was the only way she had been able to cope. Survival had been everything—her survival, her brother's survival. Constant fear had dogged her every decision. If she got it wrong and could no longer afford to keep Alex safe in his private boarding school she'd risked him being taken away from her and placed in a state home or fostered out.

Then Roque had come along—a dangerously tempting diversion.

'You were right,' she sniffed into the napkin. 'I should not have let Alex run my life for me. I should've listened when you offered me advice.'

'Was that a concession?'

If it was, he didn't sound very impressed by it.

'It is late. I need a shower. Go to bed.'

Letting her go, he swung away from her to stride back across the bedroom, all arrogant distance and touch-me-not-with-your-concession cool.

'You think you're so perfect, don't you, Roque?' Angie flung after him shakily. 'You think that because all your predictions about my brother have come true it gives you the right to take the lofty high ground. Well, I have news for you,' she said as he stopped dead. 'You were no better behaved than Alex was when it came to wanting your own way. Alex was jealous of you. What was *your* excuse for turning our marriage into a battle in which only one of you could make me dance to their tune? Which one of you was the adult?'

His shoulders flexed inside his white shirt as her final stab sank deep. 'Poor Angie,' he struck back. 'Beaten into meek submission by her warring men.'

His derision washed angry colour into her cheeks, for she had never let anyone beat her into submission—especially not Roque. 'I made mistakes,' she admitted. How could she not admit it when she'd just stood here in the room and faced them? 'I was a lousy wife to you—'

'So you were,' he agreed.

Angie sucked in a painful breath 'Well, at least I didn't go looking for comfort in another man's bed!' she hit back with shaking fervour.

Roque swung around to look at her. A sudden stark look Angie read as remorse had taken hold of his lean golden features, and her breath stalled in her throat when he opened his mouth to speak.

'Don't you dare apologise,' she heaved out shakily.

Surprise made him blink. 'I had no intention of apologising,' he stated coolly. 'Why would I, when you have just said that you were a lousy wife?'

Angie wanted to throw something at him. Instead she had to make do with clenching her hands into two tense fists, because he was already striding with laconic grace into his own dressing room, leaving her standing there feeling...

She didn't know what she was feeling, she realised as she released her pent-up breath. He tied her in knots. He'd always tied her in knots. Was he expecting *her* to apologise for driving him into another woman's bed?

A gentle knock sounding on the suite door made her hurriedly relax her taut posture before she called a polite, 'Come in.' The door opened and a little dark-haired maid dressed in pale blue stepped in. She smiled shyly at Angie and indicated she'd come to collect the supper things. Angie smiled back, managed to discover the maid's name was Maria, and after thanking her wandered into the bathroom to use up some time cleaning her teeth and brushing the damp tangles out of her hair.

When she glanced into the mirror she saw a triangular face with wide-spaced green eyes, a thin little nose and a full, soft bow-shaped mouth. A mouth that was trembling pathetically, and eyes that had darkened with hurt.

Did he truly believe he could justify what he'd done by piling the blame on to her? Obviously he did, or he would not have said it—which did not bode well for the next scene they were about the share when they climbed into that bed out there.

She turned to slump back against the washbowl, staring down dully at her bare feet, because she knew that sleep was not on Roque's agenda this time. He'd let her off the hook last night, but there was little chance he was going to do so again. And the default charge he'd laid on her this afternoon was still stinging—because, God help her, she knew she was in danger of defaulting again.

Walking back out into the dressing room, she started hunting through drawers, looking for her nightwear. Finding the right drawer in a wide column of them, she was about to pluck out a slip nightdress when she spied another nightdress folded beneath it, and a sudden light of defiance lit her up.

Throwing off her bathrobe, she let it drop to the floor, then pulled the garment out of the drawer to shake out its voluminous folds. It was a real passion-killer—a long, loose thing that would cover her from neck to feet. It had been given to her by a lingerie company aiming to reproduce the pre-Raphaelite look for its ads. She even had a copy of the photograph in her portfolio. All the other models in the picture were wearing the very latest in sensationally sexy lingerie. However, as a contrast, she'd got to look the perfect picture of pre-Raphaelite virginal white modesty because of her flowing red hair and her ability to look pale and—

'Angie, we need to talk—*meu Dues.*'

A sharp gasp of air left Angie's lungs as she spun around, then froze. Roque was standing in the opening which led back into the bedroom, his full attention locked onto her with the stunning power of a magnetic force field. Angie lost the ability to breathe at all—for he might be looking at her as if she'd just popped naked out of a birthday cake, but she could not take her eyes off *him*.

He was wearing a towel wrapped like a sarong around his hips and nothing else. The towel might reach down to his calf muscles, but it didn't stop him from looking mind-stoppingly physically gorgeous. His hair was still wet, and beads of moisture clung to his wide bronze muscled shoulders, the spread of hair on his chest. A slow, thick lethargy began creeping over her. There was no way to avoid admitting it. Looking at Roque meant looking at pure male perfection, with a horrendous amount of raw sexual promise thrown in. Her eyes felt glued to the long, sleek form of his very masculine torso, bearing the kind of muscular ridges that ignited a series of familiar stings and prickles which attacked low down in her abdomen and at the very tips of her breasts. It didn't help that she knew him, every fabulous lean, dark, intimate inch of him, knew exactly what was hidden beneath the towel and what—

'*Meu Dues,*' he said again. 'I am revisiting my perfect moment.'

Angie blinked, then jerked her eyes back to his face. Roque watched as a blush started crawling across her skin as his meaning struck home. Seeing her naked for the first time was a moment he would treasure for the rest of his life. Her shy blushing cheeks, the soft quiver of her mouth, the rippling waves of her hair falling around her face and her shoulders, the smooth flowing lines of all that amazing pearlescent skin. The way she'd stood in front of him, with her thighs pressed anxiously together and her arms crossed over her body in a manner supposed to be hiding her breasts from him. But the two perfect globes had pouted at him over the top of her inadequate cover-up.

Back then he'd felt like the rake in some costume melodrama, about to deflower the pale trembling virgin, and he'd loved it. His Portuguese blood had fired up centuries of alpha genes which he really should have been ashamed to acknowledge he had. If his great-great grandfather had been alive to witness such primitive rushes he would have been pleased. Drogo de Calvhos had been a sixty-four-year-old lech and a childless widower when he'd married the sixteen-year-old daughter of a *duc*, sold to him for the price of some disputed land bordering their two estates. Fable had it that his teenage bride had put a scar on his face, trying to fight him off on her wedding night, and his ancestor had had her whipped for her trouble. She'd given him three sons before she'd reached her twentieth birthday, and each conception had added another scar to Drogo's face.

'Go away,' gasped Angie, casting the nightdress aside in favour of stooping down to snatch up her discarded bathrobe.

For some reason he could not fathom, Roque lifted a hand to lightly stroke the side of his cheek. Perhaps it was those genes at work again, warning him that he could receive the same treatment as his ancestor if he did not tread carefully around Angie right now. He might be only thirty-two years old, not sixty-four, and this woman a now very experienced twenty-three, but the vibes were still there—the *touch me if you dare* warning buzzing in the space separating them.

'Sweet heaven,' he breathed, 'you have gained curves.'

He started moving towards her, the burning heat in his dark gaze putting Angie into a panic as she fought to pull on the robe—only to discover that the sleeves had somehow become twisted inside out.

'It's a bit late for that, *meu amante*.' Reaching out to take the tangled robe from her scrambling fingers, he dropped it back to the floor.

Angie squeezed her naked thighs together and wished every hair follicle down there wasn't tingling like mad. He was standing so close to her she could feel the warm damp heat coming off him, smell the clean sharpness of his soap.

'You—you said you wanted to talk,' she reminded him, stretching out a hand towards the voluminous nightdress.

Roque caught the hand and brought it up to his mouth. 'I don't remember.'

'W-well you did—and stop that.' She pulled her hand free. 'I n-need to…'

She lost track of what she had been going to say when he took a step closer. Instinct sent Angie falling back a step, and she came up against the drawer unit with a bump. Roque just continued to follow her, with the unremitting certainty of a man who knew exactly what was going to happen next. One of his hands lifted up, open-palmed, with long brown fingers aiming purpose-fully for the indentation of her waist. When he touched her skin she quivered, and he smiled and just kept on coming, until his hips came to settle against hers.

'Roque…' she said, meaning to follow it up with a protest, but he got in first. Low, dark and somber.

'*Sim, minha dolce*, it is I.'

He sounded so grim again suddenly that Angie forgot to protest and frowned up at him instead. 'You—you're still angry with me,' she murmured unevenly.

'I am not angry with you.'

He showed her with the nudge of his hips exactly what he was. The towel folded around his hips was damp, but it did not detract from the burgeoning force Angie could feel making itself felt. Releasing a soft gasp was all she had time to do before he lowered his dark head and captured her mouth, beginning to explore it with a slow, deep, coaxing sensuality. His other hand arrived at her shoulder, gently urging her forward until their upper bodies met.

Trying to fight the kiss, the bold nudge of his erection, and now the feel of her breasts pressing against his warm skin, Angie pulled her head back and looked into the smouldering depths of his eyes. No matter what he'd said, he *was* still angry, she saw. Frowning, she parted her lips to say so, but he just drove his tongue between the gap, and followed it up with the hungry pressure of his mouth.

With a helpless groan she squirmed against him, trying to fight the helpless meltdown she could feel taking place inside. His long fingers spanned her narrow waistline. He used them to press her up against him. He kissed her until her lips were hot and swollen, and he felt her meltdown start to show itself in the slackening of her tension.

'Tell me you want me,' he instructed, seducing her heated lips with the words.

Angie folded her fingernails into the solid satin bulge of his biceps and pushed, trying to give herself some space.

'I *will* make you say it,' he warned, when she snapped her lips shut.

'You won't,' she responded unsteadily, staring with defiance into the burning dark certainty blazing from his eyes.

Raising a hand to clasp her nape, he tilted her head back, then with a precision that set her gasping bent his dark head and closed his mouth over one small, firm pointed breast. A hot stab of pure sensation spun down the front of her body, and she released a wild choking gasp. Her fingernails dug deeper into his skin so she could maintain her balance as raw, unbridled pleasure lost her the will to put up more of a fight. Her defences crashed and burned on a swirling eddy of thick hot craving. She groaned out his name, then lifted her hips into fierce contact with his. She felt his heartbeat quicken, felt the intoxicating throb of pure male muscle swell and harden at the contact.

She wanted him. Angie finally admitted it. She wanted *this*—Roque standing over her, making her feel small and delicate and fragile with his all-encompassing superiority in height, his strength, his everything. Her fingers left his arms to graze over his taut satin shoulders, and eventually curled into his wet, clean-scented scalp so she could lift up his head.

Their eyes clashed for a split second—his lit by flames, hers alive with emerald lights. She was panting. He looked ferociously turned on.

'Yes,' she said, that was all, and he claimed her waiting mouth.

She kissed him back with the same heated urgency, clinging to him as he ran his hands down her body, shaping her ribcage, the indentation of her waist and the swell of her hips. When the towel disappeared she arched towards him with the instincts of a wanton, going in search of contact with the fierce glory of his erection. The breath left his mouth on a silken hiss and he clamped a hand around one of her thighs and lifted it, arrogant in the way he wrapped it around his waist.

He was going to take her right here up against the drawers, with no preliminaries, and she wanted him to. She didn't need preliminaries. She was so ready for him, and it was like Roque had described it—an extra pulse beat through her blood. She wanted him to lose his head and sink himself into her to the hilt.

And he knew it too. She could see the knowledge in his eyes as he drew back from the kiss to look at her. He hovered, proud against her, hot and hard, looking down at her, allowing her to press soft, urgent, needy kisses to his lips and his face.

'Say it.'

Angie released a strangled laugh, because it was crazy that he still needed to hear her say it when she was already close to coming in a shivering, quivering, static-spangled rush.

Tightening her grip on his head, she pulled his mouth down onto hers with a hungry and hot sensuous passion that should give him his answer.

Muttering something deep in his throat, he took charge of the kiss—and of Angie. He lifted her up and wrapped her other leg around him, then carried her into the bedroom and to the bed.

Her hands became restless on his body—searching, greedy. When he started teasing her with slow moist kisses to her eyes, her nose, the sensitive hollows beneath her ears, she curled in closer in such a needy way that he uttered a mocking husky laugh.

Then he speared his fingers into her hair and bent his dark head to claim her mouth again, exalted by the grateful little whimper that rolled around her throat. *Mine*, he thought with simmering triumph, even if she did not want to be his. And with a long, smooth, possessive stroke of his hand along her body he made her quiver and writhe.

As if she knew what he'd been thinking, she said, 'I hate it that you can do this to me!'

'And I love it that I can do this to you,' Roque came right back.

Then he transferred his kisses to her neck, the swelling slopes of her breasts, and Angie forgot what they were talking about because she knew what was coming. She just clung to him, and the wait was unbearable as he plied hot, moist, grazing kisses over every inch of her flesh. His hands caressed where his lips were not reaching, layering sensation over sensation with the clever use of his hands and his mouth. When he finally gave her what she was craving for and dipped a finger between her thighs she just went completely still.

Roque lifted his head to watch the glaze of desire swim across the sensual glow of her eyes and see her breathing slow right down. His own heated response flooded his bloodstream as her silken wetness enfolded his touch. He reached up to touch his lips to hers, and she raised long and dusky eyelashes so she could look at him in trancelike sensuality.

'You love this, hmm, *querida*?' he husked.

She could not find the voice to reply. She just lifted up her fingers to trace his exotic cheekbones, warmed by desire. He was so beautiful to look at her heart ached. The fingertip delicacy of his touch was so instinctively perfect she experienced its pleasure through every pore. When he lowered his head to kiss her again she melted into it in the same luxurious way she had melted elsewhere.

It didn't stay like that for long, though. Like the beautiful calm before the raging storm, he wanted more—and he knew how to extract it. His kisses grew more demanding, his caressing fingers extracting a taut restlessness from her that set her panting and needing more. Her hands were moving all over him, touching, stroking, reclaiming each ripple of pleasure he experienced, each low, dark, husky groan. He bent to suck her tight aching breasts, and she closed the long thick power of his erection in both of her hands. It swelled for her, pulsing like a separate living thing, nudging her hip and demanding more from her—which she gave. And she felt the fluttering quickening in her body, felt her senses come alive in a vibrant rush that brought them tingling to the surface of her skin. Their mouths became a hot fuse of hunger again and again and again, until she could stand it no longer,

'Roque,' she breathed desperately. 'Please...'

He reclaimed her mouth with the silken fire of his darting tongue, and continued to trace the hot, vulnerable flesh between her thighs, dipping inside her, then frustratingly out again, finding and stimulating the tiny hidden nub and circling it until she flailed in a storm of excited frustration. He sucked her nipples with a ruthlessly determined urgency that had her fingers releasing him to clutch his hair, where they stayed, helpless and useless other than to cling, because her brain and her senses were being consumed in other places.

'Please, Roque, please...' she heard herself begging in a thick, tight, anxious little voice. Then, 'Oh...' She arched her spine at a streak of glorious pleasure. 'Do that again...'

He did do it again, and again, driving her into that white-hot mindless place where only his touch mattered. The heat of his breath was on her skin, and the dark rasp of words muttered in his own language as he urged her towards that agonised peak and almost right over it. Then, with the timing of an absolute master, he came over her and took her flailing over that peak with his first long, driving stroke.

It was like coming alive after a year lost in limbo. Angie came all around him in tense, hot rippling waves that increased in power with each plunge. He was hot and hard and increasingly urgent. He kept kissing her mouth, then her throat, then her shoulder, driving her crazy, because each heated touch was like a torment that did not last long enough.

He pushed the hair back from her face and commanded, 'Open your eyes.'

Angie obeyed without a single thought that he meant anything more than to add yet another dimension to what was happening between them. Breathless, panting, eyes dark green pools of desire, she looked into his deep dark gaze and saw the flickering flames of anger a split second before he rasped harshly, 'Say farewell to your fine moral principles, Angie.' And with a final long, plundering stroke tossed her, shocked, confused, shatteringly bewildered, into the spinning world of ecstatic release.

Afterwards she felt as if she was dropping down from a very high place onto stony ground. Her body still throbbed all around him. The power of her release still sounded like a scream in her head. Roque was heavy on top of her, and the evidence that he was taking this long to find his breath was a small kind of comfort to the way he had just deliberately demolished her.

She wanted to move, but she did not want to prompt him into saying anything else. *Say farewell to your fine moral principles, Angie…* That had been a big enough bludgeon to beat her with. She'd vowed she wouldn't have sex with him, now she'd done it, and Roque had wanted to make sure that she *knew* she had done it.

He moved finally, lifting himself up on his forearms and raising his head from the warm damp hollow of her throat. He looked at her. She looked at him. Nothing— not even a glimmer of emotion passed between the two of them.

Then, with a grimace, he slid off her—and the moment he did so Angie snaked off the bed. Tears were threatening, but she refused to give in to them. She tried her best to walk in a straight line towards the archway which led into her dressing room and bathroom, but she felt so light-headed and dizzy she was afraid her legs were going to buckle beneath her.

'*Retribuição,*' he fed after her impassively. 'It means retribution,' he enlightened. '*My* retribution. I did not sleep with Nadia.'

CHAPTER EIGHT

ANGIE stilled like a frozen icicle topped by a flaming river of fire.

'The tabloids misinterpreted what they saw,' he extended in a cold, flat voice. 'So you owe me, Angie, for twelve lousy months of being labelled a faithless playboy husband. Now you will never know what I've been doing and who I've been doing it with since you walked out on me.'

'So that—just now—was your idea of revenge?' she said without turning.

'I felt I was due something.'

Angie nodded her flame-bright head. 'Then I hope it gave you…satisfaction,' she murmured, and started walking again.

'Is that all you've got to say?' He sounded so sardonic she almost turned and ran back across the room to give him what he really should be getting—which was a slap across his heartless face! But she didn't. She was too hurt and cold and—worse than both of those things—too revolted with herself for giving in to him in the first place.

'As you said to me yesterday, this is a different time and a different set of issues. I thought we were trying to rebuild something here—not trying to demolish it completely. Silly me.' She even managed a laugh, albeit a bitter one. 'I should have remembered your ruthless streak.'

'Did you hear what I said?' He sounded irritated now. 'I did *not* sleep with Nadia.'

Angie breathed short and tensely. 'Does *she* know that?'

She started walking again, and actually managed to reach the opening archway before he spoke. 'You still don't believe me about Nadia.'

It wasn't a question. Reluctant though she was to do it, Angie turned to look at him, and was surprised to discover that he'd moved without her hearing him, and now stood in the opening to his own dressing room. It felt kind of ironic that they both stood naked, with the rumpled spread of the bed between them giving evidence of what they had just shared. For they might as well both be fully dressed and facing each other across a courtroom she felt so coldly indifferent to him now.

'I liked you better when you did not resort to lying to shore up your bruised ego,' she told him. 'I saw you, you see—with my own eyes. So coming up with such a weak story now is just a bit sickening to me.'

She should have walked away then, because it had been such a good exit line, but she didn't move. She stayed to watch the frown darken his hard, handsome face.

'You cannot have seen what did not happen.'

Well, she had. 'I came back that night,' she enlightened him. 'I got halfway to Alex's school, then changed my mind. I realised you were right. I had to stop putting him first and start thinking about us. So I got my driver to turn around and bring me back to London—to the club...'

She could still see it all, as if it had happened yester-day. Still feel the same clutch of anxiety as she'd stepped into the nightclub. It had been a friend of Roque's birth-day. He'd invited a whole group of them to help him cel-ebrate it. Julian someone-or-other—she couldn't recall the rest of his name right now. Not that it mattered.

'I saw you with Nadia.'

He'd gone so still now Angie wondered if he had stopped breathing. She certainly had, but there was nothing unusual in that for her when she allowed herself to recall the scene that had murdered her marriage. And by his taut silence she knew Roque was right there with her, seeing what she must have seen then. The tiny low-lit dance floor. The slow smoochy dance. Nadia with her arms wrapped around his neck, swaying against him. Roque using his hands to hold her close.

'She was all over you, and you were loving it.'

'No.' He denied that.

'You were loving it, Roque! Do you think I can't tell when you're aroused?'

'I was not aroused!'

'You were kissing her!' Angie was charged up like a stoked fire. 'Your hands were clamped to her backside! I watched the pair of you sway to the music and I would have to be really stupid not to know you were *both* only half a step away from having sex on the bloody dance floor!'

'Don't swear,' he growled, frowning fiercely now.

'I saved myself the indignity of being noticed and got out of there as fast as I could!' Angie careered on. 'I went to Carla's and stayed there the night. She woke me the next morning with a stack of tabloids showing you and Nadia *still* wrapped around each other, entering her apartment block!'

'She was drunk.'

Angie sucked in a fire-eating breath of air.

'I did not have sex with her—'

'Don't lie!' she yelled at the top of her voice.

'She was drunk—high on something anyway!' he fired right back at her. 'I took her home and dumped her safely inside her apartment. Then—I—left!' he punched out like a violent fist. 'I went *home* and sat up all night, waiting for my *wife* to come home!'

If Angie thought *she* was angry fit to burst, Roque had now hit the same furious place.

'But you did not come back. So I started ringing people! Your brother's school had not seen you. Carla told me that *she* had not seen you!' He threw out an arm in disgust. 'How damn cruel was that? She knew we'd had a row because I told her! I was *worried* about you! Then the newspapers happened. But *still* I trusted you to come home to me, Angie. To give me a chance to explain myself! You denied me that right! You judged and condemned me without a damn hearing, then flounced off out of the firing line for months without anyone knowing where you had gone. So I deserved my moment of retribution, *minha esposa*,' he insisted harshly. 'And you know what? The way you are standing there, willing to listen to me now, infuriates me even more—because it has come twelve months too late!'

On that final stinging volley he strode into his dressing room. Ten seconds later Angie blinked as she heard his bathroom door slam shut.

Pushing her tangled hair back from her face with

trembling fingers, she let a choky shrill laugh break free from her throat.

They'd just had their fiercest row yet while standing there stark naked. How crazily bizarre was that?

Reeling around, she walked into her own dressing room. Then, because anger was still fizzing around inside her, she walked into her bathroom and slammed *her* door shut.

Was he telling her the truth? *Could* he be telling the truth?

No, she refused to believe it—could not dare to believe it. Because it would make her hidden months of misery such a cruel, hard waste.

She was about to step beneath the shower when she realised she didn't want one. Like someone struggling to stay riding on the crest of a storm tossed wave, she reeled around yet again and went back the way she had come.

The bed looked like a war zone, and for some hazy reason she set about remaking it while her thoughts and her feelings tumbled around her insides.

Then she stopped.

Well, where *were* your fine moral principles, Angie? she asked herself suddenly. You just let him make hot, passionate love to you in this very bed when you still believed that he'd cheated on you.

Her prowling restlessness sent her back into the dressing room, where she saw her bathrobe and Roque's towel lying in a snowy-white heap on the polished wood floor. Stooping to pick them up, she straightened, hugging the towelling to her and instantly inhaling the scent of Roque's soap. Tears started to push at the muscles in her throat.

If he'd been telling her the truth then he *had* deserved his moment of retribution, she forced herself to acknowledge.

And she'd deserved to be on the cruel end of it.

Twelve long, lonely months that need not have—

Then she suddenly remembered something that stopped that train of thought abruptly in its tracks.

Who the heck did he think he was trying to kid here?

Spinning around in a full circle, she scanned the room looking for where whoever had unpacked for her had placed her Harrods bag. She couldn't see it. Frustration rose up to mix with the hurt and anger already foaming in her blood. Dropping the robe and towel, she made for the nearest hanging space and dragged a long black jumper off its hanger, yanked it on over her head.

Roque was just coming out of his bathroom when she arrived in the opening, a fresh towel wrapped around his hips. He saw her and froze.

'I want to know where my bag is,' she said.

The on the face of it harmless request made him blink. Roque stared at her for a couple of seconds—at the way she was standing there in a baggy black sweater that reached halfway down her fabulous long legs, at the way she'd folded her arms across her front—before lifting his eyes to view the way her eyes were sparking green ice at him. He was glad he was wearing a towel to hide what his reaction was.

'I don't have a clue,' he answered indifferently.

'Well, I couldn't find it when I just looked for it, and I know it went into the back of the Range Rover because I saw it go in—a Harrods bag,' she described. 'It has my things in it. If you don't have it, then—' she flung out

a hand before folding it back beneath her breasts again
'—ring someone and find out what's been done with
it.'

Intrigued, despite not wanting to be, Roque went for
a dismissive shrug and strode across to his own wall
of hanging space, picked a tee shirt at random and
pulled it on over his head. 'The staff will have gone off
duty by now. It's late. Go to bed. We will find it in the
morning.'

'I want my stuff *now*,' Angie stated stubbornly.

'Well, you can't have it now!' he fired back.

He dropped the towel and pulled on a pair of jeans.
Angie got a brief glimpse of bronzed muscular flanks,
and hated it that certain muscles stung and pulsed.

Without another word she turned and walked away
again, back around the bed and into her own dressing room, where she began an angry, noisy search for
the Harrods bag. A few minutes later he arrived in the
opening, looking tall, dark and dangerous in jeans and
a white tee shirt, with his hair still ruffled and a scowl
on his too-handsome face.

Ignoring him, Angie continued with what she was
doing.

'Explain why you need the bag,' he invited abruptly.

Rummaging through a drawer, she slammed it shut
and opened the next one. 'I want my phone.'

'Leaving me again, Angie?' Roque sighed out.
'Hoping to call a cab? This is not London. Cabs don't
turn up in five minutes around here.'

'If I was intending to leave you I would have just
gone—walked back to Lisbon if I had to.' Straightening
up, she lanced him an icicle glance. 'I can't leave,'
she added, moving on to check out the bottom of the

wardrobes. 'I have to consider my brother's well-being. I want my phone so I can make you stop telling such big lies to me.'

Roque's attention was truly caught now, and this time his frown was not angry but confused. 'I do not understand.'

'I know you don't.'

She found the bag then, hidden behind a pair of long black winter boots, and bent to snatch it up. Crossing to the wall-to-wall dressing table, she tipped the contents out onto the top, found her mobile phone, and started hitting buttons as she walked over to where he stood.

'Listen,' she said, handing the phone to him, and then stood waiting for him to do as she'd said. She didn't look at his face. She didn't care what he was thinking or feeling or—anything. She just waited, with her lips sucked in at the corners to stop them from trembling, knowing exactly what he was listening to.

Nadia herself, confirming the truth about that night twelve months ago. Nadia taunting Angie with it via voicemail, describing all the other nights she and Roque had spent together while Angie had been out of the way.

She knew without looking up at him when the message had finished. She waited, without allowing herself the relief of swallowing the thick lump that had formed in her throat, for him to lower the phone from his ear.

'I saved it as evidence,' she told him. 'In case I decided I could take the humiliation of letting my lawyers listen to it for use in evidence for our div— If you're deleting it,' she broke off to say, when his fingers started hitting buttons, 'then I should tell you I've downloaded a copy elsewhere.'

'Angie—'

'As you said,' she cut right across him. 'We are doing this twelve months too late.'

Snatching the phone back, she turned and walked away from him.

'She is lying, *meu querida*,' he insisted wearily. 'It—none of what she said happened except inside her own twisted head.'

'Well, I don't suppose it matters any more.' She laid the phone down on the heap of other things she'd tipped from the bag. 'If you're telling me the truth then you've just had your payback. If Nadia is telling the truth I suppose I had mine when I kicked you out of my life.'

Wrapping her arms around the jumper, she turned and made herself look at him. He looked—stunned. Maybe even a bit shaken and pale. Crazy, she thought, how seeing him stripped of his usual arrogance made her insides start to shake.

'Now you are back...'

Not liking the way he said that, Angie frowned. She had a feeling he was thinking out loud rather than speaking to her. He even blinked slowly, as if to refocus, and then she watched him take in a short breath.

'You know something, Angie? I think I am ashamed of you,' he said, so unexpectedly that he made her blink. He grimaced and went to turn away, then changed his mind and swung back again. 'I am your husband!' he launched at her. 'Yet you preferred to believe that!' He slashed a contemptuous glance at her mobile. 'The ravings of a mean-minded bad loser out to cause trouble between us, rather than give me the right to defend myself!'

'I saw the newspapers—'

'And received a bitchy message—which, seemingly, you have hugged to yourself like a hair shirt ever since!'

She turned pale, because there was an indefensible slice of truth in that harsh statement. 'Y-you'd already told me you were going to find someone else to take my place. You—'

'And you, *querida*, still made the choice to go to your brother.'

'I ch-changed my mind and came back—'

'Exatamente,' Roque said curtly. 'You changed your mind—as was your right… As it was my right to change my mind about putting another woman in your place.'

'Oh, very slick.' Angie utterly derided that. 'I saw you with my own eyes, kissing her!'

'Sim.' He revealed absolutely no crack in his superior attitude. 'Guilty as charged. And *you* made it halfway to your brother's school before you decided to turn back.'

The parallel lines he was drawing suddenly dovetailed so neatly Angie almost choked on her breath as the two merged together. He was saying he had taken his threat as far as kissing Nadia before he'd changed his mind.

Her lips trembled and parted. She dropped her arms to her sides. She was hunting her head for a line of defence but could not find one.

As if he knew that, Roque nodded his head, spun a swift final glance of glinting contempt at her mobile, then turned and walked off.

Angie couldn't move a single muscle. The chilly wash of truth was sinking through her as she listened to the suite door open, then shut.

Could he be telling the truth?

She knew she was still hunting for a chink in his cold demolition of her totally self-righteous belief in her own version of what had happened. Face it, Angie, you need to find a chink or Roque is right!

He was certainly right about Nadia's message—she *had* hugged it to her like some self-punishing hair shirt. Her skin was suddenly riddled with a prickly quiver. Spinning round, she snatched up the phone and deleted Nadia's wretched message with tense taps of her finger, then tossed the phone away from her as if it had burned to touch it at all.

She heard the sound of another door closing, and swung around, her breath caught and her eyes glued to the archway, until it registered with her that the door she'd heard closing was the one that led out of the suite.

He'd left her alone to fester. He'd taken his bad temper off to another part of the house. The burning urge to go chasing after him almost got the better of her, but then common sense arrived, telling her to give him time to cool off.

Give them both time to cool off.

It seemed crazily fitting that when she opened the wrong drawer to look for her normal nightdress she found herself staring at a piece of white tissue paper folded carefully over something familiarly soft, with an oh-so neatly scripted label carefully pinned to it.

'My Baby's First Shawl by Angelina de Calvhos' she read with a thick, sinking swoop of her heart. Silly, soppy, sentimental…

As her lips parted and started trembling she felt a different kind of tremor take control of her throat. Reaching out, even her fingers trembled as she slowly, carefully picked up the piece of tissue and placed it gently on the drawer-top. She did not want to look inside it. She had a horrible feeling her heart was going to crack wide open if she did. Yet, with her breath caught in her chest, she still drew back the folds of tissue, then stood, feeling an odd numbness spread up from her toes.

Barely half finished and very amateur-looking, the gossamer-fine snowy white shawl had been her very first attempt at crocheting. She'd spent hours, carefully threading the fine lacy pattern, only to constantly need to unpick half of it again when she realised she'd made a mistake.

Dry-eyed, she saw herself sitting curled up in a chintzy armchair in the tiny cottage deep in the Cotswolds Carla had sent her to when she'd needed to seek refuge from the press.

And from Roque, she added as she stroked her fingers across the soft fine wool. The cottage had belonged to a spinster aunt of Carla's. She'd inherited it when the aunt died, but had rarely used it herself. 'An investment', her boss had called it. For Angie it had become her sanctuary, a place to hide away from the public eye while she nursed her wounds and nurtured the tiny life growing inside her womb. She'd found the hooks, wool and patterns languishing in a cupboard. It had just felt kind of fitting that she occupied some of her time taking on the challenge of teaching herself how to crochet.

'Bad therapy, sweetie,' Carla had drawled in her dry, mocking way, when she'd called in one day and caught her fumbling attempts to work with the hook and wool and demanded to know what she was doing. 'Maternal instincts gone mad. You should come back into the real world before you turn into one of those awful mummy frumps. I've got loads of work for a pregnant model…'

Well, not for *this* model, Angie thought sadly. A week after that conversation with Carla she'd been taken into hospital and confined to complete bedrest in an attempt to stop a threatening miscarriage. A month later it had happened anyway, for no reason anyone could give except the old one about nature taking its course.

Roque had not even known she was pregnant. She had not known it herself until a couple of weeks after their marriage fell apart. She hadn't told her brother. Only Carla knew, and the doctor she'd gone to see. After it was over she'd been glad she'd kept it to herself.

And she had no intention of telling Roque now, she thought as she folded the tiny shawl into its tissue wrapping and placed it back in the drawer. They had enough problems cluttering up their marriage without adding a lost baby to them. What would be gained from telling him now?

What was gone was gone.

Angie slid back into bed and curled up on her side. Closing her eyes, she listened to the steady pump of her own heartbeat and felt as if she was lying in the loneliest place on earth. Roque would not come back into this bed tonight—she just knew that he wouldn't. There was too much angry bitterness bubbling between them, and if he *had* been telling her the truth then…

She caught the sound of a door opening and then closing with a quiet click into its housing. Her heart missed a beat as she lay there, listening to Roque's quiet tread. The whole suite was shrouded in darkness because she'd switched off all the lights before she'd climbed into bed, so she lay listening to the rustle of clothing, then picked up the scent of brandy as he lifted the covers and slid into the bed.

'You are awake,' he said, and it was not a question.

Turning over, she peered at him through the darkness. He was lying on his back, staring up at the ceiling, the covers riding low across his chest. And he looked so very sombre Angie wanted to reach out and stroke her fingers along his unsmiling lips.

'Okay, I have been thinking,' he declared quietly. 'We do not communicate about the right things. This must change.'

Angie thought about that for a couple of seconds, then gave a jerky nod of her head, engrossed in the dark resonance of his accent, which had deepened since they'd stood flinging accusations at each other.

'I should not have brought my—bitterness about what has happened into this bed earlier. My *retribuição* crack was unforgivable in the circumstances, and I apologise for making it.'

'I—'

'Let me finish,' he cut in, and like a naughty child chided for interrupting Angie was silenced. 'The evidence of Nadia has always been stacked against me. I know that. When she lied to the press about our—involvement, I had no way of proving my innocence so I said nothing. That was also a mistake.'

'I sh-should have let you say it, though,' Angie dared to whisper.

'After witnessing that kiss?' He turned his dark head on the pillow and looked at her through the darkness. 'No.' He turned to stare at the ceiling again. 'It was not a kiss a husband should give any other woman but his wife. It should not have happened and you were right to feel cheated. If I had caught you kissing another man like that I would have ripped him limb from limb, then thrown you out of my life without conscience.'

'Not much love lost, then.' Angie could not help throwing in the jibe.

'I am Portuguese,' he claimed, as if it made him different from the rest of the human race. 'We are possessive of our women. We do not forgive infidelity. We don't like to share.'

'If that last bit was aimed at my brother, then I—'

'And your career,' Roque put in. 'Which took you away in one direction while I went off in another... Your brother was an added intrusion I did not...enjoy.'

'Alex was—'

'Your responsibility. And *he* did not like to share.'

'I warned you I would make a lousy wife,' Angie sighed out heavily, flopping onto her back.

'And you were,' he agreed.

'You shouldn't have married me.'

'I was irritated with you as my lover. My arrogance told me I could turn you into a more satisfying wife.'

Angie released a very *un*satisfied breath of air at his note of dry whimsy. It offered no answer at all as to why he'd suggested marriage—or for that matter why she had agreed. Oh, she knew that she'd been wildly in love with him. The 'first love' syndrome had grabbed a really tight hold on her. But they'd been sharing a very exciting and passionate relationship without commitment, so why had he bothered to change the status quo?

Then there was the 'no divorce' thing he'd thrown at her yesterday—or the day before that, she amended, when she remembered the lateness of the hour. What kind of man with a 'no divorce' clause built into his family pride married a woman because she irritated him as a lover?

'And I was in love with you.' He added the flat appendage as if he'd tapped directly into her thoughts.

Angie just froze as a trail of words like, *amo-te*, *eu te amo*, *eu quero te*, echoed in her head. Soul-melting endearments from a handsome ex-playboy, a guy with a fatal charm built into his genes. And she had responded to his softly spoken words with her own English versions… Yet how was it that she'd known absolutely how much *she'd* meant them while not taking on board the true worth of his words?

Then she remembered how those soul-melting endearments had gone missing within a few days of his ring sliding onto her finger, and Angie knew deep inside that she had been the one to blame. She'd continued on in her busy life with blind disregard to the fact that their relationship had changed, or that she needed to make changes along with it. Her wake-up call had arrived too late, when she'd found out she was pregnant two weeks after their marriage had blown apart.

Her eyes began to sting in the darkness as she thought about it. The horrible bad timing, the terrible hurt, the miserable weeks of loneliness when she'd hidden herself away to lick her wounds while hugging the news about their baby to herself, as if he'd forfeited the right to care.

'*W-was…?*' she prompted tremulously. 'As—as in you don't feel that way about me any more?'

Watching her through the sultry darkness, Roque saw the glitter of tears in her eyes and wanted his right to retribution back. Where the hell did she get off, daring to ask him that question after the year she had put him through?

'You think I should still love you?' He threw the loaded ball right back into Angie's court.

Pressing her trembling lips together, she gave a shake of her head, and a burning sense of dissatisfaction grabbed hold of his chest muscles, making him want to take hold of her by the shoulders and give her a damn good shake. So what was new there? he asked himself heavily. He could hardly recall a time when she hadn't annoyed him enough to make him want to shake her until she woke up and recognised what they'd had going for them once.

'A esperança é a última que morre,' he quoted heavily.

'I don't know what that means,' she whispered through the darkness.

'Then learn my language,' he suggested without remorse. He added a gruff, 'Go to sleep,' and then a sigh when he recognised he was bringing the last twenty hours in a full circle, with a gap between them in their bed as wide as an ocean.

Only this time Angie wasn't playing. 'Okay, so you're angry with me,' she accepted, drawing in a fortifying breath of air. 'I'm sorry I made you wait twelve months to tell me about Nadia. And I wish I wasn't so stubborn and unforgiving—but if you tell me what I must do one more time, Roque, I will—'

He moved without her seeing it coming. One of his arms just stretched out and appeared through the darkness to grab hold of her wrist, and the next thing Angie knew she was being hauled across the gap between them. She landed against his chest in a quiver of gasps and protests. They looked at each other—two deep-diving seconds of looking—and then his other hand arrived at the back of her head and he was pulling her down to receive the full onslaught of his kiss.

She didn't even think of fighting to get away from him this time. Instead she just kissed him back with every last bit of fevered anxiety she felt running rife in her blood. In fact she was so intent on what she was feeding into her kiss that when she felt something cool slide onto her finger she pulled her head back so hard it was a wonder she didn't snap her neck.

She stared dazedly down at him, watched a mocking little smile take control of his mouth. Then she lifted her left hand and stared at the two rings now slotted onto her finger.

She'd forgotten all about the rings again. She'd forgotten that Roque had taken them back. Her eyes were luminous even without the threat of tears as she looked back at his handsome dark face.

'A esperança é a última que morre,' he repeated softly, then pressed her back against the pillow and came over her to capture her lips with another hot, ravishing kiss. Angie's hands found his shoulders, and she set light so fast she almost hyperventilated when he snaked back from her to rear up onto his knees.

'What the hell are you wearing?' he ground out incredulously, staring down at the voluminous folds of white muslin.

'Hair shirt,' Angie whispered. 'I didn't think you would come back to this bed tonight.'

He spread back the covers so he could get a better look at the nightdress. After spending long seconds scanning her, from spiralling flame hair splashed against the pillow down to slender pink toes, he let out a lazy laugh. 'You look like Count Dracula's bride! No, don't fire up, Angelina the sacrifice.' He grinned rakishly when she tensed up. 'I like it.' Reaching down, he tugged the muslin all nice and neat around the shape of her body. 'I think it is appropriate attire for a lady about to be ravished on her wedding night.'

'Bit late for that,' Angie said, shaking out a quiver of pleasure when he ran the flat of his hands all the way up her muslin-covered legs to the feminine curve of her slender hips. 'I got to be well and truly ravished long before my wedding night—and I am not in any way, shape or form a *sacrifice*,' she added, in case he thought she was *that* sorry she hadn't let him defend himself twelve months ago.

'Don't spoil the fantasy.' Sending his hands on a further trail of her muslin-wrapped body, he shaped her narrow ribcage, then located the burgeoning fullness of her breasts. 'We will make *this* our new wedding night, and this time—' he paused to view the successful way he had outlined both budding peaks against the fine cloth with his long fingers '—we will follow it up with the honeymoon we did not manage to enjoy the first time around.'

'You—'

'Shut up now, Angie,' he growled, losing all hint of humour as he lowered his dark head, claimed one nipple in the heat of his mouth, and sucked hard on it through the muslin.

Angie forgot what she had been going to say as she closed her eyes and arched her back, setting free a helpless cry of pleasure. Her fingers dug into his hair. Her thighs sprang apart.

Roque husked out a very masculine laugh. 'Not very virginal, *meu querida*,' he murmured dryly.

'Shut up.' It was Angie's turn to call a halt to talking.

Roque's answer was the swooping glide of a long-fingered hand down between the hot juncture she'd opened up. He touched her through the muslin and sent her spinning her off into an exotic world she did not come away from for a long, long time.

Afterwards she stared up into the all-consuming darkness enfolding them and hoped—prayed—that in giving him the benefit of the doubt about Nadia she was not making the biggest mistake of her life.

CHAPTER NINE

RESTING her forearms against the rail on the sunny balcony, Angie looked down at the swimming pool situated directly below her, where Roque was currently cutting through the water like a man-eating shark.

The air this early still had a chill to it, and she did not know how he could stand it in the water, but then sharks were cold-blooded, she thought with a smile.

Not that she'd been treated to the cold-blooded, man-eating shark in him over the last three weeks. No, she'd had the very *hot*-blooded *woman*-eating shark. The one that circled her like a hunter and would pounce when she was least expecting it to devour her in a fest of passionate lust.

Lust. She pulled a face at the word, because lust was what they shared on this honeymoon. No mention from either of them since the night they'd arrived here of that other word—*love*.

Watching him cut through the water in a long, bronzed slither of supple male magnificence, she was not in the least bit surprised to feel her lust for him tangle up the sensitive muscles low down inside. Beneath the short slip of a nightdress she was wearing, her thighs shifted against a soft pulsing ache that reminded her just how passionately lustful Roque had been as recently as an hour ago, before he had left her to sleep off the effects while he'd taken himself off to his all-purpose gym before his swim.

Roque possessed vibrant energy enough to drive ten men. He was rarely ever still. If he wasn't dragging her off somewhere to show her Portugal from a proud native's perspective, he was using up some of that excess energy in dealing with his many business interests via the fully equipped office on the ground floor. When that failed to hold his restless interest he hunted her down.

As honeymoons went, theirs had been filled with non-stop passion and occasional quick trips out thrown in as respite. He'd flown them in his helicopter to Porto, then down a long stretch of the Douro River, banked by its famed hills and frilled by tier upon tier of wine terraces. And he'd really impressed her by pointing out how many of those terraced hills belonged to him or came beneath the de Calvhos umbrella. Back in Porto they'd boarded his yacht and spent a few days sailing down to the Algarve. And they'd strolled through the smaller vine terraces right here on this estate, when he'd demonstrated what went into producing a wine as exclusive as the coveted d'Agostinho label, and he'd made her drunk from tasting samples directly from the barrel, then laughed when he'd had to carry her back to his car.

He'd been relaxed and fun—a side to him she had rarely glimpsed the last time they been together. Back then they'd both been so busy, reduced to flying in and out of each other's lives with a speed and frequency that shocked and appalled her when she thought about it now. It was no wonder she'd felt wired up when he was with her and cast adrift when he was not. They'd been more like very intimate strangers, passing briefly in the warm passions of the night, than a real husband and wife. Except...

What they had now was not what she would describe as normal, Angie mused with a small frown. Because they hadn't—not once—taken a trip into Lisbon, or visited any of their old social haunts. No long leisurely meals eaten in Tavares' opulent surroundings, nor lively evenings spent with his friends at Club Lux. They had not gone near his city apartment, or strolled the shops on the Avenida da Liberdade. When she'd specially asked if they could go there he'd frowned and murmured some vague promise that they would discuss it later, then suddenly remembered a rush of calls he had to make.

Not that she wanted to shop till she dropped, or hop back onto Lisbon's social merry-go-round. She didn't. Her life had changed last year when she'd lost Roque and then their baby. Her wants and needs and ideals had changed. Perhaps his had, too. But this new life they were leading, encapsulated in a bubble, sealed off and protected from the life they'd used to live, was not sustainable. They couldn't go on for ever locking the rest of the world out.

Angie's frown deepened as she watched Roque make another looping turn in the pool and then spear back the way he had come. Yesterday Carla had called her with a business proposition that had roused her interest. When she'd told Roque about it over dinner he'd been so uncommunicative about the idea they'd almost had their first fight in three weeks.

She'd pointed out to him that if she was to live permanently here in Portugal then setting up a CGM branch here in Lisbon would be the perfect challenge for her. She'd known that by saying it she had been putting the stamp of permanency on their marriage. She'd also been aware that she was taking a huge step by if not stating it out loud then showing that she was ready to put the Nadia thing aside for good.

Roque had taken that on board, she was sure he had, because his attitude had softened and he'd started firing really impressive and well-informed questions at her about CGM, which had forced her to jump through hoops to answer and to grow quite heated when his opinions differed from hers.

They'd taken the argument to bed with them, and finished it off with a different kind of heat. And now here she was, up out of her bed hours before she normally would be, eager to strike while the idea was hot and convince him to—

Distracted from her thoughts by the familiar sound of his mobile's ringtone floating up from the terrace below her, Angie broke into an appreciative grin as she watched him haul himself out of the pool in a glorious ripple of water-washed muscle bronzed by the morning sun.

Gorgeous, she thought lushly, peering down at him like a sneaky voyeur—because he had no idea she was up here spying on him.

He picked the phone up off a table, then stood dripping water while he indulged in a sharp question and answer session in Portuguese. It had to be business, she decided, watching how, even wearing only a pair of black swimming shorts, he had taken on a whole new persona—the cold-blooded, man-eating shark kind.

Her grin widened.

Then suddenly died into stark frozen shock when the impatient snap of his voice drifted up to her. *'Para Deus causa, Nadia, irá você escuta-me!'*

For God's sake—*Nadia*?

The rest didn't matter; she would not have been able to translate it anyway. Her grasp of Portuguese was still sketchy at best, and—

Roque was still in contact with Nadia.

Angie took a jerky step back from the rail, then just stood in her flimsy, peachy strip of a nightdress, feeling the slow chilling growth of shock rise up from her feet while she listened to the impatient cut of Roque's voice fading as he strode into the house.

Silence folded around her like a huge stifling blanket. She didn't know what to do or to think. One part of her brain was throwing up all kinds of excuses—there had to be more than one Nadia out there, and maybe Nadia meant something else in Portuguese...

Or was Nadia right here in Portugal? Was she ringing Roque to arrange where they were to meet?

Are you crazy, Angie? she asked herself. You *know* that Nadia returned to live in her native Brazil last year, after she'd spilled her kiss and tell to the press, and you *believe* Roque's insistence that it was all just a pack of lies anyway.

'You are awake, *senhora*...'

Eyelashes fluttering, Angie turned to find Maria standing in the open doors which led into the bedroom, holding a breakfast tray in her hands. The little maid sounded surprised to find her out here, because she knew all about Angie's preference for lazing in bed each morning while Roque did his macho thing with the gym and the pool.

'*Sim,*' she replied, without knowing she'd said it. A dizzy sensation was beginning to spin in her head.

'You eat out here in the sun this morning, then?' Maria smiled as she stepped forward to place the tray down on the small table. 'It is such a beautiful day, no?'

'Beautiful,' Angie repeated like a dim echo, and pushed a set of icy cold fingers up to cover her mouth. It was trembling, she noticed, and the inside of her mouth and throat felt like dry sand.

Maria busied herself pouring out Angie's first cup of tea for her. As the fragrant scent of Earl Grey wafted towards her she felt her stomach churn.

Next thing she knew she was reeling around to face the doors, and heading towards them as a swirling clutch of nausea suddenly took hold. In her unsteady rush to get to the bathroom she bumped into a chair and knocked it over.

Maria straightened up with a jolt, then spun to stare at her. 'Oh, *senhora*, you are ill!' She heard the little maid gasp.

Angie forced herself to keep moving. Runway training, she kept telling herself over and over. You can make it to the bathroom before you throw up.

She was halfway across the bedroom when the suite door suddenly flew open, halting her mid-step. Turning her head, she saw Roque standing there, still wearing his swimming shorts with a towel looped around his neck. He was frowning as if he was in a bad temper.

'I have to fly to Paris this afternoon,' he growled out when he saw her.

Was Nadia in Paris?

With a muffled choke, Angie took flight on legs that

felt like fragile spindles. The archway ahead kept swimming in and out. She heard Roque say something sharp, and Maria answer him, and then the little maid's arm arrived around her waist to help support her—she had never felt so grateful for anything in her entire life.

Feeling too tall and gangly, and as weak as a rag doll, she let Maria guide her towards the bathroom. She threw up in the toilet bowl with Maria holding her hair back just as Roque arrived in the doorway. She could hear the concern in his voice as he spoke with Maria, then felt his closeness as he took over from the maid until it was over. His strong hands gently lifted her into his arms.

Angie wanted to fight him. She wanted to tell him to get off her. She wanted to scream at him to get out. But she found she couldn't raise the energy, and the dizzying sickness was already trying to pull her back down again.

Maria was still there. She could hear the two of them talking in low voices, but couldn't understand a word that they said.

Well, what did she expect? She'd married a foreigner. She was living in a foreign country and the language was still foreign to her. It wasn't to Nadia. Nadia's native Brazilian was almost an exact match to Roque's Portuguese. She was dark, like him—exotic, like him, and...

He laid her down on the bed, then stretched out to bring the rumpled sheet fluttering over her. Angie huddled beneath it, so cold she was shivering like mad.

'I'm calling the doctor,' he said harshly.

'Don't you *dare* call a doctor!' Angie shrieked out,

then groaned when it made her head feel as if it was splitting apart.

She flinched when she felt the warmth of Roque's palm on her brow. For some reason it brought her eyes flickering open. He was squatting down beside the bed, so close to her she could see tiny golden-brown shards of concern in his eyes.

'Go away,' she whispered, and squeezed her eyes shut again. She didn't want to look at him. She didn't want to blurt out the question stinging on the tip of her dry, acrid-tasting tongue.

Roque viewed her pinched pallor from the taut position of a man who was recalling the times he had cut it too fine with the use of a condom. He might not have any previous experience with morning sickness to draw upon, but his instincts had been yelling the cause at him from the moment he saw her standing there, looking pale as death, with a hand clamped to her mouth.

What else *could* be wrong with her? Maria had told him the smell of the tea had turned Angie's stomach. The maid insisted she'd been perfectly fine a minute before, enjoying the sunshine on the balcony.

'Angie...'

'No doctor,' she mumbled, completely misreading what he had been about to say.

Roque released a sigh and pressed his tense lips together, in a cowardly way glad of her interruption, because it had given him time to think. Maybe he was wrong. Maybe she had eaten something that had upset her stomach. Maybe she'd caught a bug.

He did not want there to be a baby yet. Angie was only twenty-three years old, and already she had been a mother to her brother for six years of her life. She deserved a break—a chance to learn how to be Angie. And, damn it, *he* wanted to learn more about the real Angie he had been watching slowly blossom from behind her old tough shell now that she'd passed on responsibility for her brother to him.

Was she already thinking what he was thinking? Was that the reason she had told him to go away? Was she hating him already and wishing she hadn't allowed him to coax her back into his life?

Coax? he mocked. Blackmail came closer to the truth. Coercion, intimidation—and don't forget the desire for retribution, he told himself, feeling guilt take a stranglehold on his taut throat.

Angie uncurled from her huddle and made herself sit up in the bed. She was already beginning to feel a bit better now the sickening shock had started to wear off.

'M-may I have a drink of water?' she asked, pushing back the tumbled tangle of hair from her face.

Roque stretched out a hand to pick up the vacuum flask standing on the bedside table, and poured some chilled water into a glass.

'Thanks,' she mumbled as he handed the glass to her, but she kept her eyes lowered as she sipped.

She couldn't look at him. She wished he would just go and—and get dressed, or something. Because she needed to be on her own so she could think. Drawing her knees up to her chin, she clutched the chilled glass in equally chilled fingers, glad her hair had slithered forward again and was hiding her face. *For God's sake, Nadia*, was playing over and over inside her head, alongside old lurid headlines like *'The Playboy and the Two Supermodels…'*

She took another trembling sip of her drink.

Roque continued to squat there, watching her with that brooding dark frown on his too-handsome face and giving the impression that he just didn't know what to do or say next. The air of indecisive helplessness he was emitting just did not suit him, and it niggled Angie because she knew that behind it his brain would be working. Any second now it was going to make the connection between his phone call down on the terrace and the balcony directly above it, and the idea of that happening coiled her sensitive stomach into knots.

'You m-mentioned going to Paris?' she mumbled, attempting to throw him off the scent.

He nodded his dark head. 'I received a call this morning about some business I need to attend to—but that no longer counts.' He waved a long-fingered hand in a gesture of indifference to Paris. 'Have you considered that you might be pregnant?'

It was like a shot to her blindside. Angie's chin shot up, her green eyes standing out like emerald pools of shock against the stark white colour of her pinched, strained face. It was the last thing she'd expected him to say—the *last* thing!

'Of course I'm not pregnant!' she choked out. 'I have not—no way—missed a single pill!'

She was taking the contraceptive pill? Why hadn't he known that? Roque asked himself, and tension grabbed a hold of his chest muscles as he had to control the need to release a sigh of relief.

'What gave you such a c-crazy idea in the first place?' Angie demanded, managing to turn an ever paler shade of white.

'It just came into my head,' he responded rather dryly. 'You don't have to snap at me.'

Oh, yes she did! The idea of another pregnancy would scare her witless. She didn't ever want to go through that heartbreaking trauma again!

'Well, I'm not,' she snapped, reaching out to set the glass aside before her trembling fingers dropped it. 'And if you need a reason why I'm feeling like this, then look to yourself,' she told him waspishly, fighting fear and hurt and a million other scary emotions. 'If you let me have two hours' sleep straight without wanting sex with me I feel like I'm on a winning streak—and don't look at me as if I've just stuck a knife in your ribs!'

As he rose up to his full height, Roque's chin went up, two lines of heat streaking high across his taut cheeks. 'Well, then, perhaps my trip to Paris is well timed,' he countered stiffly. 'It will allow you to sleep as many hours as you like for the next couple of nights.'

Was that where Nadia was waiting for him?

Angie threw herself back down against the bed and rolled over. 'Don't wake me up as you leave,' she flipped out, and shut her eyes tight.

A thunderous silence bounced off the walls while he continued to stand there. Angie felt as if her insides were collapsing. A baby… Didn't they have enough problems without him bringing a baby into the mix?

Tears burned like fire in her eyes, 'Will you just—go away?' she breathed thickly. 'I'm—sleepy.'

'Of course. My apologies,' he offered. 'Excuse me for delaying your much needed rest.'

Angie shivered as that crushingly impassive cool he could pull off with such chilling effect washed over her.

She listened to him striding away and pulled the covers up over her head.

She should just ask him outright about Nadia. She knew she should. She should just get it over with and spit the poisoned woman's name out of her mouth! But she couldn't. She was too scared. What if he admitted that he still had a thing going with Nadia? What if she'd misheard and made a horrible fool of herself? What if he was glad of the excuse she'd just handed him to get out of here and meet up with his on-off love in romantic Paris?

Roque cut himself with his wet razor and ripped out a curse. What kind of husband was he that he couldn't take Angie's lippy backlash when she was feeling unwell?

The arrogant, over-sensitive kind, he thought, as he tried to finish the job in hand without taking any more nicks out of his chin.

And what kind of man was he that he was preparing to leave her at all while she was feeling as she did? He was bigger than this, he told himself grimly as he pulled on the trousers to a steel-grey suit and pushed his arms into a striped shirt. Taking offence because she'd landed the blame on him for feeling ill was juvenile. He should be ashamed of himself.

Well, he wasn't going—not to Paris anyway, he decided as he knotted blue silk at his throat. He had this stuff with Nadia he needed to deal with in Lisbon. He'd been putting off facing it for too long because he had not wanted to risk Angie finding out.

His grim mouth twisted in derision at his uncharacteristic act of cowardice. One day she was going to have to know. And he was going to have to tell her before someone else did it for him.

Shrugging into his jacket, he took a deep breath and walked back into the bedroom with the intention of telling Angie that Paris was off the agenda. Only to pull to a stop when all he could see of her was the fiery top of her head.

The sight held him captive for a few seconds, a ruefully amused smile catching hold of his mouth. The last time he'd found Angie like this had been at their London apartment, when she'd foolishly believed he would leave her to sleep in a different bedroom. The rat in him then had taken the decision to haul her out of her blissful sleep. This time the loving husband in him would leave her sleeping and call her later from Lisbon, to let her know where he was.

He left the room as silently as a thief stealing away from a crime scene.

Angie sat up as the door drew shut. He hadn't even bothered to say goodbye to her.

Hurt clambered all over her insides. She hoped his fancy private plane developed engine trouble and kept him imprisoned on the airport tarmac so he couldn't keep his sleazy assignation. She hoped—

Hearing the throaty sound of a car engine, Angie slithered out of bed and walked over to the window to watch as his red Ferrari flashed up from the side of the house, then sped away down the drive with the sun glinting on its shiny bodywork. He had not been able to get away fast enough. Standing here watching him go, she felt as if he'd driven over her body without noticing in his eagerness to get to his lover.

Tears developed. She blinked them away. The rolling waves of shock and hurt still played with the muscles around her stomach. The name Nadia beat like a drum in her head.

Her mobile phone started ringing somewhere in the dressing room, and she turned in a daze and went to find it.

'Good morning, sweetie.' Carla's light, slightly dry voice greeted her. 'Do we have a deal? Are you ready to stop playing the pampered wife and start working on the Lisbon project?'

Angie blinked a couple of times before 'the Lisbon project' meant something. Trying to get her brain into gear was like crawling through mud.

'I...yes,' she answered, because saying no or that she didn't know would make this conversation just too complicated right now. 'I w-was thinking of research-ing suitable business premises today,' Angie managed to say, with reasonable intelligence—mainly because it was the truth. She *had* been intending to look for suit-able premises. 'Do you have any specific ideas in mind as to what you want?'

'Oh, *you're* supposed to know Lisbon, Angie. I've hardly ever visited the place,' Carla answered with a languid lack of interest. 'Somewhere suitably elegant with the right postcode, I suppose. I don't know. Why don't you ask Roque, since this is his brainchild? All I had to do was agree to the concept.'

Angie's head went back as if Carla had punched her. 'You—you mean *Roque* set this up?' Angie could barely get the words past her thick throat.

'He still hasn't told you?' For once in her languid life, Carla's voice sharpened.

'No,' Angie said abruptly. Not even when they'd dis-cussed it the night before.

'It appears I've let his surprise cat out of the bag, then,' sighed Carla. 'He needed to find something for you to do to keep you happy in Portugal, sweetie. And to tell the truth I didn't want to lose you completely. So I thought, if he's happy to shell out the money why not let him set me up in Lisbon? The exotic dark Latin look is very high-fashion right now. With you at the helm, scouting for new talent, we could even put ourselves a jump ahead of our competitors. And, talking about dark Latin models, now that you and Roque have resolved your differences about what happened a year ago, how would you feel about Nadia joining you in the venture?'

Nadia...? Angie suddenly felt as if she was eating glass. 'Wh-why Nadia?'

'Because she's living in Lisbon, too,' said Carla impatiently. 'Don't tell me you didn't know that either, Angie? This is really very bad of Roque—to still be keeping you in the dark about all of this. I suppose he thought it wasn't important. After all, you must believe he's telling the truth when he insists the whole Nadia thing never happened, or you wouldn't have gone back to him, would you?'

Roque *knew* that Nadia was living in Lisbon?

'No,' Angie breathed indistinctly, 'I wouldn't.'

'Well, then, have a good think about the Nadia thing. She will come in very useful since she speaks the lingo. And, like you, she's at a loose end right now.'

'She—she isn't modelling any more?' Angie tried her best to make the question sound casual.

'I know you can be blind when you want to be, Angie, but you surely have not been so blinkered that you didn't know Nadia has been out of the modelling game since she got pregnant last year? I think the baby is a couple of months old now.'

Angie was beginning to feel sick again. And she felt so cold suddenly that she didn't think she was ever going to warm up again. 'Do…?' She had to stop to swallow the thick lump in her throat. 'Do you have a contact address for her?'

'Sure. Wait a second while I access it…'

Angie waited. Angie waited and didn't breathe, and didn't allow herself to think beyond waiting.

'Here it is. Sounds very elegant. The Palácio de Ribeiro. It's—'

Angie cut the connection and tossed the phone away from her as if it burnt. The Palácio de Ribeiro was Roque's city address. It took him just fifteen minutes to walk from there to his Lisbon office building, and… and…

Nadia was living in Roque's Lisbon apartment.

Nothing could have been more black and white.

No wonder he'd spent three weeks avoiding taking her into Lisbon. He'd been scared she might come face to face with his lover before he'd worked out how he was going to convince Angie to accept his sordid little *ménage à trois*.

And a baby.

His baby?

Angie turned and ran for the bathroom. This time it physically hurt, because she was trying to throw up from an empty stomach. By the time she'd managed to make it back to the bedroom it was all she could do to sink down on the bed, where she sat with her eyes closed because the world was spinning.

It was only when she rested a hand against the

sensitive wall of her stomach, because it was still throbbing, that a sudden and terrifying thought rushed into her head.

She stared down at the hand. What if Roque was right about—?

No—no, please not that, she thought pitifully. But she was already dragging herself to her feet to go and recover her phone. Her eyes were burning, her fingers trembling, as she flicked through the menu looking for her personal calendar. A minute later she was sinking down on the edge of the bed again, a limp and quivering wreck.

CHAPTER TEN

IT HIT Roque when he was halfway to Lisbon, and he almost caused a major pile-up behind him when he slammed his foot down on the brakes.

'*Mãe de Deus,*' he bit out.

Angie had overheard his telephone conversation with Nadia.

Cursing in every language he could think of, he checked the traffic, then took his chances, swinging the long luxury car into a sleek U-turn that would send him back the way he had come. Car horns sounded in protest—he barely registered them, or the angry shouts of abuse aimed at him as he accelerated away.

Maria had told him they'd been out on the balcony when Angie became ill. His wife—his unashamedly lazy in the morning wife—had decided to get up earlier than usual, and had been standing right above him when he took Nadia's call.

His jawline fiercely clenched, he tried to remember what he'd said, but could recall hardly a damn word. Not that it mattered. He shook his grim head. He knew that he must have called Nadia by name. Just as he knew that Angie had heard him say it. And hearing him say it had made Angie sick to her stomach. It had made her break apart.

Fingers tightening around the steering wheel, he put his foot down hard on the accelerator.

Entering the master suite as Angie strode out from the dressing room, Maria pulled to a breath-catching standstill.

'You go out, *senhora*?' Maria asked, in a voice laced with disbelief—which was not surprising when the last time she'd seen her Angie had been heaving into the toilet bowl.

Now she was dressed in a breathtakingly elegant white linen dress touched with stylised brushstrokes of emerald-green. The dress skimmed Angie's long slender figure, and had *couture* sewed into every invisible seam. The neckline was square, the bodice cinched into the waist by a shiny green belt, and the skirt skimmed midway down her amazingly long thighs. And the shiny green shoes she was wearing elevated her height by an impossible five inches at least.

'To Sintra,' Angie confirmed. 'Will you ask Antonio to bring the Range Rover around to the front steps for me, please?'

'*Sim*, I will see to it.' The little maid nodded. 'You— wish Antonio to drive you?'

Angie shook her head. 'I will drive myself,' she said, for this was one errand she needed to do on her own. She was going to Sintra to find a chemist, so she could purchase a pregnancy testing kit. And she'd needed to pull on all this supermodel armour just to keep her functioning without falling into shattered little pieces.

Maria continued to hover like an anxious bird, not

at all comfortable with this turn of events. 'If—if you like, I could go to Sintra for you,' she offered eagerly. 'It will be no trouble, and Senhor Roque will be back from Lisbon soon—'

Lisbon? Angie frowned. 'He's gone to Paris, Maria,' she informed the little maid.

'No—no. He is gone to Lisbon,' Maria insisted. 'He said he had business there he must attend to this morning, but he will be back as quickly as he can because—because you are f-feeling unwell.'

So the Paris trip was yet another lie he'd told her...

'Tell Antonio about the car, Maria,' Angie breathed unsteadily.

'*Sim, senhora.*' Too well-trained to argue, the maid dipped a stiff little curtsy and whipped out of the room, leaving Angie alone to field this last hard knock to her fragile composure without a witness to watch her do it.

Somehow—she did not remember how—she found herself standing outside the *quinta*'s front entrance. The sun was shining hotly down from an azure sky. Everything around her looked clear and sharp and picture-postcard-perfect—the greens of the gardens, the bright pinks and purples of the trailing bougainvillaea against the apricot walls of the house, and the shiny black bulk of the Range Rover awaiting her at the bottom of the front steps.

She did not recall climbing into it. She did not recall switching on the engine and driving away. She fixed all her concentration on finding her way to Sintra in a car she had never driven before, on roads as foreign to her as the husband to whom she had given all her faith.

Roque slowed down to take the turn in through the gates of the Quinta d'Agostinho then powered up again to shoot the car into the tunnel of leafy trees. Coming out into the bright sunlight a few minutes later, he saw his home standing sure and solid in its elegant spread of sweeping lawns, backed by a forest of trees.

He glanced up at the balcony situated directly above the swimming pool, envisaged Angie standing there listening to the conversation taking place below her, and felt as if his skin was peeling back from his flesh as he played out what had happened next.

But that weird feeling was nothing compared to the one he experienced when he drove down towards the garages and saw that his Range Rover was missing. Diving out of his car, he strode into the house and shouted for Zetta at the top of his voice. His housekeeper came hurrying into the grand hallway from the rear of the house.

'Where is the Range Rover?' he demanded, a shade unsteadily.

The housekeeper wrung her hands together. 'The *senhora* take it out, Senhor Roque. Maria said she has gone into Sintra.'

Sintra? A wave of relief flooded through him. For a few minutes there he'd convinced himself that Angie had done a runner on him again, and was already on her way to the airport, meaning to disappear off the face of the earth.

'Why has she gone to Sintra?' He frowned, not seeing a link between the reason he had come rushing back here and their local town.

'I do not think Maria asked,' Zetta answered. 'She was more concerned that the *senhora* insisted on driving herself when she has on these very high shoes—'

Roque's tension levels shot up again. 'Are you telling me that Antonio is not driving her?'

Still wringing her hands, Zetta nodded.

'But she does not know the car. She does not know the roads. She hardly ever drives herself anywhere, and—*Mãe de Deus.*' His voice broke down into a low hoarse husk. 'She is—unwell…'

The moment Angie realised that she was completely and utterly lost came around two hours later. Pulling the car onto a clearing somewhere way up in the hills, overlooking the sea, she sat back with a sigh of defeat.

She'd found her way into Sintra by following the well-posted road signs. She'd even found a convenient car park, and her purchase now lay with her bag on the seat next to her. Everything up to that point had been so much easier than she'd expected it to be—but she'd soon learned that getting back to the Quinta d'Agostinho was a different matter altogether.

Roque's private estate was not signposted. And the road out of Sintra had taken her a different way from the one on which she'd come in. It had seemed logical that so long as she kept on driving she would eventually notice something familiar to use as a guide.

'Great logic, Angie,' she mumbled.

Now the sun was high, and the car was already stifling. She'd only killed the air-conditioning two minutes ago, when she'd switched off the car engine.

Reaching up, she ran a hand around the back of her neck and lifted her hair away from her hot skin. On the seat beside her with her bag was the half-drunk bottle of water she'd had the sense to purchase before she got herself lost. And beside it lay her mobile phone, which she'd tried to use several times only to discover there was no signal. On an act of pure frustration she'd switched the stupid thing off.

Still… With little hope that it was going to be any different this time, she let her hair fall back down onto her nape, then reached for the phone and switched it on again.

The moment it had powered up the messages began downloading like flickering shouts. Most of them from Roque, she saw. A couple from Carla, and even one from her brother, who had been calling her twice a week since he'd gone to Brazil—duty calls, to reassure her that he was enjoying himself, Angie recognised with a grimace of a smile.

About to try calling Roque again, she felt the phone suddenly leap into life in her fingers.

'Angie? *Graças a Deus.* Where the hell are you?' Roque's deep rasping voice raked into her ear.

'Lost,' she admitted. 'Up in the hills somewhere.'

'Lost? In the hills?' he repeated, as if most of Portugal wasn't covered in them. 'Why didn't you call to tell me so?'

'No signal until now,' she explained, feeling oddly as if she was having this conversation with a complete stranger rather than the husband she'd discovered was a lying cheat.

A stunning silence fell down between them for several seconds, then she heard Roque pull in a deep breath. 'Okay, so you are lost,' he murmured more calmly. 'Be a good girl and activate the car's satellite navigation system. It will pinpoint your position and then you can tell me what it says. I will come and get you.'

'But I don't want you to come and get me,' Angie told him.

'Yes, you do!' Roque exploded all over again. 'Have you any idea how much trouble you've caused by getting lost? Maria is weeping all over the place, and I was about half a minute away from calling the police. Only a madwoman drives off into the hills without knowing where she is going, so do as I tell you, Angie, and switch on the damn—'

The line went dead. Roque bit out a string of filthy curses. Lost in the hills… He turned full circle, a set of long fingers scoring through his already dishevelled hair, then grabbed hold of the back of his neck. She'd been gone for hours, so she could be anywhere.

When did he get to be so stupid? How did *she* get to drive at all in the kind of shoes Maria had described?

He tried to connect to her phone again.

Angie ignored the phone's ring while she touched buttons until she finally brought the satellite navigation screen to life, then she sat staring at the screen. It showed her a map with hardly anything on it except for a thin thread of road. All the information was in Portuguese. With no clue as to how she changed it to English, or even if she could change it, the map was, therefore, of absolutely no use.

She recovered her phone and allowed the connection. 'I've got the satellite thing working, but—'

'Angelina, I am about to lose my temper here.' Roque's grim voice cut across hers. 'So do yourself a favour and don't cut our connection again!'

'It's all in Portuguese,' she continued as if he had not interrupted her. 'You are going to have to tell me what to do so that I can understand it.'

She heard him suck in another deep breath. She felt him fighting to control his temper. Angie did not offer up any encouragement, just waited until he spoke again. 'I will talk you through it, so concentrate...'

The drive back down through the forest-strewn hills was relatively simple now she had her own personal pilot to guide her, Angie discovered. Roque had instructed her on how to make the car's computer recognise her mobile phone, and now the deep cool sound of his voice filled the car via its speakers, firing questions and directions at her as she drove. In a strange way Angie found it comforting to have him there with her, though she wasn't sure why—because she had certainly shut down from *feeling* anything else right now.

Self-preservation kicking in, she assumed, as she glimpsed signs of civilisation appearing in front of her, and only a few minutes later she was joining the main highway. Relief was a feeling, she acknowledged as she heaved out another sigh.

It was only a short second later that a red Ferrari flashed up beside her, then shot past, only to pull in front of her two metres away from her front bumper.

'Is that you?' she gasped in surprise.

'*Sim*, it is me,' Roque responded.

'But—what are you doing here?'

'I am here to make sure that you don't get lost again before I have had a chance to throttle you, *meu querida*,' he explained, so smoothly Angie almost missed the threat threading through his silken tone.

'Just—go to hell, *meu querido*,' Angie said, and switched the phone off, preferring to finish the rest of the journey following his car without having to listen to him at the same time.

She hated him, she remembered. He was a lying, cheating, self-seeking playboy. The minute she got back to the house she was going to pack her things and *leave*. Her head was aching. She hadn't eaten anything all day. She had a stupid pregnancy test lying on the seat beside her, and *he* had his mistress waiting for him not far away.

The first strangled sob tore from her as she followed him through the *quinta* gates, then into the tunnel of trees. By the time she came out again into hot bright sunlight the tears were trickling down her cheeks.

She stopped the car behind his at the front steps, then reached up to wipe the tears away with one hand while the other fumbled to unlock her seat belt. Reaching for her things from the seat beside her, she was about to open the car door when it suddenly flew open, and Roque stood there, looking less than his usual immaculate self.

Angie allowed herself a brief flickering glance at him. His hard-edged face was marblelike, the golden skin across the curving sweep of his cheekbones pulled tight. He stuck out a long-fingered hand in a grimly silent offer to assist her to alight from the car, but she ignored it, preferring to slide her long legs out over the high sill to land on slender heels the length of five-inch spikes.

The hand stretched out again, as if to steady her just in case the slender heels would not support her, and Angie quivered. 'Don't touch me,' she whispered, then brushed around him and ran up the steps to the house.

Ramming his rejected hand into a fist, Roque watched her almost twist off one of the ridiculous shoes in her rush to get away from him, and bit back a colourful oath. 'For God's sake, Angie, be careful—'

For God's sake, Angie turned into *For God's sake, Nadia* in her head, and her spine shot erect with a jerk as she strode as fast as she dared into the house

She'd already crossed the vast empty space of the grand hallway and was running up the stairs by the time Roque reached the front door. Her white and green dress clung to every slender curve and her hair hung in a rich river of fire between her taut shoulderblades. The shoes were too high. The marble staircase was unforgiving to anyone who should fall on it. He'd seen the tracks of tears streaking her pale cheeks before she'd pushed past him, and—

'Slow down before you break your neck!' he roared as he strode after her. 'You are *not* going to shake me off, Angie, so you might as well stop trying!'

Angie had reached the graceful curve of the upper landing by then, and she spun round and leant over the banister. Halfway up the marble staircase Roque paused and looked at her, and that unfair, totally unyielding crash of attraction she always felt when she looked at him caught Angie full-on. The way he was standing there, with one foot elevated to the higher step, one long-fingered hand resting lightly against the banister rail sensually—as if he was caressing the rich dark colonial wood. Everything about him was sensual, from the untidy state of his jet silk hair to the striped shirt hanging open at his throat. The unsmiling taut mouth, the slightly flaring nostrils, the deep, dark bottomless eyes looking at her with...

'You are a total womanising rat.' She broke down on the first helpless sob. 'If—if I had a knife handy I would be jumping over this rail so I could plunge it into your chest!'

Roque released a sigh. 'I can explain about Nadia—'

'Don't you *dare* use that woman's name in front of me!' she choked out. 'I don't know why you didn't marry *her*, since you obviously can't live without h-her.'

'What you overheard on the terrace this morning was—'

'Do I look as if want an explanation?' Angie tossed down at him like an electric thunderbolt. 'And anyway, it's too late. I *know* all about Nadia and her baby. I *know* you have them neatly stashed away inside your stupid Lisbon apartment.'

His expression changed. She saw the guilty flicker. 'Angie—'

'Don't you dare come up here,' she said as he started walking again. 'If you come up here I will kill you, I promise. I don't want you near me ever again!'

And with that she leapt away from the rail and ran to shut herself in their suite. She wanted to throw herself down on the bed and sob her eyes out, but knowing he could only be a few seconds behind her she locked herself inside her bathroom instead.

When she came out again she was wrapped in her bathrobe, having spent ages just standing beneath the fierce shower jets, pale as milk. The need to shed tears all over the place had gone now. In fact she felt horribly hollow and flat.

There was no sign of Roque, though she did not go looking around the rest of the suite to check. Instead she walked over to the centre island unit, slid open one of the drawers, then lifted out the tissue-wrapped parcel and laid it down gently on the top.

Perhaps it was fated that Roque should approach her right then, with the silent stealth of a mugger. The first Angie knew of his presence was when his hands came from behind her and settled on the top of the unit, effectively trapping her within the circle of his body and his arms. He'd showered too, she noticed as she picked up on the clean scent of his soap. And he was wearing a matching bathrobe to the one she was wearing.

'Let us get a few things straight while we have some calmness here,' he murmured, bringing his dark head low enough that his breath brushed her cheek. 'Nadia is *not* my mistress.'

With her head dipped, Angie responded with an inelegant sniff.

'Her baby is not *my* baby. She does *not* live in my apartment. She lives in the one *below*, with the man she *married* several months ago. *He* is her baby's father. He is Brazilian, very rich, quite old, and just out of a nasty divorce in Rio in which Nadia was cited as the adulterous cause—hence their swift move here, away from the hostile backlash.'

Angie hunched her shoulders inside the white towelling and said not a word.

Roque inhaled a deep breath. 'I know I should have told you about Nadia before now,' he continued. 'But I am stupid and arrogant. And three weeks ago I wanted to keep Nadia as a weapon to use against you if you—if you hurt me again. Also, I did not see why I should be forced into defending myself for something I did not do. Since then there has not seemed to be the right moment for me to tell you she is here in Lisbon, so I kept the information to myself—like a coward.'

When Angie still held her silence, even with the deliberate provocation he'd offered her with the coward confession, he invited, 'Will you say something? Even if it is only *I hate you, Roque*…'

'I'm pregnant,' Angie whispered.

For a few wretched seconds she thought he hadn't understood her, because he remained so silent and still.

So she tried again. 'I said I am pregnant.'

'I heard you,' he husked.

'I w-went to Sintra to buy a testing kit, and I am positively, properly p-pregnant…again.'

The last word came out all wobbly. She tried swallowing and found she couldn't. She tried blinking the moisture out of her eyes but it just swam back in. Behind her she could feel the throbbing power of his tension. Lifting her hands off the white tissue, she closed them into fists.

'Explain the *again* part,' he said finally.

Angie tried again to swallow the trembling lump in her throat, then just let it all pour out. He did not move a single muscle. He wasn't even breathing as far as she could tell. When she faltered to a halt, the final thing to tremble from her lips was, 'Now I'm scared the same thing is going to happen again…'

Trying to drag himself out of the dark place his mind had gone into, Roque blinked his eyes. The one small chink of light he could see in what she had just confessed to him was that at least this time she was standing here telling him, instead of running away to hide.

And she had every right to feel scared. *He* felt scared. And the same damn issues that had torn their marriage apart twelve months ago were still hanging around, threatening to do the same thing again.

'I bought the apartment from Nadia's husband this morning. They have decided to move to Spain.' he said, not surprised when Angie quivered in front of him. He'd hurt her by ignoring the import of what she'd said. But he was not ignoring it. He was cleaning it. 'When I explained to him the predicament I was in due to our past dealings with Nadia he was not pleased. He had no idea that she'd done to another marriage what she had done to his own. The difference for him is that he *did* have an affair with her. She *did* conceive his child—his only child. His son. And...' His voice wavered ruefully. 'He loves her. I saw the evidence in his face because I *know* how it feels to love someone so badly you are stuck with that one true love for life.'

'Badly?' Angie squeezed out.

'As in bad for me,' Roque confirmed. 'I did not want your brother nudging in between us. I did not want your career commitments to take precedence over mine. That kiss with Nadia on the dance floor was me behaving badly. When the result of it blew up in my face and you walked away from me I got what I deserved. I gave you nothing but hassle and heartache.'

'No...' At last Angie stopped just standing there, still hiding from him, and swivelled round to wrap her arms tightly around his waist. 'I was a lousy wife to you. I *let* Alex nudge in between us. I *drove* you into Nadia's arms. I was wildly in love with you but didn't know how to love you. I'm so sorry,' she finished helplessly. 'I should have told you about—about the baby. You had a right to know. Instead I hid away.'

'Because I let you down.'

Angie shook her head. 'I let *you* down. I sh-should have given you the opportunity to explain about Nadia.'

'I let you down,' he repeated grimly. 'I let you down because I was not there when you needed me more than you had ever needed me. I think that makes me a lousy husband, Angie. If you want to stick that knife in my chest I will let you.'

He was not joking. 'I think I've already done it,' Angie murmured contritely.

'*Sim*,' Roque agreed. 'Now you say you are pregnant again.'

'And I'm scared,' she repeated, in case he had missed that bit when she'd said it earlier.

He hadn't. Without the slightest of warning he gathered her up into his arms and carried her through to the bedroom. Dragging back the covers, he deposited her on the bed, then came down beside her and enclosed her in his embrace.

'You are going to stop thinking about the worst-case scenario, okay?' he instructed.

'Okay.' Angie nodded.

'Let me do all the worrying for you.' He lifted a hand to stroke her hair away from the side of her face. 'You just think pleasant thoughts from now on, and we will deal with this together—as we should have done the time before.'

Angie nodded again.

'No more running around in high-heeled shoes. No more getting lost in hills. And no more fights about stupid Nadia,' he added. 'In fact, no more fights at all.'

'Okay,' Angie agreed.

'First thing we do tomorrow is go and see a doctor. If necessary we will fly over to London and consult with a—'

'I hope you feed me before then,' Angie posed wistfully. 'I haven't eaten a thing today and I'm starving to death.'

'Why didn't you say so before?' He was already trying to get up when Angie grabbed hold of him and brought him back to her.

'No, don't go,' she breathed tautly. 'I like it when you hold me. It makes me feel—safe.'

'Loved,' Roque said with a faint edge of tension as he came back into her embrace. 'The word you hesitated over using is *loved*.'

'Loved and safe, then,' Angie extended, then her beautiful green eyes misted over and her soft mouth trembled. 'I love you so much,' she whispered softly. 'I was so miserable when I thought I'd lost you.'

That edge of tension left him, and he gathered her closer so he could cover her mouth with a slow, incredibly tender kiss.

Of course the kiss didn't stay slow and tender. It never could for them. As the passion intensified and their legs tangled together and their breathing quickened, Angie was not in the least bit amused when he suddenly drew back.

'We can't,' he groaned out hoarsely, flinging himself flat onto his back. 'We have to think about the baby now.'

He was oh-so right, and Angie just didn't know what so say. Sorry seemed appropriate, because she just couldn't imagine how they were going to manage for long months without indulging their desire for each other—if she carried this baby through to the end.

'I could always…' She fed a hand down his long tense body, only to have Roque snatch it away.

'I wasn't complaining,' he said frowningly. 'Don't even think like that again.'

'Sorry,' whispered from her lips in genuine contrition. 'I was being—impulsive.'

'You were being adorable,' he groaned, rolling over to gather her in close again. 'We will just have to practise self-control, that's all.'

'Or…we could get up and drive into Lisbon to see the doctor now. Check out what's safe for us and what isn't?'

Eyes like black caverns spun with hints of bronzed mockery captured hers. 'You insatiable witch,' Roque murmured.

Angie just looked up at him and said nothing. He shifted his gaze to her defiantly pouting mouth. A lazy teasing smile spread across his own mouth, then suddenly died again.

'Okay, let's go,' he announced.

The water was glorious, all warm and silkily soapy. Angie lay in it, feeling like an exotic siren being pampered by her loving slave.

'If this bump grows any bigger we will have to install a deeper bath,' Roque complained as he stroked the flat of his hand over her tightly swollen abdomen.

'You love this bump,' Angie murmured lazily. 'You love getting into this bath with me.'

Water sloshed as he shifted his position and came to stretch out at her side, his long, lean bronze-skinned body the perfect contrast to Angie's pearly white slenderness—not including the bump.

'It works for us, my voluptuous one,' he teased her, stroking his fingers around the soapy globe of one lush breast. 'When I am ready, I can slide inside you with the minimum of effort required on your part—and don't you just love it when I do?'

The roaming hand slid lower, meandering away from her breast so he could replace his fingers there with his mouth. Angie stirred on a sensuous murmur of pleasure. The roaming fingers dipped between her thighs, sending her eyelashes fluttering upwards and her head turning on its waterproof pillow.

'Kiss me,' she begged.

Her handsome slave complied. Her arms lifted up, then fell again around his neck, and he made the kiss mimic the sensuous action of his caressing fingers.

It was all so gloriously beautiful she murmured, 'Love you,' against his lips.

'Show me,' he encouraged, and she did show him. She wasn't so restricted by her advanced pregnancy that she could not indulge him as much as he was indulging her.

The first few months had meant weeks of restraint and carefully controlled anxiety, until she'd finally accepted that she was not going to miscarry this precious baby as she had their first child. These last few months had been filled with the most wonderful moments of pure happiness and exquisite lovemaking, with days filled with planning for their baby, and nights filled with perfect passion offered by the man who loved her more than she'd ever dared believe was possible.

She loved to feel his senses quicken for her. She loved

to see the burning heat of his desire for her blaze in his eyes. She loved it when he came over her, as he was doing now, and made that first slow drive with his hips that joined them. She loved to see the fierce depth of his desire for her strip everything but his love for her from his beautiful face.

Reaching up, she touched his lips with her fingers, and smiled tenderly when he kissed them. Then she wasn't smiling—she was drowning, in him, and in what he could make her feel.

Later they lay together in their bed, with the winter moonlight tracing a path across the windows. Angie felt her baby give her a pummelling kick, and smiled when Roque soothed his son with a stroke of his hand.

'To think,' she said, 'we almost lost all of this.'

It didn't seem possible they had come so close to the brink.

'*A esperança é a última que morre,*' Roque murmured.

'You've said that before.' Angie turned to look at him. 'What does it mean?'

One of those impassive smiles she found difficult to read passed across his face. 'Hope is the last one to die,' he translated.

He had never lost faith.

'Oh, Roque, come and look at this,' Angie called softly.

She was leaning on their balcony rail, looking down on the pool terrace below. Feeling the stroke of his hands as they claimed her waist, Angie indicated with her head to the sunny terrace, where her brother Alex sat on a sun lounger with their son sitting within the protective circle of his strong tanned legs.

Alex was reading out loud from one of his course books, while six-month old Luis listened, his attention fixed on his uncle's face and the melodious resonance of his voice.

'Do you think we have produced a genius?' Roque posed dryly.

'They get on like a house on fire.' Angie smiled. 'My handsome grown-up brother and my beautiful son.'

'I am feeling left out again,' her handsome husband murmured.

'Oh, dear.' She turned around to look at him. 'Three—I have *three* demanding men to deal with,' she sighed.

'And you love it.' Roque had no sympathy. 'Your beautiful son had you to himself all morning. Your handsome brother had you to himself all afternoon. When is it my turn?'

As if he did not know, thought Angie, as she laughed and allowed him to draw her in through the balcony doors.

Angie sent him a questioning look when he stepped around her to pull the doors shut. 'I am saving your blushes because you are about to get noisy,' he explained.

Angie blushed anyway. 'You are—'

'Mad for you,' Roque inserted, silencing her with his first scorching kiss.

VOWS MADE
IN SECRET

LOUISE FULLER

To my husband, Patrick, who provided inspiration not just for the love scenes but the emotional conflict!

CHAPTER ONE

SCOWLING, A LOCK of dark hair falling onto his forehead, Laszlo Cziffra de Zsadany stared at the young woman with smooth fair hair. His jaw tightened involuntarily as he studied her face in silence, noting the contrast between the innocence of the soft grey eyes and the passionate promise of her full mouth.

She was beautiful. So beautiful that it was impossible not to stand and stare. Such beauty could seduce and enslave. For such a woman a man would relinquish his throne, betray his country and lose his sanity.

Laszlo smiled grimly. He might even get married!

His smile faded and, feeling restless and on edge, he leant forward and squinted at the cramped, curled inscription at the bottom of the painting. Katalina Csesnek de Veszprem. But even though his eyes were fixed intently on the writing his mind kept drifting back to the face of the sitter. He gritted his teeth. What was it about this painting that he found so unsettling? But even as he asked himself the question he shrank from acknowledging the answer.

Anger jostled with misery as he stared at the face, seeing not Katalina but another, whose name was never spoken for to do so would burn his lips. Of course it wasn't so very like *her*; there were similarities, in colouring and the shape of her jaw, but that was all.

Disconcerted by the intense and unwelcome emotions stirred up by a pair of grey eyes, he glanced longingly out of the window at the Hungarian countryside. And then he froze as he heard an unmistakable hooting. It was bad luck to hear an owl's cry in daylight and his golden eyes narrowed as he uneasily searched the pale blue sky for the bird.

From behind him there was a thump as Besnik, his lurcher, sat down heavily on the stone floor. Sighing, Laszlo reached down and rubbed the dog's silky ears between his thumb and forefinger.

'I know,' he murmured softly. 'You're right. I need some air. Come.' Standing up straight, he clicked his fingers so that the dog leapt lightly to its feet. 'Let's go! Before I start counting magpies.'

He wandered slowly through the castle's corridors. The wood panelling on the walls gleamed under the low lights, and the familiar smell of beeswax and lavender calmed him as he walked down the stairs. Passing his grandfather's study, he noticed that the door was ajar and, glancing inside, he saw with some surprise that the room wasn't empty; his grandfather, Janos, was sitting at his desk.

Laszlo felt his chest tighten as he took in how small and frail Janos appeared to be. Even now, more than six years after his wife Annuska's death, his grandfather still seemed to bear the burden of her loss. For a moment he hesitated. And then, softly, he closed the door. There had been an almost meditative quality to his grandfather's stillness and he sensed that Janos needed to be alone.

He wondered why his grandfather was up so early. And then he remembered. Of course. Seymour was arriving today!

No wonder Janos had been unable to sleep. Collecting art had been his hobby for over thirty years: a personal, private obsession. But today, for the first time ever, he would reveal that collection to a stranger—this expert, Edmund Seymour, who was arriving from London.

Laszlo grimaced. He instinctively distrusted strangers and he felt a ripple of dislike for Seymour—a man he'd never met, and to whom he had never so much as uttered a word, but whose company he would now have to suffer for weeks.

Pushing a door open with his shoulder, he glanced warily into the kitchen and then breathed out slowly. Good! Rosa wasn't up. He wasn't ready to face her gimlet eye yet. Apart from his grandfather their housekeeper was the only other person from whom he couldn't hide his feelings. Only, unlike Janos, Rosa had no qualms about cross-examining him.

Pulling open the cavernous fridge, he groaned as he saw the cold meats and salads arranged on the shelves.

And then, despite the rush of cold air on his face, and the even colder lump of resentment in his chest, he felt his mood shift and he closed the fridge door gently. Food had been a comforting distraction during his grandmother's long illness. But by the time of her death it had become a passion—a passion that had led to him financing a restaurant in the centre of Budapest. The restaurant had been his project: it had been a risk, and a lot of hard work, but he thrived on both and he was now the owner of a staggeringly successful chain of high street restaurants.

Laszlo lifted his chin. He was no longer just Janos's grandson but a wealthy, independent businessman in his own right.

He sighed. Not that he wasn't proud of being a de Zsadany. It was just that the name brought certain responsibilities along with it. Such as Seymour's impending visit. He gritted his teeth. If only the blasted man would ring and cancel.

As if on cue, his mobile phone vibrated in his pocket. Clumsy with shock, and a ridiculous sense of guilt, he pulled it out with shaking fingers: it was Jakob! Relief, and the tiniest feeling of regret, washed over him.

'Laszlo! I thought you'd be up. I know you'll have forgotten, so I've just rung to remind you that we have a visitor arriving today.'

Laszlo shook his head. Typical Jakob—ringing to check up on him. Jakob Frankel was the de Zsadany family lawyer, and a good man, but Laszlo couldn't imagine letting his guard down with him or any other outsider. Not any more: not after what had happened the last time.

'I know you won't believe me, Jakob, but I did actually remember it was happening today.'

He heard the lawyer laugh nervously.

'Excellent! I've arranged a car, but if you could be on hand to greet—?'

'Of course I will,' Laszlo interrupted testily, irritated by the tentative note in the lawyer's voice. He paused, aware that he sounded churlish. 'I want to be there,' he muttered roughly. 'And let me know if I can do anything else.' It was the nearest he got to an apology.

'Of course. Of course! But I'm sure that won't be necessary.' Jakob spoke hurriedly, his desire to end the conversation clearly overriding his normal deference.

Laszlo murmured non-committally. For most of his life Janos's hobby had seemed a strangely soulless and senseless exercise. But Annuska's death had changed that opinion as it had changed everything else.

After her funeral life at the castle had grown increasingly bleak. Janos had been in a state of shock, inconsolable with grief. But once the shock had worn off his misery had turned into a kind of depression—a lethargy which no amount of time seemed able to heal. Laszlo had been in despair; weeks and months had turned into years. Until slowly, and then with increasing momentum, his grandfather had become almost his old self.

The reason for his recovery, like all catalysts for change, had been wholly unexpected. A stack of letters between Annuska and Janos had reminded him of their mutual passion for art.

Tentatively, not daring to hope, Laszlo had encouraged his grandfather to revive his former hobby. To his surprise, Janos had begun to lose his listless manner and then, out of the blue, his grandfather had decided to have his sprawling collection catalogued. Seymour's auction house in London had been contacted and its flamboyant owner, Edmund Seymour, had duly been invited to visit Kastely Almasy.

Laszlo grimaced. His grandfather's happiness had overridden his own feeling but how on earth was he going to put up with this stranger in his home?

Jakob's voice broke into his thoughts.

'I mean, I know how you hate having people around—' There was a sudden awkward silence and then the lawyer cleared his throat. 'What I meant to say was—'

Laszlo interrupted him curtly. 'There are more than thirty rooms at the castle, Jakob, so I think I'll be able to cope with one solitary guest, don't you?'

He felt a sudden, fierce stab of self-loathing. Seymour could stay for a year if it made his grandfather happy. And, really, what was a few weeks? Since Annuska's death time had ceased to matter. Nothing much mattered except healing his grandfather.

'I can manage,' he repeated gruffly.

'Of course…of course.' The lawyer laughed nervously. 'You might even enjoy it. In fact, Janos was only saying to me yesterday that this visit might be a good opportunity to invite some of the neighbours for drinks or dinner. The Szecsenyis are always good fun and they have a daughter around your age.'

In the early-morning light the room seemed suddenly grey and cold, like a tomb. Laszlo felt his fingers tighten around the handset as his heart started to pound out a drumroll of warning.

He took a shallow breath, groping for calm. 'I'll think about it,' he said finally. His tone was pleasant, but there was no mistaking the note of high-tensile steel in his voice. 'I mean, our guest may simply prefer paintings to people.'

He knew what his grandfather really wanted, and why he had inveigled Jakob into suggesting it. Janos secretly longed to see his only grandchild married—to see Laszlo sharing his life with a soulmate. And why wouldn't he? After all, Janos himself had been blissfully happy during his forty-year marriage.

Laszlo's fingers curled into his palms. If only he could do it. If only he could marry a perfectly sweet, pretty girl like Agnes Szecsenyi. That would be worth more than fifty art collections to Janos.

But that was never going to happen. For he had a secret, and no matter how many dinner dates his grandfather engineered, a wife was most certainly not going to result from any of them.

'Now, you *have* read my notes properly, haven't you, Prue? Only you do have a tendency to skim…'

Pushing a strand of pale blonde hair out of her cloud-grey eyes, Prudence Elliot took a deep breath and counted slowly up to ten. Her plane had landed in Hungary only an hour ago, but this was the third time Uncle Edmund had rung her to see how she was doing: in other words, he was checking up on her.

Edmund paused. 'I don't want to sound like a nag, but it's just… Well, I just wish I could be there with you…you *do* understand?'

His voice cut through her juddering, panicky thoughts and her anxiety was instantly replaced by guilt. Of course she understood. Her uncle had built up the auction house that bore his name from scratch. And today would have undoubtedly been the most important day of his career—the pinnacle of his life's work: cataloguing reclusive Hungarian billionaire Janos Almasy de Zsadany's legendary art collection.

With a lurch of fear, Prudence remembered the look of excitement and terror on Edmund's face when he'd been invited to the de Zsadany castle in Hungary. His words kept replaying in her head.

'The man's a modern Medici, Prue. Of course no one actually knows the exact contents of his collection. But a conservative valuation would be over a billion dollars.'

It should be Edmund with his thirty years of experience sitting in the back of the sleek, shark-nosed de Zsadany limousine. Not Prudence, who felt she could offer little more than her uncle's reputation by proxy. Only Edmund was in England, confined to bed, recovering from a major asthma attack.

Biting her lip, she glanced out of the window at the dark fields. She hadn't wanted to come. But she'd had no choice. Edmund owed money, and with debts mounting and interest accruing on those debts the business was in jeopardy. The fee from the de Zsadany job would balance the books, but the de Zsadany family lawyer had been adamant that work must start immediately. And so, reluctantly, she'd agreed to go to Hungary.

She heard Edmund sigh down the phone.

'I'm sorry, Prue,' he said slowly. 'You shouldn't have to put up with my nagging when you've been so good about all this.'

Instantly she felt ashamed. Edmund was like a father to her. He had given her everything: a home, a family, security and even a job. She wasn't about to let him down now, in his hour of need.

Taking a deep breath, she tried to inject some confi-

dence into her voice. 'Please try not to worry, Edmund.
If I need anything at all I'll ring you. But I'll be fine. I
promise.'

He rang off and gratefully Prudence leant back against
the leather upholstery and closed her eyes until, in what felt
like no time at all, the car began to slow. She opened her
eyes. Two tall wrought-iron gates swung smoothly open to
let the limousine pass, and within minutes she was looking
up at a huge, grey stone castle straight out of a picture book.

Later she would realise that she had no memory of how
she got from the car to the castle. She remembered only that
somehow she had found herself in a surprisingly homely
sitting room, lit softly by a collection of table lamps and
the glow of a log fire. She was about to sit down on a faded
Knole Sofa when she noticed the painting.

Her heart started to pound. Stepping closer, she reached
out with one trembling hand and touched the frame lightly,
and then her eyes made a slow tour of the walls. She felt
light-headed—as though she had woken up in dream. There
were two Picassos—pink period—a delightfully exuber-
ant Kandinsky, a Rembrandt portrait that would have sent
Edmund into a state of near ecstasy, and a pair of exquisite
Lucian Freud etchings of a sleeping whippet.

She was still in a state of moderate shock when an
amused-sounding voice behind her said softly, 'Please—
take a closer look. I'm afraid the poor things get completely
ignored by the rest of us.'

Prudence turned scarlet. To be caught snooping around
someone's sitting room like some sort of burglar was bad
enough, but when that someone was your host, and one of
the richest men in Europe, it was mortifying.

'I'm so—so sorry,' she stammered, turning round.
'What must you...?' The remainder of her apology died
in her throat, the words colliding into one another with
a series of shuddering jolts as her world imploded. For

it was not Janos Almasy de Zsadany standing there but Laszlo Cziffra.

Laszlo Cziffra. Once his name had tasted hot and sweet in her mouth; now it was bitter on her tongue. She felt her insides twist in pain as around her the room seemed to collapse and fold in on itself like a house of cards. It couldn't be Laszlo—it just couldn't. But it was, and she stared at him mutely, reeling from the shock of his perfection.

With his high cheekbones, sleek black hair and burning amber eyes, he was almost the same boy she had fallen in love with seven years ago: her beautiful Romany boy. Only he most certainly wasn't hers any more; nor was he a boy. Now he was unmistakably a man: tall, broad-shouldered, intensely male, and with a suggestion of conformity that his younger self had lacked. Prudence shivered. But it was his eyes that had changed the most. Once, on seeing her, they would have burnt with the fierce lambent fire of passion. Now they were as cold and lifeless as ash.

She felt breathless, almost faint, and her hand moved involuntarily to her throat. Laszlo had been her first love—her first lover. He had been like sunlight and storms. She had never wanted anything or anyone more than him. And he had noticed *her*. Chosen *her* with a certainty that had left her breathless, replete, exultant. She had felt immortal. The knowledge of his love had swelled inside her—an immutable truth as permanent as the sun rising and setting.

Or so she'd believed seven years ago.

Only she'd been wrong. His focus on her—for that was what it had been—had burnt white-hot, fire-bright, and then faded fast like a supernova.

Prudence swallowed. It had been the ugliest thing that had happened to her. After the fierce bliss of what she'd believed was his love, that disorientating darkness had felt like death itself. And now, like a ghost from paradise lost, here he was, defying all logic and reason.

Surely he couldn't be real? And if he was real then what was he doing *here*? It didn't make any sense. She stared at him, groping for some kind of answer. Her stomach lurched as she remembered the last time she'd seen him: being pushed into the back of a police car, his face dark and defiant.

Laszlo didn't belong in a place like this. And yet here he was. Standing there, as though he owned the place.

She felt her stomach lurch. In the back of her mind, pushed down in the darkness, she'd always imagined that he'd drifted into bad ways. So to watch him saunter into the room was almost more than her brain could fathom. Helplessly, she racked her brain for some shred of explanation.

'Wh—what are you doing here?' she stammered, her voice sounding small and shrunken, like a soul facing purgatory.

Laszlo stared at Prudence, his handsome face cold and blank. But inside it was as though he was falling from a great height. His mind was racing, explanations tumbling over one another, each one more desperate and untenable than the last. And all the time, like a silent movie, the short, doomed pretence of their love played out before his eyes.

Aware that he was playing for time, he felt a rush of anger. But words had literally failed him—for he had blotted out all traces of her so completely that just looking at her made him feel dizzy.

'I could ask you the same question,' he murmured.

And then, with shock, he remembered that it had been only that morning that his hunger-fuelled brain had conjured up her memory. He shivered as the hairs stood up on the back of his neck and he remembered the cry of the owl he had heard earlier. Had he somehow summoned her here?

The part of his mind not numb with shock pushed the suggestion away irritably: of course he hadn't. Clearly she hadn't come looking for him, for her own shock was unmistakable. So what exactly was she doing here?

Eyes narrowing, he stared assessingly at her and waited for answers.

White-faced, Prudence stared back at him dazedly. She must have fallen down a rabbit hole, for what other explanation could there be? Why else was Laszlo Cziffra here in this isolated castle in the Hungarian countryside? Unless—her blood turned cold—could he be working for Mr de Zsadany?

Her mind cringed from the possibility and, remembering his blank-eyed indifference when she'd told him she was leaving him, she felt suddenly sick. But that had been seven years ago. Surely after all this time they could treat each other with at the very least a polite neutrality? But instead of cool curiosity, he was watching her with a sort of icy contempt.

'I don't understand—' She broke off, the colour draining from her cheeks as he walked slowly across the faded Persian carpet towards her. 'What are you doing here?' she said again. 'You *can't* be here.'

Watching the shock on her face turn to horror as he approached, Laszlo felt the floor yaw beneath him like a wave-tossed ship. But he had no intention of revealing to Prudence how strongly he was affected by her presence. Or her evident dismay at seeing him again.

Breathing deeply, he steadied himself. 'But I am,' he said slowly. 'Why are you trembling, *pireni*?'

She tried to ignore it. Just as she was trying to ignore how handsome he was and his nerve-jangling nearness. But the familiar word of endearment seemed to grow to a roar inside her head, drowning out her answer to his question.

For what felt like a lifetime they stood, staring at one another in silence, as they had done a hundred…a thousand times before.

The man's voice, when it came, startled both of them.

'Ah, there you are! I'm sorry I'm late. The traffic was terrible.'

A plumpish, middle-aged man, with thick, dull blonde hair and a panicked expression on his face, hurried into the room. Turning to Prudence, he shuffled some files under his arm and held out his hand.

'I'm so sorry to have missed you at the airport, Miss Elliot. You got my message, though?'

Still speechless with shock, Prudence nodded. She had felt a momentary spasm of relief at the man's arrival. But now it would appear that her relief was premature. For his words had made it painfully clear to her that Laszlo's presence was a shock only to *her*.

The man glanced cautiously at Laszlo and cleared his throat. 'I see you two have already met. So let me introduce myself. Jakob Frankel. I work for the law firm that represents Mr de Zsadany. May I say on behalf of the family how grateful we all are for you stepping in at the last moment. It was really very kind of you.'

Laszlo felt his guts twist. His brain was struggling to give meaning to what was happening. Jakob *had* told him that Edmund Seymour was ill and that someone else was coming in his place. Typically, he'd forgotten—for one stranger was no better or worse than another. But suddenly Jakob's words seemed to take on a new and wholly unpalatable significance: Seymour's replacement was *Prudence Elliot*. And that meant she would be living under his roof for the foreseeable future!

'It's my pleasure,' Prudence said hoarsely.

The lawyer nodded and, looking nervously from Prudence to Laszlo, said, 'Everyone is most grateful.'

Prudence smiled weakly and opened her mouth to speak but Laszlo interrupted her.

'Miss Elliot could buy her own castle with the fee we're paying her. I don't think she needs our gratitude as well.'

Flinching at the undertone of hostility in his voice, Prudence felt rather than saw Laszlo's dark, probing gaze turn towards her. Her breath, suddenly sharp and serrated, tore at her throat and she touched her neck nervously. She still had no idea what he was doing here but he must be important, for the lawyer was clearly deferring to him. The thought somehow exhausted her, and she felt suddenly on the verge of tears.

This wasn't supposed to be happening. It was bad enough feeling out of her depth professionally. But now there was Laszlo, staring at her with those cold, dismissive eyes, and all she could think was that he could still make her feel like nothing. How he had made her feel like nothing seven years ago. Swallowing, she gritted her teeth. At least she'd fought for their relationship; he, on the other hand, had been too busy doing whatever he'd done to get himself arrested.

And she *wasn't* nothing. In his words, she was being paid enough to buy a castle to do this job and that was what she was there to do. Her job. It didn't matter that once upon a time, her love hadn't been good enough for him.

Lifting her chin, she turned towards the lawyer. 'You're very kind, Mr Frankel,' she said clearly. 'Thank you for allowing me to come. This is a marvellous opportunity for me. I just hope I can live up to your expectations.'

'Oh, I wouldn't worry about that,' Laszlo murmured softly. 'We have very low expectations.'

There was another long, tense moment of silence and then Frankel gave a nervous laugh. 'What Mr Cziffra is trying to say—'

'Is that Miss Elliot and I can take it from here,' Laszlo finished smoothly.

The lawyer looked at him doubtfully. 'You can?'

'I think I can manage.' Laszlo's voice was as cold and

flat as an Arctic ice floe and Prudence shivered as Frankel nodded, his plump face flushed.

'Of course,' he said hastily. 'Of course.' He turned towards Prudence.

'You'll be in safe hands, Miss Elliot! After Mr de Zsadany, no one knows more about the collection than his grandson.'

The shock was like a jolt of electricity.

Prudence felt her whole body still and then start to shake. The room was spinning at the edge of her vision. Janos Almasy de Zsadany was Laszlo's grandfather! But how could he be? Janos Almasy de Zsadany was a billionaire several times over. Laszlo was a Romany—a traveller who lived in a trailer. How could they possibly be related?

With an almost painful stab of hope she wondered if she had misheard Frankel and she turned to Laszlo, expecting, praying he would still be staring at her with the same cold, uninterested expression. But she saw instead that he was staring at her with a look of pitying scorn and horror.

Her stomach convulsed with fear. Frankel was telling the truth.

Heart thumping, feeling dizzy and sick, she glanced numbly at the lawyer. But he seemed unaware of the turmoil he had created with his simple statement of fact. Fighting her misery, she glanced back at Laszlo. There was no denial on his face—no embarrassment or confusion, and she stared at him, unable to ignore, even in her misery, his luminous, impossible beauty.

He looked up and she flinched as he met her gaze, the softness of his mouth only seeming to emphasise the hard challenge in his eyes.

Frankel coughed. 'Right. In that case I'll be on my way. Goodnight, Miss Elliot! I'll see myself out, Mr Cziffra.'

'Thank you, Frankel.' Laszlo stared steadily at Prudence, his eyes glittering like shards of yellow glass. 'Enjoy the rest of your evening. And don't worry. I'll take good care of Miss Elliot.'

Prudence felt her stomach turn to liquid as Laszlo turned towards her and nodded.

'I promise I'll give her my full and undivided attention.'

The table lamps felt suddenly like spotlights, and although the room was warm she felt cold and shivery. She watched Frankel leave with a mounting sense of dread, every nerve in her body straining to breaking point. She wanted to run after the lawyer and beg him to stay but her body was rooted to the spot. Numbly, she stared at the paintings on the wall. Just moments ago they had given her such innocent pleasure. But not any more. Now they seemed like cruel-eyed onlookers, mocking her stupidity.

The anaesthetic of shock and bewilderment was starting to wear off and she felt a sudden stabbing surge of irritation. Okay, it was awkward and stressful for both of them to be thrown together like this, but surely she had a far greater reason to be upset than him? Surely she deserved some answers here? Her lip curled. In fact, how could he just stand there and not offer one word of explanation?

Glancing at his expressionless face, she gritted her teeth. Quite easily, it would appear. Her chest tightened. He hadn't changed a bit. He was still putting the onus on her to resolve everything. As though he were a witness rather than a central protagonist in what was happening.

'Pretending I'm not here isn't going to make this go away!' she said slowly. Willing herself to stay as cool as she sounded, she lifted her chin and met his gaze. 'We need to sort this out.'

Laszlo stared at her. '"Sort this out"?' he echoed softly. His mouth tightened as he suppressed a humourless laugh. There was nothing *to* sort out! Except out of which door he would throw her! 'Is that what we need to do?' His eyes met hers. 'So. You're Seymour's replacement?' he said coolly.

Heart thumping against her ribcage, Prudence nodded. Keeping her eyes straight ahead, she cleared her throat. 'And you're Mr de Zsadany's grandson!'

She fell silent and waited for his answer. But he did nothing more than nod. Turning her head, she clenched her fists: the words *incorrigible* and *impossible* were ricocheting inside her brain. Was that it, then? No explanations. Not one word to acknowledge the impact and implication of those words.

As though reading her mind, Laszlo sighed. His eyes looked through her and past her as he spoke. 'My mother was Zsofia Almasy de Zsadany. She was Janos's daughter and only child.'

It was like hearing a marble statue speak and her heart flinched at the chill in his voice.

'She met my father, Istvan, when she was sixteen. He was seventeen, a Kalderash Roma. Both their families opposed the match but they loved each other so much that nothing could keep them apart.'

His eyes gleamed and she felt a jolt of pain at the accusatory barb of his words.

'They were married and I was born nine months later.'

Prudence stared at him numbly. Who *was* this Laszlo? And what had he been doing living in a shabby trailer in England? Had he been rebelling? Or estranged from the de Zsadanys? Her head was swimming with questions. From knowing next to nothing about him she suddenly had so much information she could hardly take it all in. But her heart contracted as she realised that even the small things he had shared with her had been half-truths.

'Why were you there? In England, I mean?'

He frowned. 'After my parents died I spent time with both my families. My grandfather wanted me to go to school. To be educated. So I stayed in Hungary during term-time, and in the holidays I went and visited my father's family, wherever they happened to be living.' His eyes gleamed remorselessly. 'I wanted to be loyal to both my mother *and* my father.'

She forced herself to meet his gaze. 'I see,' she said slowly. 'But you didn't want to be open and honest with me?' She felt a sudden rise in tension as his eyes slid slowly and assessingly over her rigid frame.

'No. I did not,' he said finally.

Prudence gaped at him, her pledge to stay calm and detached now completely forgotten. 'Didn't you think it might have been better, not to say *fairer*, to share the whole truth with me?' she said furiously. 'You know—the fact that your grandfather was one of the richest men in Europe? And that you lived in a castle surrounded by priceless works of art?'

He looked away from her and shrugged. Prudence felt almost giddy with rage. How dare he just stand there and shrug at her? As if it didn't matter that he'd lied to her. As if *she* didn't matter.

'What difference would it have made?' he said flatly. 'There were lots of facts you didn't know about me—why focus on that one?' His face twisted. 'Unless, of course, it wasn't the truth you wanted to share. Maybe there were other things you'd have liked to share. Like my grandfather's money.'

The breath seemed to snarl up in her throat. 'How can you say that?' She stepped towards him, her body shaking with anger. 'How can you even suggest—?' Her head was spinning, nerves humming with rage and frustration. 'Don't you dare try and twist this, Laszlo. You lied to me!'

Laszlo's face was suddenly as pale and rigid as bone and she had to curl her fingers into her hands to stop herself from flinching at the hostility in his eyes.

'I didn't lie,' he said coldly. 'I *am* half-Romany and I *did* live in a trailer.'

'Oh, that's okay, then,' Prudence said sarcastically. 'Maybe it was your other half. The half that lived in a castle. Perhaps *he* lied to me?'

Anger was bubbling up inside her, her breath burning her throat. *She* wasn't the one who'd lied about who she was. She winced as her nails dug into her skin. Had he actually told her the truth about anything?

Laszlo met her gaze. 'You believed what you wanted to believe.'

Prudence shook her head in disbelief. 'I believed what you encouraged me to believe,' she said furiously. 'There's a difference.'

There was a dangerous silence and then his eyes narrowed.

'You're missing the point, Prudence. It doesn't matter what someone believes if they don't have faith.' His voice was ragged, frayed with a bitterness she had never heard before. 'Without that it's all just words.'

She sucked in a breath. 'Yes, it is. *Your* words. The lies you told me.' Her heart was pounding; her hands were tight fists against her sides. 'Don't try and turn this into some philosophical debate, Laszlo. I'm upset because you lied to me and you took away my choices.'

'So now we're even,' he said coldly.

CHAPTER TWO

SHE STARED AT him blankly. Even? *Even!*

'What that's supposed to mean?' She flung the words at him, wishing they were sticks or stones or better still bricks. But he didn't reply. Instead he made an impatient sound and she watched helplessly as his face closed tight like a trap. Her muscles were aching with the effort of not picking up a lamp and beating him to death with it. How could he *do* that? Just switch off in the middle of a conversation and take himself outside of it?

Feeling a familiar cold, paralysing panic, she wrapped her arms around herself. But of course she didn't need him to answer anyway. She knew exactly what he was talking about.

An undertow of defiance tugged at her frustration and slowly she shook her head. 'No, Laszlo. If you're talking about the fact that I ended our relationship, then we are *not* even. Not even close to being even.'

Her whole body was suddenly shaking and she wrapped her arms more tightly around herself. Walking away from Laszlo and from her romantic hopes and dreams had been hard—one of the hardest things she'd ever done—and it had taken every ounce of willpower she'd had. But if he'd wanted to, if he'd wanted her, he could have stopped her; she'd given him every chance to change her mind. Only he'd barely uttered a word when she'd told her that she was leaving him. Certainly not the sort she'd craved. He'd let her go and that had been his choice.

A sudden, suffocating misery reared up inside her as, with a shudder, she remembered just how cold and unapproachable he'd been.

She stood rooted to the spot, numbed and struck dumb at her own stupidity. No wonder he'd been so secretive—smuggling her into his trailer and carefully sidestepping her requests to meet his family. Fool that she was, she'd been too dizzy with love, too in thrall to the way her body had softened and transformed beneath his touch, to wonder why. Besides, she'd been flattered at the start, at least, for she'd believed that he wanted her all to himself. He'd stolen her heart and her virginity in quick succession and all the while he'd been living a lie.

She looked at him wearily. But why did this lie matter, really? After all, she couldn't change the past. Or change the fact that he hadn't loved her enough to fight for her. Her mouth twisted. This discussion was a dead end. There was no point in trying to talk about their relationship now: it was seven years too late. And besides, she had a new life now. Maybe not the one she'd been hoping for, but a good life, and she wasn't about to let him pick up her world and smash it to smithereens.

Her pulse fluttered into life and she glanced at the door, wishing she could go back in time to the moment before she'd walked through it. And then, with a start, she remembered that even if that had been possible it simply wasn't an option. Edmund needed this job. That was why she had come to Hungary. And she needed to focus on that fact and not get sidetracked into a post-mortem of her romantic past.

She took a calming breath. The cataloguing was more important than her feelings. Not that she had any feelings for Laszlo any more. At least not any that should get in the way of what was essentially a job like any other. Their relationship was history and, while clearly she would never have chosen to meet him again, let alone work with him, there was no reason not to treat him like any other client—albeit one who was difficult, bordering on the socially inept.

Fighting down the urge to bolt through the door, she lifted her chin and met his gaze. She wasn't going to let his inability to let go of the past upset her. She would be calm and efficient—a detached professional.

'This is getting us nowhere, Laszlo,' she said firmly. 'I'm here to do a job for you and your grandfather.'

Biting her lip, she paused, her muscles tightening again. Did Janos know about her relationship with his grandson? That could be awkward. But then her body relaxed. Somehow she didn't think so. It was a long time ago, and they'd never met, and Laszlo had probably had hundreds of girlfriends since her. Her cheeks grew suddenly hot and quickly she pushed that thought away.

'I know he wants to start on the cataloguing as soon as possible, so why don't we put aside our differences and try and concentrate on making that happen for him? Can we do that? Can we call a truce?' She gave a small, tight smile and clenched her hands into fists to stop herself from crossing her fingers.

Laszlo stared at her speculatively. She wanted this job. It was obvious from the conciliatory note in her voice and the slight increase in tension around her shoulders. His gaze drifted hungrily over her neck to the pulse beating in the hollow at the base of her throat. To anyone who didn't know her she looked like the perfect English Rose, pale and demure. But he knew the other Prudence. The one beneath that calm, poised exterior, who had wrapped herself around him with passion and fervour. That contrast, and the knowledge that he alone possessed that other, hidden Prudence, had excited him unbearably. With a spasm of disbelief, he realised it still did.

Feeling his body stiffen, he lifted his gaze and smiled at her almost mockingly. 'Since you put it so nicely—'

She stared at him warily. She hadn't expected him to come round so easily. But then, with Laszlo you never knew what to expect. 'Thank you,' she said stiffly. 'I must say I'm a bit surprised—'

He smiled coolly. 'I know how much women love surprises.'

Nodding, she forced herself to breathe slowly. Perhaps she could make this work. She just needed to stay focused on what was important: the fact that Laszlo was nothing more than a client. She looked up and found him watching her. A tingle of heat ran down her spine. She could almost see his desire—feel him wrapping it round her like a dark velvet cloak.

Her cheeks were burning. Quickly, before the sudden softness in his eyes could rattle her even more, she looked away. She was here to work and it didn't matter that she and Laszlo had once shared a passion so pagan, so consuming, that the outside world had ceased to exist. Now their relationship needed to work only on a business level.

She met his eyes. 'And I know men hate delays.' She paused and cleared her throat. 'So I suggest we discuss what happens now.'

Laszlo stared at her. A peony-pink flush had crept over the skin on her throat and his gaze drifted down over the pale grey blouse that clung to the soft swell of her breasts, then lower still to where the smooth downward curve of her hips and waist pressed tight against the fabric of her skirt. She was so close they were practically touching and, breathing in the familiar scent of jasmine, he found himself almost paralysed with longing again.

Breathing in sharply, he gritted his teeth. He had spent so long hating her, hating what she had done to him, that he had never supposed that he might still want her.

And yet apparently he did.

He stared at her, confused. He wanted her. But he also wanted to punish her. And yet even that wasn't wholly true, for he couldn't help but admire her. After all, how many other women—particularly one as shy and unworldly as Prudence—would stand their ground in this situation? Not that it surprised him. She had always possessed that quality of being in a state of quiescence, of teetering on the edge. His jaw tensed as her misty grey gaze rested on his face. Only now was not the time to be thinking about Prudence's finer qualities. Better to concentrate on her flaws.

'You tell me. Talking was always your thing, wasn't it? For me, actions speak louder than words.'

He watched colour creep across her cheeks. Saw the moment that she relaxed, the tension leaving her body, making it softer and more vulnerable.

Prudence felt her cheeks grow warm. She needed no reminder of how eloquent his actions had been. Particularly not now, when she needed to keep her thoughts in some semblance of order. But his smile was like a beam of sunlight breaking through cloud. She just wanted to follow it…place herself in its path.

Focus, she told herself firmly. She cleared her throat and began to talk quickly. 'As I said before, I know how keen your grandfather is to begin the cataloguing. So I think we should push on with the original timeframe.'

He stepped towards her and she tensed, her body suddenly a helix of tendon and muscle.

'You're the expert,' he murmured.

Blushing, Prudence swallowed. His voice was such a captivating mix of soft and seductive. She felt heat begin to build inside her and for one brief moment allowed herself to remember the touch of his fingers, travelling over her skin with the virtuosity of a concert pianist. How the rippling rhythms of their bodies had quickened and inter-twined to a breathless cadence.

Prudence took a deep breath. Surely she couldn't still ac-tually find him attractive? She must have more sense than that. But what had sense got to do with lust? No woman alive could stand next to Laszlo Cziffra and feel nothing.

Somewhere in the castle a door slammed and Prudence started forward with surprise. For a moment her hands grazed his chest as she swayed against him and then, breathing unsteadily, she teetered backwards. They were standing inches apart now. He was so close she could feel the heat of his skin. Her heart was pounding as though she'd been running and her body was trembling helplessly. He smelt of newly mown hay and rain-soaked earth and she felt almost dazed with longing as every inch of her reacted to him.

'Castles were built to keep out arrows and cannon fire. Not draughts,' he said drily.

Still horrified by the revelation that her body apparently had no loyalty to her heart, Prudence dragged her gaze away, hoping that he hadn't noticed or, worse, correctly interpreted her physical response to him.

'Weren't they?' she mumbled, her cheeks flushing. 'Wh—what was I saying? Oh, yes. The timeframe. Three weeks is a typical estimate for a preliminary assessment. It's important to be thorough at that stage.' She frowned. 'And don't worry. If I have any problems I can speak to Mr Seymour. In fact, I'll be in close contact with him the entire time.' She gave a small, tight smile. 'I find it help-ful to have another point of view. For clarity.'

Her smile faded and she stared at him nervously, aware of a sudden stillness in him, a slight narrowing of his eyes, although she couldn't quite understand what had changed. But then, why should she care? She was here to work, and Laszlo's moods were no longer her concern.

Clearing her throat, she straightened her shoulders and forced herself to ignore the undertow of apprehension tugging at the back of her mind. 'A-and obviously I'm happy to discuss any concerns Mr de Zsadany has,' she stammered. His eyes clashed with hers and despite herself she felt another twinge of foreboding.

'Obviously…' he said coolly. 'I know how you love to discuss problems.'

Her heart was thumping hard. There it was again: a tiny but deliberate dig. He was taking what was nothing more than a casual, unpremeditated remark and making it something personal, to do with the past. *Their* past. She felt sudden swift anger. Hadn't they agreed to call a truce? This was going to be hard enough as it was, without him making a difficult situation worse with his snippy double-edged comments.

Her mind was so churned up with emotion it took her another couple of moments before she understood just *how* difficult the situation was going to be. For it wasn't as if she was just going to *work* with Laszlo—her blood seemed to still in her veins—she was going to have to live with him too.

A tremor grew at the back of her neck. Of course she would have to live with him. But not like this. Not dreading his every remark—not deliberately having to misunderstand his every insinuation. She needed to make it clear now that she would not tolerate being treated like that.

'I don't *like* discussing problems.' Returning his gaze coldly, she lifted her chin. 'It's just that I think communication is key to a successful relationship.'

She had meant to sound assured, without being overtly confrontational. But she knew the moment she spoke that it was the wrong thing to say. For he went entirely still and his eyes locked onto hers like an infrared missile seeking its target.

Swaying, she took a faltering step backwards. 'I didn't mean us—'

'Don't bother! I already know pretty much all there is to know about your views on relationships.'

Watching the shock and confusion bloom on her face, Laszlo felt a surge of satisfaction.

His voice was little more than a rasp. 'You explained them to me in great detail when you walked out on me— *Prudence.*'

She flinched as he turned towards her and spat her name into the air as though it were a poison he had inadvertently swallowed.

'In fact...' He paused, his lip curling with contempt. 'You made it abundantly clear how pitiable I was to have ever imagined that our relationship might work, given the range and depth of my flaws.'

'N-no. I didn't—' Prudence began shakily, shocked and unnerved by the level of venom in his voice. But her voice died as he stepped towards her and she saw real anger in his eyes.

'Oh, but you did.' His face was tight with emotion. 'Only you were wrong. They weren't *my* flaws. They were yours!' he ground out between gritted teeth. 'You were just too weak and snobbish—'

'I was *not* weak and snobbish.' The injustice of his words melted her shock and suddenly she was coldly furious. 'I just didn't want to pretend any more.'

'Pretend what? That you loved me?' His face was blunt, angular with hostility.

Liquid misery trickled through her. 'That we had anything in common.'

He shook his head. 'Like loyalty, you mean? Maybe you're right. We certainly felt differently about *that*!'

'You don't need to tell me about the differences between us,' she snapped, stung into speech by the censure

in his voice. 'I know all about them. They're why our relationship didn't work. Why it could never have worked.'

Her throat tightened as he looked at her coldly.

'Our relationship didn't fail because we were different.
It failed because you cared more about those differences
than you did about me,' he snarled. 'Tell me, *pireni*, how
are you finding my communication skills now? Am I making myself clear enough?'

Her heart gave a sudden jerk as abruptly he turned and
walked towards the fireplace.

For a moment she stood frozen, gazing speechlessly at
his back. Anger was building inside her, displacing all other
feeling, and suddenly she crossed the room and yanked
him round to face her.

'That's not true! I *did* care—' She broke off. Rage, hot
and unstoppable, choked her words. 'Don't you dare try and
tell me what I felt.' She set her jaw, her eyes narrowing. 'If
I cared about the differences between us it was because,
yes, I thought they mattered. Unlike you, I like to talk about
the things that matter to me. And, crazy though this may
sound, I try and tell the truth. But what would *you* know
about that? The truth is like a foreign language to you.'

She watched his eyes darken with fury, the pupils seeming almost to engulf the golden irises.

'The truth?' he said savagely. 'You left me because you
thought I wasn't good enough for you. *That's* the truth.
You're just too much of a coward to admit it.'

Silently, Prudence shook her head. Not only because she
was disagreeing with him but because she was too angry
to speak. She hadn't even known she could feel that angry.

Finally, she found her voice. 'How dare you talk to me
about the truth when we're standing here in this castle?
Your castle. A castle I didn't even know existed until today.'
Her eyes flashed with anger. 'And just because I wanted to
talk about the leaks in the trailer and the fact that we didn't

have enough money to buy food for more than a couple of days didn't mean I thought you weren't good enough!'

'Those things shouldn't have mattered. They didn't matter to *me*,' Laszlo snarled.

'I know!' she snarled back at him. 'But they did to me. And you can't punish me for that fact. Or for the fact that it worried me: how we felt differently about things. We disagreed about stuff and that was going to be a problem for us sooner or later, only you wouldn't admit it,' she raged at him. 'So it wasn't me who was a coward. It was you.'

She took a sudden step backwards as he moved towards her; his face was in shadow but the fury beneath his skin was luminous.

'I am not the coward here, Prudence,' he said quietly, and his dispassionate tone was frighteningly at odds with the menacing gleam in his eyes.

Prudence felt her insides lurch. Beneath the chill of his gaze her courage and powers of speech wilted momentarily and she felt suddenly defeated. Suddenly she didn't want to talk any more. What was the point? Judging by the last twenty minutes it would only hurt more than it healed.

When at last she spoke, her voice was defeated. 'This is going nowhere,' she said wearily. 'I know you're angry. We both are. But can't we just put our past behind us? At least until after the cataloguing is complete?'

Laszlo stared at her, his eyes glittering with fury. 'The *cataloguing*? Do you know what my grandfather's collection means to him? Or why he decided to have it catalogued?' He shook his head. 'After everything that's happened between us, do you really think I'd trust *you*, of all people—?' He broke off and breathed out unsteadily.

Prudence felt a stab of fear. What was he trying to say? 'But you can,' she said shakily. 'I'll do a good job. You have my word.'

He winced as though she had ripped a plaster from a

scab. 'Your *word*?' he repeated. He tilted his head. 'Your word…' he said again.

And this time the contempt on his face felt like a hammer blow. Her mouth had gone dry.

'I—I only meant—' she stammered, but he cut across her words with a voice like a flick knife.

'It doesn't matter what you meant. We both know that your word is worthless.'

'What are you talking about?'

Balling his fists, feeling sick to his stomach, Laszlo shook his head. He felt an odd rushing sensation in his head, like a sort of vertigo, and words and memories hurtled past him like debris from an explosion. What kind of woman *was* she? He had long known her to be snobbish and weak-minded, but this—this refusal to acknowledge what she'd done—

His jaw tightened.

'I honoured you with a gift. The most important gift a man can give to a woman. I made you my wife and you threw it in my face.'

Prudence gaped at him, shock washing over in waves. She opened her mouth to deny his claim but the words clogged her throat. His *wife*? Surely he didn't really think that they were actually *married*? Her heart was pounding; the palms of her hands felt suddenly damp. Married? That was ridiculous! Insane!

Dazedly she thought back to that day when she'd been led, giggling and blindfolded, to his great-uncle's trailer. Laszlo had been waiting for her. She felt a shiver run down her spine at the memory, for he'd looked heartbreakingly handsome and so serious she had wanted to cry. They'd sworn their love and commitment to one another, and his great-uncle had spoken some words in Romany, and then they had eaten some bread and some salt.

Coming out of her reverie, she stared hard at him wordlessly. There had been no actual marriage. It had been no more real than his love for her. But it had been part of the fantasy of their love. And now he was destroying that fantasy. Taking the memory of something beautiful, innocent and spontaneous and turning it into a means of hurting her.

Her vision blurred and she felt suddenly giddy, as though she were teetering on the edge of a cliff-face. 'You're despicable! Why are you doing this? Why are you trying to ruin that day?'

'Ruin it?' His features contorted with fury. 'You're the one who did that. By walking out on our marriage.'

Her pulse was fluttering and despite her best efforts her voice sounded high and jerky. 'We're not married,' she said tightly. 'Marriages are more than just words and kisses. This is just another of your lies—'

Her voice trailed off at the expression of derision on his face.

'No. This is just the ultimate proof of how little you understood or respected my way of life. For you, my being Romany was just some whimsical lifestyle choice.' He watched the blood suffuse her face and felt a spasm of pain. 'You liked it that I was different—an outsider. But you didn't expect or want me to stay like that. You thought I'd just throw it off, like a fancy dress costume, and become "normal" when it came to the rest of our lives.' His eyes hardened. 'That's when you started whining about the mess and the moving around. But that's what we do. It's what *I* do.'

'Except when you're living in a castle,' she said shakily.

His gaze held hers. 'You're going off topic, *pireni*. It doesn't matter where I lived then or where I live now. We're still married. I'm still your husband. And you're my wife.'

She felt a stab of shock—both at the vehemence in his

voice and at the sudden spread of treacherous heat at his possessive words.

Turning her head, she swallowed. 'What happened in that trailer wasn't a wedding, Laszlo. There were no guests. No vicar. No witnesses. We didn't give each other rings. We didn't even sign anything. It wasn't a wedding at all and I'm not your wife.'

Laszlo forced himself to stay calm. He had too much pride to let her see that her horrified denial had reopened a wound that had never fully healed—a wound that had left him hollowed out with misery and humiliation.

Shaking his head, he gave a humourless laugh. 'Oh, believe me, *pireni*, I wish you weren't—but you are.' His fingers curled into the palms of his hands. 'In my culture a wedding is a private affair between a man and wife. We don't register the marriage, and the only authority that's needed for it to be recognised is the consent of the bride and groom.'

Prudence felt a vertigo-like flash of fear. She shook her head. 'We're not married,' she croaked. 'Not in the eyes of the law.'

The change in him was almost imperceptible. She might even have missed the slight rigidity about his jawline had the contempt in his eyes not seared her skin.

'Not your law, maybe.' He felt a hot, overpowering rage. 'But in mine. Yes, we were married—and we still are.'

Closing her eyes, she felt a sudden, inexplicable sense of panic. Laszlo clearly believed what he was saying. Whilst she might have viewed the ceremony as a curious but charming dress rehearsal for the vintage-style white wedding she'd been planning, the marriage had been real to him. Nausea gripped her stomach. What did it really matter if there was no certificate? It didn't mean that the vows they'd made were any less valid or binding.

Heat scorched her skin. *What had she done?* She looked

up and his gaze held hers, and she saw that he was furious, fighting for control.

'Laszlo, I didn't—'

His voice was barely audible but it scythed through her words and on through her skin and bone, slicing into her heart.

'This conversation is over. I'm sorry you had a wasted trip but your services are no longer required.'

Prudence looked at him in confusion, her face bleached of colour. 'I—I don't understand...' she stammered. 'What do you mean?'

Laszlo rounded on her coldly. 'What do I *mean*?' he echoed. 'I mean that you're fired—dismissed, sacked. Your contract is terminated and this meeting is over. As of this moment I never want to see your face again.' He turned back towards the fire. 'So why don't you take your bags, turn around and get out of my house? *Now.*'

CHAPTER THREE

PRUDENCE FELT THE floor tilt towards her. She reached out and steadied herself against the back of an armchair. 'You can't do that,' she said slowly. 'You can't just fire me.'

'Oh, but I can.'

Laszlo turned and looked at her, full in the face, and a shudder raced through her as she saw to her horror that he meant it.

'But that's so unfair!' Her voice seemed to echo around the room and she gazed at him helplessly.

'I don't care.'

He spoke flatly, his jaw tightening, and with a spasm of pain she knew that he didn't. Knew too that it wouldn't matter what she said or did and that it had probably never mattered. She had lost the job the moment Laszlo walked into the room. She just hadn't realised that fact until now.

She stared at him, shock and disbelief choking her words of objection. But inside her head there was a deafening cacophony of protest. He couldn't fire her. What would she tell Edmund? And what about their debts to the bank and the insurance company?

'No.'

The word burst from her lips like a flying spear. Laszlo stared at her calmly. Firing her seemed to have lanced his fury and he seemed more puzzled than angry at her outburst.

'No?' he murmured softly. 'No, what?'

She glared at him, her cheeks flooding with angry colour. 'No, I won't leave. I know I made a mistake, but it all happened years ago—and anyway you can't fire me for that. Apart from anything else it's got nothing to do with my ability to do this job.'

'It's got *everything* to do with your ability to do this job,' Laszlo said coldly. 'You lack conviction and loyalty and I don't employ people without those qualities.'

Prudence sucked in a breath, hating him more than she had ever hated him before. 'Stop it!' she hissed. He was so self-righteous and hypocritical. How dare he act as if he had the moral high ground? He'd lied to her. And he was the one who'd broken the law and been arrested for who knew what! Perhaps he should examine his own failings first instead of focusing on hers.

She opened her mouth to tell him so and then closed it again. There was so much history in this room already. Why add more? She breathed out slowly.

'Stop sitting in judgement on me! You're not some innocent victim here, Laszlo. You lied. Maybe that doesn't matter to you, but it does to me.' She stopped, her breathing ragged. 'Only I'm not using it to get at you. I wouldn't stoop that low.'

Laszlo looked at her for one long, agonising moment.

'Really?' he said coolly. 'I wonder…' He ran his hand over the dark stubble grazing his chin. 'Just how badly do you want this job, Prudence? Are you prepared to beg for it?'

She felt nausea clutch at her stomach. 'You're a monster!' His eyes were cold and implacable.

'This is payback! Firing you makes us quits, *pireni*! And, believe me, you've got off lightly. If there were still wolves in Hungary I'd throw you to them. So if I were you I'd walk out of here while you still can.'

Prudence stared at him, her chest blazing with anger.

'What does *that* mean? Are you threatening me?' she asked tightly.

Laszlo stared at her in silence, his eyes glittering with mockery. 'Threatening you? Of course not. But this discussion is over, so I think you should accept that and walk away.' His jaw tightened. 'That shouldn't be a problem for you. After all, you've had lots of practice.'

Anger swept through her. 'Oh, you think you're so clever, don't you? Well, let's get one thing clear. This discussion is *not* over.'

He gazed at her impassively in silence. Finally he said, almost mildly, 'Then I suppose you'd better start talking. Although I'm not quite sure what difference you think it will make.'

She stared at him in confusion. How did he *do* that? Only moments earlier his anger had been incandescent beneath his skin. Now he was prepared to grant her an audience. It was impossible to keep up with him. She gritted her teeth. But hadn't it always been this way between them, though? With her trying to chase the moods which ran like quicksilver through his veins?

She lifted her chin. But the blood was humming in her ears and she felt suddenly hot and stupid in the face of his cool composure. Was she just expected to somehow plead her case while he stood there like some hanging judge? Fixing her gaze on the wall behind him, she swallowed.

'I admit I made mistakes back then. But you're punishing me for them *now*. How is that reasonable or fair?' She paused and heat burnt her cheeks as he stared at her. For a moment his eyes fixed on her, as though her words had meant something to him, and then he shook his head slowly.

'Fair?' he echoed. '*Fair!* Since when did you care about fairness? You dumped me because you didn't want to live in some tatty trailer.' His eyes hardened. He, on the other hand, would have been content to sleep under the stars if she was with him. Shaking his head, he gave a humourless laugh. 'How was that fair to me?'

Blood colouring her cheeks and collarbone, Prudence flinched, his bitterness driving the breath from her lungs. It was true—she *had* said words to that effect—but she hadn't meant them, and whatever Laszlo might think, she'd been so madly in love then that she would have lived in a ditch with him if he'd asked.

All she'd wanted was for him to repudiate her fears that he'd lost interest in her or, worse, found someone else. Only he'd been so dismissive. And bored. As if she was a nagging child. So it had been impossible to tell him the truth, for that would have meant revealing the depth of her love. She'd been too upset to do that, but just angry enough to want to provoke him and hurt him for not loving her. And so instead she'd lashed out at him about the mess and the cold and the rain.

Prudence felt a trickle of misery run down her spine, but then, almost in the same moment, she shook her head, anger filling her. He was taking what she'd said out of context and—surprise, surprise—ignoring the part he'd played.

Damn it! Unlike her, he'd actually thought they were married! So why hadn't he done more to make it work between them? Did he think that relationships just sustained themselves? A lump formed in her throat. It certainly seemed that way. She'd gone to him for reassurance but he'd left her no choice but to walk away, and it had been the hardest choice she had ever made. Even talking about it now made her heart swell with grief.

She lifted her chin. 'We're not going to go there, Laszlo. I am not going to talk about the past with you any more.' Heart thumping, she took a breath. 'If you wanted to discuss our relationship you should have done so at the time. Frankly, now it's irrelevant.'

Her grip tightened on the chair as he stepped towards her. She felt her stomach swoop. Close up, his beauty was radiant and piercing—like a flaming arrow. His eyes were more golden, his skin smoother, the angles and shading of his cheekbones almost too perfect to be real.

'I don't agree. I think it's entirely relevant, given that you have brought our past back into my life.'

Her mouth trembled. 'That's not true, Laszlo. It was you who contacted Seymour's.'

She stared at him indignantly. If he hadn't wanted anything to do with her then why had he chosen to use her uncle's firm? Only of course he didn't *know* it was Edmund's business. He didn't even know her uncle's name, let alone what he did for a living. She shivered. Somehow now didn't seem like the best time to tell him.

Trying to ignore the pounding of her heart, she swallowed. 'I know how you hate being responsible for anything, but this is *your* mess.'

'And we both know how you hate mess, Prudence,' he said smoothly.

'I didn't care about the stupid trailer!' she snapped, her temper rising. 'You just focused on that and wouldn't listen to me. It wasn't a criticism of you, or your precious Willerby Westmorland! It's just who I am.' Her heart was thumping so hard it hurt. 'I don't like mess. I like things tidy and in order and that's why I'm good at my job. Maybe if you'd thought about that instead of sneering at me—'

'I'm not sneering, *pireni*.' His face shifted, and meeting her angry gaze, he shrugged. 'And you're right. Maybe I did focus on that remark—'

He stopped and Prudence gaped at him speechlessly. Was that some kind of apology?

His eyes locked with hers and he sighed. 'But I'm not going to change my mind, Prudence. You do understand that, don't you?'

'Yes,' she said stiffly. 'But, given that it's probably not just your decision to make, I've decided it doesn't matter.'

Laszlo frowned. 'You think there's a higher authority than me?'

His eyes gleamed with sudden amusement and she felt her stomach flip over.

'I hope so—for Mr de Zsadany's sake.' Wondering again if Janos knew of her relationship with Laszlo, she felt a stab of pain. He was such a fraud. Why, if he'd believed himself to be married, had he kept her existence secret?

Forcing herself to stay focused, she lifted her chin. 'Seymour's is the best there is. Giving this job to another firm would only demonstrate how unqualified you are to have anything to do with the cataloguing.' Hers eyes flashed challengingly at him. 'I mean, you don't even *like* art!'

'I appreciate beauty as much as the next man,' Laszlo said softly.

'Really?' Prudence retorted. 'How do you work that out? The only time we went to see an exhibition together you spent your entire time in the café.'

Laszlo shrugged, his gaze sweeping slowly over her face until heat suffused her skin.

'I can think of better things to do in a darkened room. You, of all people, should know that.'

Prudence stared at him, trembling, dry-mouthed; her body suddenly a mass of hot, aching need. He let the silence lengthen, let the tension rise between them.

'Or have you forgotten?' he murmured finally. 'Perhaps I should jog your memory.'

He watched her eyes widen and felt his groin tighten in response. But almost immediately he closed his mind to the tormenting tug of hunger.

'But I digress. I don't need to like art, Prudence. I just want to support my grandfather and be there for him—'

'Good luck with that!' Prudence interrupted him crossly.

'*Being there* for someone generally requires an element of reliability or commitment, you know.'

She glared at him as his gaze rested on her accusing face.

'Meaning…?' he asked slowly.

'Meaning that *you* can't commit to the next five minutes.' She stared at him incredulously. 'Don't you know yourself at all? Trying to pin you down to a time and place is like asking you to give up your soul or something.'

A slight upturn of amusement tugged at the corner of his mouth. 'Ah, but at least you admit I have a soul.'

And then suddenly he smiled, and it felt like the sun on her face. Despite her brain warning her not to, it was impossible not to smile back—for it was a glimpse of the Laszlo she had loved so very much. The Laszlo who, when he chose, had been able to make her laugh until she cried. But then her smile faded and she reminded herself that *this* Laszlo had cold-heartedly used his power to avenge himself, regardless of the consequences to her or her family.

She frowned. 'Life can't always be improvised. Sometimes you have to do boring things too—like learn lines and turn up on set on time.'

Laszlo stared at her, a muscle working in his jaw. 'You're comparing our relationship to a film?'

'Yes. I am.' Prudence lifted her chin. 'A very unmemorable silent film, with poor casting and no plot.'

She felt the hairs stand up on the back of her neck as he smiled again and shook his head slowly.

'I think your memory is playing tricks on you, *pireni*. There were some very memorable scenes in our film. Steamy too. Award-winning, even.'

'For the best short film?' she snapped.

'I was thinking more hair and make-up,' he said, his eyes glittering.

She couldn't resist. 'Yours or mine?'

'Oh, definitely mine,' he whipped back.

There was a silence, and then both of them started to laugh.

Prudence stopped and bit her lip. 'Can't we stop this— please, Laszlo?' She saw the indecision on his face and for a moment she faltered, and then she said quickly, 'It's brutal. And senseless. We're just going round and round in circles, and all this name-calling isn't going to change the fact that your grandfather wants his collection cata- logued and I'm here to do it. So let me do it, Laszlo: for him. For your grandfather.'

Their eyes locked: hers bright and desperate, his, dark and unreadable. She swallowed hard, trying to find the words to change his mind.

'If I lose this contract you won't just be punishing me,' she said steadily. 'Other people will suffer—people you've never met…people who've done you no harm.'

She held her breath and watched his face, trying not to let her desperation show.

'Please, Laszlo. Please don't make this personal. Just let me do my job and then I'll be out of your life for ever.'

There was a tense, expectant silence as he studied her face. She wanted this job, badly, and he wondered idly just how far she would go to get it back. Immediately prick- ling heat surged through him and his groin grew painfully hard. He gritted his teeth, shocked by the intensity of his body's response.

It would be easy to give her a chance. His chest tight- ened painfully. But why should he? After all, she had never given their marriage a chance, had she? His face hardened. Did she really think that she could somehow emotionally blackmail him into forgetting the past and the harm she had done to him? And what about his family? What about *their* pain?

He remembered the long days and nights spent watching his grandmother's health fade, the years spent living with the guilt of not having given her the great-grandchildren she'd so longed for.

Prudence held her breath, watching a sort of angry bewilderment fill his eyes. The tightness around her heart eased a little: maybe all was not lost yet.

'Can't we just forgive and forget?' she said softly. He looked up and she hesitated. 'Please, Laszlo. I don't believe you really want to do this.'

His face was stiff with tension. Slowly he shook his head. 'Then you clearly don't know me at all, Prudence.' His mouth was set in a grim line. 'I *want* to let you stay. For my grandfather's sake, you understand. But I can't,' he said simply. 'You see, I'm half Kalderash Roma. We don't forget or forgive.'

He paused and his voice, when he spoke again, was like the sound of a tomb sealing.

'And you're still fired.'

Prudence gazed at him in shock, her ragged breathing punctuating the silence in the room. A sense of impotent despair filled her and then something else: a hot and acrid frustration that burnt her stomach to ash.

'I see. So it's not your choice.' Her hands curled into fists. 'How convenient for you to be able to blame your stubbornness and your spite on genetics.'

His narrowed gaze held hers. 'I'm not blaming genetics. I'm blaming *you*.'

'But not yourself?' She stared deep into his eyes. 'Nothing is ever your fault, is it, Laszlo?' she asked flatly. 'You just saunter through life, expecting everyone around you to take responsibility for the nasty, boring bits.' Smiling bitterly, she shook her head. 'I thought husbands and wives were supposed to give and take. Not in *our* marriage, though!'

She tensed as he stepped towards her, his eyes suddenly gleaming like wet metal.

'So now you're my wife? Interesting! As my charms

clearly weren't sufficient to persuade you of that fact seven years ago, I can only imagine that my grandfather's wealth is a more compelling reason for you to belatedly acknowledge our marriage.'

Prudence glared at him. 'How dare you? I couldn't care less about your grandfather's wealth.'

'Just about my poverty?' he said bleakly.

'No!' Biting back the hundred and one caustic responses she might have made, she shook her head. 'This isn't about wealth or poverty. This is about what's happening here and now. About how you're prepared to make everyone suffer—me, Edmund and all the people who have worked so hard to make this happen.' She ticked them off on her fingers. 'All because you're so blinkered by your stupid male pride that won't see sense!'

'And you're so blinkered you couldn't see beyond my trailer to the people living inside,' snarled Laszlo.

'That's not true,' Prudence said hotly. 'If I didn't see those people it's because you would never introduce me to anyone.'

His eyes narrowed. 'You're such a hypocrite. You didn't want to be part of their lives any more than you really wanted to be part of mine.'

For a moment she didn't reply. It was true. She hadn't wanted to be part of his life: she'd wanted to be all of it. As he'd been all of hers.

She shook her head. 'You don't know what I wanted.' She shivered on the inside. He never had.

Feeling suddenly close to tears, she clenched her fists, struggling to find a way past her misery.

'Fine! Have it your way! I was everything you say and worse,' she said flatly. 'That doesn't mean I'm not good at my job. But if you fire me you'll never know. Until you're stuck with a second-rate replacement.' She paused and shot him a challenging glance. '*If* you can find one, that is.'

'Oh, that shouldn't be a problem. I had no trouble replacing you last time,' he said softly. He watched the colour leave her face.

'I'm not surprised,' she said hotly. 'Being the grandson of a billionaire and owning a castle must have a lot of pulling power with a certain kind of woman.'

Watching his eyes narrow at her insult, she felt a flicker of triumph that blotted out the misery of his words.

'It's nice to know that you took your wedding vows so seriously,' she snapped. 'Having vilified *me* for not believing our marriage was real. Who's the hypocrite now?' Breathing deeply, she let her eyes meet his—steel clashing with bronze. 'We could stand here trading insults all night, Laszlo, but this isn't about our personal qualities. It's not even about us. There are other people involved. Not just people, but family. Just remember how anxious your grandfather was to get started. Don't his feelings count?'

She paused as, with a jolt, she suddenly realised that Mr de Zsadany was sort of her family too. Shock swept over her in waves. She stared at him, legs shaking, stomach plummeting. Suddenly she had to know for certain.

'Is that why he chose Seymour's?' she blurted out. 'Because he thinks I'm your wife?'

Laszlo stared at her calmly. 'No. He doesn't know we're married. No one does except my cousin and my great-uncle. I didn't see the point in upsetting everyone.' His eyes hardened to stone. 'Especially not my grandfather. He wasn't strong enough to deal with it.'

She felt dizzy, sick with wretchedness. 'I'm sorry. I really am.' It sounded so inadequate, even to her. 'But surely that makes this easier? My staying, I mean?'

She took a step back from the white heat of his anger.

'*Nothing* about you being here is easy.'

'I just meant—'

'I know what you meant,' he said bleakly. 'I know you better than you know yourself.'

Her misery gave way to fury. 'Stop being so sanctimonious. You've just spent the last half-hour telling me how contemptible I am for not believing in our marriage but you didn't even tell anyone about us.'

She glowered at him.

'You don't actually feel any more married than I do, do you, Laszlo? What's upsetting you is the fact that *I* didn't think our marriage was real.' Biting her lip, she pushed a strand of tousled blonde hair behind her ear. 'That's what this is really about. That's why you're punishing me. Not because you really care about our marriage. If you did then how could you treat me like this? I mean, do you honestly think that any *normal* man would fire his own wife?'

She flinched as he raised his eyebrows, his lips curling in disbelief and contempt.

'That would depend on the wife...' he said slowly.

He studied her face, noting the small frown between her eyes, the delicate flush colouring her cheeks. She was so disingenuous! His feelings about their marriage might not be consistent or rational, but at least he hadn't deleted its very existence. He frowned. He should hate her—and he did. And yet his body was responding to her just as it had done in the past.

She shook her head. 'You can't use our marriage against me, Laszlo. Married or not, you never really let me in.'

She swallowed. Except when they'd made love. But there was more to a relationship than just lovemaking. Like trust and honesty and a willingness to share.

Sighing, she shook her head. 'I get that your life was complicated. I even sort of see why you didn't tell me everything at the start. But nothing changed after we "married". You still kept me on the outside.'

She met his gaze, her hurt and anger clearly visible in her eyes.

He felt his chest tighten painfully. 'You didn't give me a chance. You barely managed to stay around long enough to digest the bread and salt we shared at our wedding. Besides, you're just talking about details.'

'Details?' Prudence stared at him incredulously. '*Details!* Your grandfather is a billionaire and you call that a *detail*.'

She shook her head. She felt light-headed—almost dizzy. How could he stand there with that contemptuous look on his face as if he was the one who'd been tricked?

'You're unbelievable! You deceived me. And you kept on deceiving me.' Her voice sounded jagged. 'Not just about some tiny, stupid detail but about who you *were*. Don't you see how that makes me feel?' She stopped abruptly, like a train hitting the buffers.

Laszlo's face was cold and stone-like. 'I imagine it feels no worse than realising my background had some bearing on your feelings for me.'

The contempt in his eyes seemed to blister her skin.

'Besides, my grandfather's wealth is not pillow talk: I don't discuss the state of his finances with every woman I sleep with.' He gave a short laugh.

Prudence felt the room lurch as the implication of his words sank in. She clenched her hands together to stop them shaking.

'I wasn't "every woman". I was your wife. Or have you forgotten?'

He shook his head slowly. 'I try to forget every day, *pireni*. One day I may finally do so. But, either way, I will never forgive you. And you're still fired.'

There was a frozen silence. Prudence could taste rust in her mouth—the corrosive tang of failure. Her body felt limp, spent, her mind reduced. She had no words left inside—or none that had the power to reach him anyway. It was over.

And now that it was, all she wanted to do was get away from him as quickly as possible, with all that remained of her dignity.

'Fine. Then perhaps you could call me a taxi for the airport? I should like to leave as soon as possible.' Her head suddenly felt impossibly heavy, and she pressed her hand against her temple.

Laszlo watched her. Even though anger still festered inside him, he found himself reluctantly admiring her courage in defeat.

'If that's what you'd prefer,' he said.

His voice was that of a stranger: polite, solicitous, but remote. It pricked her like a needle and she felt a cold, creeping numbness begin to seep through her body at this poignant reminder of the irrevocable shift in their relationship.

'Our car is at your disposal, of course.'

Prudence shook her head. 'Thank you, but no thank you,' she said stiffly. 'I'd be happier making my own way.' She hesitated and then, lifting her chin, said flatly, 'I don't know what you're going to say to your grandfather, but please would you pass on my apologies for what's happened? I really am sorry for any inconvenience this may have caused him. And I'm also sorry not to be meeting him. He sounds like a remarkable man.'

Pausing, she stared fixedly at a point above his head.

'And there's something else—' Noticing the irritation on his face, she shook her head. 'It won't take long.'

He nodded but suddenly she found she couldn't speak. She knew what she needed to say—she just wasn't certain of how to say it. She just knew that as long as she remained 'married' to him her life would never be her own.

Gritting her teeth, she drew a quick breath—for what more had she to lose?

'If I'd known you were here I never would have come.

But…' She paused and took another breath. 'But I'm glad now that I did. Seeing you again has made me realise that I need to draw a line under what happened between us.'

Her face felt suddenly hot and dry and her unshed tears felt like a burden of lead. But she would not cry. Not until she was on that plane home.

Watching his eyes narrow, she smiled stiffly. 'Don't worry. I'm not going to go over it all again. Let's just agree that we were both too young and we made mistakes.' She hesitated. 'But we're older now, and wiser, and so we can put them right.'

'Put them right?' echoed Laszlo. His words were expressionless but there was a glimmer of emotion in the hammered gold of his eyes.

'Yes,' Prudence said flatly. She swallowed. 'I mean obviously neither of us wants to meet again. So I think we should take this opportunity to sort our relationship out once and for all.'

The air felt suddenly tight around her. Gasping, she lifted her chin and found herself on the receiving end of a bone-chilling stare.

'I see. So what exactly are you suggesting?' Laszlo said softly.

Prudence tensed. Whatever inner strength she had, it wasn't enough. Not nearly enough to dig a hole big enough to bury the past and the pain. And she was done with digging. She needed closure. Something formal. Something that would let her get on with her life. And now maybe she'd found it.

'Our marriage is over. We both accept that. All I'm suggesting is that we make it official. I think we should get a divorce, however we do that.'

Her voice trailed off and there was a small, tight pause. Her cheeks felt hot.

Suddenly her heart was beating like a drum and she

found herself babbling. 'It's been seven years, Laszlo. Our lives have moved on. We just need to tie up all the loose ends.'

It was the wrong thing to say. She watched his shoulders stiffen with a tension that thinned the air between them.

'Is that what I am?' he said, his gaze probing her face with such fierce intensity that suddenly she was holding her breath. 'A *loose end*?'

She ignored his question. 'I don't want this hanging over me. Without a divorce we'll both be trapped by something neither of us wants any more. I want my freedom.'

'Freedom?' Laszlo demanded.

She flushed. 'I want closure. I want to move on,' she said urgently.

'You want to move on…' Laszlo lifted his eyebrows. He looked at her impassively but there was a dangerous glint in his eyes.

'Stop repeating everything I say! Yes, I want to move on.' Prudence jerked her chin up. 'I have a career now. And if I meet someone…'

Suddenly he was no longer coolly aloof but intent and alert.

'Did you have a particular someone in mind?'

He spoke softly—courteously, even—but there was no mistaking the hostility and challenge in his voice.

Prudence stared at him, transfixed. 'No. I don't. Not that it's any concern of yours.'

His eyes clashed with hers and she tensed in their glare.

'No concern of mine? And how do you come to that conclusion, *pireni*?'

'Easily,' she said irritably. 'We haven't seen or spoken to one another for seven years. We have no claim on each other whatsoever.'

Laszlo's eyes lifted to hers and with shock she saw passion and possession in their burnished depths. 'And yet here you are: my wife.'

Heat rose up round her neck, coiling tendrils over her face and throat.

Shaking her head, she took a small, hurried step back from the intensity of his eyes.

'You know what? Forget it! Let's just leave it to the lawyers.'

Her heart was thumping and her palms felt suddenly damp as he shook his head slowly.

'I don't believe in divorce.'

She stared at him in silence, her skin prickling beneath his gaze. 'So what are you saying?' Her voice rose. 'That we carry on as though none of this happened?' It was her turn to shake her head. 'Laszlo, that's *insane*! Why on earth would you want to do that? You don't even *like* me.' She paused, her colour rising betrayingly. 'And I certainly don't like *you*!'

'Is that right?'

He gave her an infuriating smile and she gritted her teeth together.

'Yes, it is. It's been a long time since I've been susceptible to your charms.'

Her pulse twitched at the lie and she had to clench her hands to stop them covering the tips of her breasts, which were pushing treacherously against the thin fabric of her blouse.

'Are you sure about that?' he whispered.

Transfixed, Prudence caught her breath. Her skin was taut and tingling, as though a storm was about to break, and as his eyes travelled questioningly over her trembling body she felt a slow, rippling swell of tension rise up inside her. He stepped towards her and her stomach plummeted. She knew she should protest, or push him away, and she opened her mouth. But no words came, for something in his gaze had drained the last atom of resistance from her.

'Let's just see, shall we?' he murmured softly.

Imprisoned by a hope, a longing she knew she should resist, she felt her body melt as he brought his lips down on hers with a fierce urgency. And then there was no one but him, his insistent mouth on hers, and a swimming giddiness tugging her down into darkness.

He tasted sweet and salty. And hot. Her eyelids fluttered and her mouth opened and then she was kissing him back greedily, her lips bruising against his. And all the time heat was climbing inside her, spiralling upwards. Frantically she squirmed against him, pressing her body to his, her hands tugging at his shirt, plucking clumsily at the buttons.

He kissed her hungrily, with lips that formed no words but spoke of danger and of something like belonging, and his kisses made her feel fearless and strong.

She heard him groan, and then abruptly he released his grip and stepped away. She opened her eyes and stared at him, confused, feeling a coldness against her skin where moments earlier she had felt the pressing warmth of his lips and fingers. Her body was trembling like a leaf in the rain and hastily she clutched at one of the armchairs for support.

There was a long, pulsing silence and then Laszlo shook his head and said quietly, 'Not susceptible?'

Prudence gazed at him, dazed; her brain felt fogged and her lips were tingling and tender from the heat of his kiss. She could hardly believe what had just happened—what she had let happen.

'We shouldn't have done that,' she said shakily. 'It was a mistake.' She took a step backwards, her eyes darting frantically around the room.

Laszlo studied her coolly. 'No. Our marriage was a mistake. That…' He stared mockingly at her swollen mouth.

'That was just a demonstration of how little you know yourself.'

Somewhere in the castle a clock began to chime and, frowning, Laszlo glanced at his watch. His face darkened and he shook his head, his mouth set in a grim line.

'It's too late now for you to catch a flight home.'

There was a tense silence and then finally, in a voice that made her stomach turn in on itself, he spoke.

'You'll have to stay here tonight.'

He stared at her coolly, his eyes dark and implacable.

'But don't get any ideas. I'm only letting you stay out of the goodness of my heart.' His eyes glittered. 'Nothing's changed, Prudence. You have one night and one night only.'

She found herself holding her breath as he studied her face.

'After that I don't ever want to hear from you or see you again,' he warned softly. He studied her coldly. 'A word of advice, though. I wouldn't bother trying to pursue this matter outside of this room. The stakes are too high. It won't just be your pride that gets hurt.' He paused, his eyes fixed to her face. 'I'll ruin Seymour's too.'

In other words, she just had to accept her dismissal in silence. *Unfair dismissal,* her brain screamed. He couldn't just fire her like this.

Only he could. And he had.

Worse, there was nothing she could do about it. The De Zsadany Corporation was a huge, global company that had almost limitless funds and an entire publicity department at its disposal. She felt a shiver of apprehension. There was no doubt in her mind that if she tried to challenge Laszlo he'd use every weapon in his armoury to wipe not just her but Seymour's off the face of the earth.

It was bad enough that she was going to have to tell him that she'd lost the de Zsadany contract; she certainly wasn't going to do anything else to jeopardise Edmund's livelihood.

She shivered at the intensity in his expression as he spoke again.

'I don't suppose you'll want to hang about, so I'll arrange for a taxi to be waiting at…shall we say six-fifteen?'

Prudence nodded mutely.

'Good.' His mouth twisted into a grim smile. 'And make sure you're in it. Otherwise you, your family and all those nice people at Seymour's will live to regret it.'

And with that he turned and walked out of the room.

Her heart pounding erratically, Prudence stared after him. A rising hysteria was scrabbling inside her like a trapped animal. She'd ruined everything—and not just for Edmund.

She shivered. Seven years ago she'd vowed to forget him. Some mornings she'd barely been able to drag herself out of bed. Only one thought had kept her from pulling the duvet over her head: that in time she would be able to think of Laszlo Cziffra with nothing more than a bruised sadness. And one day she might just have managed it.

Her face quivered. One fervid, feverish kiss later and how foolish that hope seemed. For now she saw that it didn't really matter how much time she had. Seven years or seven hundred—it would make no difference. It would never be long enough for her to forget Laszlo and how he had made her feel.

Prudence lifted a hand to her mouth, remembering the burning heat of his kiss. How he could apparently still make her feel.

CHAPTER FOUR

LASZLO WOKE WITH a start. His room was dark and cold but it was not the cool night air which had shaken him from sleep. He shivered and rolled onto his side, feeling his heart drumming against his chest. It had been a long time since 'the dream' had woken him—so long he had almost forgotten the mixture of apprehension and panic that followed in its wake. Of course the feeling of dread would subside, but Prudence Elliot wasn't just haunting his dreams now. She was here, in his home, sleeping under his roof, her presence tugging at him like a fish hook.

Scowling, he rolled onto his back. In the darkness, he felt his cheeks grow warm.

Last night Prudence had accused him of being a coward and a liar. Her accusations—so unexpected, so bitter—had left him breathless; and now they lay lodged under his heart, cold and solid like stone. He rolled back onto his side, trying to shift the memory of her words, but the empty space beside him seemed only to strengthen their tenacity.

He felt misery swell in his chest.

Once upon a time he had imagined Prudence lying next to him in this very bed—had imagined bringing her to the castle as his new bride, even pictured her face, her surprise and excitement. He frowned. And now she was here. Only she was sleeping in a guest room and she had come not as his wife but as an unbidden, unwelcome intruder.

He grunted crossly. No matter. She would be gone soon enough. His breathing sounded suddenly harsh in the darkness, and anger, frustration and resentment fused in a rip tide of emotion.

Gritting his teeth, he shifted irritably beneath the sheets, knowing that sleep was inconceivable now. He fumbled in the darkness for the bedside lamp and a soft light illuminated the room. Squinting, he rolled onto his side. What the hell was wrong with him? Prudence's imminent departure should have comforted him, so why was the thought of it making him feel more tense?

He swallowed. Guilt. That was why. Picturing his grandfather's disappointment, he frowned through the ache in his chest. But what choice had he had? Working with her, living with her, would have been intolerable. Laszlo shivered, his jaw tightening. Firing her had been the right, the only thing to do. And it should have been the end of it. Only then she'd told him she wanted a divorce.

He winced inwardly: *divorce*. She'd thrown the word at him carelessly, almost as an afterthought. But to him it had felt like a punch to the head. Grimacing, he punched the pillow in return and lay back again. She had been so insistent—she who had never known her own mind, who had questioned every tiny detail. Demanding her freedom! Freedom from something she'd never even believed in.

The only thing that had mattered had been hurting her and proving her wrong, and so he'd kissed her. And, feeling her melt against him, he'd felt a surge of triumph. Only now the triumph had faded and he was lost—swept far away, a stranger to himself, his entire body a quivering mass of frustrated desire.

Damn her! He shouldn't be feeling like this; after all, he hated Prudence Elliot. A muscle flickered in his jaw and suddenly, remembering her mouth beneath his, his body instantly and painfully tightened. He rubbed his hands tiredly over his face. Okay: he wanted her. That was undeniable. Maybe *hatred* was the wrong word. It certainly didn't do justice to this whole set of feelings that were plaguing him now. Not that he even really knew what they were. Just that his life had grown infinitely more complicated and less certain overnight.

Abruptly he tired of his thoughts and hoping to shift the uneasy, shifting mass of arguments inside his head, he switched off the lamp and stared at the window, watching the light creep under the curtains. And then, feeling suddenly drained, he slid down under the bedclothes and sleep came at last as the sun began to warm his room.

It was time to leave.

Pressing herself into the corner of the taxi, Prudence sat back and, closing her eyes, said a silent farewell to Kastely Almasy. It should have been a relief to leave, to know that this was the end. But as the car accelerated down the drive she was fighting hard not to give in to the sense of failure and desolation that filled her chest. How could it have come to this?

Sadly, she remembered the first time she'd seen Laszlo. It had been at a funfair, and even though she'd been almost intoxicated by the lights and the noise, the screaming and too much sugar, she had still lost her footing when she'd noticed him standing slightly aloof from the crowd. His dark-eyed beauty had been like a shot of neat alcohol. A rushing, teasing dizziness she could still remember. In that moment, she had fallen swiftly and irrevocably in love and later lying in his arms, she had felt invincible in the sanctum of their intimacy.

Prudence sat up straighter, her jaw tightening. But that had been seven years ago. Now all that remained of that exhilaration and ecstasy was a crushing hangover. She sighed irritably. Tiredness was making her self-indulgent.

Last night sleep had eluded her. Images from the evening, dark like wine, had spilled and spread through her dreams: Laszlo's brooding gaze, the sensual curve of his mouth, his strong hands reaching out to pull her closer...

Her body stilled as she remembered the fierce, vivid pleasure of his kiss and how badly she had wanted him to keep kissing her and touching her and—

Abruptly, her eyes opened. And what? She caught her breath. Wasn't letting him kiss her a big enough mistake? Perhaps she should sleep with him too, just to make her humiliation complete? Maybe then the message would get through to her. That his kiss had been nothing to do with passion and everything to do with power.

She should have slapped him or pushed him away—or better still run away. But of course she'd done nothing of the sort. Her body had been utterly beyond her control— her hunger, her need for him, hot and unstoppable like lava. Even though he'd been so cruelly vindictive and unreasonable, everything and everyone—her family, her career, her pride—had been surrendered to the honeyed sweetness of his lips and the warm, treacherous pleasure gathering inside her.

Wincing, Prudence bit her lip. What had happened last night shouldn't have happened. But it wasn't surprising that it had. Last night their past had dropped into the present like an atom bomb. She and Laszlo had been like the survivors of a blast, staggering around, unable to speak or hear. Physical intimacy had been inevitable, for they had both been wounded and needing comfort. And besides, sex had always been the way they'd communicated best.

She stared bleakly out of the window, feeling the comet's tail of his caresses trailing over her skin, and then she shivered, feeling suddenly empty and drained. Now was not the time to be indulging in fantasies. Laszlo Cziffra might still be her 'husband' but he was not her lover. He was the enemy, and that kiss had been a ruthless demonstration of his power—not some resurrection of the passion they had once shared.

She lifted her chin, feeling anger effervesce inside her. How dare he twist what had been beautiful and blissful between them for his own ends! He was a monster! A bullying, manipulative monster. For all that talk of being married was just that: talk. After all, what kind of a husband would sack his own wife?

Seething with frustration, she glanced out of the window at the wall that edged the estate, her thoughts scampering in every direction. How could he just fire her anyway? She frowned. She, or rather Seymour's, had been hired by Mr Janos de Zsadany—not Laszlo Cziffra!

She felt another spasm of anger and then suddenly, unthinkingly, leant forward and hammered on the glass behind the taxi driver's head.

'Stop! Stop the car, please!'

She was out of the taxi before it had even ground to a halt and she caught a glimpse of the driver's startled face as she half stepped, half fell onto the road.

'S-sorry,' she stammered breathlessly. 'I didn't mean to scare you. It's just that I've realised there's something I need to do back at the castle.' She felt her cheeks burn as the man stared at her incredulously. 'I just remembered it. Just then,' she said hurriedly. 'So I'll just go back and...'

Her voice tailed off as he frowned and, suddenly remembering that she needed to pay, Prudence reached hastily into her handbag. But the driver shook his head.

'No. No need. It is settled. No need for money. But no need to walk. I take you back, yes?'

Prudence felt a sudden twinge of alarm. What exactly was she doing? And then, with shock and something like excitement, she realised that she didn't know—and what was more, she didn't care. All her life she'd made plans and followed the rules and what good had it done her?

She shook her head. 'No,' she said firmly. 'No, thank you. It's not far and I'll enjoy the walk. If you could just get my suitcase from the boot?'

She waited impatiently as the driver got out of the car and went round to the rear of the vehicle, releasing the boot to take out her case. He placed it beside her and she pulled up the handle and tilted the case back onto its wheels. She smiled her thanks at the driver and then turned and, heart thumping in her chest, began to walk back towards the castle.

Part of her expected to hear the driver call out, or turn the car round, but nothing happened and after a few moments she realised that for the first time since she'd agreed to go to Hungary she felt oddly calm—happy, even.

Finally she reached the tall iron gates. She stopped and drew a deep breath and, reaching out, pulled firmly on the handle. And pulled and pulled—and pulled again, and again, with increasing desperation. But it was no good: the metal creaked but the gates stayed obstinately shut.

For a moment Prudence stood pink-cheeked and panting, and then she let out a low moan. Of course—they were electric. She glanced wildly around for a bell but there wasn't one. There wasn't even a nameplate. How was she supposed to get back in?

She stared up and down the road but there was no sign of anyone, and finally she turned back to the gates, feeling her earlier bravado slip away. So that was that. Her one and only act of rebellion—over before it had even started. Looking up, she stared sadly at the stone wall.

Or was it?

Frowning, she glanced down at her high-heeled court shoes, and then in one swift movement she had kicked them off and tucked them firmly into her suitcase. Perfect! She took a couple of steps backwards and stared assessingly at the wall, and then, with as much strength as she could manage, she hurled her midsized case upwards. Holding her breath, she watched as it flew high into the air and over the top of the wall. It landed with a heavy thump on the other side.

Sighing in relief, she grabbed hold of one of the damp stones and began to pull herself up. It was easier than she'd thought it would be, and climbing down was easier still. She had just stepped back from the wall with a self-congratulatory smile when abruptly she felt a sudden rise in tension. The air stilled and her skin began to prickle. And then the breath seemed to ooze out of her lungs like a balloon deflating as she heard a familiar voice.

'Good morning, Miss Elliot! I'd like to say it's a pleasure to see you again but we both know that wouldn't be true, don't we?'

Prudence reluctantly turned round to find Laszlo watching her, his hands in his pockets, his face, as usual, unreadable. Dressed casually in jeans and a black polo shirt, his hair tousled, he looked younger, more carefree than he had done last night, but there was an intensity to his stillness that felt almost predatory to her.

'This dropping in on me is becoming a bit of a habit, isn't it? If I didn't know better I'd say you had designs on me,' he observed slowly. 'I must say that I'm a bit surprised— although perhaps *surprised* isn't the right word. *Shocked* might be better; or *outraged*—or perhaps *offended*. Given that you appear to be in the process of breaking into my home.'

Laszlo thrust his hands deeper into his pockets. Actually, as he'd watched her clamber down the wall he'd felt something closer to fear than anger—for what would have happened if she'd fallen and he hadn't been out walking the grounds?

Even though she was back on solid ground, Prudence felt her nerves scrabbling frantically for a footing. A sidelong glance at Laszlo did nothing to improve her composure: he seemed almost preternaturally calm. But there was no point in her having come back if she was going to let him intimidate her from the outset and, gritting her teeth, she held her head high and met his gaze defiantly.

Finally he shook his head and said lightly, 'So. Did you come back to rob me? Or just to check that you'd finished me off with your suitcase?'

Prudence stared at him, her face white with shock. 'Of course I didn't come back to rob you!' She stopped speaking suddenly, momentarily confused. 'Wh—what do you mean, finish you off?'

Laszlo raised his eyebrows. 'What do I mean?' he repeated quietly, his expression cryptic. 'I mean I was taking an early-morning stroll, quite happily minding my own business, when suddenly I was nearly poleaxed by *that*.'

He glanced behind him and Prudence saw her suitcase lying on its side in the grass.

'That *is* yours, isn't it?'

She bit her lip and he watched her eyes darken, the black swallowing the grey, and then slowly she was smiling, and then she burst out laughing.

'I'm sorry,' she mumbled. 'It's not funny. I'm sorry—I really am.' She bit her lip again and tried to stifle a giggle as he shook his head, his eyes gleaming and golden beneath their dark lashes. And then, just as suddenly, his jaw tightened and it felt as if a bucket of cold water had been thrown into her face.

'It's a miracle you didn't injure someone. My grandfather often rises early and walks around the grounds.' He looked at her evenly. 'But I suppose no one was actually hurt, so I'll accept your apology. However, that doesn't explain why you're sneaking over my wall just minutes after I saw you leave in a taxi.'

Prudence felt her face turn hot with embarrassment and

fury. 'I wasn't *sneaking*!' she snapped. 'I had to climb over the wall because the gates were locked.'

Again Laszlo raised an eyebrow.

'Indeed they are,' he said softly. 'They keep out unwanted visitors. Usually.'

Feeling clumsy under his cool scrutiny, but refusing to be intimidated, she turned to face him. 'I am *not* an unwanted visitor. I am here to do a job—a job I was hired to complete by your grandfather. You might want to send me packing but it's not your choice to make.'

Laszlo studied her impassively. He'd thought nothing could ever surprise him again after finding Prudence in his sitting room last night, but that was before he'd watched her scramble back into his life over a huge stone wall. And now she was refusing to leave unless his grandfather agreed to it.

Fingering his phone in his pocket, he looked away and gritted his teeth. It would be the work of moments to call the taxi driver back and double…triple his fare to take her away. So why was he hesitating?

He glanced back at her and his groin tightened. *That* was why! He felt heat slide over his skin and wondered if she had any idea how incredibly sexy she looked. Was this really the same shy girl he'd married seven years ago? Standing there barefoot on his lawn, her hair tumbling over her shoulders, her breasts thrust forward like a modern-day Semiramis.

He shook his head, to clear it of this arousing, unsettling chain of thought, and as if on cue she stepped forward, eyes flashing, ready for battle. 'I won't leave on your say-so, Laszlo. You'll have to drag me kicking and—'

'Okay. Okay.' He raised his hands in surrender. 'Give me your bag!'

Prudence looked up at him suspiciously. 'Wh—why would I want to do that?'

Their eyes met and the silence between them rose and fell in time to the sound of her heartbeat.

'So I can carry it for you. I don't usually conduct business on the lawn. Let's go somewhere more private. And safer!'

She heard the smile in his voice and, glancing up at him, she felt her stomach flip over as his eyes locked on hers. 'Trust me. This lawn's actually much more dangerous than it looks.'

She felt the hairs rise on the back of her neck and suddenly breathing was a struggle. 'No, thanks,' she said hoarsely, averting her gaze. 'You probably just want to throw me in the moat or something.'

Laszlo shook his head and looked up at her speculatively through thick dark lashes.

'That definitely won't happen.' He paused, the corners of his mouth tugging upwards. 'We haven't had a moat since the sixteenth century.' Glancing up at the sky, he frowned. 'Besides, it's about to start raining. I'm too much of a gentleman to leave you to your one-woman protest, and rain means my hair is going to get wet. And you know what happens when my hair gets wet…'

Shaking her head, she gave a small reluctant smile. 'Gentleman? More like gentleman of the road!'

He winced as a drop of rain hit his shoulder. 'Come on, *pireni*! You know how much I hate it when my hair goes curly.'

Breathing unsteadily, her heart banging against her ribs, Prudence frowned.

'I promise I won't do anything you don't want me to,' he said lightly.

He watched the colour spread over her cheeks as she hesitated, and then she nodded. And then the clouds split apart and they ran as rain thundered down.

'This way!' he shouted over his shoulder as water

splashed at them from every direction, and then, as one, they burst through a heavy close-boarded door into an enormous empty barn. 'We'll have to wait here until it stops!' He glanced down at her feet. 'Are you okay? You didn't cut yourself or anything?'

He had to yell to make himself heard and she shook her head dumbly. Was she okay? She was in a barn, alone, standing with a soaking wet, panting Laszlo. How was that ever going to be okay?

Her eyes fixed on his rain-spattered shirt, the definition of hard muscle clearly visible against the damp fabric. Instantly she felt a familiar tingling ache low within her pelvis: she knew exactly what lay beneath that shirt. She could feel a yearning deep inside for the ceaseless touch of his hands, his lips—

And then the air slammed out of her lungs as he suddenly shook his head like a dog.

Abruptly she heard the rain stop.

He looked up at her and Prudence felt her pulse jump.

'I don't want to have to drag your grandfather into this, Laszlo. I just want you to give me my job back,' she blurted out.

Laszlo studied her calmly. 'I know what you want,' he said slowly, and his shimmering golden gaze slipped over her skin in a way that made her stir restlessly inside.

Flustered, almost squirming with tension, she lifted her chin. 'Do you?' she said challengingly.

His eyes gleamed and the trace of a smile curved his lips for the briefest of moments—and then his smile faded. Staring at her broodingly, he let his gaze drift over her soft pink mouth and felt his body respond instantaneously. It had always been like this with Prudence—this fierce, relentless tug of physical need like a terrible, aching hunger that must be satisfied.

He frowned. He felt as if he was teetering on the brink of something.

'Okay,' he said softly. 'You can stay. The job is yours.'

Heart thumping, Prudence bit her lip. Had he really changed his mind? Or was this some sort of cruel game? But one look at his face told her that incredibly, unbelievably, he was telling the truth. She turned away to hide her confusion as instead of relief a spasm of doubt ran through her body.

'And you're sure about this?' she said slowly, looking up at him and frowning. 'Only it all seems a bit sudden. You changing your mind like this.'

Laszlo forced himself to meet her eyes. He was just going to have to hope that she accepted his volte-face as evidence of his impulsive nature. But the truth was that he was struggling to make sense of his decision too. 'You know me, Prudence. I can't resist a fork in the road. It's in my blood.'

Prudence stared at him suspiciously. She could hardly refute his claim; his mercurial moods and erratic behaviour had overshadowed their entire relationship. However, if this was going to be a business relationship, they needed to deal in fact. It didn't mean that he could try to fob her off with some flowery, meaningless nonsense.

'You're going to have to do better than that, Laszlo.' She shook her head. 'Why have you changed your mind?'

There was a loaded silence and then he shrugged. 'Seymour's are the best, and I want the best for my grandfather.' He surveyed her calmly. 'So, do we have a deal, then?'

She nodded slowly.

His smile tightened. 'But don't think that just because I've changed my mind anything has changed between *us*. I may be willing to forget the past for my grandfather's sake, but I haven't forgiven you.'

Nor was he entirely sure that he'd done the right thing,

letting Prudence stay. But it would be for only a matter of weeks, and *he* would be calling the shots. Breathing out slowly, he felt a twinge of satisfaction—for now that he'd rationalised his behaviour, he saw that it would be immensely gratifying to have his beautiful English wife at his beck and call.

Staring defiantly at his face, Prudence clenched her fists, resentment curdling in her throat. She should be feeling relieved—ecstatic, even—for she'd fought to keep her job. But now the full consequences of having achieved that goal were starting to dawn on her and she felt more cornered than anything. He was in control here and she knew that. Worse—he did. And even worse than that was the knowledge that she still responded to the maleness of him with an eagerness that shocked her.

Her pulse leapt. Could she really do this? Work and live with Laszlo? Remembering the heat of his lips on hers, she felt her body still and her breath snag in her throat. How could she still want him? After everything he'd done and said? It was incomprehensible. But while her heart might have hardened against him, her body still melted at his touch. Not liking that fact didn't make it any less true.

She turned to face him and found him watching her impassively. Looking away again, she swallowed. If ever she was weak and stupid enough even to *imagine* kissing him again, she'd need to remember that look—right there—to remind herself that Laszlo had coldly and without any compunction discarded her. No kiss and no caress, however sublime, could change that.

'I understand,' she said crisply.

It was on the tip of her tongue to say that receiving his forgiveness was not exactly top of her agenda, but she had no desire for yet another confrontation—and then she sucked in a breath as she realised that her inadequate instinct for self-preservation was the least of her worries.

'What about your grandfather?' she said abruptly. 'What are you going to tell him? About us?'

For a moment he said nothing, and she held her breath, and then he turned to look at her, his eyes so golden and fierce it was like looking into the sun.

'What would you have me tell him? That I've deceived him for the last seven years?'

His voice seared her skin and she shook her head. He looked away, his mouth thinning to a grim line. She swallowed and took a stinging breath, hating herself but knowing that there was no avoiding it.

'And my contract?'

Laszlo studied her for a moment. 'Will be signed this morning. But until then shall we shake on it?'

Prudence stared at him in silence, her skin prickling. Taking a deep breath, she nodded and offered him her hand. His fingers brushed against hers, and then she gave a sharp cry of surprise as his hand slid over her wrist and he jerked her towards him, hard and fast, pulling her body close to his lean, muscular torso.

'Let me go,' she said, trying desperately to yank herself free.

She struggled against him but he simply drew her closer, clamping her body against his until he felt her resistance subside.

'No. Not until you and I have got a couple of things straight.'

Prudence gritted her teeth. 'Isn't that something to do when we sign the contract? You know—with a lawyer present.'

Her stomach flipped as she felt him weave his fingers through her hair, his hand holding her captive.

'You'll get your contract, Prudence. But we need to lay down a few ground rules just between the two of us.'

He tilted her face up towards him and her skin grew warm beneath his glimmering hypnotic gaze.

'Firstly, you're here to work. And whatever you might like to think, *I'm* your boss and I'll be working closely with you on this project. This is something my grandfather has asked me to oversee. So if you don't think you can stomach taking orders from me then I suggest you climb back over that wall right now.'

Clenching her hands into fists, she counted to fifty under her breath. Finally, after a long pause, she said stiffly, 'I understand.'

Their eyes met and he nodded.

'Good. Secondly, you will restrict your remarks to matters relating to the cataloguing. You will most certainly not discuss anything to do with our previous relationship or the existence of our marriage with anyone. And I don't just mean my grandfather.'

Prudence stared at him, her mouth trembling. 'Oh, don't worry—I don't intend to tell *anyone* about our marriage; it's not something I actually go around boasting about.'

His hand twisted in her hair and she squirmed in his grip as he jerked her closer. 'Finally,' he said softly. 'Something we can agree on.'

Her eyes slammed into his like thunderclouds colliding with the sun and then she shook her head wearily. She was beginning to wish that she'd just stayed in the taxi.

'You know what? I actually don't want to have anything to do with you when I'm not working. That's *my* ground rule. I came back for my job and that's what I'm going to do: my job. Not gossip about a marriage I didn't even know was real and that quite frankly was so long ago and so short I can't really remember it anyway!'

His eyes met hers and she held her breath, her blood humming in her veins.

'Oh, but I can,' he murmured.

His hand slid down her neck, cupping her chin, the thumb strumming her cheek, stroking slowly, steadily, until she arched helplessly against him, feeling his hard strength, his raw desire, and wanting more of both.

'I can remember every single moment.'

Prudence swallowed. She opened her mouth to speak, tried to lift her hands and push him away, but her brain and body refused to co-operate. Her head was spinning and she could feel her insides tightening, desire mingling with frustration and anger. And then he shifted against her so that the hard muscle of his thigh pushed against her pelvis.

She moaned softly, tipping her head back as his lips caressed her neck, moving slowly, deliberately over her throat and back to her mouth, and then her lips parted and he lowered his mouth to hers. Tingling currents of sensation snaked across her skin and, reaching up, she curled her fingers through his hair and drew him closer, gripping him tightly, for it felt almost as though she might disappear into the kiss itself.

And then, slowly at first, and then with a jolt, her brain seemed to awaken from a deep sleep and she broke free of his arms.

The air on her skin felt sudden and sharp, like a knife, and she rubbed her hand against her mouth as though to remove all traces of his dark, compelling kiss.

'We shouldn't have done that.'

Her voice was raw, her breathing coming in panicky little gasps. It had been wrong. And stupid and dangerous. A shudder ran through her. But how could it be wrong when it had felt so good and so right?

Laszlo watched her shake her head, a fierce, urgent heat flaring in his belly. He wanted her so much he could hardly stand. And she had wanted him—she still did. He could see that in the dark turbulence in her eyes and in the convulsive trembling of her skin.

'What are you talking about?' His voice was taut, his breathing fraying apart as he spoke.

'I don't want that—I don't want you—' she began.

Laszlo cut her off incredulously. '*That* was you not wanting me?'

Biting her lip, she shook her head, too horrified by the violence of her response to him even to try to dissemble her desire for him. 'No. I *do* want you.' Shivering, she took a step backwards, staring at him with wide-eyed agitation. 'But we can't. It would be wrong—' She looked frantically past him, trying to locate the door in the gloom of the barn.

Laszlo frowned. 'Wrong? How could it be wrong? We're married—'

It was her turn to look incredulous. 'It's not about whether we're *married*, Laszlo!' She shook her head again. 'It's not appropriate, our doing that, when—' She was struggling for words. 'I mean, you hate me.'

'I don't hate you,' he said slowly, and he was surprised to find that it was true. He didn't.

There was a shocked silence and she met his gaze.

'But you don't like me, and I don't like you, and we certainly don't love one another.' Her voice sounded wooden but her breathing was calmer now and she lifted her chin. 'This is just sex.'

'This is *not* just sex,' he said, speaking with slow, clear emphasis. 'You clearly haven't had much in the way of sexual experience if you think *that* was just sex.'

Her face coloured. 'You're right. I haven't. But when I make love to someone it will be because I love them and *only* because I love them. Not because of anything else.'

Knowing just how good that 'anything else' could feel, she clenched her fists against the treacherous warmth seeping over her skin.

'So, no, Laszlo. I'm not going to have sex with you in a barn even though we may be married.'

Crossing her arms in front of her body, she stared at him defiantly.

Laszlo studied her in silence. Had he really thought she would sleep with him? And would he have respected her if she had? He smiled grimly. Would he have respected *himself*? After all, he'd kissed her twice in twenty-four hours, each time telling himself it was the last time—each time, telling himself it was a mistake, that whatever desire he felt was just some reflex kicking in…a habit from the past. But why, if that were true, did he want to keep on repeating those mistakes? And go on repeating them.

He felt his body stir again and frowned. His mistake had been to believe he was over her—for he saw now that, like a virus in his blood, his longing for her had simply lain dormant until she'd walked back into his life yesterday and turned him inside out.

His jaw tightened. He needed some way to cure himself of this sexual power she had over him. Only he was so wound up he was finding it hard to think. All he knew was that his body was pulsing with frustration.

'Okay,' he said finally. He watched her breathe out. 'Look. We've both had a lot to take in. And we're still coming to terms with—' he waved his hand towards the roof of the barn '—everything. So I think we should cut ourselves a bit of slack. How about we go up to the castle and have some breakfast?'

Prudence nodded wordlessly. Her brain was in overdrive. Why had she said she 'might' be married to Laszlo? And why did the thought of being his wife make her stomach turn over and over in helpless response to him? Her mouth tightened. It was foolish and distracting. Even if she accepted his version of events, it was still not something of which she needed to be reminded. Particularly as she seemed determined to give in to the intense sexual chemistry between them at every opportunity.

Pushing back her shoulders, she reached behind her neck and smoothed her hair into a ponytail. Her body clearly had very poor judgement when it came to men and she would need to be on her guard at all times—otherwise this arrangement simply wouldn't work. And that was what she was here to do: work. Not concoct some parallel life in which she and Laszlo were happily married.

She realised that he had spoken again. 'Sorry—what did you say?'

He stared at her speculatively. 'I said that I'll introduce you to my grandfather after breakfast. And then we can sort out where you're going to sleep. It shouldn't be a problem. We have twenty bedrooms at the castle. Eighteen spare, that is.'

His groin tightened painfully as an image of her lying naked beside him in his bed slid into his head and he took a deep breath. Maybe their sleeping under the same roof was not such a good idea after all. Not unless he was prepared to sleep standing upright under a cold shower.

Prudence was clearly having the same thought.

'Why don't I just stay in a hotel?' she said quickly.

'That won't be necessary.'

A muscle flickered in his cheek. There was another option—only up until that moment the mere thought of suggesting it would have appalled him. But nothing was the same any more. Looking up at Prudence, he cleared his throat. 'There's an empty cottage on the estate. It's small. But it's clean and private and a lot cosier than the castle.'

His eyes blazed.

'Just don't get *too* cosy! As soon as the cataloguing is complete I want you out of my life and I never want to see you again.'

CHAPTER FIVE

'AND THIS IS one of my favourite pieces in the entire collection!' Janos de Zsadany took a step back and stared intently at the portrait of a girl clutching an open green fan. 'Annuska and I gave this to Zsofia for her sixteenth birthday.' He turned towards Prudence and gave the faintest of smiles. 'I think secretly she'd been hoping for a horse. But thankfully she was enchanted.'

Prudence gazed at the portrait. 'It's beautiful!' she said slowly. 'Were you specifically looking for a Henri?'

Janos shook his head. 'No. Not at all. But when Annuska and I saw this painting we both knew it was the one. She reminded us so much of Zsofia. Not just in colouring. It's her expression.' He smiled ruefully. 'My daughter often used to look at me like that. You know—that mixture of love and exasperation.'

Prudence bit her lip. She had suddenly realised that they weren't talking about some random young woman but Laszlo's mother. 'I'm sure it was just her age,' she said hesitantly.

She felt suddenly sick with guilt. Janos was talking so openly about such a private matter with the woman who was secretly married to his grandson. But what choice did she have? She sighed. It had been easy enough to agree with Laszlo not to discuss their marriage with anyone. It was not even that hard to convince herself that it was all for the best. Only now, faced with Janos's gentle courtesy, their subterfuge made her feel shabby and sly.

She sucked in a breath and managed a polite smile. 'Whatever your reasons, it was a good choice, Mr de Zsadany.'

Janos laughed. 'I think so too.' He beamed at her. 'I think we're going to get along very well, Miss Elliot.' He frowned. 'But could I suggest we do away with all these formalities, or we'll spend most of our time together repeating each other's names. Please call me Janos!'

Smiling, she shook his hand. 'Prudence,' she said firmly. 'And thank you, Janos, for making me feel so welcome.'

He bowed. 'No. Thank *you* for making this happen. You've made an old man very happy. And, as sorry as I am that Seymour was unable to be here, I'm in no way disappointed by his replacement. Don't worry, though! I won't tell anyone. It can be our little secret.'

'A remote castle in Hungary and a beautiful woman with a secret. How intriguing! It sounds like the plot for some kind of historical romance.'

They both turned to find Laszlo watching them from the doorway. His eyes fixed on Prudence and then his gaze shifted to his grandfather, his face softening into a smile.

'So!' He walked into the room and stopped in front of the painting, frowning. 'What's the big secret, then?'

He was still smiling, but his voice was blunt—like a knife against a whetstone. Since her arrival he'd been tormented by dreams of Prudence naked in the barn, and yet every time he'd met her she'd been polite but glacially remote. His smile tightened. It was an icy aloofness that appeared to be reserved only for him, for she'd established a sweetly flirtatious rapport with his grandfather.

Shaking his head, Janos patted his grandson on the arm. 'Oh, I was just trying to reassure Prudence that her presence here was in no way a disappointment. In fact, I'm rather hoping she might agree to be a charming, if sadly temporary, addition to our bachelor evenings of chess and backgammon.'

Forcing herself to look straight ahead, Prudence managed a faint smile. 'That would be lovely, Mr de— I mean Janos. But I wouldn't want to intrude.'

Janos shook his head. 'Not at all. You're a long way from home,' he said firmly. 'And while you're our guest it's our job to make you feel welcome—isn't it, Laszlo?'

Prudence caught her breath as Laszlo gave the ghost of a smile and nodded slowly. 'Of course, Papi,' he said stiffly. 'But right now you need to go downstairs and find Rosa. Apparently you're supposed to be discussing curtains?'

Janos frowned. 'Ah, yes. The curtains. I hadn't forgotten. I just rather hoped Rosa had.' He ran a hand over his face and cast an apologetic glance towards Prudence. 'If you'll excuse me, my dear? Perhaps, however, I can persuade you to join Laszlo and myself for lunch?'

Watching Janos leave, Prudence felt a pit open up in her stomach and the air seemed suddenly to swell in the pulsing, steepening silence. Since arriving at the castle three days ago she'd made a point of staying in the cottage outside of work hours, and had hardly seen Laszlo except at mealtimes, when she'd found his marked courtesy towards her both grating and depressing. Only now here they were: alone. There was nowhere to hide from his dark, probing gaze. Or from the fluttering, shivery anticipation squirming inside her.

Biting her lip, she reached up to tuck her hair behind her ear before remembering that, as usual for work, she'd tied it back into a low ponytail.

'I don't have to come to lunch. I could say I have work to do. Or that I've got a headache.' She spoke quickly, desperate to say something before her body began to slip apart and she couldn't even think straight, far less talk.

Laszlo stared at her, his face expressionless, and then he

said coldly, 'I'd rather you didn't keep lying to my grand-father, Prudence.'

She glared at him. 'I'm not lying. I *do* have work I could be doing.' And, turning, she began to rifle pointedly through a pile of papers on the desk.

'And the headache?' Laszlo said relentlessly.

Gritting her teeth, Prudence turned back to face him. 'Also true—and standing right in front of me!' she snapped.

Laszlo stared at her for a long, long moment, until finally he began to drift around the room. From the corner of her eye, she watched furtively as he walked up to his mother's painting and idly ran a finger down the frame.

'Don't you have somewhere to be?' she snapped finally.

Turning, he shrugged, and then in a voice that made the hairs on the back of her neck stand upright, he said mildly, 'I have a cure for headaches.'

His eyes locked onto hers and she felt heat break out on her skin. Clenching her fists, she gave him an icy glare. 'So do I. Painkillers. In my handbag.'

Laszlo frowned. 'You shouldn't take pills for a headache. They're not a cure. You need to treat the cause, not the symptom.'

Prudence glanced at him irritably. 'I'm sorry, I didn't know you were a doctor. Is that another of your parallel lives?'

A muscle flickered in his cheek. 'I don't like you taking drugs.'

'It's a painkiller!' she said through gritted teeth. 'And I'd be grateful if you kept your remarks to matters relating to the cataloguing. That is unless you think my drug-taking is affecting my job—'

She gazed at him in astonishment as he began peering under tables and rifling through canvases. 'Be careful! Don't touch them without gloves.'

She hurried across the room, and then her feet stuttered to a halt as he turned to face her.

'Wh—what are you doing?' she stammered. His eyes rested on her face and, legs shaking, she pressed her knees together as her body tightened automatically in response.

'I'm looking for your high horse,' he said softly. 'Or is he in stables with all the others?'

Prudence swallowed. 'Very funny! I don't know why you're making fun of me. It was you who said we couldn't discuss anything apart from the cataloguing. I'm just following the rules.'

'But I make the rules. And I can change them too.'

She held her breath as his eyes locked onto hers. Then, abruptly, he walked towards the window and glanced outside.

'What you need is some fresh air,' he said smoothly. 'And some sunlight. A walk, maybe. You used to like going for walks.'

Prudence licked her lips. A sudden, all too vivid memory of where a walk with Laszlo might lead flashed into her head and she felt heat rise up inside her. Cheeks burning, she fumbled for the remnants of her anger—for something that would banish the slow, treacherous thickening of her blood.

'Okay. I'll go for a walk before lunch. Satisfied? And now, if you don't mind, I have work to do.'

Desperate for him to be gone, she put her hands on her hips and stared pointedly at the door. But instead of leaving he simply stood and watched her in silence until she thought she would scream.

'Why are you still here?' she snapped finally. 'Don't you have some suits of armour you could polish or something? I thought you had a job running a restaurant.'

He shrugged, shook his head. 'A chain of restaurants actually. But no. I'm entirely unoccupied.'

Her eyes narrowed. In other words, he was bored. And she was—what? The entertainment? 'Well, I'm not,' she said flatly. 'So why don't you go climb your towers and survey your estate?'

'Turrets…' Laszlo murmured. 'From the Italian *torretta*. They help protect a castle from hostile intruders. At least, they're supposed to.' He raised an eyebrow. 'I'm ready when you are,' he added softly.

Prudence felt a niggle of dread. 'Ready for what?'

He frowned. 'Our walk, of course.'

His eyes were fixed on her shocked face and she shook her head. Her heart was suddenly pounding so hard she could hardly hear herself.

'I said no, Laszlo!'

She took a step back and Laszlo stared at her mockingly.

'Come on! You need some fresh air. And besides, Rosa gave me some linen to bring over to the cottage. I'll never hear the end of it if I let you carry it. So either I can come with you now or I can drop by later.'

Prudence stared at him in silence; she felt like a mouse cornered by a cat. But surely she was being over-anxious? She glanced down at her demure navy blouse and olive-coloured work trousers. It wasn't as though she was dressed for seduction. Besides—she bit her lip—she didn't want him turning up at the cottage at night!

'Fine. Let's get it over and done with, then. But I'll need to take one of these boxes back with me, so you'll have to wait until I've sorted out the paperwork.'

Five minutes later she was walking resentfully towards the cottage, trying to ignore the fact that Laszlo was strolling alongside her, clutching what appeared to be nothing more burdensome than a pile of tea towels. To add insult to injury, the document box she'd chosen to bring with her seemed to have doubled in weight since they'd left the castle and her arms now felt as if they were on fire.

'Here. Let me.' A lean brown hand reached out towards her.

'I can manage,' she muttered, but Laszlo ignored her feeble resistance. Tugging the box out of her hands, he tucked it under his arm before continuing to saunter calmly by her side.

Determinedly she carried on walking, staring fixedly at the horizon until finally, and to her infinite relief, she saw the roof of the cottage come into view.

She stopped and turned towards him.

'Thanks very much. I think I can take it from here.' Looking up at him, she blinked, feeling suddenly hot and stupid as he smiled at her coolly.

'You know, it's hotter than I thought,' he murmured, glancing up at the midday sun. 'Perhaps I could just grab a glass of water?'

She caught the glint in his eye and gritted her teeth; he'd be asking for a pot of tea and biscuits next. Quickening her pace, she marched across the grass, fuming in silence.

Suddenly he was beside her again. 'Why aren't you talking?'

Eyes flashing with fury, she spun round to face him. 'Mainly because I have absolutely nothing to say to you.'

She watched the corner of his mouth tug upwards.

'Oh, I think you've got plenty to say to me,' he said softly.

Feeling hopelessly out of her depth, she let out a breath and pointedly looked in the other direction.

Laszlo watched her intently. 'Perhaps you're right,' he murmured. 'I've always thought talking was overrated and I can think of much better things to do with your mouth.'

Her chest grew tight. Things were getting too complicated. Breathing was suddenly difficult, and hastily she began to walk down the sloping path that led towards the cottage. The path was still damp from some overnight rain, and as her shoes slithered beneath her she almost fell. Her heart jerked as Laszlo reached over and caught her hand to steady her.

'Careful,' he warned softly. 'Or is walking with me so traumatic you'd rather break your own neck?'

Knocked off balance by the unexpected gentleness in his eyes, she stood half swaying against him. Her blood was singing and heat and confusion crackled under her skin. Looking up, she saw that the sky had grown dark. The air felt suddenly viscous and heavy. A storm was coming.

'It's these shoes. The soles are slippery,' she mumbled, her cheeks suddenly hot.

'Don't worry. I've got you,' he said calmly.

Holding her breath, she felt his grip on her hand tighten as the first drops of rain splashed onto her face.

They ran towards the cottage, stopping at the door to face one another.

'I guess I don't need that water any more,' he said hoarsely.

Heart pounding, Prudence stared at him. She knew he was giving her a choice. But what choice was there really? Wordlessly she stepped towards him and then, by way of reply, she reached up, slid her arm around his neck and pressed a desperate kiss against his mouth.

Groaning, he pulled her against him, pushing the door open with his body and kicking it shut behind them both. Her mouth parted beneath his and he pulled her towards him, capturing her face between his hands. Grunting, he pulled lightly at the knot at the nape of her neck, tugging her hair free, weaving his fingers between the silken strands.

She moaned, curling her fingers into his shirt, and he deepened the kiss, slowly, languidly sliding his tongue between her lips, teasing her, tasting heat and sweetness. He felt her stir restlessly against him and he groaned softly, his groin tightening in response as she kissed him back, pressing her mouth to his, then catching his lower lip between her teeth.

Senses swimming, he lifted his mouth, his breath snagging in his throat as her hands slid under his shirt, and then he turned his head, breaking the kiss. His pulse seemed to trip and stumble as the scent of her, warm and clean and sweet, filled his nostrils.

'Prudence...' he murmured softly. She looked up at him and his stomach clenched, his body growing painfully hard. He saw the struggle within her eyes that so sharply echoed his own. 'Don't be afraid. I won't hurt you.'

The tension inside him was fast, dark and swirling, like a spring tide rising. He could barely breathe for wanting her. Suddenly he was fighting to stay calm.

Reaching out, he touched her cheek gently. 'Do you want this?' he asked roughly. The air felt suddenly thick in his throat and he could barely speak. 'Do you want me?'

She looked up at him and their eyes met, and then she nodded, and her face seemed suddenly to open and uncurl like a flower feeling the sun.

Slowly he let out his breath, and as he traced his thumb over the soft fullness of her mouth, he heard her gasp. A fierce heat engulfed him, for it was the sound of surrender. Desire leapt in his throat and, leaning forward, he lowered his head, brushing his lips over hers.

'I want to see you. All of you,' he whispered hoarsely.

In the darkness of the room her eyes looked feverish, almost glazed, and her soft pink mouth was trembling. Reaching out, he undid the fastening of her trousers and gently pushed them down over her hips. Straightening up, he watched dry-mouthed as she unbuttoned her blouse with trembling hands and shrugged it off, so that she was undressed except for the palest pink bra and panties.

Time slowed and Laszlo gazed at her, heart thudding, wordless, waiting. Heat seemed to burn every inch of him and his head was spinning wildly.

'Take them off,' he said finally, and slowly she unhooked the bra and peeled it from her shoulders.

His breath rasped in his throat as he stared at her small upturned breasts. She was so beautiful. Helplessly, he reached out and pulled her towards him, sliding his hands slowly up her thighs, over her hips and waist to her breasts, his thumbs brushing against them until he heard her cry out in pleasure.

Then suddenly, he was guiding her back towards the sofa, tugging his shirt off at the same time, wanting to feel the touch of her skin against his. Breathing deeply, he wrenched off his shirt. His eyes never leaving her face, he moved swiftly towards her, straddling her legs and pressing his mouth against the petal-smooth softness of her throat, then lower to the curve of her breast. His lips grazed the rose-coloured nipple, feeling it quiver and harden, and then his mouth closed over the tip, his tongue sliding over it, taking his time.

Blood was roaring in his head, swelling and rolling, humming like a cloud of bees about to swarm. Blindly he reached out and cupped her bottom, lifting her against him. He heard her gasp, felt her arch closer as his hands moved slowly over her hips and between her thighs. He felt her still beneath him as his hand caressed the apex of her thighs, brushing over the already damp silk. Gently he slid her panties over the curve of her bottom. Her fingers gripped the muscles of his arm and she whispered his name, and then her hand moved down over his chest and stomach and she was tugging at the buckle of his belt.

He groaned as she unzipped him, her fingers curling around him, freeing him. Trembling, his breath quickening in his throat, he shifted his weight, moving between her knees, spreading her legs. Her hips lifted to meet him and he pushed up, entering her with a gasp. He heard her answering moan of pleasure and began to move, thrusting inside her.

She clutched him tighter, her body shuddering, her hands tangling through his hair, pressing against him, pressing and pressing—and then she tensed and he heard her cry out. As he felt her flower beneath him he thrust hard, his muscles rippling, his breath choking in his throat and his body spilling inside her.

He lay still and spent. Her body was still gripping him tightly, and gently he caressed her warm, damp skin, feeling the spasms of her body fade. The sound of the rain was deafening now and he was grateful, for it blotted out the frantic beating of his heart.

Breathing unsteadily, he buried his face in her neck, trying to sort out his thoughts. It had been inevitable, he told himself bleakly. Since that moment in the barn the sexual tension between them had been ratcheted up to breaking point. Every single time they'd met it had felt like a minor earthquake. And today, finally, they'd snapped. His heart began to beat faster. It was only natural.

He frowned. But that didn't make it right. He glanced down at the woman lying in his arms. In the barn, he had ached with wanting her. Her refusal to give in to the powerful sexual attraction they had for one another had been infuriating, not to say painful. He sighed. But now he wondered whether by giving in to that hunger he'd merely set himself up for another sort of discomfort.

His breathing slowed. Hypothetically, it was easy to fall into bed with a woman to whom you had no commitment. There was no need for post-coital conversation or affection. No need even to see her again. But Prudence wasn't just any woman. She was his wife and pretty much nothing about their relationship was easy.

Feeling her shift against him, he frowned. Now he'd added another layer of complexity to their already tangled relationship. In fact, he was struggling to work out how to even describe what was going on between them—for while he was ostensibly her husband, he was also her boss…and now her lover.

Lightly, he traced a finger down her arm. He must have been crazy to let her stay and work for him, and crazier still to end up sleeping with her. But how was he supposed to resist her when everywhere he looked she was there? Laughing with his grandfather or bending over a notebook, her bottom jutting so alluringly towards him… His face darkened as he felt her stir beside him. It was too late to worry about resisting her. The only question that remained was what he should do next.

Shifting his weight slightly, he turned his head and stared down into her face.

Prudence looked up at him in silence. Her head was still spinning but she didn't want to speak anyway. For to speak would be to break the spell. Drifting her fingers over the flat muscles of his stomach, she bit her lip. It had felt so good—too good, she thought, heat colouring her cheeks as she remembered the sharp intensity of her climax. But then, making love with Laszlo had always been shockingly exciting. It was hardly surprising that her body still responded to him so fiercely.

She felt a twinge of alarm. Hardly surprising, but not particularly sensible. Her eyes closed. There was nowhere to hide from what she'd done.

She'd made love with Laszlo. A man who had broken her heart seven years ago and made her feel worthless and stupid. A man who, she'd since found out, had lied to her for the entire length of their relationship but who held her responsible for ending their affair. Her eyes opened. Oh, if that wasn't messy enough, he was both her boss and apparently her husband too.

She shivered and, frowning, he pulled her against the warmth of his chest.

'You're not cold, are you?'

She managed a weak smile. 'No. I was just listening to the storm. I think it's moving off.'

Laszlo reached out and cupped her chin with his other hand. 'It's not, you know. It's right here. In this room. Can't you feel it?'

His fingers began to drift languidly over her stomach and lower, to the triangle of soft curls at the top of her thighs. She knew she should push him away, tell him to stop, but already she could feel her pulse quicken in response.

'We need to get dressed,' she whispered quickly, for soon she wouldn't be able to speak or think or even be aware of anything except the ruthless seeking rhythm of his caresses. 'For lunch.'

His fingers stilled and then she felt a sharp tug, like a fish hook in her stomach, as his warm palm slid over her breast, pulling gently at the nipple until she felt soft and hot and aching inside.

'I can't wait that long,' he murmured, catching her hand and pushing it down towards his groin. 'I'm too hungry.'

Without giving her a chance to reply he lifted her hips and drew her against him, his mouth stifling her soft gasp of excitement. And even though something deep inside her knew she was heading for disaster she arched herself willingly against him as the fierce heat swept over her again.

CHAPTER SIX

GLANCING UP AT the window, Prudence frowned as a few small drops of rain hit the glass. Mr de Zsadany—she still thought of him as that privately—had given her the afternoon off and she'd been hoping to walk into the nearby village. Now that plan would have to wait. She sighed. Not that it mattered really; she had a stack of books by her bed or she could even just watch some old black and white movie on TV.

She bit her lip. Only that would mean going back to the cottage. Her face flared, as it did every time she remembered that scene inside the living room: she and Laszlo, their bodies fused together, moving effortlessly against and inside each other, outside of time and reality. Her happiness had been absolute—and for the first time in such a long while she had felt savagely alive.

Only now, back in reality, she had to face facts. She'd simply picked up from where she'd left off seven years ago. Only at least then they'd actually been in love—or she had. And to Laszlo, at least, she had been—her mind shrank from the words—his wife.

Crossly, she snatched up a pile of papers and stuffed them without her usual care into a file. Now she was nothing more than a fool and a clichéd fool at that. She shook her head. The castle might be a romantic setting but the truth was more prosaic: she'd just slept with her boss. Like some naive heroine in a lurid story, she'd allowed herself to be swept away by a tide of fate and coincidence. And lust!

She blinked. What was *wrong* with her? She had practically *invited* him to have sex with her. Her stomach clenched and she felt a pang of queasiness. How *could* she? Knowing what she knew about him and how he felt about her. For someone who'd vowed never to fall for his charms again, she'd certainly fallen into his arms with almost embarrassing alacrity.

Biting her lip, she picked up a paperweight and thumped it down on top of a pile of certificates. Who was she trying to kid? What had happened between her and Laszlo had been inevitable. But also horribly confusing. Lying in his arms had felt so natural, so familiar—as if she still belonged to him. And afterwards, when he'd pulled her against him, kissing her passionately right up until the moment before he'd calmly ushered her into lunch, that too had felt as if it meant something.

She frowned. But it hadn't. What they'd shared had just been sex. And after seven years of occasional dates and virtual celibacy, what she'd been feeling had simply been loneliness and lust. Only it had been impossible for her to see that, because intimacy with Laszlo shouldered out all rational thought.

She sighed. It was too late for regrets. All she could do now was keep her distance. Which shouldn't be hard, given that shortly after she'd let him take what he wanted he'd simply disappeared, slipping away like a swallow at the end of summer.

Picking up a box of files, she glanced round the empty room dispiritedly and sighed. Wouldn't it be wonderful if she could make her longing for him disappear just as easily?

An hour later, hair newly washed and dressed in a faded sundress, she wandered slowly around the garden behind the cottage. She felt slightly calmer now, restored by the fresh air and the sunlight. The rain had stopped, the sky was a clear blue and a light wind brushed her bare legs as she crossed the lawn.

With a cry of pleasure she spotted a cherry tree and, after pulling down a handful of the gleaming dark fruit, she bit into one. It was perfectly ripe and a sharp sweetness filled her mouth.

And that was when she saw him, walking slowly towards her across the grass.

It was all she could do to keep breathing. She stood, tracking him with her eyes, until he stopped in front of her. There was a roaring sound in her ears and her pulse scampered like a mouse across the floor as his gaze met hers—golden, steady and unwavering.

'I've been looking for you,' he said quietly.

Skin prickling, she stared at him in silence, hardly able to believe it was him.

'It's my afternoon off,' she said finally, glancing at him and then quickly looking away. 'Can't it wait until tomorrow? I'll be back at work then.' The gentlest of breezes caught her hair and, suddenly conscious of his focus, she felt her face grow warm.

'It's not work-related,' he said softly.

Their eyes locked and Prudence flushed. 'Then we have nothing to discuss.'

He laughed softly. 'In other words, we have a lot to discuss. Let me guess: you're mad at me for going off like that?' He lifted his hands in a gesture of surrender. 'I'm sorry I disappeared. I had to be somewhere. But if it's any consolation I've been thinking about what happened a lot.'

Prudence stared at him in silence. 'Did something happen?' she said slowly, trying to affect an air of nonchalance. 'I didn't notice. Just like I didn't notice that you'd disappeared.'

A slow smile spread across his face and then, shaking his head, he reached out towards her. Her heart contracted. It would have been so easy to give in, to let him take her into his arms, to lean in to his warmth and strength. But instead she raised her hands, curling them into fists.

'Don't!' she said fiercely. 'Don't even think about it! Honestly, Laszlo. You're unbelievable. Did you really just think you could roll up after two days and expect to carry on like before?'

His eyes narrowed. 'I said I was sorry. What more can I say?'

She stared at him helplessly. 'What *less* could you say? You didn't even say goodbye. But don't worry, I'll say it for you now. Goodbye.'

She turned to walk away but he reached out and grabbed her arm.

'Let go of me!' Jerking her wrist, she tried to pull herself free, but he merely tightened his grip.

'I'm sorry, okay?'

Shaking her head, she tugged herself free of his hand. 'It's *not* okay. How could it ever be okay?' She grimaced. 'Laszlo. We broke the rules.'

'I'm aware of that. But I don't see why you're getting so upset about it. We're both consenting adults.'

Gritting her teeth, she took a step towards him. 'It's not that simple.'

His face stilled and her skin seemed to catch fire beneath his gaze.

'Oh, but it was. Simple and sublime.'

She caught her breath, achingly aware of just how sublime it had been. How sublime it had always been. For a moment she hovered between desire and anger, and then anger won.

'It's not simple and you know it. It's a mess,' she snapped.

He studied her dispassionately. He hadn't intended to

argue with her. On the contrary, he'd been looking forward to seeing her again despite the fact that she was right: it *was* a mess. He smiled grimly. After they'd made love he'd held her in his arms, trying to rationalise his behaviour, and on some levels it had been easy to explain. It was perfectly natural for any man to be attracted to any woman— and what man wouldn't be attracted to Prudence? She was beautiful and clever and poised.

His face tightened. Only then he'd started to think about their marriage, and about lying to his grandfather, and suddenly he'd wanted to be free of the tangled mess of his thoughts. A flush coloured his cheeks. And so he'd simply walked out, fully intending to stay away until the cataloguing was complete. Only after just two nights he'd changed his mind, driven back to the castle by a sudden inexplicable need to see her smile.

She wasn't smiling now. Her face was taut and strained, and he knew that his sudden disappearance had angered and hurt her. *Hell!* Why couldn't she just accept his apology and move on?

He stared at her coldly, his dark hair falling across his forehead. 'What do you want me to say, Prudence? I thought you enjoyed it. I certainly did.'

She was staring at him as though he were speaking in Mandarin.

'This isn't about whether I *enjoyed* it or not.'

'Then you really don't know yourself at all, Prudence. You slept with me for the same reason I slept with you. Because what we have is incredible. Physically, we couldn't be better matched.'

Prudence blushed, heat seeping over her throat and collarbone. There was a loaded silence.

'Fine. I agree,' she admitted finally. 'But that doesn't change the fact that our doing what we did makes everything so much more difficult. Even you must see that.' She stared at him agitatedly. 'I can't believe you just *left*. That you didn't think we should at least have one tiny conversation about it.'

He shrugged and glanced across the lawn, his gaze drifting away towards the horizon. 'What's there to talk about?'

'Everything!' she cried. 'You. Me. Us. My job. Our marriage. Where do you want to start?'

He stared at her, his golden eyes reflecting the early-afternoon sun. 'At the beginning.' He gave her an infuriating smile. 'When we got married. Which makes you my wife.'

She gazed at him helplessly. 'Only I don't feel like your wife, Laszlo! It still doesn't feel like a real marriage to me. But even if it did we haven't been together for seven years. We broke up—remember? And now we've crossed a line.' She bit her tongue. 'I know couples who split up do end up sleeping together and it's understandable. I mean, everything's so familiar and safe and easy.'

Feeling his steady gaze on her, she paused, blushing, for none of those adjectives bore any relation to her intimacy with Laszlo.

She glowered at him. 'But they have a one-night stand! They don't have to live and work with each other afterwards. We do—and I don't even know how to describe our relationship any more, let alone how to make it work.' She felt a spurt of anger. 'Everything's so messy and confusing, and you just stand there and do nothing like it's all going to just fall into place—'

'And what are *you* doing, *pireni*?' he interrupted her harshly. 'I fail to see what you think you're actually achieving here. You're just asking me unanswerable questions.' His mouth twisted. 'What happened between us in the cottage isn't the problem, Prudence. *You* are. You turn everything into an inquisition. Hell, seven years ago you turned our relationship into an inquisition.'

Prudence choked in disbelief. 'An *inquisition*? Did you ever stop and think *why* I asked all those questions?' She shook her head, bunching her hands into fists. 'No. Of course not. Our relationship was never about me, was it? It was only ever about you and your needs.'

Misery washed over her in waves and she curled her fingers into the palms of her hands to distract herself from the pain.

'I asked questions because I wanted answers. I wanted to know you; to understand you. But you made me feel like I was an intruder in your life. When you were there you never wanted to talk and then you'd disappear for days and I wouldn't know where you were. And you just expected me to put up with it.'

Laszlo shook his head in frustration. 'Not this again. You knew I didn't have a nine-to-five job. You knew I sometimes worked away for days at a time. And you knew I'd be back.'

'No, I didn't.' Her voice sounded suddenly loud and harsh. 'I *didn't* know that.'

Her whole body was shaking and she stopped, breaking off as she saw from his face just how baffling and irritating he found her insecurities. She bit her lip. She'd had reason to feel like that. Only aged twenty-one she had felt too unsure of his love, too aware of how boring he found any sort of soul-searching, to blurt out her life story.

'I didn't know,' she said again, more quietly this time, for the old pain was welling up, making her hurt inside.

'Meaning what, exactly?'

His face was like stone and she looked away from it. 'I know it sounds crazy but I *didn't* know that you'd come back. Every time you disappeared I thought that was it. And I couldn't bear it.'

Laszlo said nothing and she felt the pain inside her spread. But had she really thought he would want to understand now, after seven years of hating her, just because they'd had sex again?

'Why did you feel like that?'

His voice was so gentle it startled her, and she looked up, half thinking that someone else must have asked the question.

'Did you feel like it right from the start?'

She nodded slowly, suddenly deprived of speech. Looking up, she saw him frown.

'But if you felt like that,' he said softly, 'then why did you stay with me?'

Prudence sighed. There in that one sentence was why their relationship had ended. For surely he knew the answer to that—just one look at her face had been enough for her Uncle Edmund to guess the truth.

She'd stayed because she'd fallen deeply and desperately in love with him.

Those few short weeks with him had been the most incredible, the most exciting time in her life. Exciting but terrifying, for Laszlo had unlocked a part of herself that she'd denied and feared in equal measure: a part of herself that she'd spent most of her life trying to repudiate or forget.

And here, now, after everything they'd done and said, she was afraid of giving too much away. Or, worse, destroying the memory of their time together, the time when she'd loved him and believed he loved her. Her lip quivered. She might no longer love Laszlo, but part of her still wanted to protect and preserve her memories.

'Like I said, I was acting a little crazy.' She smiled weakly.

Laszlo studied her. 'You were never crazy. Anxious and insistent, yes. And sweet, gentle and sexy.' His gaze rested on her mouth. 'Not crazy, though.' He paused, his eyes cool and unreadable. 'But why does that mean you didn't think I'd come back. I mean, I admit I was unreliable. But I was *reliably* unreliable: I always came back.'

He was attempting a joke and she tried to smile. But instead, to her horror, she felt hot tears sting her eyes and she shook her head.

Laszlo stared at her with a sort of bewildered anger and then his jaw tightened. 'So you're saying it's my fault? I made you feel like that?'

But Prudence didn't answer; she couldn't. Not with Laszlo standing so close. He wouldn't understand her fear, the creeping uncertainty. He was just so certain of himself—so sure and utterly without doubt.

'Please. Tell me. I want to know,' he said slowly.

Some roughness in his voice made her lift her head. And then, after a moment, he reached out and touched her hand, uncurling it with his fingers.

'I might even be able to help.'

Heart pounding, she took a deep breath. 'It wasn't you.' She gave him another weak smile. 'Although you didn't help much.' Her heart twisted. 'It was me. I was just waiting for it to happen. Waiting for you to leave and not come back. Like everyone else.'

She felt close to tears again, remembering the waiting, fearing, hoping that it would be different—

'Who's everyone else?' Laszlo frowned, his face darkening. 'You mean other men?'

Prudence laughed. 'What other men? There haven't been any. Not really since us—and certainly not before.' She shook her head, frowning. 'No. I mean my mum—and it's a long story. You won't want to hear it.'

Laszlo stared at her intently. 'I do want to hear it. Tell me about your mum.'

His face was focused on hers, the golden eyes calm

and dispassionate and yet warm like the sun. She let out a long breath.

'My mum met my dad when she was nineteen. They got married and had me. And then he left her.' Her mouth trembled. 'He came back, though. He always came back after a bit. While he was away she'd be frantic, and sometimes she'd go out looking for him.' The skin on her face felt suddenly scorched. 'Or for someone who'd make her forget him. She'd leave me. On my own. For hours. Sometimes all night. I hated it, being alone in the house in the dark.'

She swallowed, lowering her gaze.

'I always knew when she was going to go out. And I'd try and stop her. Stall her by asking questions.' She bit her lip; her questions to Laszlo seven years ago had stemmed from the same fear. Letting out a long breath, she shrugged. 'She nearly always went out, though. Then one day my dad never came back. Just cleared out their bank account and disappeared. It turned out that he was married already— to two other women. So really they weren't even married,' she said flatly.

'And you thought I'd do that to you?' Laszlo's voice was neutral but his mouth was set in a grim line.

Prudence couldn't meet his eyes. 'I suppose, deep down, I did. I assumed the worst.'

And that was why she'd walked away. Because she'd been scared. Scared that the worst was already happening, and that if she stayed her life would settle, like her mother's, into a pattern of rows and pleading and disappearances and lies.

Looking up, she met his gaze and they stood staring at one another, the silence between them broken only by the humming of the bees and the faint sound of a tractor on the breeze.

'I didn't give you much reason to hope for the best, did I?' Laszlo said softly.

He scanned her face, seeing what he'd failed to see before: a young woman seeking reassurance. Not once had he stopped and thought to ask himself *why* she had been so anxious. Instead he'd convinced himself that her constant need for reassurance had demonstrated a feebleness of character unbecoming in his wife.

Reaching out, he pushed an unsteady hand through her hair and pulled her gently towards him. For a moment he imagined burying his face against the doe-soft smoothness of her neck, but then he frowned.

'You were my wife. I should have known these things about you. And the fact that I didn't is my fault,' he said slowly. 'But you're right. You *did* assume the worst. Only I'm not your dad.' She stiffened at his words and he grimaced. 'And you're not your mum, Prudence! From what you've just told me, she doesn't sound like the sort of maddeningly stubborn woman who'd climb over a massive wall to demand her job back.'

Blushing at that image of herself, she looked up at him. He smiled at her slowly, his eyes glittering with an emotion she didn't recognise.

'I wasn't that stubborn until I met you,' she said carefully, her grey eyes issuing him with a challenge.

Watching the colour return to her cheeks, Laszlo felt a flicker of admiration rise inside him. She was brave. Braver than he'd thought. Braver than himself. He knew just how hard it was to reveal the truth about yourself to anyone.

Loosening a strand of her hair, Laszlo curled it round his finger. If only they could go back to bed, so she could curl her body around his as she'd done at the cottage.

As though she could read his mind, she looked up and sighed.

'So what are we going to do? You said you'd been think-ing about us a lot?'

They were back where they'd started. He frowned. 'Not us. It. About *it*. The sex.'

Her shoulders felt leaden and she was suddenly more tired than she had ever been in her life.

'Of course. My mistake!' she said wearily. 'I seem to be making a lot of those. Look, Laszlo. What happened between us isn't going to happen again. I don't want to sleep with you—'

'Yes, you do,' Laszlo interrupted her, his voice sharp and sure like a scalpel. 'You want me as much as I want you. And until you stop torturing yourself about that it won't stop, whether you're in London or in Hungary, mar-ried to me or not. You told me you wanted a divorce so you could move on. But you didn't even know we were mar-ried. Now that's *crazy*, Prudence.'

A muscle tightened in his cheek.

'I agree. We need to move on but what's holding us back is not some vows we made. It's this thing we have. This incredible need for one another. I'll "divorce" you, if that's what you want. But you need to accept that no piece of paper, or whatever it is you're hoping to get, is going to bring you physical closure.'

Prudence felt herself frown. What he was saying made sense. Being unaware of her marital status hadn't stopped the memory of him casting a shadow over her sexual rela-tions with other men. A light blush spread over her skin. Their touches, their kisses, had seemed like insipid, infe-rior copies of the fierce, primal passion she had shared with Laszlo. But how was she ever to move on if she couldn't stop this burning want she had inside her for him?

She shook her head. 'I don't understand. Are you say-ing you *do* want a divorce?'

His eyes darkened. 'The divorce is irrelevant. You have

to face the truth. We want each other. And that want is holding us back from living freely.'

'What are you suggesting?' she asked slowly.

He studied her face. The air was suddenly thick between them.

'I think we should keep on sleeping together,' he said softly. 'The truth is we both want to. And maybe that's what we need to do to get each other out of our systems for good.'

She stared at him, stunned into silence not just by his words but by her body's instantaneous response to them.

Finally, she shook her head again. It wasn't worth the risk. 'So your solution to this mess is to make our lives more complicated? What happened at the cottage was understandable—'

'It was incredible,' he corrected.

Ignoring his comment, and the traitorous heat rising up inside her, she forced herself to concentrate. *'Understandable,'* she repeated firmly. 'But it was spontaneous. A one-off. What you're suggesting would be deliberate and repeated. We can't do that.'

'It's nothing we haven't done before.' He spoke quietly but his eyes were fierce.

She blinked. 'No. Laszlo. *I* haven't done this before. Had an affair with my estranged husband, who doesn't even like me and also happens to be my boss! It's just wrong on so many levels.'

His gaze flickered over her face and he smiled a smile that lit up his eyes like the sun, spreading radiance and warmth over her.

He shook his head, his eyes glittering. 'No. What we share could never be wrong, Prudence,' he said softly. 'I agree, it's not a conventional arrangement, but what we have is so extraordinary, so overwhelming. Look, I don't know if it'll work, but when I'm holding you in my arms it feels like we know everything about each other. It's like our own perfect private communion.'

Gazing up into his face, Prudence felt herself wavering. She knew she should turn him down but the pull of his words was so powerful. She could no more resist him than the tide could resist the tug of the moon.

Laszlo let out a breath. His heart was pounding. Looking down, he saw with surprise that his hands were shaking and he wondered why. He gritted his teeth. It was frustration, he told himself. Two days spent thinking about Prudence's delectable body and his own body was hovering on the edge of meltdown. Particularly with her standing so close, looking so desirable.

And she was so very beautiful. Her eyes were shimmering like beaten silver and he could smell the sweet honeyed fragrance that clung to her skin and hair. But truthfully it wasn't just about her beauty. It wasn't even about the sex. Her bright enthusiasm for art, her doggedness in getting back her job, her sweetness with his grandfather—all charmed him, delighted him.

'It's not just the physical,' he said finally. 'I like spending time with you.'

Prudence swallowed. Her grey eyes flashed with reproach. 'Only when it suits you.'

Seeing the indecision in her eyes, he was on the verge of simplifying everything by pulling her into his arms and melting her resistance with the heat of his kisses. But something held him back—some confused idea that this was not the moment for passion.

Besides, he had something better in mind.

CHAPTER SEVEN

'COME WITH ME. I have something I want to show you.'

He held out his hand and after a moment Prudence took it. They walked slowly together over the rough, springy grass until finally they reached a copse of stunted, low-branched trees and he stopped and gently disengaged his hand.

'What are we doing?' she asked.

'We're meeting him here,' he said, turning to face her.

'Meeting who? Where? We're in the middle of a field.'

Grinning, he shook his head. 'We're meeting my cousin. And this is not a field. It's an apple orchard. My apple orchard,' he said softly, taking her hand in his again. 'A long time ago the estate used to make all its own cider.'

Biting her lip, she looked at him nervously. 'Your cousin? Won't that be a little awkward? I mean, he knows we're married...'

Her voice sounded shrill and shaky and, frowning, Laszlo pulled her towards him.

'Take it easy. I have about thirty cousins. This is a different one.' Gently, he pushed a strand of hair behind her ear. 'This is my cousin Mihaly.' He paused and studied her face speculatively. 'He doesn't know we're married. Only my great-uncle and my cousin Matyas know.'

He grimaced.

'And they're not here. Not that they'd say anything to anybody anyway,' he said slowly. 'I promise. You'd have more luck having a conversation with Besnik than you would at getting a word out of either of them.'

Squeezing her hand, he squinted into the horizon. 'There he is.'

He lifted his arm and waved at the outline of a man riding on horseback.

'That's Mihaly.'

Feeling somewhat calmer, Prudence let out a breath as he raised his hand to greet his cousin.

'Mihaly! How are you?'

Smiling shyly, Prudence turned to where Laszlo was waving and then gasped softly. Not at the dark-haired man sliding off the bare back of a sleepy-eyed white cob, but at the caravan behind the horse.

'Oh. That is so beautiful,' she whispered. 'Is that a *vardo*?' Blushing, she glanced at Laszlo and he nodded slowly.

He dropped her hand and walked swiftly towards his cousin. The men hugged one another and then Laszlo turned. Reaching towards Prudence, he tugged her forward by the hand.

'Mihaly, this is Prudence. She's working for my grandfather. Prudence—my cousin Mihaly. He's like a brother to me and he's a good friend. Just don't let him sing to you.'

Mihaly grinned and inclined his head. 'And don't let *him* play a guitar.' He winced. 'I'm still having trouble in this ear. And now, cousin, where do you want me to put this—because I need to be getting back?' He turned towards Prudence and grinned sheepishly. 'My wife is having our fifth child any time now, so I need to get home as soon as possible.'

After much manoeuvring, Laszlo and Mihaly finally managed to guide the *vardo* between the apple trees and across the fields to the cottage. Having detached the shafts from the pulling harness, Mihaly waved cheerfully and rode away.

Prudence stared at the *vardo* in wonder. 'When I was a little girl I had a storybook with a picture of a *vardo* in it. But I've never been this close to one before,' she murmured.

'Take a look inside.' Laszlo gestured towards the *vardo*. 'There's a bed and a dresser and a stove.'

Prudence climbed up the steps and then trod lightly inside the *vardo*. It was just perfect, with intricately painted roses and castles and bright embroidered cushions. She swallowed and climbed back down.

There was a moment's silence and then Laszlo said quietly, 'So, what do you think?'

His voice sounded hesitant and, glancing across, Prudence saw that his expression was strained—anxious, almost. Guiltily she remembered how he'd accused her of shunning his family. Clearly he wanted to know what she thought of his cousin.

She smiled. 'He seemed nice.'

Laszlo laughed. 'Not Mihaly! The *vardo*. Do you really like it or are you just being polite?' He stared at her, his gaze intent, a line of doubt on his forehead.

'N-no, of course I'm not just being polite,' she stammered. 'It's beautiful. Really. You're very lucky,' she said teasingly. 'A castle *and* a *vardo*! That's just plain greedy.'

He grinned, and then his expression shifted, grew serious. He looked at her levelly. 'Actually, the *vardo* isn't mine. I've just been holding on to it for someone.'

She held her breath, sensing a tightness in him—a sort of eagerness. 'Whose is it?' she whispered. But even before he could reply she already knew the answer to her question. 'Is it mine?' she asked hesitantly.

He nodded, watching as her look of shock and confusion turned to happiness. 'It was supposed to be my wedding gift to you.'

He hadn't planned on telling her that the *vardo* was hers. He'd simply wanted to show it to her, for he'd known that it would soften her. A woman would have to have a heart of stone not to be ensnared by the romanticism of a real gypsy caravan.

She turned to smile at him and he smiled back. But his smile was hollow, for seeing her genuine pleasure made him feel shabby and manipulative and he felt a stab of jealousy. With shock, he realised that he wanted to *share* in her happiness. That he actually *liked* making her happy.

A muscle flickered in his jaw. 'It's more of a curio than anything. We wouldn't have lived in it, obviously—'

'Why not?' She frowned, instantly defensive. 'It's beautiful and romantic and it's got everything you need—'

'Everything but a toilet and a shower and hot running water.' He smiled ruefully. 'Give me a Willerby Westmorland any day!' His eyes gleamed. He watched her with mild amusement. 'And there's nothing romantic about not being able to wash,' he added drily.

'Why did Mihaly have it?' She glanced up at him tentatively.

His eyes met hers. 'He and my uncle restore *vardos*. They've been holding on to it for me.'

He paused and Prudence felt her face grow warm.

'That's where I went the other day,' he said softly. 'After I ran away. I went to my uncle's and I remembered it was there. Only I couldn't bring it back because one of the wheels was damaged. So Mihaly said he'd bring it over to me today.' His golden eyes moved over her face like the sun. 'I wanted you to see it before you leave,' he added calmly.

His matter-of-fact tone went some way towards taking the bite from his words but Prudence still heard the blood rush inside her head and felt her stomach clench as she came crashing down to earth. But of course she was going to leave. Her contract wasn't permanent and Laszlo had just agreed to divorce her. So why did she feel so cold? As though she'd suddenly stepped into the shadows?

Pushing that troublesome question away, she took a step towards the *vardo*.

'Is it really mine?' She turned to face him. 'I mean, could I spend the night here?'

He took so long to answer that she thought he hadn't heard her, but then he stared at her, his eyes impossibly gold and translucent, like clear new honey, and nodded. She hesitated, suddenly tongue-tied and blushing.

'I mean, with you.'

The words caught in her throat and the air felt suddenly charged around them. Their eyes locked and then slowly he walked towards her. Sliding his hands through her hair, he tipped her face to his.

'Me? Stay in your caravan?' Frowning, he pretended to think. 'Are you sure? I don't know. That sounds complicated,' he whispered.

She pulled away from him and held out her hand. 'Then I think we should keep things simple,' she murmured. 'Stick with what we do best.'

And then, taking his fingers in hers, she began to lead him up the steps into the *vardo*.

Prudence woke to the sound of birdsong. The *vardo* was warm with sunlight and for a moment she lay sleepily on her back, revelling in the ache of her body. Then, rolling over, she reached out and touched the space beside her in the bed. The sheets were still warm and, closing her eyes, she breathed in Laszlo's clean, salty, masculine smell.

In the last few days when they'd been together every private moment had been spent in bed. And every night Prudence lost count of the number of times they made love. At first, despite lack of sleep, she hadn't wanted the morning to come, for fear that daylight would break the spell between them. But on waking that first morning, without any apparent effort on their part, everything had fallen quite naturally into place, and now their days and nights had slipped into a pattern.

Most mornings Laszlo would wake long before she did—often before dawn. Sometimes he would get up and dress and return, waking her with breakfast. Other times he would reach out for her in the darkness, pressing her body against his, the beat of his blood in time to her heart…

At the memory of the way his mouth sought out hers, of his hands so gentle, yet demanding, she felt a familiar ache deep inside her pelvis that made her press her legs together. Blushing, she gave a squirm of pleasure. The sex was so good, and his desire for her was so intoxicating, so quick, so urgent—like pollen bursting from a flower. He made her feel so alive, utterly unlike herself. Lost in him she became passionate, brave and wanton.

She bit her lip. But soon it would be over. She would be back in England and back to a life without passion; a life without Laszlo. Slowly she rolled out of bed and sat up straight. A hard knot was forming in her stomach. She had spent the last week living in the moment, trying not to think, and more particularly trying not to think about the future. Easy at first, with the days and nights stretching out ahead of her, to do just that. Easy, too, to accept the rationale for what they were doing and ignore the fact that physical intimacy encouraged the senses to play all kinds of stupid, dangerous tricks on the mind.

Sighing, she lay back down and rolled onto her side. She had no one to blame but herself, for Laszlo had never offered anything other than sex. In fact, he couldn't have made it clearer that their affair was simply a finite means to an end—a way for both of them to find sexual closure. But being with Laszlo seemed to be doing little to reduce her hunger for him. Instead the hours she spent in his company seemed only to remind her why she'd fallen in love with him seven years ago.

'I don't normally like talking about work over lunch...' Janos paused and glanced apologetically around the dining room table. 'But I just wondered, Prudence, how you think the cataloguing is going?'

Prudence frowned and put down her fork. It was a perfectly reasonable question, but there was a tension in the old man's voice that made her hesitate and, looking across at him, she felt a ripple of concern when she saw that he looked drawn and tired.

'It's early days,' she said slowly. 'But we are making progress.'

Looking across at his grandfather, Laszlo frowned. 'You look a bit pale, Papi. Are you feeling all right?'

Janos shook his head. 'I'm fine, Laci. I'm just being a silly old man.'

Laszlo frowned. 'I doubt that,' he said firmly. 'What's up? Is something worrying you about the cataloguing?'

The old man shook his head. 'It's nothing, really. It's just that it all seems to be taking so much longer than I expected.'

Prudence felt her chest squeeze tight with guilt. All she'd been thinking about for the last few days was Laszlo; everything else—Edmund, England and even the cataloguing—had been pushed to the periphery of her mind.

'Please don't worry, Janos,' she said quickly. 'I should have warned you. This part is always incredibly slow-moving. There's always lots of gaps in the paperwork.'

'Particularly when a collection is owned by a forgetful old fool who can't remember what he bought or when and where he bought it?' Janos said slowly.

Prudence shook her head. 'Not at all. You'd be surprised how many people own art that's worth thousands of pounds—hundreds of thousands of pounds—and yet have no paperwork at all.'

'They need Prudence to come to their rescue,' Janos said, his smile returning.

Laszlo leant back in his chair, his face impassive. 'They can't have her. She's ours!'

His eyes gleamed with an intensity that made her lose the thread of what she was saying and she felt her skin turn to liquid.

Resisting the tug of his gaze, she cleared her throat. 'I'm sorry you've been worried. I know it can be a bit overwhelming…' She hesitated. 'I don't know how you feel about this, but I'm sure Edmund would be a good person to talk to about it.'

Janos nodded slowly. 'Certainly, my dear—if you think he'd be happy to give me an opinion?'

Grimacing, she laughed. 'Knowing Edmund, I'm sure he'll be more than happy!' She bit her lip. 'I don't always like what my uncle has to say, but maddeningly he's quite often right.'

Her words were simply meant to reassure Janos but, feeling a prickle of heat on her skin, she looked up and found Laszlo watching her.

'Is that so?' he said flatly. 'Your *uncle* is a man of many talents!'

His eyes locked onto hers and her heart began to pound, for she saw that while his face was still and calm, his eyes were alive with anger.

'How *fortunate* for all of us,' he said slowly.

Laszlo felt a sickening wave of nausea. His stomach twisted. Edmund Seymour was Prudence's *uncle*!

It was as though a tide had receded, revealing jagged rocks beneath a calm blue sea.

It was bad enough that he hadn't known until now exactly who Edmund Seymour was in relation to Prudence. But for her to suggest that Seymour now be allowed to give his 'opinion'— It was intolerable.

He gritted his teeth and then, turning to his grandfather, smiled gently. 'Papi, I'm going to sort this out. I want you to take the rest of the day off.'

He held his hand out towards his grandfather.

'You can go and put your feet up and read one of those interminable Russian novels you like so much.'

Waving away Janos's words of protest, he chivvied his grandfather out of the room.

'No, Papi. I insist. Prudence and I can manage.'

At the door, Laszlo stopped and turned, and she felt her pulse slam against her skin as his eyes fixed coldly on her face.

'Oh, don't ring your uncle just yet. I've got an opinion of my own I'd like to share with you first. Wait here!'

A moment later, her face still scalded with colour, Prudence sat staring nervously around the dining room. Looking down at her plate, she pushed it away. Could she have misunderstood the implication of his words? But she knew she hadn't, and she knew that something had happened to change the mood between them. She frowned. Only *nothing* had happened. Part of her job was to reassure the client, and that was what she'd done. Her mouth tightened into a grim line. It most certainly *wasn't* part of her job to try to second-guess Laszlo's moods.

Ten minutes later she bit her lip in indecision and then, abruptly pushing back her chair, she stood up. Typical Laszlo! Telling her to wait and then forgetting all about her. She shook her head irritably. Unlike him, she actually had work to do. But first she would ring Edmund. After all, what possible objection could he really have to her speaking to her uncle?

Laszlo caught up with her just as she reached the cottage. 'Where the hell do you think you're going? I told you to wait!'

His voice, dark with fury, swung her round mid-stride. She stared at him, struck by the cold, angry beauty of his face.

Forcing herself to stay calm, she shrugged and said flatly, 'I did wait. But you didn't come back and I have notes to write up. So, if you don't mind—'

'Oh, but I *do*. We need to talk.'

She flinched at the biting tone of his voice but drew her head up to meet his gaze. 'I'm sorry you feel like that, but I'm busy now,' she said carefully. 'Maybe we can talk later.'

Turning, her heart pounding in her chest, she walked quickly up the path and opened the front door of the cottage. Before she could shut it, Laszlo had followed her into the living room.

'What are you doing?' She stared at him furiously. 'You can't just barge in here!'

'Don't you *ever* walk away from me.' His face was twisted with anger. 'I told you to *wait*!'

She lifted her chin, eyes blazing. His high-handed manner was setting her teeth on edge. 'I did,' she shot back at him. 'But if you think I've got all day to sit around and wait for you—'

'My grandfather was upset. I was trying to make him feel better. But maybe you don't care about that.' His eyes were hardening like lava cooling.

'That's not true, Laszlo. I *do* care about your grandfather,' she said shakily. 'And I want to help. That's why I'm going to speak to my uncle.'

She stared at him in helpless silence as he shook his head.

'No, you're not.'

His voice scraped over her skin, hostility palpable in every syllable.

'Not if you want to keep this job!'

Prudence took a step backwards, the unfairness as much as the autocratic tone of his command leaving her feeling almost winded. She felt dizzy. He'd gone completely mad. That was the only explanation.

'What *is* your problem? You're not making any sense. If Edmund hadn't been ill he'd have been here instead of me. And you were fine with that. Only now you're telling me I can't even *ring* him?'

Incandescent with anger, Laszlo stared at her. She was right. His behaviour was irrational. Except that it wasn't. Only he couldn't explain that to her. Not while he was still reeling from this revelation that Edmund Seymour was the man who had ruined his life.

His chest felt tight and he took a calming breath. Finally, he said flatly, 'We made a deal. I told you that if you couldn't work for me then you should leave.'

'Any deal we made *didn't* include pussyfooting around you when you're having some sort of temper tantrum!' She glared at him. 'This has nothing to do with our deal and you know it. You're just angry because I wasn't where you wanted me to be. Well, now you know what it feels like!'

There was a moment's savage silence and then she took a breath. What were they doing? Tearing each other apart over a phone call?

Feeling suddenly calmer, she shook her head and said slowly, 'I didn't just leave to make you angry. I really did— really *do*—have a lot of work to do.'

She bit her lip. Had they naively expected that the anger and resentment from their past would magically dissipate just because they'd started sleeping together again? If so, they'd been grievously mistaken. The fragile peace they'd shared for more than a week was over, and sadly she realised that it had been as illusory as every other aspect of their relationship.

'But my advice would still be to contact Edmund.'

His eyes narrowed. 'I see. I suppose you think you know better than I do what's best for my grandfather?'

Biting her lip, she nodded. 'In this instance—yes. He's worried about the cataloguing and Edmund can help him,' she said simply. 'Sometimes you just need a different point of view to solve the problem.'

Catching sight of the ineffably contemptuous sneer in his eyes, she felt a ripple of anger snake over her skin.

She took a deep breath. 'You know, the trouble with you, Laszlo, is you're just so certain you're right you just can't imagine that there might be another point of view.'

'Not true.' His voice was dangerously soft. 'I know everything there is to know about other points of view. Particularly your uncle's.'

There. He'd said it. It was as though he'd taken off a particularly scratchy sweater. She stared at him, her eyes blinking in time with her scattering thoughts. 'What do you mean? You've never even spoken to my uncle. He spoke to your grandfather and Jakob.'

He smiled slowly and she felt the breath squeeze out of her lungs.

'Not about the cataloguing...' he said softly.

'I don't understand,' she said faintly.

'Then let me explain.'

His voice seemed to slice her bones away from her flesh and she felt her legs starting to sway.

'Seven years ago I went to your home.'

Her head jerked up and, despite the pain in his own heart, he felt a sharp sting of satisfaction at the shock in her eyes.

He looked at her steadily. 'I went to talk to you.'

Prudence's heart seemed to stop. 'I don't believe you,' she said weakly.

'That doesn't stop it being true.'

His voice trapped her, pulled her in. 'You're lying,' she whispered.

But she knew that he wasn't, and her face felt hot, and she suddenly couldn't breathe. Looking up, she saw the anger and the pride in his eyes. She took a step backwards.

Watching her back away, Laszlo felt a ripple of rage—even now she was trying to evade what she'd done.

'Only you were out. Shopping…' He spat the word out with derisive emphasis. *'Shopping!'* There was a tense, choking silence and he shook his head. 'How do you think that made me feel? To find out that while I was sitting in some stinking police station my wife was out shopping.' He laughed without humour. 'Sorry. My mistake. You didn't actually think we were married, did you?'

She clenched her fists. She had resolved never to mention his arrest. But now his sneering contempt unleashed the pent-up fear and pain.

'What should I have been doing? We were over. Your criminal activities were no concern of mine.'

'They took me in for questioning. And then they released me without charge,' he said slowly, his face tight with hostility. 'Only you didn't know because you were out *shopping*.'

She shook her head, trying to stay focused. He didn't have the upper hand here—didn't have it full stop! All he'd done was lie and deceive her.

She glowered at him. 'We were over—'

'We were *not* over. We'd had a row. Do you really think I'd just let you throw away our marriage like that?' he said savagely. The air was quivering between them.

Prudence shook her head. 'I asked you how much effort you'd give to make our relationship work.' Her voice broke. 'Do you know what your answer was? You said that *any* effort was too much!'

'I was just angry with you! I'd just walked in the door. I was tired. I wanted a shower.'

Eyes blazing, she stepped towards him. 'And that meant you could give up on our relationship?'

'No. But as you keep on reminding me, I had to go to the police station!' His mouth twisted. 'I couldn't leave. You, on the other hand, were free. I came to find you as soon as I got out. You didn't come to see if I was all right.' He stopped and shot her a look of pure exasperation. 'I know that you didn't think our marriage was real. And, yes, we'd broken up. But didn't you feel bound to me in *any* way?'

The bitterness in his voice felt like a slap to her face.

There was a pulsing silence and then he shook his head. 'I could never work out what had changed. You seemed different that day. Not yourself.'

Prudence stared at him, trying to keep her expression steady. She could feel something like panic building up inside her.

He gave her a long, hard look. 'But then I met your uncle and it all kind of fell into place.' Smiling grimly, he nodded. 'You're right about his opinions, by the way. I didn't like what he had to say. In fact, I was quite upset by his point of view. But funnily enough I wasn't surprised by it.' He looked across at Prudence, his eyes glittering with sudden savage fury. 'But then, how could I be? I'd already heard it before—hadn't I?'

Prudence stared at him, frozen to the spot, struggling to swallow her shock. 'I don't understand…' Her voice shrivelled as she felt the blistering anger of his gaze.

'Oh, I think you do.'

There was a moment's dead silence and then, in a voice that chilled her bones, he went on.

'When I'm struggling with something, I always find it helpful to have another point of view.'

She felt the blood drain from her face as she recognised her own words.

Watching her reaction, he clenched his jaw. 'It was quite eerie, actually. Hearing your words come out of his mouth. It was a faultless performance. You must have rehearsed a lot.'

'N-no…' Prudence stammered. 'No. It wasn't like that.' She shivered as the temperature in the room plummeted.

'It was *exactly* like that, Prudence. Or are you telling me he told you to stand by your man?'

Looking at her paper-white stricken face, he felt suddenly sick inside.

'No. I thought not.'

A muscle flickered in his jaw and he regarded her for a long, excruciating moment.

'You should have waited to hear what I had to say. But you didn't. You chose to listen to someone who'd never met me. Who despised the very idea of me.'

Laszlo leant forward, his face dark with fury.

'Do you know he called me a liar and a charlatan? Told me he knew all about my "sort".'

He gave a humourless laugh and Prudence felt her cheeks burn. She shook her head desperately.

'He didn't mean because you're a Romany,' she mumbled.

Laszlo smiled derisively. 'Please! Do you think I'm stupid?'

Miserably, Prudence shook her head. 'No. But I know he wasn't talking about that. He was just worried about me. About where it would all end. I think he thought I was turning into my mum.'

She looked away, fighting tears; fighting memories.

'You'd been gone for ten days, Laszlo. I didn't know what to think. I'd left so many messages, and then Edmund came home from work and found me crying.' She gave a small strangled laugh. 'I think it really scared him.' She drew a jagged breath. 'Especially because I hadn't really told him and Daisy much about us. Just that I was seeing someone I'd met at the fair.'

Prudence stared blankly around the sitting room. 'I *did* talk to Edmund, and he gave me advice. But he didn't change my mind,' she said slowly. 'When I came looking for you—after I'd spoken to him—I still wanted us to work. I would have done anything to be with you.' She paused and shivered, her lip trembling. 'But, like I told you before, you didn't even try and reassure me.'

Her voice petered out and Laszlo frowned. It was true. He *hadn't* tried to reassure her. And he saw now that the repercussions of her parents' bigamous marriage had affected not just Prudence but her aunt and uncle too. They had looked after her, brought her up. His breathing was suddenly harsh. How must it have felt for Edmund to see the girl he thought of as a daughter weeping hysterically over a man? A man who seemed in many ways to resemble her perfidious father?

Prudence took a breath and looked up at him sadly. 'Edmund told me what he thought I should do. But he also said that the decision must be mine.' She bit her lip and her eyes felt suddenly hot with tears. 'And it was. You didn't seem to care one way or another. That didn't seem to be a good basis for a relationship. So I ended it.'

Her stomach was contorting, as though her misery was actually alive inside her.

'Edmund didn't wrong you. All he and Daisy have ever done is try and protect me. You can think what you like. The truth is our relationship ended not because of other people or their opinions but because the sum of what we held back was greater than what we shared. We only really shared our bodies.'

Laszlo stared at her in silence. She had never looked

more beautiful or vulnerable. But for once he couldn't lose himself in the soft beauty of her face. His skin was prickling with what he knew to be guilt. Guilt and regret. Having grown up in the shadow of her mother's disastrous love affair, she'd met him before she'd had a chance to realise that she wasn't her mother but her own person.

Now he understood just how lonely and frightened she must have felt when confronted by his baffling absences and moodiness. His head jerked up, his cheeks burning. He had told her he would never forgive her for what she'd done. Now he saw that it was he who needed forgiveness. He had been her lover and, in his mind at least, her husband. The one man who should have restored her faith in men and, more importantly, in herself.

And what had he done to reassure her?

Nothing.

No wonder she had sought comfort from the one man who had always been there for her and never let her down.

'You must love them very much,' he said finally.

He saw the flicker of emotion in her grey eyes.

'They're not perfect.' She smiled weakly. 'But they're my family, Laszlo, and I love them. I trust them too.'

'More than you trusted me?'

His question caught her off guard and she swallowed hard. She was so tired—more than tired…she was drained. Meeting his gaze, she saw from the tension around his eyes that her answer mattered to him. It would be easier to placate him; quicker to give him some glib answer that would end this row, so she could crawl off and lick her wounds. But she was done with lying to him. No matter what the consequences, she wanted to confront the past—the whole of the past. Not keep holding back or editing out the most painful parts.

Finally, she nodded.

The gold of his eyes began to flicker with outrage.

'What did you *want* me to say?' she said, annoyed by his reaction. 'Haven't you learned *anything* from the past? Our marriage might be over but I want—' She stopped. Her voice had turned husky with emotion but she didn't care. 'I need to be honest with you. And I'd like to think you want that too. So the answer is *yes*, Laszlo. I trusted them more than I trusted you. Or myself.'

His mouth set in a grim line, Laszlo stared at her for a long moment.

'I want to be honest with you as well,' he said quietly. 'You were right to have doubts about me. Right not to trust me.'

She stared at him dazedly. 'Wh—what do you mean?' she stammered. She felt almost physically sick at the expression of guilt and remorse on his face.

He watched her in silence, a muscle working in his jaw. 'I was holding back. Holding back the truth about my grandfather. And you sensed that and that's why you didn't trust me. Add that to all my comings and goings, and I'd say you had a very strong case for ending our relationship.'

He sucked in a breath.

'In fact, I'm surprised you stayed with me for so long.' His face tightened and then slowly, his hand shaking slightly, he reached out and stroked her cheek. 'I've not always been a kind person, *pireni*. Or a fair one.'

He let out the breath.

'When you broke up with me I blamed your uncle. And then I blamed you.' He gave a small, tight smile. 'And then I blamed both of you.' He sighed. 'But I can't blame anyone but myself for what happened. All I did was fuel your doubts and then get angry that you doubted me,' he said quietly. 'Too angry to look deeper.'

He opened his mouth to say something else and then stopped.

Prudence felt her spine stiffen, her hurt somehow tempered by the inevitability of the familiar way his face closed over. Had she really expected Laszlo to open up to her? Surely she knew him well enough to know that he would always have secrets to keep.

Frowning, Laszlo glanced away from the tears gleaming in her eyes. He didn't want to hurt her. She had been so open, so brave. But there was so much he couldn't explain.

'I'm sorry about everything,' he said slowly, 'but I'm glad we had this conversation.' There was a moment of uneven silence, and then his face creased and he added softly, 'And I'm glad you're here.'

He saw the pull of his words on her face and then his chest tightened as he watched a tear trickle down her face.

'Don't cry!' Impulsively Laszlo reached out and brushed his fingers gently over her cheek. Their eyes locked and then he sighed again. 'We certainly didn't make it easy for ourselves, did we, *pireni*? I just assumed that our marriage would somehow magically work, and you were convinced it would fail!'

He tilted her face to his and cupped her chin in his hand.

'We didn't get everything wrong, though, did we? I mean, most couples would kill to have the sort of chemistry we share.'

She knew he didn't really mean his words to be taken seriously, but something about his remark depressed her. It was the truth, probably, she thought miserably. For Laszlo, any discussion about their relationship would always lead back to that one thing.

Glancing down at her, Laszlo frowned again. He knew he'd hurt her, and he wanted more than anything to pull her into his arms, but much as he desired her he suddenly didn't want to use sex to blot out emotion.

'Look, don't worry about the cataloguing.' He paused and took a breath. 'I'm going to ring your uncle later and talk it all through with him. You don't think he'll recognise my voice, do you?'

Prudence hesitated a moment, her grey eyes searching his face. She knew he was trying to make amends and it was novel at least to have Laszlo be the one to make a peace offering. Shaking her head, she gave him a weak smile. He grinned at her and his obvious relief that he had made her smile made her heart wobble.

'Good. I don't want him charging over here to rescue you.' He paused. 'You don't *want* to be rescued, do you?'

Prudence shivered. Of course she didn't—but it might have been better if she had. Her feelings were becoming more and more confused, and harder and harder to contain.

She shook her head. 'No. I don't want to be rescued.'

His face flushed and she felt her pulse start to quicken, for he looked heartbreakingly like his younger self.

'I promise I'll be on my best behaviour,' he said slowly. 'I won't say or do anything annoying.'

She laughed softly. 'Let's not tempt fate!'

Looking down at her, Laszlo smiled crookedly. 'How reassuringly superstitious of you,' he said softly. 'My sweet Romany wife.'

She gazed at him, hypnotised by the soft darkness of his eyes and the even softer darkness of his voice. And then her heart twisted inside, for Laszlo's words were not a promise for the future but a simple statement of fact.

Trying to ignore the tangle of emotions her thoughts provoked, she glanced at one of the clocks—surely sense demanded she should leave before she said something she'd regret?

'I should go and find your grandfather, but he usually has a nap about now.' She bit her lip. 'I don't know what to do...'

Laszlo frowned. 'Maybe I can help with that.'

Sliding his fingers through her hair, Laszlo pulled her towards him, his expression thoughtful.

'Let's see…' Turning her hand over, he stroked the centre of her palm and then, lifting her hand, slowly ran his tongue along the lifeline until she squirmed against him. 'Hmm…' he murmured softly. 'Your skin's so smooth it's difficult to read the future. But…'

His gleaming golden gaze rested on her face, making her feel hot and tingly all over.

'I *can* see that there's a tall, dark, handsome man in your life.'

Prudence wriggled free and shook her head, trying not to laugh. 'Really? I wouldn't say Jakob is tall.'

He grinned at her. 'The man I'm talking about is definitely not a lawyer. He's just as smart, but he's witty and cool and sexy…'

He laughed softly as, heart pounding, she tugged her hand away. 'And bordering on the delusional?' she said quickly.

She wanted him so much. And when he held her close like this, his body so warm and hard against hers, everything inside her seemed to unravel and fly apart.

Hoping fervently that her feelings weren't showing on her face, she took a deep breath and lifted her chin. 'Or maybe you just need your eyes tested?'

He smiled—a long, curling smile that whipped at her senses.

'Quite probably. No doubt my eyes have been damaged by years of living in this gloomy castle.' He pressed his body against hers. 'Maybe I should keep you where I can see you,' he murmured possessively.

And then his hand tightened in her hair and, dropping a fierce kiss onto her lips, he pulled her into his arms.

CHAPTER EIGHT

FROM THE WINDOW of his bedroom Laszlo stared out at the cloudless blue sky and scowled. Rising early, he had gone for a walk before breakfast in the fields that surrounded the estate. Usually he enjoyed the silence and the crisp, early air—but not today. For once he had found it hard to take pleasure in the peace and beauty. Instead his thoughts had been dogged by scenes from last night. And now yesterday's conversation with Prudence was playing on repeat inside his head, so that rather than slip back into bed beside her, he'd returned to the castle.

His chest grew tight. Feeling distinctly uncomfortable, he closed the window. But there was no way he could shut out the unpalatable truth. He had treated her badly. And a weaker person—the person he'd so arrogantly assumed Prudence to be—would have been crushed.

Only she hadn't been crushed. And she hadn't given up either. In spite of her youth and inexperience, and in the face of his evident and repeated reluctance to talk about anything, she had still tried to make it work. His mouth tightened. And it was still the same story now. When fate had thrown them together he had used his power and position to punish her, but even then she hadn't walked away. She'd just climbed over the wall and refused to leave.

He suddenly grinned. He loved it that she was so bloody-minded. And beautiful. And brave. She was everything he'd wanted in a wife. And then his smile faded. Why was he using words like *wife* and *love*? He didn't *love* Prudence, and soon she wouldn't even be his wife. In fact, soon she wouldn't even be in the country. With a growl of frustration he clenched his hands. Everything seemed to have backfired. Letting Prudence back into his life and into his bed seemed to be having quite the opposite effect to the one he'd imagined.

For a start, sleeping with Prudence didn't actually seem to be killing his desire for her. If anything he wanted her more. In fact, he couldn't imagine a time when he *wouldn't* roll over in bed to find her lying next to him.

Worse, the anger he had felt when he'd found her in his study seemed to have faded to be replaced by a sort of nervous anticipation. He gritted his teeth. If he hadn't known better, he might have said that he had some sort of *feelings* for her.

A muscle flickered along his jaw. Only of course that would be ridiculous. His 'feelings' were just a trick of the senses. As Prudence had so rightly pointed out yesterday, the only time they ever felt comfortable being open and honest with one another was during sex, and no doubt his emotions were just the after-effects of intimacy. Add to that his guilt at having treated her so shabbily and it was no wonder he was feeling confused.

He let out a breath, pleased to have found a rational explanation for his discomfort. Glancing out of the window, he could just see the roof of the *vardo* and, whistling softly, he turned towards the door.

Sifting through the papers in his lap, Janos gave a small cry of triumph and beamed at Prudence.

'I've found it. *Finally.* That *is* a relief!' Glancing up, he looked at the grandfather clock in the corner of the sitting room and frowned. 'I can't imagine where Laszlo is.' He shook his head. 'Sometimes I think he's less house-trained than Besnik. At least Besnik remembers mealtimes.'

Closing her laptop, a blush creeping over her cheeks, Prudence said shyly, 'Actually, he told me he's going to be a little delayed.'

Her blush deepened. She was still reeling from the unfamiliar experience of Laszlo earnestly *telling* her that he was going to be late.

Studiously avoiding Janos's eyes, she added, 'I think there was some problem over at the top field.'

Janos gave her a searching look. 'I see.' There was a pause, while Prudence gazed in concentration at the lid of her laptop, and then he said slowly, 'I think I might need to speak to your uncle later.'

Prudence looked up at him. 'Wh—why?' she stammered. 'Is there a problem?'

Janos shook his head, a small smile tugging at the corners of his mouth. 'Don't look so worried, my dear. I'm just wondering whether I can persuade him to let you stay for ever! First you manage to single-handedly organise forty years of paperwork concerning my collection, and now—far more impressively—you've trained my grandson to apprise you of his movements.'

Prudence drank a mouthful of coffee, finding it suddenly difficult to swallow. 'I don't think that's all down to me,' she said, blushing again.

Janos laughed. 'It's certainly not down to *me*! But don't worry. You won't have to stay in this draughty old castle for ever. I know you must be missing your family.'

She smiled. 'I did miss them at first. But you've made me feel so welcome. And I love the castle,' she said simply. 'It's such a perfect setting for all your beautiful things.' Biting her lip, she paused. 'Actually, it really reminds me of one of my favourite places—the Soane's Museum in London. Sir John Soane used to live there, with all these incredible works of art and sculptures and clocks—just like you do there. It's an amazing place.'

She shook her head slowly.

'Edmund says I treat it like church: I always go there if I have something to celebrate or if I feel sad—' She broke off in astonishment as the clocks throughout the castle began to strike the hour. 'Is that the time? Perhaps I'd better just run down and tell Rosa that Laszlo is—'

'Laszlo is what?'

Dressed casually in jeans and a faded grey sweatshirt, Laszlo strolled into the room, Besnik following at his heels. Reaching his grandfather's armchair, he bent down and kissed Janos gently on the head, then turned to Prudence, his gleaming gaze making her stomach flip over.

They shared a brief burning silence and then he said, almost conversationally, 'That I'm starving? Or that I'm on time? Hard to say which would give her greater pleasure!'

Dropping onto a sofa, he sat back and his eyes drifted over her lips. Her breath stuck in her throat.

'How are you today, Prudence? Are *you* hungry too?'

His voice was teasing and warm, and she felt a corresponding heat across her skin. She glanced nervously over to Janos, for she was always worried that he would sense the tension between her and Laszlo. But she saw with relief that he had returned to sifting through his paperwork. She still disliked having to lie to him, but it was not for much longer. And then she would be back in England and she would have to lie only to herself.

She felt a jolt of misery. *Don't go there,* she told herself, sitting up straighter. *This was only ever going to be temporary. Nothing has changed.*

She took a deep breath. Only it had. She hadn't meant it to change, but it had. Like a tsunami warning, a cool voice inside her head kept urging her to get away from the strike zone. But she couldn't. Her only option was to stay detached. It was only sex, after all.

She shivered. But what was going on inside her heart had nothing to do with sex. Her lower lip quivered as miserably she realised that Laszlo had been right all along. A piece of paper meant nothing. For in her heart she would always be married to Laszlo.

Shifting in her seat, she tried to steady her nerves. *It's all in your imagination,* she told herself angrily. But it wasn't. She loved him, and all she really wanted to do was forget everything that had happened between them and start again.

Looking up, her eyes collided with the stinging intensity of his gaze and she felt a spasm of pain—a pain that she knew no amount of distance in time or place would ever lessen. She might be in love with him, but he had simply and expediently reduced their relationship to the physical.

Heart pounding, fighting her misery, she looked away and said hastily, 'I'll just go and tell Rosa you're here.'

'Not necessary,' Laszlo said softly. 'I told her on my way up. Oh, and Jakob rang to say he'd be over this evening.'

He sat back, letting his long legs sprawl negligently in front of him, but despite his relaxed pose Prudence could almost see the restless energy coming off him in waves.

For a moment the room was silent, and then Janos looked across at his grandson thoughtfully. 'Incredible. You're on time *and* you remembered to give me a message!'

Laszlo shrugged. His face was neutral, but his feet were tapping out a rhythm on the carpet. 'Just keeping you on your toes, Papi.'

Janos studied his grandson benignly. 'There's nothing wrong with my toes. You, on the other hand, are about to wear a hole in one of my favourite rugs. Did Jakob say what time he'd be over?'

Frowning, Laszlo pretended to think. 'He did. Now,

what did he say…? Oh, yes. About eight.' He grinned at his grandfather. 'Oh, ye of little faith!'

Shaking his head, Janos laughed. 'I'm impressed, but still a little shocked.'

'I don't see what the fuss is all about,' Laszlo grumbled. He turned to Prudence, a curve of amusement tugging at the corner of his mouth. 'What do *you* think, Prudence? Can't a leopard change his spots?'

Conscious of Janos's presence, she bit her tongue—but the desire to tease overwhelmed her. 'I'm not sure. Is that how you see yourself? As a leopard?'

She paused, mesmerised by the hunger burning in his golden eyes and the rough shadow of dark stubble grazing his jaw.

'You're more like a wolf really,' she murmured, her blood slowing in her veins at the intensity of his gaze. 'A tamed wolf that'll come inside the house but only if the door is left open.'

Their eyes locked and she felt a shiver of quicksilver run down her spine. Suddenly her heart was pounding, and the only sound was the rain falling on the window and the strained intake of their breath.

And then Janos cleared his throat. 'I believe the word you're looking for is *liminal*,' he said mildly. 'It means to occupy a space on both sides of a boundary—or in this case threshold.'

For a moment Prudence stared at him blankly, all thoughts, all words gone. And then, colour burning her cheeks, she straightened up abruptly and the spell was broken.

'Liminal… I must remember that,' she said weakly, finding speech at last.

Janos nodded. 'I believe architects often refer to hallways as "liminal" spaces.'

Prudence shifted in her chair, uncomfortably aware that she'd been too consumed with longing to hide her emotions. But if Janos was aware of her feelings he was hiding it well, for he merely smiled and returned to reading his papers.

Her heart was thumping painfully hard. Breathing out, she looked up and found Laszlo watching her almost hungrily through the thick dark lashes that fringed his eyes.

'If I'm a wolf, does that mean you're a lamb?' he said softly. Her heart lurched against her ribs.

He was exactly like a wolf: a predatory, single-minded wild animal. And she felt exactly like a lamb that had stumbled into his lair. Only perhaps because finally—privately—she had admitted her love for him it suddenly felt like the most important thing in the world to disagree.

Taking a deep breath, she summoned up a casual smile. 'Oh, I'd probably be something very prickly and shy—like a hedgehog.'

Laszlo grinned slowly. 'Hedgehogs aren't always prickly. When they relax and feel safe their quills lie flat.'

Their eyes met and she had to curl her fingers into the palms of her hands to stop herself from reaching out and pulling his mouth against hers. 'Then what happens? You eat them, I suppose?'

She blushed as he lifted an eyebrow.

'That would depend on the hedgehog.'

Janos shook his head. 'He's teasing you, my dear. He's never eaten a hedgehog in his life.'

Smiling weakly, Prudence sat up straighter, flattening herself against the back of the chair. Her skin felt hot and prickling, quite as if she were growing spines, and she had to ball her hands into fists to stop herself from rubbing her arms.

'What about you, Janos?' she said quickly, turning away as Laszlo mouthed the word *coward* at her. 'What animal are *you* like?'

Janos put down his papers and frowned. 'Judging by

the state of my memory, I ought by rights to be a gold-fish,' he said ruefully.

They all burst out laughing.

Grinning, Laszlo reached across and squeezed his grand-father's hand. 'You're such a fraud, Papi! Your memory's better than mine. And as for Prudence—' He shook his head. 'Hers is *too* good! I'd like her to forget the odd thing.'

He paused and, unable to resist the pull of his gaze, Prudence looked up helplessly.

He gave her a crooked smile and then his expression shifted, grew suddenly serious. 'Actually, there's quite a lot of things I'd like her to forget.' He hesitated, as though groping in his mind for a word or phrase, and then said quietly, 'Quite a lot I'd want to change too.'

She stared at him uncertainly, her stomach suddenly churning with nerves and confusion. His voice was strained—she might even have described it as anxious. But of course that must be her nerves playing with her imagination, for his face was neither.

Something passed through his eyes, and then abruptly he stood up and walked over to his grandfather.

'Papi! I've got some news! Something I want to share with you!'

Looking up, Janos chuckled and shook his head slowly. 'I *knew* there was something. I don't know about a wolf, but you've been like a cat on a hot tin roof all morning! Come on, then—out with it. What's your news?'

'Kajan is here!' Laszlo spoke softly but his eyes were bright.

Prudence smiled politely. She had no idea who Kajan was, but his arrival was obviously welcome, for both men were beaming at each other.

'He arrived last night, after you'd gone up to bed. I helped him set everything up in the top field. Everyone else should be arriving today.'

He hesitated and Prudence felt her scalp begin to prickle, for she could hear the pent-up excitement in his voice.

'Mihaly wants to christen Pavel this weekend. And they've asked *me* to be his godfather.' Then he grinned as Janos stood up shakily and pulled his grandson into his arms.

Watching them together, Prudence felt suddenly utterly out of place—as though she had gatecrashed a private party. Inside, her heart felt leaden. Lying in his arms that morning, her body aching and sated, their closeness had felt like the natural, unfeigned intimacy of any normal couple—it had been easy to pretend to herself that theirs was just an ordinary relationship.

But now, like a spectator watching from the sidelines, she felt a stab of despair. Who was she kidding? She had no right to stand up and congratulate her lover with a hug. Nor would she ever see his godfathering skills put into practice with their own children.

Forcing herself to push away that troubling thought, she smiled brightly and said, 'Congratulations. That's wonderful!'

Releasing his grandfather, Laszlo turned towards her. She was about to repeat her congratulations when something on his face stopped her.

'Thanks.'

He stared at her with such bleakness that she felt cold on the inside.

And then his face twisted into a smile as his grandfather patted his arm and said shakily, 'I'm very, *very* proud of you. I'm sorry, my dear!' Janos glanced at Prudence. 'It's just that this is quite a moment for both of us.'

She smiled at Janos. 'Of course it is! And I'm very pleased for both of you.' Her gaze flickered towards Laszlo and she said carefully, 'What are your duties? Is it quite a hands-on role?'

His eyes fixed on her face and she saw a ripple of some nameless emotion stir the surface.

Then, glancing away, he shrugged and said stiffly, 'It can be.'

His voice was flat, with no trace of his earlier joy, and she could almost see him withdrawing from the conversation—withdrawing from *her*. She stared at him in misery and confusion.

'I'm sure Mihaly will want you to be involved,' she said slowly. 'He obviously thinks a lot of you.'

He shrugged. There was a short, tense silence and then, not looking at her, he said coolly, 'I'm his cousin. Relatives are always chosen to be godparents.'

'I didn't know,' she said stiffly.

'Why should you?'

The coldness in his voice held a warning. It felt like a slap to the face and, biting her lip, she looked away. She felt suddenly foolish and tired—for how could she ever have imagined that they were close?

Oblivious to the tension in the room, Janos beamed. 'He's following a great tradition, Prudence. Both his father and his father's father had many godchildren between them, and I know Laszlo will be the same. He is much loved.' His face softened and he glanced at Prudence conspiratorially. 'And this will be good for him. Being shut up in this castle with only an old man for company has made him far too serious about life.'

Avoiding Laszlo's gaze, Prudence licked her lips. 'He *can* be a little intense,' she said carefully.

Janos snorted and Laszlo looked up and shook his head. 'I *am* still in the room, you know,' he said drily.

Prudence eyed him sideways. His mood seemed to have shifted again, and not for the first time she wondered what actually went on inside that handsome head of his. She watched in silence as he sighed in mock outrage.

'Some of us don't spend all day just looking at pretty pictures, Papi. So, now that my character is slain—laid bare and lifeless for all to see—can we move on? I've got a lot to organise.'

He was smiling again and Janos laughed.

'Is that right? I'll remind Rosa of that later!' Reaching into his jacket pocket, he pulled out a small leather-bound notebook and a fountain pen. 'We're all going to be very busy for the next few days. You too, my dear,' he said, smiling warmly at Prudence. 'Outsiders don't generally get to go to Romany gatherings, but you're our guest, so you'll be welcomed as one of the family.'

Prudence felt the blood drain from her face. She glanced anxiously across at Laszlo, to gauge his reaction to Janos's words, but he was leaning forward unconcernedly, scratching Besnik's ears. Perhaps he hadn't heard—for surely if he had he would be making some sort of objection? After all, he wouldn't actually *want* her mixing with his family. It had been nerve-racking enough meeting Mihaly.

Janos looked up and frowned. 'I imagine Kajan will be wanting a *bolimos* after the christening?' He turned towards Prudence. 'Kajan is the most senior member of the Cziffra family. Between the two of us, we brought Laszlo up.'

Feeling slightly sick, Prudence nodded weakly. If only Laszlo would pay attention!

She felt a swell of relief as he looked up distractedly and frowned. Thank goodness! Now he would intervene and tell Janos that she couldn't possibly come to some intimate family gathering.

But after a moment, he simply nodded and said, 'Yes. I was thinking we might hold it in the barn. We'll need that much room for the tables and the dancing.'

Janos glanced across to where Prudence sat, quietly frozen, looking at her hands. 'A *bolimos* is great fun. It's like a huge feast and party combined. And the whole *kumpania* turn out for one. Men, women, children… So you'll have a chance to meet everyone.'

Prudence forced herself to smile. 'That's really very kind of you, but I don't think I should intrude—'

Frowning, Janos glanced up at the clock. 'Nonsense. Laszlo—make Prudence see sense. I am going to find Rosa, and then we'll all have a glass of champagne to celebrate.'

Wordlessly, Prudence watched him leave, and then, turning to Laszlo, she said breathlessly, 'Why didn't you say something? You know I can't come!'

He narrowed his eyes. 'Seriously? You're worried about *intruding*? Shall I remind you of how you got your job back?'

'Of course I'm not worried about intruding,' she said crossly. Why was he being so obtuse? 'If you won't say something then I'll have to speak to your grandfather…'

He frowned. 'It's just a christening and a party.'

She looked at him incredulously. 'But you don't know who's going to be there. What if someone recognises me?'

He shrugged. 'They won't. But even if they did, like I said, they wouldn't say anything.' He studied her for a moment with that mixture of bafflement and irritation she knew so well, and then, at last, he said softly, 'Besides, they won't remember you. There were always loads of *gadje* girls hanging round the site. I doubt they could tell any of you apart.'

Prudence shivered. She felt numb inside. How could a few randomly combined words cause so much pain? And how could he be so insensitive, so brutal when he'd been so loving just hours ago? But then, love had nothing to do with his earlier tenderness during sex. His kisses and caresses were simply designed to excite and arouse. Any impression of feeling was a mistake on her part.

'I see.'

Her response was automatic. She'd just needed to say something—anything to slow the suffocating, relentless misery rolling over her. And it worked, for anger was slowly supplanting the exhaustion.

'Let's hope that's true for both our sakes. And now I think I'll go and look at some pretty pictures!'

She stood up quickly, but he was quicker.

'I'm sorry!'

His voice was so taut, so savage that it took her a moment to understand that he was apologising.

'What?' she said dazedly. 'What did you say?'

She watched him shake his head, saw muscle tighten beneath his shirt and thought that she must have misheard him.

And then he said quietly, 'I'm sorry. I shouldn't have spoken to you like that. I didn't mean what I said.'

His words seemed to be scrabbling out of his mouth, and with shock she saw that there was fear and misery in his eyes.

'I'm sorry,' he muttered again. 'Don't go. Please.'

Prudence regarded him in silence. Even though he'd hurt her so badly, she felt an urge to reach out and comfort him. Stifling it, she lifted her chin. 'Why did you say it, then?'

He shook his head again. 'I don't know. To hurt you, I suppose.'

She stared at him. 'Why do you want to hurt me?' she said slowly. 'I thought we were past all that. You said you wanted me to forget and that you wanted to change—'

Laszlo grimaced.

'And I meant it,' he said shakily. 'But then, when I told my grandfather this morning about being a godfather, I just kept thinking about all the lies I've told him and how badly I treated you—' His face twisted. 'I just don't think I can stand up in front of all those people and make promises.'

Prudence swallowed. She felt helpless in the face of

his uncertainty, for Laszlo had always been so sure, so secure in his beliefs.

'Why not?' She looked up at his face and then, taking a breath, reached out and took his hand. 'Why not?' she repeated.

He stared down at her hand almost in bewilderment, and for a moment Prudence thought he would push it away. But instead his fingers tightened on hers and she had to bite back tears.

'Surely you, of all people, don't need to ask me that?' he said quietly.

His eyes fixed on her face and she realised with astonishment that she did. She had actually forgotten what had happened between them. Her breath stilled. Forgotten and forgiven—for of course she loved him, and what purer form of love was there but forgiveness?

'Mihaly wouldn't have asked you to be a godparent if he didn't think you could do it.'

He looked away, his face creasing with frustration. 'I told you. Mihaly chose me because I'm family. And family comes first,' he muttered hoarsely.

Prudence's eyes blazed. 'And who knows that more than you? Janos told me how you stayed with him the whole time your grandmother was ill. And you're still here now, taking care of him.'

She paused, her words and the emotion behind them choking her.

'Look at *me*!' she commanded. 'You even let me stay to make him happy. Despite everything that had happened between us you let it go. For *him*.' She shook her head. 'You're strong and loyal and kind. And I think you'll be a wonderful godfather.'

There was a moment's charged silence and then Laszlo lifted her hands to his lips and kissed them tenderly. 'So.

When did you become my number one fan, *pireni*?' he murmured unsteadily.

Lost in the golden softness of his gaze, she let out a long, shaking breath. 'I'm not saying there's not room for improvement...' she said slowly.

He smiled and she saw that his misery and confusion was fading and his confidence had returned too, and also a peace that hadn't been there before—as though something...some burden...had been lifted from his shoulders.

'Is that so?' he asked lightly. 'Perhaps you could give me a little bit of guidance. Point me in the right direction!'

He ran his hand lightly down her arm, his fingers brushing against her breast. She nodded, grateful that his words required no answer, for her mind was struggling to think of something other than the touch of his hands on her skin.

But even as she let him pull her closer her relief was tinged with confusion. Not so many days ago she had hated Laszlo. Now she was championing his cause, and with a joy almost like a jolt of pain she realised that for the first time ever he had needed her.

She felt his hand moving rhythmically over her back, lower and lower. But what did any of that matter really? She might love Laszlo, but for him this relationship was only ever going to be about great sex. Nothing would change that. But she could change how she reacted to that fact like when she'd been a child and she'd wanted a star for her birthday. Eventually she'd got over it and settled for a dolls' house. That was what you did when you wanted the impossible. You took what was offered instead. And if all Laszlo could offer was passion, then she wasn't going to dwell on the impossible.

'Why are you shivering? Are you cold?'

'No,' she said and swallowed.

Gently, his breathing not quite steady, he pulled her closer. She felt the warmth of his body against her and some of her confusion seemed to go away. And then his arms tightened and, leaning against him, she reached up and pulled his mouth onto hers, kissing him with fierce desperation.

Blindly, he pulled her closer, pressing her against him, deepening the kiss, tasting, teasing, tracing the shape of her lips. Prudence whimpered. Her skin was squirming with tension, drops of pleasure spreading over her skin in rippling concentric circles. She could feel her body melting; feel his hardening, the swollen length of his arousal pressing against her pelvis.

His grip tightened in her hair and she felt him shudder—and then he groaned softly and pushed her away.

'Wh—what's the matter?' She took a step backwards, gripping his shirt to steady herself. 'Why have you stopped?'

Laszlo gave a strangled smile. 'I want to tear all your clothes off.' He glanced over his shoulder. 'But Rosa will be up here any minute. We need some place private.' He felt a flash of panic: he sounded like some gauche teenage boy.

'So take me somewhere private. Somewhere I can tear your clothes off,' she said slowly.

Groaning, he lowered his mouth and kissed her fiercely. And then from the hallway there was the sound of voices and laughter and he tore his lips away from hers. They stared at each other, panting, and then finally he held out his hand.

'Come with me!'

CHAPTER NINE

HAND IN HAND they ran, giggling like teenagers, past an open-mouthed Rosa, along corridors and up staircases, until finally he stopped and they stood panting in front of a door.

Heart thudding, feeling a knot of tension in her stomach, Prudence stared at him. 'Where are we?'

He was silent, and then abruptly he leant forward and, tipping her head back, kissed her hard—kissed her until she couldn't think or speak or breathe.

He lifted his head and stared into her eyes. 'Somewhere private,' he said softly. 'My bedroom.'

With infinite tenderness he ran his fingers over her trembling cheek, his eyes fixing on hers.

'You don't need to worry about being disturbed. No one comes up here but me.'

She stared at him for a long moment, her chest tightening, for she knew he was trying to let her know that this was important to him. Wordlessly, she nodded, her breath sharpening at the blazing, possessive intensity of his gaze, and then his head dropped and his mouth captured hers, parting her lips and kissing her passionately.

Suddenly he was pushing her backwards, through the door and across the room to the bed. Her hands slid over his back and through his hair, and then she cried out hoarsely as his lips slid down her neck and over her throat and collarbone, grazing her nipples through the thin fabric of her blouse.

One hand was on her hip, the pressure making her squirm against him. Her eyes closed as his warm breath caressed her throat. She felt cool air on her thighs as slowly his fingers pushed up the hem of her skirt. And then his hands moved higher and gently he pulled the silken strip of her panties from her.

He lifted his head and gazed down at her, breathing unsteadily, his eyes dark with passion. 'You are so beautiful,' he murmured. 'And I want you so much.'

Dry-mouthed, she watched him slide down the bed. 'What are you—?'

But her words died on her lips as he dipped his head and lowered his mouth to the small triangle of damp curls at the top of her pelvis. She gasped, squirming beneath his touch, almost frightened at how badly she wanted him to keep touching her. Her pulse was pounding; her skin felt hot, burning with a fierce white heat. Inside she was tightening, her body tugging her towards the darkness.

Curving her back, she balled her hands into fists, curling and uncurling as she felt his warm, flickering tongue probe and caress. Suddenly her head was spinning. She clutched him closer and a fluttering, dancing pleasure shimmered over her skin, growing faster and stronger, quickening in time to her pulse, until finally her body tensed and she arched her pelvis against his mouth, burying her hands in his hair.

She lay spent and shaken, and then he slid back up the bed. She shuddered helplessly as his tongue found the soft swell of her breast. Moaning softly, she pulled frantically at the buttons of his fly, her breath stuttering in her throat as she felt the hard, straining male flesh as she eased his jeans down.

At the touch of her hand he groaned and, reaching out

blindly, she pulled him inside her. His hips lifted to meet hers and he thrust deep inside, then deeper still, his mouth capturing hers. She gripped his arms, her body throbbing in response, moving and shifting frantically against him. His hands tightened convulsively in her hair and his mouth sought hers. Her muscles clenched and, digging her nails into his back, she cried out loud as her entire body jerked against his. And then she heard his own cry as he tensed, arched and drove himself inside her.

Later, their bodies aching and sated, they lay entwined on his bed.

'I meant to ask you something, earlier.'

His deep voice broke into her thoughts and she tipped her head up to gaze at him. 'What is it?'

He smiled, his eyes lighting up as they moved over her face and body. 'I wanted to ask you why you came back. The second time, I mean.'

She frowned. 'I told you. To get my job back.'

He nodded. 'But there are other jobs. Surely no job was worth having to put up with me?' Raising his eyebrow, he studied her face, watching the slow flush of colour spread over her skin.

'I didn't want to let my uncle down.'

She looked up at him, her eyes wide with misery and confusion, and he felt a sudden fiercely protective rush towards her.

'You didn't. But if you'd told him who I was he wouldn't have wanted you to stay—?'

She shook her head. 'I couldn't tell him. He needs the money,' she said flatly. 'Edmund's stupidly generous with everyone and he's got in a muddle. Anyway... Your fee will make everything okay. That's why I had to come back.'

His eyes were warm and clear, like single malt whisky. 'I see. So you put up with me to make your uncle happy? Despite everything that happened between us, you let it go? For *him*.' He shook his head. 'I think that makes *you* pretty strong and loyal and kind too.'

Recognising her words, Prudence blushed.

Laszlo frowned. 'You know, we might be more like one another than we care to admit. I think if we'd concentrated on how similar we are, rather than focusing on our differences, we could've made it work.'

Smiling, she slid her hand low over his belly, watching his eyes close with relief—for her sadness was almost too much to bear beneath his gaze. They had wasted what they might have had and yet she knew that one word from him and she would have given their marriage another chance.

But Laszlo was only talking about the past. Words like *if* and *could've* held no promise of a future they might share. Her throat was suddenly thick and tight with tears, and then she felt his hand curl underneath her and, closing her eyes too, she let the fire building inside her consume her misery...

Later, running her hand lightly over his hair-roughened skin, still intoxicated with happiness at how much he'd wanted her, Prudence buried her face against the hard muscles of his chest.

'You smell gorgeous,' she murmured. Tilting her head back, she met his eyes. 'Like woodsmoke and lemons and salt, all mixed up.'

Laszlo held her gaze and then gently kissed her on the lips. 'How is that "gorgeous"? It sounds like kippers to me.'

Laughing softly, she cuffed him playfully around the head and then, giving a shiver of pleasure, snuggled against him. She felt ridiculously happy and safe. Outside the sun was shining weakly, and she could hear birds singing, but it was what was inside his room that mattered. Just her and Laszlo: perfect and complete. Here they could laugh and kiss and touch, and the uncontrollable, intrusive demands of the outside world would just pass them by.

Drowsily, she pressed herself against him.

She didn't remember falling asleep. With a sigh, she rolled over onto her side and, opening her eyes, found Laszlo, fully clothed, sitting on the edge of the bed watching her.

'You got up…' she murmured sleepily, stretching out under the sheets.

Smiling, he lowered his head and kissed her—a teasing caress of a kiss that made her feel hot and tense, made her want him all over again.

'Why don't you come back to bed?' She sat up, the sheet slipping down over her body, exposing her breasts, and watched his gaze darken and grow blunt and focused. She shivered with anticipation.

'I want to….'

He ran his fingers over the smooth, flat curve of her abdomen and she swallowed as a prickling heat spread over her. 'But…?'

He glanced at her regretfully and then shook his head. 'But I can't. I just went downstairs to grab some food and my uncle collared me—now I've got to paint the barn with my cousins.' Glancing from her breasts to her reproachful face, he groaned. 'Don't look at me like that! If I don't go down they'll come looking for me—'

Glancing towards the door, he frowned and picked up one of his sweaters from a nearby chair.

'In fact, I wouldn't put it past them to come barging up here anyway. Let's get you decent.'

Prudence frowned. 'I can just get dressed and go.'

She watched his face shift, grow hesitant, and then he shook his head slowly.

'No. I don't want you to leave.'

Her heart gave a tiny leap. His desire for her to stay was obviously nothing more than that: desire. But he clearly didn't want her to leave, which was something.

Feeling suddenly wicked, she leant against the pillow and let the sheet slip even lower. 'Won't they knock?' she asked mischievously.

He glared at her. 'No. They won't. Now—arms up,' he said firmly.

Pretending not to notice how aroused he was, Prudence raised her arms with exaggerated slowness. Swearing softly under his breath, he slid the jumper down and over her head.

'That's better,' he said, breathing out. Grimacing, he shook his head. 'You are going to pay for that later, *pireni.*' His body stiffened painfully as he heard her breath quicken. 'Damn it!' Shaking his head, he laughed softly. 'You have got to stop taking advantage of me. Or at least feed me first. If we hadn't missed lunch I'd never have gone downstairs and Kajan wouldn't have collared me.'

Food. Lunch.

Prudence stared at Laszlo, frozen in horror as her stomach suddenly gave a loud grumble of complaint.

'Oh, no! W-we missed lunch!' she stammered, staring at him in dismay.

Laszlo shrugged.

'It's cool. I saw Papi and told him you were lying down.'

She gaped at him. 'Up *here*?' she squeaked. 'You told him I was in your bedroom?' Her cheeks felt suddenly hot, and she felt panic rising like a storm inside her.

Laszlo frowned. 'I'm thirty, Prudence, not fourteen. I don't have to ask permission to take people up to my room. Anyway, don't look so worried.' He leant forward and kissed her. 'He was fine about it. He told me to let you sleep. Said that you'd been working far too hard. And Rosa was just worried that you'd starve. Which reminds me...'

Pausing, he stood up and walked across to the chest of drawers, picked up a plate covered with a napkin.

'I made us a picnic.' He grinned, his eyes gleaming.

'Oh, and there are cherries. Unless you want to wait till I get back for dessert?'

She rolled her eyes at him and laughing softly, he sat down on the bed beside her.

While they ate he told her stories about the castle and explained some of Hungary's complicated history. Then, when they'd finished, they fed each other cherries until there was nothing but stones and stalks left. Finally Prudence looked up and kissed him softly on the lips.

'Thank you. That was delicious. Some quite surprising taste combinations. I like that.'

She was teasing him and he grinned.

'I know you like to mix your flavours up.'

She shivered as his warm hand touched the bare skin of her leg.

'But what if I could only give you bread and cheese? Would you be happy with that?' he asked slowly.

'Yes,' she said softly. 'If you were there I'd eat old shoe leather.'

His eyes were dark and unreadable and then, glancing away, he looked round the room speculatively. 'Maybe you should just stay here in the tower? You could be my very own Lady of Shalott.'

She looked at him levelly, trying to ignore the steady, soft touch of his hands. Trying to stop herself from reading too much into his remark. She smiled. 'Doesn't she die alone and heartbroken?'

Laszlo frowned.

'Yes, she does. I'd forgotten that part. I wasn't really thinking about the poem. I just remember the painting by Waterhouse.' He smiled at her mockingly. 'Okay. What about Rapunzel? She saves her prince and they live happily ever after.'

Not trusting herself to speak, Prudence glanced away. *Could* she save Laszlo? Would he ever let her get close to him? She felt a flicker of hope. Maybe they could live happily ever after—maybe that was why fate had thrown them back together.

Her breathing slowed. Wrapped up in his bed sheets, it was easy to forget that none of this was real, for his words were so seductive. But her relationship with Laszlo would end soon, and there would be no happy-ever-after. And his words were designed to captivate and ensure that he got what he wanted. She sighed. What she had wanted too, at the beginning. Only now she wanted more.

And then, remembering how he'd held back from her just yesterday, she felt her stomach tighten. There was no point in hoping for any kind of reconciliation. What kind of marriage could they really have without trust and openness on both sides? Not that Laszlo had any interest in rekindling their relationship anyway. To him, this was and had only ever been a finite fling. Any seduction on his part was simply a means to an end. She needed to remember that when his poetic words started making her believe in fairy tales.

Composing herself, she smiled. 'I'm not sure. I don't remember Rapunzel throwing suitcases at her prince,' she said teasingly.

He gave her a crooked smile. 'That's because her pointy hat got in the way.'

She giggled as he reached over and pulled her closer.

'Not that you've thrown anything at me for days. Except the odd insult!' His eyes moved across her face slowly. 'I meant what I said. About you staying. I mean, why does all of this have to end?'

His arm tightened around her waist.

'I admit when you arrived it was difficult. We had a lot of things to sort out. But that's done now.'

His face was tense with concentration; she knew he was choosing his words carefully.

'We could just carry on doing what we're doing, couldn't we? We both want it. And I want you more than I've wanted any other woman.'

She felt a twitch of longing between her thighs, but it was tempered with sadness. It was flattering to be so desired, only she wanted so much more. But the thought of leaving him was so dreadful to contemplate that there was really no point pretending that she would refuse a relationship on whatever terms he offered.

'Just you and me? Just the two of us?' she said lightly.

He nodded, but his expression was suddenly serious. 'Just the two of us,' he echoed. 'That could work.'

Silence fell and then abruptly, Laszlo stood up.

'I'd better go. But you'll stay, won't you?'

She nodded slowly and watched him leave and then, sighing, she fell back onto the pillows.

She hadn't meant to fall asleep again. But somehow she had. It was the second time she had woken up in Laszlo's bed. Only this time she was alone in his room, and she felt his absence like an ache inside. Hugging his jumper against her body, she drew some comfort from his scent, and then rolling over, she gazed around the room.

It was a beautiful room, with high ceilings and deep, wide-set windows. Unlike all the other rooms she'd seen at the castle, there were no paintings or mirrors on the pale grey walls and it was sparsely furnished. Just an armchair, the curved wooden bed she was lying on and a chest of drawers.

And then she noticed the photograph.

For a moment, she stared at it blankly, wondering why she hadn't noticed it before, for it was the only ornament in the room. Then, pushing back the sheets, she walked across the carpet and, feeling slightly guilty, reached out and touched the framed black and white photograph.

Her mind was humming. Thoughts and feelings were buzzing through her head. And then she breathed in sharply. The two people in the photograph were Laszlo's parents. She was sure of it. The family resemblance was there in every line and curve of their faces. They were so beautiful, so young. But what drew her eye was not their youth or beauty—it was the intensity of their focus. They literally seemed to have eyes for no one but each other.

Prudence swallowed. She had never seen a photo of her own parents together. In fact, the only picture she had of her father was from a newspaper. Someone—probably Aunt Daisy—had cut out the report of a trial involving her father. She'd found it, yellowing and fading, hidden inside a book.

She was gazing so intently at the photograph that she didn't hear Laszlo come in.

'Pick it up, if you want.'

Jumping slightly at the sound of his voice, she turned round, a faint blush colouring her cheeks. 'You always seem to catch me snooping,' she grumbled.

Watching her worry the soft flesh of her lower lip, he felt a sudden twitch of desire. Even wearing his tatty jumper, with her hair tousled from sleep and her pink mouth bruised from his kisses, she looked sexier than hell.

He gave her a faint smile. 'Snooping…breaking and entering? Prudence, I have a feeling you're not in Surrey any more!'

There was a short, tense silence and then he reached out for her as she stepped towards him and they kissed fiercely.

Lifting his head, he dragged his mouth away from hers. 'I missed you.' He felt her arms tighten around him.

'I missed you too,' she murmured, burying her face against his chest.

Finally she gestured towards the photograph and frowned. 'Sorry…' She hesitated. 'They're your parents, aren't they?'

He nodded slowly, his golden eyes studying her warily. 'Yes.'

'Is that before or after they were married?'

'After,' he said shortly.

She wanted to ask more, but the brusqueness of his tone seemed to discourage any more talk in that direction, so instead she glanced around the room and said lightly, 'It's not how I expected it to look. Your room, I mean.'

'What were you expecting? Shawls and knick-knacks and bargeware?' Seeing from her guilty expression that she had, he grimaced and shook his head. 'I've had my fill of castles and roses—excuse the pun. But why do you care what my room looks like?' And then he frowned. 'Oh, I get it. You think it somehow reflects *my soul.*'

His earlier tension seemed to have shifted and his eyes were laughing down at her.

She blushed. 'I did an Art History degree, remember? I can find tragedy and torment in two squares of maroon and red.'

Grinning, he took her hand and held it against his lips. 'So what do you think my room says about me?'

She lifted her head. 'I think it says you ran out of picture hooks. Either that or you're a philistine.'

She yelped as he made a grab for her.

'Just because I don't want a bunch of Old Masters cluttering up my walls, it doesn't make me a philistine.'

He spoke flippantly, but there was an edge to his voice and she turned to face him.

'I was joking. Truly. I know you're not a philistine,' she said slowly.

She watched his face grow taut.

'Because of my grandfather?' He shrugged. 'That's rather a simplistic point of view. I would have thought you'd be the first person to understand that blood can be no thicker than water.'

He looked away, and her cheeks burning, Prudence stared at his profile helplessly. There was something pushing to get out from behind his anger. Something that he'd wanted and failed to tell her yesterday and she needed to find some way—some words—to reach him.

Holding her breath, she followed his gaze. He was looking at the photograph of his parents.

'What were they like?'

He was silent so long she thought he wasn't going to reply, and then his shoulders rose and fell and he said quietly, 'They were perfect.'

Her heart was suddenly pounding. It was an odd word to use, but it was the way he said it—so wearily, so unhappily—that made her feel as though she were breaking in two.

Her eyes fixed on the photograph.

'You look a lot like your mother,' she said carefully. 'But your eyes are just like your father's.'

Laszlo watched her glance anxiously from the photo back to him. 'At least I inherited *something* from them.'

He hadn't meant his remark to sound so sharp, and his neck tensed as she turned to look at him.

'What does that mean?'

Instead of answering he gave a casual shrug and leant forward, intending to kiss her. Kiss away his pain and confusion.

But, stepping backwards, she stared at him confusedly. 'I want to help—'

'I don't want your help!'

He spoke quickly—too quickly—and she lifted her head, her eyes suddenly darker than steel, her voice glacier-cold. 'But you *do* want to have sex with me?'

As he met her gaze, he felt relief, for her anger was so much easier to respond to than her concern. 'I don't see a connection.'

'I want you to stop pushing me away.'

'I don't push you away. I can barely keep my hands off you.'

'I'm not talking about that. That's just sex.'

She looked away. There was a pulsing silence. A muscle flickered in his jaw and he groped for something to take the pain from her eyes. And from his heart.

'I'm sorry. I don't want to.' His face was suddenly stiff with tension. 'I'm not trying to push you away—' Prudence stared at him anxiously. She could almost feel the weight of misery in his heart.

'But you are pushing *something* away. Or someone…?'

It was conjecture—nothing more than a feeling—but his face tightened.

'Is it your mum and dad?'

He looked almost dazed, and then his eyes seemed to scramble away from hers. There was a silence, and then he said quietly, 'I let them down. And not just them. My grandparents too.'

'I don't understand…' she said slowly. And then suddenly—incredibly—she did. 'Are you talking about our marriage?'

Even as he nodded, she was shaking her head.

'No. Laszlo. That doesn't make sense. None of them knew about our marriage. So how could you have let them down?'

His face quivered. 'You're right. You *don't* understand.' He frowned. 'Even now people in my family talk about my parents. They were so perfect together. And they made everything look so effortless. Marriage. Love. Life.'

He grimaced. Even the difference in their backgrounds had been no obstacle to their happiness; instead their passionate belief in each other had simply blurred the lines between the Romany and non-Romany world.

'And you wanted to be like them.' It was a statement not a question.

After a brief hesitation he let out a breath and nodded. 'I wanted what they had. That passion—that rightness.' He gave a twisted smile. 'I think, actually, it'd be more accurate to say that, as their son, I *expected* it. As my right. And I thought I had it.'

'Why?' she whispered.

And she was suddenly more grateful than she'd ever been that it was his turn to speak, for she couldn't have opened her mouth again without crying.

'I met you.' He smiled again, but this time his smile seemed to illuminate his whole face. 'And I was desperate—no, *determined* not to lose you. We married and everything was perfect. At first.'

She stared at him, feeling a spasm of nausea. 'And then I ruined it?'

Abruptly he grabbed her arms and shook her, his face tightening with anger. 'No. You *didn't* ruin it. You were just young and nervous and inexperienced.'

She struggled against him, words tumbling haphazardly from her lips. 'You were young too.'

'Spoilt and arrogant is what I was! I was used to getting what I wanted,' he said harshly. 'And what I wanted was for you to make our marriage work—because I sure as hell wasn't going to. I just assumed everything would fall into place.' His eyes fixed on her face. 'I was wrong.'

'We were both wrong!' she raged back at him.

His hands dropped to his sides and he let out a ragged breath. 'I thought it'd be easy.'

He frowned, remembering how inadequate he'd felt. How lonely too—for he'd been too proud to admit his problems to anyone.

'Only it *wasn't*. And when it got hard I blamed you. I pushed you away,' he said quietly. 'I'm the one that ruined everything, *pireni*! I hurt you and I lied to you, and because of my arrogance and stubborn pride I let you go when I should have done everything in my power to make you stay. And then I had to lie to both my families. All my grandmother wanted was to see me happily married before she died, and I messed that up too.'

His voice cracked and he lowered his head.

'I never meant to hurt you, Prudence. You have to believe me. I just wanted it to be perfect.'

Feeling tears prick the backs of her eyes, Prudence shook her head. 'I know,' she said softly. 'And I don't blame you for what happened.'

Her throat tightened. It was no wonder he'd reacted so badly when their marriage had seemed to falter.

Reaching out, she took his hand and squeezed it. 'You know this morning, when you said we're more alike than we thought? You were right. Our parents' marriages influenced us way too much.' She laughed weakly. 'I actually think it was some kind of miracle that we even got together in the first place.'

Gripping his hand, she dragged him across the room.

'Listen to me, Laszlo!' She picked up the photo, brandishing it like a weapon. 'I've spent years looking at photos, paintings and sketches. And it's true what they say: every picture *does* tell a story. And this is *their* story. Not yours.'

She put the frame down carefully.

'I don't have a photo of you, but if I did it would tell me your story. The story of a young man who made some mistakes but who is loyal and devoted to his family and who has learned to forgive and trust.' Her eyes flared. 'You haven't let *anyone* down. Your parents' marriage may have looked easy from the outside, but you only knew them as a child. And I'm sorry that your grandmother didn't know about our marriage, but you made her very happy, Laszlo. And you took care of her—just like you're taking care of Janos now.'

He caught hold of her arm and pulled her tightly into his arms, burying his face in her hair. 'I don't deserve you,' he murmured.

For a long, long time, he just held her, his warm breath on her neck. Then at last, he sighed.

'Talking is so tiring. How do women do so much of it?'

She pulled back slightly and smiled up at him. 'We *are* the stronger sex,' she said quietly.

He nodded, his face serious. 'Stronger. Wiser. You're probably the wisest woman I've ever met, Prudence Elliot. The most beautiful. Most compassionate. Most forgiving.' He sighed again.

'If only I could make a proper Hungarian goulash I'd be perfect,' she said shakily.

He smiled weakly. 'I've had enough of perfection. I'm happy with what I've got.'

Standing on tiptoe, she pressed her mouth against his. 'Me too!'

He kissed her back fiercely and then, groaning, broke away from her. 'You know, all that talk about goulash has made me think about food again. How about we go downstairs and show Rosa where she's been going wrong all these years?'

Later, lying with Prudence curled against his body, Laszlo felt strangely calm. He'd told her everything, and she'd listened while he talked. Not once had she judged him. Instead she'd given him the courage to face his fear. A fear that had chafed at him for so long and corroded his relationship with the only woman he'd ever loved.

Closing his eyes, he felt his heart contract almost painfully.

The woman he still loved. His wife.

His hand tightened around her body and he was suddenly close to tears, for he had so nearly lost her again.

And then he almost laughed out loud as he remembered their teasing conversation of earlier. For he was the one who was trapped in the tower, and *she* had rescued *him*.

Abruptly, he felt his chest grow tight. And then, like a balloon popping, his happiness burst. His relationship with Prudence would soon be over and all his thoughts of love and marriage were just speculation and hope. At no time had Prudence even hinted that she wanted to give their relationship another chance.

He frowned. Come to that matter, he hadn't either.

In fact, he'd made it pretty clear that their relationship was nothing more than a cathartic fling that would terminate at the same time as her period of employment at the castle.

Opening his eyes, he stared bitterly at the photograph of his parents. He needed to show Prudence he'd changed. Words wouldn't be enough this time. But, having convinced her that all he wanted was a loveless affair, how was he going to persuade her that he wanted to give their marriage another chance?

CHAPTER TEN

'ARE YOU READY?'

Laszlo's voice drifted up the stairs, causing Prudence to glance in dismay at the discarded clothes strewn across her bed. So far she was wearing only her underwear and her shoes.

'Nearly!' she called out quickly.

'Nearly? How is that possible? You've been up there for hours...' His voice trailed off as he stepped through the doorway. 'Nice dress,' he said slowly. 'Where's the rest of it?'

She glared at him. 'This isn't the dress. It goes underneath.'

His eyes slid over the sheath of satin.

'And what goes underneath that?' he murmured softly.

'Nothing. That's the point.'

He grinned. 'It's a very good point. Very convincing, in fact.' He walked across the room and kissed the corner of her mouth. 'Although if you took it off I think your point might be clearer still.' He pulled her towards him and kissed the soft hollow at the base of her neck.

She looked into his eyes and gave him a teasing smile. 'Really? You don't think it might be a little risqué for the party?'

She squirmed against him and he looked down at her, his gaze darkening.

'Hell, yeah! I'm the only person who gets to see you

naked,' he growled, lowering his mouth onto hers and kissing her fiercely.

Head spinning, Prudence clung to him, feeling heat—scorching, dizzying heat—wash over her. Just as she thought her legs would give way, she heard him swear softly under his breath.

Groaning, he broke the kiss and released her. 'I can't believe we have to go to this damn party. I've already spent all day with my family.'

He stopped and stared incredulously at the pile of clothes on the bed.

'You're not going to say you don't have anything to wear, are you?' he said slowly.

'No. Yes. I don't know… It depends.'

He frowned. 'On what? What about the dress you chose in Budapest?'

She bit her lip. 'I did get a dress. Only now I'm not sure if it's more of an evening one than party.'

Laszlo winced. 'Can't it be both? We *are* going to an evening party, after all.' His eyes lit up hopefully. 'If you're really worried then maybe we should just stay here?'

Smiling, she shook her head. 'Nice try! But we're not bailing. What would your family think?' She frowned. 'I don't know why you don't want to go anyway.'

Throwing himself down onto the bed, he pushed the dresses to one side and pulled a pillow behind his head. 'Because I want to stay *here*,' he said sulkily. 'And, as it's taken you nearly two hours *not* to get ready, I think the party will probably be ending by the time you're dressed.'

Laughing, Prudence picked up a scarf from the back of a chair and threw it at him. 'It's easy for men!' she said, reaching round and sweeping her long blonde hair into a loose topknot. 'They just put on a suit!' Glancing at him, she felt her smile fade and gave a small cry of exasperation. 'Only you're not!'

Winding the scarf around his neck, he looked up at her calmly. 'Not what?'

'Wearing a suit!'

Looking down at his jeans and shirt, Laszlo frowned. 'What's wrong with this?'

She glowered at him crossly. 'You're joking, aren't you? Laszlo! I thought you said everyone was dressing up?'

He shrugged. 'They are. And I *have* dressed up; this is the shirt I bought yesterday. Anyway, it's my party—I can wear what I like.' Reaching out, he grabbed her hand and pulled her next to him on the bed. 'What's wrong?' he said gently.

'I don't want to let you down in front of your family.'

'How could you ever let me down? If it hadn't been for you I might never have gone through with being Pavel's godfather.' He pressed her hand to his lips and kissed it tenderly. 'Besides, you'd look beautiful wearing that rug.' He glanced at the riotously patterned Afghan carpet on the floor and grimaced.

Stroking his hair off his forehead, she smiled weakly. 'They won't be looking at me anyway. You're the godfather, remember?' Her eyes grew soft and misty. 'The very handsome, very serious godfather.' She hesitated. 'I'm so proud of you.'

He pressed his thumb against her cheekbone. 'You're a good person,' he said softly, leaning forward so that his warm breath tickled her throat. 'Good enough to eat.'

His words excited her unbearably, and she could feel heat pooling between her thighs. Cheeks burning, she gritted her teeth, trying to stay calm. 'You don't want to spoil your appetite. And I need to get dressed,' she said lightly.

He sighed. 'I still don't really get why you're so worried, *pireni*. Although I suppose I'd probably feel the same if I was in your shoes.'

Summoning up a smile, Prudence looked down at her

high-heeled black court shoes. 'If you were in my shoes I think you'd bring the party to a standstill!'

He grinned. 'Don't tempt me!'

His eyes met hers and she felt a shiver of desire run over her skin as Laszlo ran his hand slowly up her leg and then abruptly rolled to the other side of the bed.

'You know what? I don't care what you wear.' He groaned. 'But you *have* to put some clothes on or I won't be responsible for what happens.' He stood up. 'In fact, just to be on the safe side, I'm going to go back to the castle. If I put a couple of fields and metre-thick stone walls between us I might just be able to keep my hands off you until after the party!'

He paused and pulled her scarf more tightly around his neck.

'Oh, and I *might* change into something that's a bit more "evening and party wear"!'

She giggled and their eyes met.

'I'll be back to pick you up later…ish.' Blowing her a kiss, he grimaced and shook his head. 'The things we do for love!'

After he'd gone, she spent at least ten minutes mulling over his words. Finally she roused herself. It was just a phrase—a jokey remark that people used all the time. She would be crazy to read anything more into it.

Twenty minutes later she slid a lipstick across her lips and stared critically at her reflection in the dressing table mirror.

She turned her head from side to side. The neckline was perhaps a little lower than she'd normally wear, and her pinned-up hair would probably not survive the dancing, but overall she was satisfied. Still staring at her reflection, she bit her lip. She seemed to be looking at two separate versions of herself. One was serene and cool, the deep smoky grey of the long silk dress highlighting her classic English rose skin and fair hair. The other Prudence was visible only in her eyes, which were dark, apprehensive. Aroused by Laszlo's imagined response to her transformation.

She heard a knock at the door and felt a stab of excitement. *Laszlo!*

Heart pounding, she opened the door—and took a step backwards, her hand over her mouth. He looked impossibly handsome in a classic black dinner jacket, his snowy white shirt unbuttoned at the neck, bow tie hanging loose around the collar.

'It—it's a dinner jacket,' she stammered.

He glanced down at himself nonchalantly. 'This old thing? I found it at the back of my wardrobe,' he murmured.

He smiled, his teeth gleaming in the darkness. She saw the flare of approval and desire in his face and felt her body respond.

'You're beautiful, Prudence,' he said softly. Reaching out, he tugged gently at a tendril of honey-coloured hair, shaping the curl between his fingers. 'I love your hair up like this. You're like a goddess—an Aphrodite.'

Prudence stared at him breathlessly. He was more beautiful than any god she could name. And sexier too, with his shirt open and his eyes dark and teasing.

'That would explain why I can't ever seem to get warm. I should really be on some hot Greek mountain,' she said lightly, her heart banging against her chest.

He studied her in silence. 'Speaking of cold…are you going to invite me in or shall I just wait out here?'

She blushed. 'Sorry. Of course—come in. I just need to get my bag.'

Shutting the door behind him, Laszlo pulled off his jacket and hung it carelessly over the back of the sofa. He sat down in one of the armchairs, picked up a magazine and began to flick through it.

After a moment he sighed and put his feet up onto the

coffee table. 'What do women put in their bags anyway?' he said idly.

Prudence smiled. 'All the things men keep in their jacket pockets. Money, keys, lipstick…'

'I don't have any lipstick,' Laszlo said sadly.

She laughed softly. 'You don't have any money or keys either.'

Grinning up at her, he tugged her leg and she let herself fall into his lap.

'Is that so? How would you know? Or have you been going through my clothes as well as breaking into my house?'

He shook his head and, laughing, she wriggled free of his hands. Standing up, she pulled down his jacket and began patting the pockets one by one.

'See?' she said triumphantly. 'Empty. Oh—' Her fingers touched something small and rectangular and then suddenly she was holding a small velvet-covered rectangular box.

'What's this?'

Frowning, Laszlo stood up. He paused and then swore softly under his breath. 'Damn it!' He shook his head and then smiled ruefully. 'That was—is actually for you.'

She stared at him, too shocked to speak. 'For me?' she said finally. 'What is it?'

His eyes met hers and he laughed quietly. 'Open it and see!'

Heart pounding, she felt her mind dance forward as she lifted the lid—and then she gasped. 'Oh, Laszlo. It's beautiful.'

He nodded. 'It's to match your eyes.'

She stared at the luminous grey pearl necklace in silence, shivers running up and down her spine. 'It's truly lovely. But I didn't get *you* anything,' she said, looking up at him anxiously.

A dark flush coloured his cheeks. There was a pause, and then he shook his head slowly. 'It's not from me.' He cleared his throat. 'It's from my grandfather. He would have given it to you himself, but he got tied up on the phone and he wanted you to have it before the party.'

Prudence blinked 'Your grandfather?' She swallowed. Her skin felt hot and raw; his gaze was blistering her skin. She felt stupid and naive. Keeping her gaze averted, she breathed in deeply. 'That's so sweet of him. But I can't possibly accept it.'

Laszlo frowned. 'You must. Please. He chose them himself as a thank-you for all your hard work.'

She bit her lip. 'He didn't need to thank me. Not with something as beautiful as this. Shall I wear it tonight?' she said shakily.

Nodding, he reached out and took the necklace gently from her hand. 'It's not as beautiful as you. Now, stand up and turn round!'

She turned away, feeling her skin tingle as his warm fingers slid over her.

'There! Let me see…'

She turned back towards him slowly and lifted her head. Their eyes met and her pupils shrank beneath the intensity of his gaze.

'You don't need any jewellery. Your eyes and lips are your jewels,' he said roughly.

Breathing deeply, he stepped away, his eyes narrowing.

'And now I'd like to give you *my* gift. I'm sorry it doesn't quite match up to my grandfather's.' He smiled ruefully. 'If he'd been any other man I would have punched him on the nose. But what could I do? He's my grandfather!'

'*Your* gift?'

He reached down and pulled a small embellished leather bag from beneath his shirt. 'It's a *putsi*. It means "little

pocket". It's traditional for Romany women to carry one.'
He looped the cord over his hand and held it out to her.

'It's beautiful,' she croaked.

Her heart was racing, and she knew that her feelings were all over her face, but she was too happy to care. Her whole body felt as though it were filling with light.

With hands that shook slightly, she turned the bag over. It rattled softly. 'Is there something inside it?'

He nodded. 'Amulets. Magic charms.' He shrugged. 'They're supposed to bring good luck. Ward off evil. If you believe in that sort of thing.'

She nodded, unable to speak.

'Just don't open the bag,' he said, deepening his voice dramatically. 'Or the magic will fail.'

Shivering, she looked up with wide, uncertain eyes.

He pulled her towards him, laughing softly. 'I'm kidding. You can open it if you want.'

She began to pull clumsily at the drawstring and then, looking up, saw him watching her. Her fingers faltered.

'I think I'll wait,' she said slowly. 'Save my luck for later.'

Gently, he reached up and stroked her cheek. 'You don't need luck.' He glanced at the soft curve of her waist beneath the clinging silk and frowned. 'But if we don't go right now there's no amulet on earth that's going to stop me ripping that dress off you!'

'I'm ready!' she said hastily.

Reaching down, she picked up her small beaded evening bag, opened it and put the *putsi* inside. Then, looking up, she smiled at him shyly.

'Thank you, Laszlo. I'll keep it close to me always. And I love it just as much as the pearls.'

He watched her coolly, back to his old inscrutable self.

'It's my pleasure. And I'm pleased.' He grinned. 'Utterly unconvinced, but pleased.'

He turned towards the door but she put her hand on his arm. 'Wait!' Their eyes met and then she blushed and pointed to his neck. 'What about your bow tie?'

Glancing down, he frowned. 'Oh... I gave up,' he said simply. 'Papi can do them in his sleep, but he was busy on the phone, and every time I tried to talk to him he shooed me away,' he grumbled.

Their eyes met and she burst out laughing. 'You are *such* a spoilt baby.' She reached out and did up his top button. 'Your grandfather was probably talking to the caterers. Now, lift your chin!' Deftly, Prudence twisted the black silk between her fingers. 'Turn around!' Stepping backwards, she stared at him assessingly. 'Perfect!' she said softly.

He grinned slowly. 'Me? Or the bow tie?'

Rolling her eyes, she picked up the pashmina she'd had the foresight to buy at the airport and slid it over her shoulders. She let out a breath.

Laszlo looked at her enquiringly. 'Ready?'

'No. But do I have a choice?'

He kissed her lightly on the lips. 'Not any more. Come on! Let's go!' He gave Prudence his arm and, opening the front door, stepped into the night air.

She gave a gasp of surprise, for, leading away as far as the eye could see, hundreds of tiny flickering flares edged the path up to the castle. 'That's so pretty!'

Shaking his head, Laszlo laughed. 'They're supposed to stop us breaking our necks. But I suppose they *do* look a bit like fireflies.' His golden eyes gently mocked her excitement. 'It all adds to the magic of the occasion. For the women and children!'

Prudence laughed. 'Don't make me use my *putsi*,' she said teasingly.

'There's nothing wrong with a bit of magic.' Laszlo grinned. 'I'll remind you of that later, when my Uncle Lajos starts doing conjuring tricks.'

The noise of laughter and music greeted them as they walked along the gravel path towards the barn and Prudence squeezed Laszlo's arm nervously.

She had enjoyed the christening more than she'd expected. The tiny church had been bright with sunlight and filled with flowers. And seeing Laszlo hold Pavel in his arms, his unguarded face still with pride, she could have wept with love and envy. Laszlo's family had been polite and friendly. But now the darkness felt intimidating, and she suddenly wished that she was walking in as his wife.

Shivering, she pushed the thought away. 'It sounds like the party's already started,' she said quickly. 'How many people are coming?'

Laszlo shrugged. 'I don't know. Probably a hundred—maybe more.'

Prudence felt her feet stutter to a halt. 'A—a *hundred*?' she stammered. 'A hundred people?' She stopped and stared at him incredulously. 'Why didn't you tell me?'

He gazed at her with a maddening lack of concern. 'I thought you knew? Did you think it was just the guests from the christening?' He laughed softly. 'No. This is *everyone*.' Frowning, he took her hand in his. 'Does it matter? I mean, they're all family...'

Swallowing, she smiled weakly. 'Is that why there were more women than men at the church?'

He grinned. 'They didn't all come to the church. A lot of the men think that priests take away your manhood. Mine seems fine, though!' His eyes gleamed in the darkness.

She knew he was teasing her, trying to make her relax, but she couldn't. Feeling suddenly queasy with panic, Prudence clutched his arm more tightly.

Laszlo gave her hand a comforting squeeze. 'You did the hard part this morning. It'll be fine. They're going to love you. Trust me.'

Trust: how could so much be wrapped up in that one little word? 'Okay.' Heart pounding, she nodded. 'Okay. But you have to trust me too, Laszlo. That's how trust works.'

In the darkness, she couldn't tell if he'd taken in her words or not. She opened her mouth to speak again, and then, behind them, the door to the barn opened and light and noise and colour hit her like a physical blow.

'Laszlo! *Laszlo!*'

Prudence stared in astonishment round the barn. All around her, hands were reaching across and patting Laszlo on the back, pulling him by the arm, calling out his name. Turning towards her, he grinned and shouted back something in Hungarian, or maybe Romany. But the noise in the barn made it impossible for her to do anything but smile and nod.

Children were running around, darting through the crowds of smartly dressed adults, laughing and shouting. Some men dressed in dark suits and waistcoats were singing, stamping in time to guitars, and men and women, old and young, were dancing in a mass of people that seemed to fill one end of the vast barn.

Laszlo guided her into a part of the barn that had been screened off as a cloakroom. He turned to her and grinned. 'Now, *this* is a party. A Romany party!' he whispered in her ear.

She nodded. 'A hundred people?' She glared at him accusingly as he led her back into the main barn. 'There must be well over two hundred!'

He glanced round the room. 'Nearer three, I'd guess.' His eyes were light and teasing.

She shook her head. 'You're incorrigible, Laszlo Cziffra! You knew *exactly* how many people were coming—and I bet you were always going to wear a dinner jacket, weren't you?'

'No.'

His smile sent shivers up and down her spine.

'I was always going to wear a suit. But then I thought tonight was special—'

He turned as a dancing couple barged into him and apologised. She blinked in confusion. What did he mean by 'special'? She felt his hand tighten on hers and looking up, found him watching her, his gaze fierce and glittering.

'We need to talk.'

Wordlessly, she nodded—and then, glancing over his shoulder, she noticed a middle-aged couple watching them curiously.

'Not here,' she murmured, flinching as another couple skimmed past Laszlo's back.

Frowning, he put his arm round her protectively. 'Shall we go outside? It's quieter there…less chance of injury.'

'Yes.' She paused. 'But could we find your grandfather first? I want to thank him for the necklace.'

Laszlo studied her face and then nodded slowly. Scanning over the heads of the dancers, he pointed across the barn. 'He's over there! And there's Mihaly too.' He gripped her hand tightly. 'Don't let go. I don't want to lose you.'

He turned and began to push his way through the crush of people, pulling her behind him. Every few metres he was stopped by guests and Prudence found herself being introduced to a baffling array of people. Finally they reached the other side of the barn, where tables and chairs had been set up and trestles of food and drink lined the walls.

'Laszlo!' Mihaly reached out and yanked his cousin into a crushing embrace. He took a step back and, glancing down at Laszlo's suit, grinned wickedly. 'What's this? They've got you being a waiter at your own party?'

Pushing Laszlo under his arm, he sidestepped in front of Prudence and bowed.

'Miss Elliot! You look beautiful! I wonder, may I have this dance with you?'

He gave a yelp that turned into a laugh as Laszlo grabbed him from behind and punched him on the arm.

'No. You may not!'

Still laughing, Mihaly held out his hand to Prudence. 'Don't listen to him, Miss Elliot.' He gestured towards an elderly woman sitting by the dance floor, a walking frame by her side. 'That's my great-aunt. Laszlo danced with her once! Just *once*!'

He and Laszlo both burst into laughter, but there was no mistaking the possessive note in his voice as Laszlo pulled her against him. 'Prudence won't be dancing with anyone but me. And *you're* going to need a walking frame too, cousin, if you don't back off!'

Trying to ignore the warm rush of pleasure at his words, she glanced anxiously over to where Janos was talking to another elderly man. 'I must just speak to your grandfather,' she said quietly.

Janos broke off his conversation as she approached him. He smiled warmly. 'You look quite lovely, my dear.'

Prudence blushed. 'Thank you so much, Janos. It's such a beautiful necklace.' Standing on tiptoe, she reached up and kissed Janos gently on the cheek.

Smiling, he patted her on the hand. 'It's my pleasure.' He glanced over Prudence's shoulder to where Laszlo and Mihaly were still fooling around with each other. Sighing, he shook his head. 'They act like children when they get together, but it's nice for me to see Laszlo having fun.'

His face clouded.

'I know it must appear to you that he's had a charmed life, living here in a castle surrounded by priceless works of art. But he's known a great deal of unhappiness,' he said quietly. 'He's seen so much sickness and death and grief.' He smiled sadly. 'Of course I love having my grandson live with me, but he's spent far too much of his life cooped up in the castle with me.'

He hesitated.

'We're too shut off here. It's made him push away the world. Turn away from life itself. But you coming here has changed that. He seems so much happier.'

Prudence blushed. 'I don't think I can really take the credit for that.' She swallowed. 'But I'm glad he's happy. He deserves to be. Even though he's so incredibly annoying and stubborn...' Her mouth twisted. 'I don't think I know anyone quite like him!'

Janos burst out laughing. 'Nothing you can't handle, I imagine?'

She laughed. 'No. I think we've pretty much worked out our differences.' Biting her lip, she hesitated. 'But I think it's not just Laszlo who's changed. You've changed too.'

Janos nodded. 'Yes. I have.' His eyes flickered with excitement. 'And there may be more changes to come. But none of it would have happened without your hard work and patience.'

Prudence glanced down to the necklace gleaming at her throat. 'Hmm... Pearls for patience? I think I should quit while I'm ahead.'

Janos smiled. 'It's a fair exchange! And happily Laszlo actually remembered to give you the necklace.' He frowned. 'I wasn't entirely sure he would. He can be a little forgetful.'

'Jakob's not forgetful!' Laszlo slid between his grandfather and Prudence. 'What are you talking about, Papi? He's got an excellent memory. Or were you casting aspersions on *me*?' He smiled mischievously at Janos, who shook his head and began to speak in Hungarian.

For a long moment Laszlo said nothing. His expression didn't change, but something in his gaze seemed to reach out to her—she could almost feel his hands on her skin, even though they were standing apart.

Finally both men nodded and then, his face softening, Laszlo held out his hand. 'Dance with me?'

Prudence felt the air squeeze from her lungs and for a moment time seemed to stop—and then slowly she smiled.

The rest of the party passed with unconscionable speed. Later, Prudence would try to piece the evening together. She had danced and eaten, and talked until her voice was hoarse from trying to compete with the music. And then finally the music had slowed and the lights had dimmed and Laszlo had held her tightly against him. They'd danced until suddenly Janos had been there, telling them that he was tired and was going to go home to bed.

'I'll walk you home, Papi. I could do with some fresh air,' Laszlo said, pulling his dinner jacket from the back of a chair. He turned to Prudence, his eyes locking onto hers. 'Shall I come back for you?' he asked quietly.

She shook her head. 'No. I'll come now.'

Smiling, he slipped his jacket over her shoulders, and together the three of them walked up to the castle.

Inside the hall, Janos turned and frowned.

'Are you all right, Papi?' Laszlo stared at his grandfather.

'Oh, I'm fine. The fresh air's just woken me up.' Janos hesitated. 'I wonder… Do either of you feel up to a nightcap?'

Glancing at one another, they both nodded simultaneously.

Janos beamed. 'Wonderful. Let's go and warm up.'

In the study, a fire was flickering in the grate. Laszlo leant over and banged the glowing logs with a poker, and flames leapt up as though defending themselves.

'Sit down by the fire, Papi. Prudence—come here,' he ordered.

Janos sat down and glanced apologetically around the room. 'I'm afraid I may have been a little disingenuous.' He smoothed an imaginary crease from his trouser leg. 'You see, I have something I want to discuss with you both. I was going to wait until tomorrow...' Lifting his head, he frowned. 'But it's been playing on my mind.'

Prudence looked down at her hands in her lap, feeling Laszlo's gaze on the side of her face.

'So? What is it, Papi?'

Janos paused. He looked alert and animated, the vigour in his eyes belying his age. 'I'm thinking about making some changes. And I'd be quite interested in hearing what you think.'

Laszlo raised his eyebrows. 'Not the moat again, Papi?' he said slowly.

Janos shook his head and gave a reluctant smile. 'No. Not the moat. Although it *does* have something to do with the castle.' Pausing, he glanced across at Prudence. 'It was you, my dear girl, who gave me the idea.'

Prudence gaped at him. 'I did?' she said incredulously.

There was a moment's silence, and then Laszlo cleared his throat. 'So. Don't keep us in suspense, then, Papi. What's the big idea?'

Smiling, Janos shook his head. 'You're just like your mother. Always so impatient.' He looked up at his grandson, his expression tender and hopeful. 'All my life I've been surrounded by beauty. Now I'd like to share my good fortune with other people.' He paused again, his eyes bright, almost feverish with excitement. 'And that's why I want to turn the castle into a museum.'

CHAPTER ELEVEN

THERE WAS A stunned silence in the room. Finally Laszlo shook his head. 'I'm sorry. Did you just say you wanted to turn the castle into a *museum*?' He gave his grandfather a long, searching look. 'Why on earth would you want to do that?'

Janos raised his hands placatingly. 'To give something back, Laszlo.'

Laszlo frowned. 'You *do* give something back. Quite a lot of "something", if that last meeting we had with the accountants is anything to go by.'

Janos shook his head. 'Yes. I give to charity. But this would be different.'

His frown darkening, Laszlo began pacing the room. 'Different?' He gave a short laugh. 'It would definitely be *different*. And disruptive—and intrusive. Have you really thought what it would be like to have a bunch of people wandering about in our home?' Stopping in front of his grandfather, he stubbed the carpet with the toe of his shoe. 'I just don't understand why you would want to do this. And why now?'

He shot Prudence a questioning glance.

'*Is* this something to do with you? What did you say to him?'

She stared at him, confused. 'I—I don't know—' she stammered.

Reaching out, Janos patted the chair beside him. 'Laszlo!

Laszlo! Sit down. Prudence and I were talking about her life in England and she mentioned the Soane's Museum. That's all.'

Prudence watched as Laszlo allowed his grandfather to pull him into the chair.

Janos frowned. 'I'm so sorry.' He glanced at Prudence apologetically. 'I should have waited until tomorrow. We're probably too tired and emotional after the party to be having this sort of conversation.' His voice trembled. 'It was thoughtless of me. I suppose I've just had this idea buzzing around my head for so long now that I forgot it would be new and shocking to you.' He sighed. 'And I just wanted to share it with you both.'

Taking his grandfather's hand, Laszlo squeezed it hard. He looked so young and troubled that Prudence turned away.

'I'm sorry, Papi,' she heard him say softly. 'Of course I want to share your idea. I just wasn't expecting it.' He smiled weakly. 'But I want to hear all about it. So—how will it all work?'

Janos smiled back at him. 'It's not going to happen overnight. Someone from the Museums Committee is coming over in a couple of weeks, to take a look at what we've got here, and then I think there will be a lot of long but necessary meetings. Quite possibly the castle will be ready for visitors by the end of next year.'

Laszlo nodded slowly. 'And how will that work? I mean having visitors. You're not expecting me to give guided tours or anything?' He spoke lightly but his face had tightened.

Laughing, Janos shook his head. 'No, Laszlo. You won't be giving tours around the castle. We won't have much to do with the visitors at all.'

Laszlo frowned. 'Given that they'll be wandering around our home, I think we *will*.'

There was a long, strained pause and then Janos coughed.

'The castle won't *be* our home when it's a museum, Laszlo. By the time it opens to the public we'll have moved out.'

'Moved out?' Laszlo said slowly. 'Moved out of the castle?' He shook his head. 'Papi… What are you talking about? This is your home. *Our* home. It's been in our family for hundreds of years!'

'I know—and I love this castle. It's been an enormous privilege to own such an incredible building. But, my darling boy, it's not a home any more.' He put his hands on his grandson's shoulders and said roughly, 'This castle is a museum in everything but name. And we both need to accept that and move on.'

For a moment the room hummed with a silence that was broken only by the spitting of the fire, and then finally Laszlo nodded.

'I know,' he said quietly. 'I suppose it's just that it's taken me a long time to think of it as home and now—' He cleared his throat. 'But you're right. It's ridiculous, the two of us rattling around here like this.' He managed a small smile. 'Have you told Rosa yet?'

Shaking his head, Janos frowned. 'Not yet. I wanted to speak to you first.' He screwed up his face. 'I must admit I'm a little worried about telling her.'

Laszlo pursed his lips. 'She'll be fine once she gets used to the idea.' He smiled. 'And as long as she gets to fuss around *you* she'll be happy wherever she lives.' Looking up at his grandfather, he hesitated. 'Which sort of brings me to my next question… Where exactly are you planning on us living?'

Janos let out a breath. 'That would rather depend on Prudence.'

Prudence felt her fingers curl painfully around her glass as both men turned to stare at her. 'M-me? Why does it depend on *me*?' she stammered.

'Because I was rather hoping that after the cataloguing is complete you might consider staying on,' Janos said gently. 'That's why I want you to be here now. So I can ask you if you would like to be the museum's curator.'

Prudence stared at him speechlessly. Stay on? In Hungary? With Laszlo?

Finally, she found her voice. 'I—I'm not… I don't know what to say…' she faltered.

Janos laughed. 'Of course you don't. How could you? Please don't look so worried, Prudence. I'm not expecting you to give me an answer right now,' he said hastily. 'I'm just hoping you might think about it over the next few days. Or weeks. Take as long as you like.'

Heart pounding, Prudence gave a weak smile. 'Thank you. And thank you for thinking of me,' she said slowly.

Janos laughed. 'My dear, I didn't think of anyone else.' He frowned. 'I must confess before you came I was quite worried about how everything would work. You know— having a stranger in our home. But you coming here has been a blessing.' He glanced across to Laszlo, his lined face creasing into a smile. 'And you're part of our family now—isn't she, Laszlo?'

Almost intoxicated by hope and longing, Prudence glanced across at Laszlo—and her bubbling happiness began to ebb away. For, meeting his gaze, she saw from his face that he shared none of her pleasure or excitement.

She felt panic clutch at her chest as he stared at her in silence, smiling unsteadily, a strange, unfamiliar light glittering in his eyes.

Abruptly he stood up and cleared his throat. 'I'm going to go back to the party. Make sure everything's okay. And you need to get some sleep, Papi. It's been a very long night for you. And this can wait until morning. We don't want to push Miss Elliot into a decision she regrets.'

Her body tensed as he turned, but he didn't even look at her as he walked out of the room. Pain and panic tore through her as she watched him leave. For one terrible, agonising moment she wanted to go after him and pull him back. Demand that he stay and explain. But she stopped herself. Laszlo had never been much good with words, but on this occasion he didn't need to be. He didn't need to explain anything. His actions were loud enough.

He didn't want her to stay.

He didn't want her at all.

It was nearly time to leave. The *vardo* gleamed in the late-morning sun. Gently Prudence ran her hand over the gold-painted scrolls and garlands and bouquets of flowers. It was truly a labour of love. For the craftsman who'd made it, at least. She bit her lip.

Slowly she walked up the steps, touching, feeling the wood smooth and warm beneath her fingers. Picking up a pillow from the bed, she closed her eyes and inhaled: woodsmoke and orange blossom. It was his scent, but even as she inhaled it seemed to fade. Opening her eyes, she crawled onto the bed and stared bleakly out of the window. From where she lay the castle seemed to fill the tiny square of glass entirely, blocking out the light.

Just as Laszlo had dominated her life from the moment she'd met him seven years ago.

Rolling onto her back, she closed her eyes.

They had come so close to making it work.

Yesterday, for the first time ever, he had opened up to her about so many things. His family...his fears. Her breath caught in her throat. He had needed her emotionally—wanted her support. And she had let herself believe that it meant something, for it had felt as if something had changed between them. As if there had been some shift in the fundament of their relationship.

Her heart gave a painful lurch. But of course, as with so much of their relationship, nothing was what it seemed.

She shivered, remembering Laszlo's face when Janos had called her one of the family. She could have ignored his reaction. Let it go. As she'd let so many other things go because she'd feared losing him. But she didn't fear losing him any more.

On the contrary—what she'd feared most was that she wouldn't be strong enough to leave him.

Her eyes grew hot and damp. It had been so, so hard the last time. She drew in a breath. But she had got over it eventually. And she would do so again. In time, and with distance between them. Which was why she'd gone to find Janos that morning and told him that she needed to go home for a few days. She'd used the excuse that she needed to talk through his offer with Edmund and he'd agreed immediately, as she'd known he would. Jakob had even pulled strings so that a seat had been found for her on a plane leaving that evening.

Opening her eyes, she covered her mouth with her hand, trying to hold back her misery. Part of her wanted to stay. The part that felt as if it was disintegrating. But what would be the point? Her love wasn't enough for Laszlo; *she* wasn't enough for him.

She lifted her chin and the knot of misery in her stomach began to loosen. She was not about to crumble. Laszlo might not love her but she still had her self-respect. And if she wanted to avoid the same fate as her mother, diminished and worn down by unrequited love, she needed to get away from him.

That meant leaving Hungary. And never coming back.

It was the first time she'd acknowledged that fact— if not out loud then in her head. But she knew it was the right—the only choice she had. She needed to be where her judgement wasn't skewed by her heart. That was why she was going home to her family.

She glanced up at the sky and frowned. And why she needed to start packing.

Back at the cottage, suitcase packed, she walked dully from room to room, checking for anything she might have forgotten. With a stab of pain she noticed Laszlo's dinner jacket, hanging on the back of the kitchen door. He'd draped it over her shoulders when they'd left the party and she'd still been wearing it later when, dumb and still shivering from shock, she had let Janos get Gregor, the handyman and chauffeur, to escort her back to the cottage.

She lifted her chin. She would give it to him at lunchtime. Despite eating breakfast at the cottage, she'd resigned herself to the fact that seeing him one last time was inevitable. At least with Janos there there would be no risk of her losing control and throwing a bowl of soup in his face.

But at lunchtime Laszlo's seat was conspicuously empty.

Janos was apologetic. 'He didn't come down for breakfast either. He's probably with Mihaly,' he said, trying to sound encouraging as Prudence tried and failed to eat the delicious lunch Rosa had made especially for her. 'I'm sure he'll be here any moment.'

But he hadn't appeared.

Later, waiting at the airport, she felt almost sick with nerves, for part of her had stupidly hoped that he would come after her.

It was only when she was boarding the plane that she knew that it was really, finally over.

Glancing wearily out of the window, she watched the patchwork of green and brown fields disappear beneath the clouds. It was better that it had ended like this, with her on her own. There would be nothing to haunt her now, for that last evening in Janos's study seemed to have fled her memory.

Outside, everything had turned white, and she felt

something like peace slide over her. For even though it had been hard to leave, and it was going to be much, much harder to learn to live without him again, she didn't regret what had happened. Finally she could accept that she and Laszlo would never have a future together. And, more importantly, she'd learned that there was nothing to fear from the past: her mother's choices did not have to be hers.

She had the power to shape her life. Finally, she could face the future without fear or regret.

She shivered. Closing her eyes, she shrugged her coat over her body. But that was the future—right now she just wanted to get warm. Only, huddling into her jacket, she doubted she would ever feel warm again...

Staring at the museum's sprinklers longingly, Prudence sighed. If only she could set them off... But, even though it was her last day at work, she couldn't imagine herself ruining hundreds of priceless artefacts in exchange for one blissfully cool shower.

She scowled. London was in the grip of an Indian summer and she was sick of the heat. Tucking a strand of limp hair behind her ear, she took a breath of warm air and began to speak.

'And this is the cast of the Belvedere Apollo.' Gesturing to the statue in front of her, Prudence turned to the crowd of tourists gathered expectantly around her and smiled. 'It's a copy made for Lord Burlington in Italy, sometime around 1719. Before it came to the museum it was held at Chiswick House.'

She paused and glanced around at the faces staring up at her. Since leaving Seymour's she had been working part-time at the museum, and although she'd enjoyed it she was looking forward to leaving. These people were her last tour group. And after that—

She bit her lip. After that she'd take it one day at a time.

What was important was that Daisy and Edmund had been so understanding and so supportive. About everything. And, although she would of course like to get a place of her own, she had agreed to keep on living with them for the immediate future.

She looked up and took a breath. 'The Belvedere Apollo takes its name from the Belvedere Palace in the Vatican, where it has resided since the early fifteen-hundreds. The sculpture depicts the Greek god Apollo as an archer. He is nude except for his sandals and a robe slung over his shoulders.'

Pausing, she took another breath. It felt hotter than Greece in the museum, and suddenly she remembered the crisp, cold mornings in Hungary. For a fraction of a second, her smile faltered but, gripping her clipboard tightly, she ploughed on.

'That concludes our tour this morning. If you have any questions, please don't hesitate to ask. I hope you enjoy the rest of your visit to the museum and your stay in London. Thank you.'

Picking up her handbag from behind the desk, she walked towards the hallway, where the air conditioning greeted her like a fridge door opening. Fanning her face, she sat down and closed her eyes.

'Excuse me?'

For a moment, her brain was in free fall and then her eyes flew open as she thought she recognised his voice. But it couldn't be him, could it? Why would Laszlo be in London? He hadn't even bothered to say goodbye.

The sun was in her eyes. At first she could make out only a blurred dark shape. But then she saw his outline, and the breath seemed to freeze in her throat.

He stepped out of the light and she felt her legs slide away from under her.

He caught her as she fell.

'Here…'

She felt his hands, warm and firm, guide her into a seat. Her head was spinning.

'Drink this.'

Water from the water cooler. So cold and fresh it might have come from one of the streams that criss-crossed the fields around his castle.

She moaned and Laszlo crouched down by her side, holding a glass to her lips.

'Just sip it.'

The noise of traffic surged into the room as downstairs a door was opened.

'Are you okay, Miss Elliot?' Now Joe, the doorman, was leaning over her. 'Do you want me to get a doctor?'

She shook her head. 'No. Thank you.'

And then Laszlo stood up, his body screening her from Joe's anxious face. 'I've got it from here.'

He spoke pleasantly, but some alarm must have shown on her face, for Joe stood his ground. 'And you are, sir...?'

'I'm her husband!'

There was a tense silence, and then she heard Joe's feet retreating across the tiled floor.

She was suddenly furious. 'What are you doing here?'

He ignored her question. 'Finish your water.'

'Answer my question!' She glared at him.

He studied her impassively. 'I will. After you've finished the water.'

Swallowing her anger first, she drained the cup and handed it to him. 'Now answer my question!'

'Surely you should be answering *my* questions? After all, you *do* work here.'

She stared at him in disbelief and then, reaching up, pulled her name badge off her shirt and dropped it in the bin. 'Not any more!' She glared at him and then abruptly stood up. 'Goodbye, Laszlo!' she said quietly. 'I hope you enjoy the rest of your visit to the museum and your stay in London.'

He regarded her calmly and then, as she took a step forward, moved in front of her.

She shot him a frustrated glance. 'Could you move, please?'

He stood silently in front of her and she shook her head and looked away from him. 'You can stand there all day if you want. I'm used to silent men made of stone.' Her hands clenched at her sides. 'But it won't change anything. I have nothing left to say to you.'

He waited until finally, reluctantly, she turned to face him. 'Quite a lot to write, though, it would appear,' he said. 'About ending our marriage.'

She watched wordlessly as he reached into his pocket and pulled out an envelope. Her skin was suddenly tight across her face and she felt cornered. And then she met his gaze, for she wasn't going to let him intimidate her.

'What about it?' she said shortly. 'I told you in Hungary that I wanted a divorce. I still do. There's no point leaving things as they are.'

'And how *are* things?' His voice was hoarse. 'You see, I thought you were happy.'

She shook her head in exasperation. 'I was. I *am*. But when did my happiness matter to you, Laszlo? You only care about yourself, and you didn't look too happy when your grandfather asked me to stay on as curator. Or when he called me one of the family.'

She felt a stab of pain at the memory and suddenly could barely see his face through her tears.

'In fact, you were so happy you walked off.'

His face tightened. Running his hand through his hair, he said slowly, 'I didn't want you to—'

'Didn't want me to stay. I know—'

'No.' He cut her off. 'I didn't want my grandfather to

rush you. You seemed unsure, and he was so desperate for you to agree. I thought he'd just keep on pushing and—'

'And you thought I'd say yes?' Her voice rose and she shook her head. 'So you decided to talk it over with me and your grandfather.' She paused, her lip curling contemptuously. 'Oh, no. You *didn't*. You walked out.'

Laszlo looked at her, his expression bleak. Finally he nodded. 'Yes. I walked away. I didn't know what else to do. So much had happened between us, but so much still wasn't resolved. Like us being married. I knew if you agreed to take the job then you'd come back. And not just for a couple of weeks this time.'

Prudence felt like throwing up. 'Imagine that,' she said flatly. 'No *wonder* you couldn't wait to get away.'

She took a painful breath as he shook his head.

'I wasn't thinking about me. I knew *you'd* have a problem with that.'

Staring at him incredulously, she gave a humourless laugh. 'Not as big a problem as you.' Pausing, she gritted her teeth. 'I don't really understand what you're trying to say, Laszlo. But you know what? I don't care any more.'

'I do!'

He practically shouted the words and she took a step back from him.

'I care. And I cared in Hungary. You *hated* lying to my grandfather about us. And I knew it would be a problem doing it again. And for so long. I thought if he pushed you, you'd panic and say no—'

His voice cracked and she stared at him in shock.

'And I didn't want you to.'

For a moment she thought she must have misheard him. She opened her mouth and then closed it again. Her breath was burning her throat. 'Why?' she said shakily. 'Why didn't you want me to say no?'

He stared at her and then bowed his head. 'Because I love you.'

Her heart twisted inside her. 'Don't say that, Laszlo.'

Tears sprang to her eyes as he reached out and, taking her hands, raised them to his lips.

'I *will* say it.'

He looked up and she saw that his face was wet with tears.

'I will say it. And I'll keep on saying it until you believe me. I love you. I only worked it out when we talked about my parents and their marriage, and I realised that I'd only believed in *their* love and not mine.' He grimaced. 'I should have just come right out and told you, but...' He smiled weakly. 'I'm so bad at this stuff.'

He shook his head.

'I have trouble explaining it to myself. Let alone to the person I'm so scared of losing.'

She stared at him in exasperation. 'So you thought it would be a good idea to make me believe that our relationship was only about sex?'

'I'm an idiot.'

'So it wasn't?'

He screwed up his face. 'Maybe a little bit—at the beginning. When I was angry and mean.' He let out a ragged sigh. 'But I'm only flesh and blood, and I don't think you have any idea how sexy you looked in that blouse and skirt and those heels.'

He bit his lip.

'But it changed. *I* changed. I wanted more. I wanted my wife back! I was going to tell you before the party but I bottled out.' Letting go of her hand, he sighed. 'If only I'd let you open the *putsi* when you wanted to,' he said sadly.

Prudence reached into her handbag and pulled out the small leather bag that she hadn't been able to face discarding.

He stared at it as though mesmerised. 'Open it!'

His voice was husky and she pulled clumsily at the cord. With shaking fingers she tipped the bag upside down and into her hand tumbled an acorn, a key and a beautiful diamond ring.

She felt suddenly faint again. But this time with happiness. 'Oh, Laszlo!' she whispered.

'Prudence—' He reached out hesitantly and, taking the ring from her hand, slid it onto her finger.

'I thought you didn't want me,' she said, tears rolling over her cheeks.

He stepped close to her and took her hands in his. 'And I thought you didn't want *me*.' His voice cracked. 'After the party I went to Mihaly and I told him everything.' He clenched his teeth. 'He told me to stop being such an idiot and tell you how I felt.' He smiled ruefully. 'Actually, he didn't quite use those words. They were slightly more colourful.'

Prudence laughed.

His smile faded. 'But when I got back to the castle you'd gone.' He took a breath. 'Then I lost it and I told my grandfather everything as well.'

Prudence bit her lip. 'And...?'

Frowning, Laszlo pulled her closer. 'He told me I was an idiot too.'

She pulled away slightly and smiled. 'I wish I'd stayed after all,' she said teasingly. There was a brief silence, and then she said hesitantly, 'Were they angry?'

Laszlo shook his head. 'No. They were delighted. In fact, I think they thought I was quite lucky to catch you. And they love you already. Almost as much as I do.' His face tightened, grew suddenly strained. 'I just wish my grandmother was here. She so wanted to see me married and with a family of my own.'

He gave her an unsteady smile.

'I'm warning you now. You think my grandfather was pushy about you taking the curator's job? Just wait until my aunts hear that I'm married!'

'Never mind your aunts. What about *you*? Do you want children?'

He grinned. 'Yeah, I do. Loads. At least seven.'

'Seven?' she squeaked.

He nodded, suddenly serious. 'One for every year we were apart,' he murmured, tightening his grip around her waist.

She smiled. 'I see. I suppose we should get started, then?'

He grinned. 'Definitely! I'd like to be a father as soon as possible. Like in about nine months. Do you think that's possible?'

She kissed him gently on the lips. 'I can do it in seven.'

He looked at her blankly. 'Seven? You mean nine.'

In reply, she took his hand and put it gently on her stomach. 'No. I mean seven.'

He stared down at the slight bump of her belly. 'Really?'

She nodded. 'Really!'

Pulling her gently into his arms, he closed his eyes, too choked to speak. 'Only another six to go,' he whispered against her cheek—and then abruptly, he released her and took a step back, his face clouding over.

'What is it?' She stared at him anxiously.

He let out a long breath. 'Everything moved pretty fast after you left. Papi and Rosa have moved into the cottage, but…' He frowned. 'As of tomorrow I'm going to be homeless.'

'Oh,' she said slowly. 'Actually, this really is my last day at work. So, as of now, I'm unemployed.'

They stared at each other in silence, and then both of them burst out laughing.

'For better for worse,' he said softly.

She felt his gaze drift over her face. 'For richer for poorer!' she murmured.

He grinned, and then his smile faded. 'Don't worry. I'm not going to make you live in a trailer.'

'I don't mind—' she began, but he shook his head, grimacing.

'No. But I do.' A faint flush coloured his cheeks. 'I know I shouldn't really say it, but I don't really like living in trailers.' He shivered. 'They're even draughtier than the castle!'

Prudence giggled.

Reaching down, he picked up her hand and fiddled with the ring on her finger. 'I guess, with the pregnancy and everything, you'd like to live near your family?'

Frowning, she nodded slowly. 'Actually, I *am* living with them. They wanted to be there to help me when the baby comes.'

He stared at her anxiously. 'And that's what you still want, is it?'

Smiling weakly, Prudence leant against him and rubbed her cheek against his. 'No. I want to live with my husband. But I *do* want to be near them.' She sighed. 'It's such a shame. The cottage next door came up for sale and that would have been perfect. But it never even went on the open market. Apparently the buyer offered twice the asking price. I'm not sure why…'

Laszlo gazed at her steadily. 'Maybe he liked the location.' His hand tightened around hers and their eyes met.

She stared at him, confused. And then she realised that he was waiting—waiting for her to understand. '*You* bought it?'

He nodded, his face creasing into a smile. 'Yes. I think your neighbour thought I was insane.' He groaned. 'It's probably the first time ever that a Romany has paid more than the asking price!' His smile tightened. 'But I had to have it. You see, I wasn't sure you'd even speak to me—'

'So you thought you'd stalk me?' Prudence shook off his hand. But her eyes were dancing.

'I thought if I lived next door you wouldn't be able to avoid me,' he said softly. 'Then all I'd have to do was wear down your resistance.'

'Is that right? And how, exactly, were you going to do that?'

She felt her stomach flutter as his eyes narrowed.

'Let me show you,' he murmured, and then he pulled her into his arms and kissed her until, for the third time that afternoon, she thought she'd faint.

* * * * *

LET'S TALK
Romance

For exclusive extracts, competitions
and special offers, find us online:

  facebook.com/millsandboon

 @millsandboonuk

 @millsandboon

Or get in touch on 0844 844 1351*

For all the latest titles coming soon, visit
millsandboon.co.uk/nextmonth